Itchy Donner

A Novel

Doug Lambeth

Sashee Press
Pullman, Washington

Published by:

Sashee Press

Pullman, WA

ISBN 978-0-9728-2182-7

This book is a work of fiction. Names, characters, places and incidents are products of the author's imagination or are used fictitiously. Any resemblance to actual events or locales or persons, living or dead, is entirely coincidental.

Ard1651@hotmail.com

Additional copies are available at: www.lulu.com

Itchy Donner

I sat beside my mother with my hand clasped in hers, as we slowly moved away from that quaint old house on its grassy knoll, from the orchard, the corn field, and the meadow; as we passed through the last of our land, her clasp tightened, and I, glancing up, saw tears in her eyes.

Eliza Donner
April 15, 1846

Chapter One

They say Itchy Donner was born during a blizzard, on a night much like the long winter nights in 1847 when his starving ancestors shivered in tents and toyed with the idea of eating the people next door.

Of course, Itchy and his mother Irene always corrected the cannibal misconception.

"Our ancestors," Irene would say, her voice cracking with indignation, "were not cannibals. It was the Murphys and the Graves'. And that horrible Keseberg! He was the worst. But the Donners never resorted to such things. They—we—are an honorable family."

Oddly, Irene wasn't truly a Donner. Her ex-husband Red claimed the Donner connection, but Irene felt that her kinship—though by marriage—entitled her to both the glory and defense of the famous family. Red vanished a few months before Itchy's birth and hadn't been seen since, so over the years Irene made sure that Itchy learned everything there was to know about his illustrious heritage.

"Your great-great-great grandparents were the bravest pioneers, Itchy," she'd tell him while he cooed and gurgled in his crib. "I think you're brave just like great-great-great Gramma Tamsen Donner. Do you want me to tell you about great-great-great Gramma Tamsen again?" Itchy, eight months old and far more interested in chewing his toes than learning the family story, burbled in a way that Irene took as a "Yes."

"Tamsen wanted to be a botanist. A botanist! Can you believe that? A pioneer woman in 1846 with a bunch of kids, traveling across the plains in a covered wagon, but she took the time to study plants. And when she got to California, great-great-great Gramma Tamsen wanted to start a girls' school. Isn't that something?"

Itchy grinned a toothless, gummy smile. Irene knew she was getting through to the baby. He always smiled like that when she told him Donner Family stories.

Itchy had been christened Jacob George Donner—Jacob and George being the names of the Donner brothers who made up the Donner Party. But shortly after his birth, Irene noticed that Itchy constantly scratched at a little red patch by his left eye. Doctor Fleming, who came to the Tamarack clinic every Tuesday afternoon, told Irene that the red spot was just a little skin irritation and nothing to worry about. But Itchy wouldn't stop fussing over the rosy patch, and Irene came to call him "Itchy Baby." It got shortened to Itchy, and soon the name stuck. All of Irene's family called him Itchy, the town knew him as Itchy, and pretty soon Irene was just about the only person left in Tamarack who remembered that his real name was "Jacob George." Such is the way of nicknames.

As Itchy grew the patch grew, spreading red and scaly across his cheek and onto his back and chest.

"Appears to be a bad case of psoriasis," Doctor Fleming told Irene when Itchy was four. "We can treat it with creams and lotions, and it'll come and go. But it's probably something Itchy's going to have to deal with all his life."

Irene wept bitter tears that night. Her baby, the creature that was her only reason for living, was cursed with a flaw. The poor little guy was almost—she hated to think of the word—disfigured. The grief of Itchy's imperfection left her despondent.

But Irene was blessed with a resilient spirit, much like her in-law ancestors, and she soon came to terms with Itchy's ailment. She comforted him when the outbreaks were raw and painful, and as he got older and had to endure teasing from other kids, Irene spent many an hour gently pep-talking Itchy out of self-pity or resentment.

"Remember your kin," she often told him. She liked the way "kin" sounded, so close, so intimate and friendly. "Remember George and Jacob, and Tamsen, and Eliza and Elitha and Frances. Do you think they ever complained or got down on themselves when adversity struck?" Irene loved the word "adversity." She didn't have any schooling beyond Tamarack High, but she read constantly, absorbing words and meanings, and she always, *always* found ways of using the words to teach Itchy life lessons—usually somehow connected to the tragic Donner pioneers.

Itchy was in preschool when he first started asking the "Daddy" questions.

"How come other kids have daddies and I don't?" he asked one day as Irene walked him home. An unusual balmy wind had swept over Tamarack the night before, turning the snow into a dirty slush that squished under their boots. An inversion trapped woodsmoke over the valley in a bluish haze, and Irene's breath hitched—although she wasn't sure if it was the sweet, stinging smoke or Itchy's question.

"You have a daddy, Itchy. You know that. His name is Red."

"Why?"

"Why what?"

"Why is he red?" Itchy giggled. Itchy liked to scrawl crayon pictures of red giants on rough scratch paper, and Irene wondered if they were his imagined portraits of his never-seen father.

"That's his name, silly," Irene smiled. She tousled Itchy's thin brown hair. She loved the sensation of touching him. Sometimes she couldn't believe that she'd actually created another human being. She moved her hand along his cheek. His rashy blotches were pale and faded at the moment, lying in wait for the unknown signal that would fire them up and make him scratchy and miserable.

"Why's his name Red?" Itchy asked for the ten-thousandth time. Irene wondered why five-year-olds never got tired of asking the same questions. He had to remember the answer; he wasn't stupid. She decided it must be the comforting habit of having the same conversation over and over. It was like a prayer. Asking about Red made him feel safe.

"His name is Red because when he was a little boy he had red hair."

"So...it's like my name?"

"Sort of." She always hated this part of the conversation, because it forced them to talk about Itchy's psoriasis, and Irene preferred avoiding the subject. "Nicknames usually start when people are very young."

"Do you have a nickname?" Itchy asked. This was new. He'd never asked that question before.

Irene hesitated. "I don't believe I do, Itchy."

"How come?"

"I guess it's because I'm not that special. You have to be special to have a nickname. Like you. Only somebody really special can be called 'Itchy'." Irene was proud of her answer. She'd read books and seen *Oprah* episodes on dealing with children who had illnesses or defects, and they all said that pumping up the kids' self-esteem was very important. By the smile on Itchy's face she knew she'd said the right thing.

"I think you're special," Itchy said, serious and beyond his years. "Even if you don't have a nickname like me."

"Thank you, Itchy."

They walked hand in hand through the slush and haze and disrepair of their decaying little hometown. They climbed a steep, rutted street, and icy runoff gushed over their boots. At the top of the street sat their singlewide trailer, the one place in the world where Irene and Itchy Donner were safe— safe from the hard world outside and the frigid winter winds that had killed so many unlucky Donners in the past.

"I wish that kid wouldn't come over here," A. Jackson Flynn grumbled as he poured himself a glass of Glenlivet. It had been a rough day at work; the Tama-rack Logging and Milling Company was hemorrhaging money, and A. Jackson didn't know how to stop it.

His wife Miriam delicately sipped her glass of Merlot. A. Jackson had no-ticed lately that she always seemed to have a glass of wine in her hand, no mat-ter the time of day.

"He's Sara's friend. She needs friends." Miriam swirled the lovely, deep red wine and then downed it. She carefully refilled the glass and started over with the swirling and sipping.

"Yeah, well, I'm not all that hot about Sara seeing the kid. He's poor, he's got that rash—"

"It's psoriasis, it's not contagious."

"It's nasty," A. Jackson said. The Glenlivet scorched his lips. He wasn't a wine fan like Miriam. He wanted his liquor strong and painful. "The kid gives me the creeps. If he's anything like his old man, he's gonna be big trouble some day." A. Jackson rubbed his forehead. The hair was receding quickly, and he noticed in the mirror the other day how old he looked. His strong jaw, always his most attractive feature, had begun to soften, and he feared the day when he turned jowly and squishy, with curly nose hairs and droopy beagle ears, like the old men he used to make fun of. Losing the family fortune and closing down the little town of Tamarack could age you quickly, he realized.

Tamarack began life in 1867, twenty years after and thirteen hundred miles to the north of the Donner Party's winter misery. Like all little logging towns, Tamarack grew in boom and bust spasms. Fortunes made, fortunes lost, and many a logger killed in the woods. The pattern repeated decade after decade and it seemed it would never end. The woods were boundless, the country's log appetite insatiable.

But end it did. As the technology improved, greed overcame common sense, and by the middle of the twentieth century Tamarack was running out of wood. The market collapsed, and so went Tamarack.

Since the '70s, Tamarack had lurched along, a lost little backwater eking out survival from second growth woods and faraway timber sales. The town claimed seven hundred souls, plus-or-minus the occasional oldtimer called home to Jesus or ill-timed baby arriving to underemployed women like Irene Donner. Some outsiders passed through, but they were few. The heart of Tamarack were the families who'd been there forever—families like Irene's, the Weatherlys. Irene's dad Bill Weatherly spent his life in the woods like his father and grandfather. And, like them, Bill Weatherly died in the woods. The cedars and firs could be formidable opponents.

There were other family dynasties in Tamarack like the Pandolas and the Bents, the Lanes, the MacGregors—all intermarried so that it seemed that everyone was a cousin or in-law of everybody else. Red Donner once told Irene, "No wonder this little chickenshit town is so fucked up. You're all workin' off of too few chromosomes." Red was drunk when he'd said that, and Irene refused him sexual favors until he apologized. But Red had a point. To an outsider like him, Tamarack could be closed and wary like small towns are to anyone whose roots aren't generations long.

The only family that was different was A. Jackson's. The Flynns had owned the mill for as long as anyone could remember. Old Patrick Flynn had made his fortune in San Francisco during the gold rush. He hadn't been foolish enough to take his chances in the gold fields—only men without imagination did that. Old Patrick realized that the real gold rush was selling to the would-be miners. He cornered the market on gold mining gadgetry, cheerfully fleecing newly arrived, naïve '49ers from innocent points east out of their life savings. He became one of the wealthiest citizens of the young San Francisco, and when the gold rush's easy money played out, he set his sights on timber. Old Patrick had vision and faith, he knew that the future of the west was unlimited—especially once the railroads came. He moved to wilds of what would become Idaho, founded the city of Tamarack, and began cutting trees. Old Patrick never looked back, and by the time he died in 1884, he'd become the richest man in the Pacific Northwest.

His heirs weren't as cunning—or lucky—and by the time his great-great grandson A. Jackson Flynn inherited the family business, the fortune had dwindled. The Flynn family still ran the town, such as it was—A. Jackson was the mayor—and they still owned the mill, but nowadays they were like any other small backwoods business—debt-ridden and barely hanging on. The Flynns lived better than their neighbors only because they lived in Old Patrick's mansion, which, though weather-beaten, was still remarkable.

A. Jackson—A. for Antoine, his hated, unused first name bestowed by his French- Canadian mother—was fighting a losing battle to restore the Flynn family glory and wealth. He ruled his business and town with a fierce capitalist benevolence that made him both admired and feared. Locals complained about his high-handed imperiousness. Irene Donner found him arrogant and rude, but even she had to admit that without A. Jackson Tamarack would be a ghost town. Red had hated A. Jackson—Red always had trouble with authority—and butted heads with him whenever their paths crossed. Red was a logger; he worked hard, drank hard, and hated hard. A. Jackson was everything Red despised, "a smart-assfuck rich fratboy who never got his hands dirty." After Red disappeared and Itchy was born, Irene unexpectedly got to know A. Jackson and his sad, quiet wife Miriam. Itchy shared crayons in kindergarten with A. Jackson's daughter Sara, and they became fast friends. As they grew their friendship grew, much to A. Jackson's chagrin.

A. Jackson was never mean to Itchy, and since Sara was so fond of Itchy he never spoke ill of him within Sara's earshot. But Sara's playdates at Irene's singlewide mortified A. Jackson. "Our little girl shouldn't be at that...place. It's not dignified," he told Miriam. So Itchy began spending time at their mansion, which annoyed A. Jackson just as much. He couldn't win.

A. Jackson didn't understand why Miriam wasn't bothered by Itchy. She was even more of a snob than he was, having grown up in Seattle as the spoiled daughter of a doctor and college professor. She'd met A. Jackson at a fraternity party, and he'd swept her off her feet with his stories of his family's triumphs and romantic tales of the town he owned. The reality hit Miriam hard, though, when she married A. Jackson and moved to the sad little town of Tamarack. Although she loved Old Patrick's mansion, she was lonely. Even after fifteen years she knew almost no one in Tamarack, and didn't really care to. There were no women of her class, and other than frequent trips back to Seattle, Miriam had little to live for except her afternoon wine. A. Jackson was beginning to realize that his wife's acceptance of Itchy had more to do with the numbing effects of Merlot than anything else.

"Itchy's a sweet little boy," Miriam said as she sipped her wine. "And Sara adores him."

"Jesus, don't say that. It sounds like you've got them married off already."

"Would that be so bad?" Miriam asked.

A. Jackson didn't respond. He loved Sara fiercely, with a feral protective-ness that frightened him. She was scrawny and gangly, with bleached-out eye-lashes and spattery freckles. Sara defined homely. A. Jackson saw the reality, but that only made him love her all the more. He'd do anything to protect her. Besides, Sara made A. Jackson smile. He was a humorless man; frivolity struck him as a waste of time. There was money to be made, and serious, adult things to be done. Humor was a waste of time. But Sara was different. She was bright and witty for a child, and her insatiable interest in the world amused A. Jackson.

"Daddy, did you know?..." was the preface to most of Sara's comments to her father. She was forever reading, absorbing useless little facts that she proudly parroted with the earnest seriousness of near-religious discovery. Sara arrived home most days with armloads of new library books, and she spent hours roaming the Internet, hunting for knowledge, clicking the links to a world she found fascinating.

"Are they up there on the damn computer again?" A. Jackson asked Miriam as he refilled his glass with Scotch. This was going to be a half-bottle night.

Miriam smiled. "I suspect they're looking for Itchy's relatives."

A. Jackson sighed. "I guess it's better than porn sites." He gave Miriam a perfunctory kiss on the forehead. "I need to go crunch some numbers for awhile."

Miriam nodded. He left his wife in the parlor sipping her Merlot and went into the mansion's leather-bound office. He heard Sara and Itchy chattering upstairs. Most annoying. He'd have to do something about it.

But right now he needed to figure out a way to save his livelihood.

*   *   *

Most people in Tamarack couldn't afford computers, so, other than the library, the Flynn mansion was the place to be. Itchy Donner and Sara sat side-by-side in front of her computer, pounding an intricate duet of keyboard strokes. Itchy wasn't interested in the rest of the world like Sara was. He cared about only one thing: The Donner Party.

"Wow," Itchy said as they stumbled across yet another Donner Party website. Itchy was only eleven, but even at that tender age he was amazed at how obsessed the outside world was with his ancestors. "That's...twenty-five sites so far today." They kept score as they bounced from Donner site to Donner site. He scratched at a hot, crusty patch in his armpit. It was a bad day for the psoriasis.

"Does it have pictures?" Sara asked. Sara liked the old pictures they found of Itchy's great-great-greats, but she was *really* interested in pictures of the bones of the dead people who got eaten. They never found any pictures like that—but there were still a lot of places to look and she forever hoped.

"Just the usual ones of Eliza and Elitha and Patty Reed," Itchy said. He sniffed and rubbed his nose. A slimy smear slicked the sleeve of his cheap flannel shirt. Itchy's nose ran most of the time. He got teased at school for both his itchy red patches and his endless snot. Sometimes he felt like the unluckiest kid in the world. If it wasn't for the Donner Party....

He quickly navigated the website, sizing it up as yet another non-informative Donner backwater, and clicked on to the next.

Itchy loved the afternoons he spent at Sara's house. It was so different from his mom's rickety singlewide—not that he hated his home or anything. But the Flynn mansion was big and warm and solid. And it had a computer, the best thing of all! Sara's mom was always nice to him, feeding him cookies and pop and junk food that Irene never allowed. Irene was convinced that garbage food made Itchy's psoriasis worse. Itchy realized that Irene was probably right to forbid Ding Dongs and Doritos and Skittles, but he was a kid—he couldn't resist his cravings for the food all the other kids ate.

The one bad thing about Sara's house was her dad. Itchy could tell that he didn't like him. Irene had told him that Sara's dad and Itchy's dad didn't get along, so Itchy naturally assumed any problems Mr. Flynn had with him weren't his fault. It never occurred to Itchy that A. Jackson disliked him because he was scaly and snotty and friends with Sara. Itchy had suffered more than his fair share of bullying and mindless cruelty from mean kids at school who made fun of his essential Itchy-ness, but he was still innocent enough to give adults the benefit of the doubt. Itchy figured that grown-ups couldn't be as mean as kids.

Itchy had a lot to learn.

"Are there any bone pictures?" Sara asked breathlessly as Itchy clicked through the new Donner site.

"No. I told you, I don't think anybody took pictures of the bones. They didn't do stuff like that back in 1847."

"There has to be bone pictures. We just need to look harder."

Itchy sighed. Sara was okay for a girl, but sometimes she didn't get the point. This was his *family* they were talking about. He wasn't sure he wanted to see bones of somebody he was related to. It was creepy. It surprised Itchy that Sara was so interested in bones anyway. That seemed like more of a guy thing.

"Look at this," Itchy said. He clicked to a grainy, old-time photo of a grubby-looking prospector holding up some rotten pieces of wood. "I haven't seen this one before." The text said that it was taken in 1886 at the Donner campsite at Alder Creek. The wood was supposedly part of the Donner's wagon. "Wow," Itchy said, gazing at the screen. "Can you believe that?"

Sara shrugged, less than impressed. "It's okay, I guess."

Sometimes Sara made Itchy mad. That she let him use her computer to look for Donner Party stuff was pretty cool, but she didn't show enough interest in his major discoveries. It was like she didn't care as much as he did.

"Alder Creek was where the Donners camped," Itchy added.

"Uh-huh." Sara was starting to get bored. "If we can't find bone pictures, maybe we should look for some other stuff like dinosaurs or *Harry Potter*."

"Everybody thinks the Donners camped with the other people like the Reeds and Keseberg down by Donner Lake, but they didn't," Itchy said, ignoring her suggestion. "They were up by Alder Creek. That's one of the reasons they didn't eat anybody...or get eaten. At least until the end." Itchy sounded a little sad, but he always did when he thought about what happened to Tamsen Donner. Yuck.

Sara frowned at Itchy. "How do you know your relatives didn't eat anybody? Everybody says they ate people."

"They didn't!" Itchy snapped, bordering on a shout. His voice was the squeaky little grunt of a pre-adolescent, thin and weak and a bit pathetic. The kind of voice that other kids mocked. "The Donners never ate anybody!"

"But what if they did?" Sara asked. Unreasonably, as far as Itchy was concerned.

"They didn't. That's all. I know. They were my relatives."

"Maybe they lied," Sara offered. "Eating people isn't the kind of thing you brag about."

"They never lied about *that*!"

Sara wasn't necessarily accusing Itchy's ancestors of cannibalism. It just seemed to her that Itchy was awfully sure of something he couldn't prove, especially since a lot of the stuff they read said that the Donners *did* eat people. They had to survive, Sara reasoned. She didn't hold it against them.

"Let's look for something else," Sara said. She didn't want to fight with Itchy, and she noticed that the red patch on his face was starting to flare up. Whenever Itchy got mad or excited the red stuff glowed. It was like blushing, except worse. Sometimes Itchy's itchiness grossed her out, but she liked him anyway. He was the only boy in school, in town, who treated her like just another kid. Since her daddy was mayor and rich and owned the mill, sometimes the other kids were mean, or worse—they ignored her. She and Itchy needed to stick together. They both knew what it was like to be smart outcasts.

"I think I have to go home now," Itchy said, sniffing back a snot river. He scratched at his psoriasis patch like a dog with fleas. Sara heard the hurt in his voice and felt her usual guilt stabs. She felt guilty a lot. Itchy was her best friend, after all, and if he wanted to use her computer to look for his Donner Party stuff, then she shouldn't crab at him to do something else. She'd heard her daddy say that lots of times to her mom: "Quit crabbing at me, Miriam. You don't know how much stress I'm under." Sara always felt bad when Daddy sounded like that; when the word "crab" came up, it usually meant her parents would be fighting for the next hour or two, and she'd have to take refuge in her room to leave them to it. She didn't want to crab at Itchy. Someday, when she was grown-up, she never wanted her future husband to tell her to quit crabbing. That was her goal.

"Let's look for some more Donner things then," she said, and Itchy immediately brightened. She watched him as he happily scanned the web for more information about his long-dead relatives. She smiled at the sudden awareness that she had the power to make somebody else happy.

That made *her* happy.

Irene waited impatiently for Itchy to get home from the Flynn mansion. She'd gotten off work early—none of her regulars wanted perms, thank God, which always took forever. Her mom Jacqueline, who owned the Tamarack Salon, had growled in her leathery smoker's voice, "Get along home for Itchy, honey. Make him some supper." She was in the midst of highlighting Helen Bent's thinning hair. Jacqueline always made fun of old Helen to Irene. "Hell, she'll be as bald as half the old geezers in town before long. I only highlight two hairs at a time." Jacqueline loved to gossip about their customers. In Jacqueline's opinion, the vast majority of Tamarack women were vain and stupid and crass. Only she and Irene had any semblance of style, and sometimes she wasn't so sure about Irene.

Jacqueline Weatherly opened the salon shortly after her husband Bill had been crushed to death by a hundred-foot cedar. She'd been christened Alice at birth, but an intense teenage obsession with all things Jacqueline Kennedy Onassis made her change her name in the late '60s. To Jacqueline, *Jacqueline O* was everything good and saintly: stylish, beautiful, a dignified widow, brilliant. A nobody named Alice in a bumwad, jerkwater town would never amount to anything. As a Jacqueline, though, there might be a chance....

So Alice became Jacqueline, dedicated to beauty and style, and when some hapless friend or acquaintance would accidentally call her Jackie, they'd get a burning glare and a frosty, "Jackie is a white trash name. My name is *Jacqueline.*" When the real Jacqueline died in '94, Tamarack Jacqueline was inconsolable for weeks. It was like part of her had died.

Irene put up with her mom's pretensions, but she found the whole hero-worship thing silly. Irene believed in the here and now, that you had to be proud of who *you* were, not mimic somebody else. She didn't see the irony of her own Donner family pretensions. But she loved her mother in all her goofy Jackie-O glory, and she enjoyed working with her and being her business partner. Jacqueline was only sixteen years older than Irene, so they were more like girlfriends than anything else.

As Irene waited for Itchy, she wondered if her mother was right about Itchy's friendship with Sara Flynn. Jacqueline was always saying that Itchy shouldn't hang around with "that little rich girl." Jacqueline was acutely aware of class distinctions.

As Irene sat worrying—sometimes it seemed to her like all she did was worry about Itchy—the phone rang. It must be Itchy calling, she thought.

"Hello?"

Silence. Sometimes Itchy goofed around and tried to fool her with silly trick voices, so Irene waited. Her sweet little Itchy was being a cut-up again. But as she waited, she sensed that something was different. Still no sound.

"Hello?" she repeated, a little louder, a little concerned.

Nothing. Then—

Irene heard a gaspy breath. And nothing more.

She slammed the phone down. She shivered, even though the baseboard heater was cranked to high and the singlewide sweltered. The *gasp*. The sound, the phone call with no voice.

Red....

Red used to pull that crazy stuff right before he ran off. When he was out drinking with his buddies he'd call to check up on her, to make sure she was home and alone. Red wasn't convinced that the baby Irene carried was his— based on what, Irene never knew. Red wasn't always logical. So he'd call, crazy drunk, and he wouldn't say anything, he'd just listen. And breathe.

As Irene shivered at the thought of Red, the door flew open and in popped Itchy. As soon as she saw his grinning, rashy face, as he dropped his backpack and pulled off his coat, Irene went to him and hugged him tightly.

"Mom?!" Itchy said. He was getting to the age where hugging him was like hugging a cat.

"I love you, sweetie," she said. Itchy squirmed away, embarrassed. Sometimes he thought his mom was the weirdest person in the world.

"What's for dinner?" he asked, scratching at his side.

He hurried off into the kitchen to raid whatever morsels he could find.

Irene watched him, smiling, but unsettled.

God, I hope that wasn't Red, she thought.

We are now four hundred and fifty miles from Independence. I never could have believed we could have traveled so far with so little difficulty. The prairie between the Blue and the Platte rivers is beautiful beyond description. Indeed, if we do not experience something far worse than we have yet done, I shall say the trouble is all in getting started.

Tamsen Donner

June 16, 1846

Chapter Two

Sometimes Father Ray believed he was the loneliest man in Tamarack.

It wasn't just the priest part, the tending-to-the-flock-while-nobody-tended-to-you business—although that certainly didn't help. It had more to do with the isolation of fraud. Of living a lie.

Because Father Ray was a liar through and through.

It wasn't the in-your-face kind of lie, the get-out-of-trouble fib or a fuzzy sin of omission. Father Ray's lies were life lies, devotion lies, the cruelest, most unforgivable kind of lies. Father Ray's loneliness sprang from his heart, because you can't live a lie and be happy.

Father Ray didn't believe in God anymore.

And he was secretly in love with one of his parishioners.

Today, on a chilly October morning, the 28th Sunday in ordinary time, when the readings were Isaiah 25, Philippians 4, and Matthew 22, Father Ray stood at the pulpit in Our Lady of the Woods Catholic Church in Tamarack, Idaho and delivered his sermon. The comforting interpretation of the scripture readings passed through his lips, but Father Ray wasn't thinking about the words. He gazed out over his sparse flock—some, mostly the elderly, hanging on every word, others, eyes glazed, daydreaming, fidgeting kids, yawning teens...all the usual devout and not-so-devout, but Father Ray wasn't paying attention to any of them.

He saw only one.

Irene Donner.

Because Father Ray, shepherd of Our Lady of the Woods flock, was madly in love with her. And because he loved Irene Donner, he stopped loving God. And even stopped *believing* in God.

It puzzled Father Ray how his belief had shriveled away in direct proportion to his mad infatuation with Irene. It was as if he couldn't hold both, there wasn't enough space inside him for belief and love. Or maybe it had more to do with sin. Because loving Irene was a biggie, the kind of sin that shuts you down forever, that turns you away from God. *Forever and ever, Amen.* Not that love was bad, mind you, but this was forbidden love, taboo, and he had to make a choice: priest or not. Love God, love Irene. Pastor, leader, husband, love. Woman.

Sex.

Oh, that was a big one. Father Ray was besotted with sexual thoughts, the same thoughts that troubled the few who still bothered to come to confession on Saturday afternoons. The "Bless me father for I have sinned, it's been two weeks since my last confession, I've had impure thoughts" people. Nobody in Tamarack who came to confession wanted to have face to face reconciliation sessions; they were all the old school—hide behind the screen and beg for forgiveness, take their three *Hail Marys* and four *Our Fathers* and their fresh absolution and go back out into the world. Hiding behind the screen was good for Father Ray, because he feared that his own disbelief and filthy sins would show up on his face like a beacon and give his secret away.

He'd talked to his own confessor about his problems, although he didn't mention Irene specifically. He'd couched it more as a general lack of faith, and Father Martin, his confessor down at the archdiocese, had given him the usual holy boilerplate that Father Ray knew by heart. Pray, seek strength, *blah-blah-blah*. Nothing new or helpful there. So Father Ray stewed in a foolish, unrequited love fog of guilt and desire, and he knew that his weakness would someday destroy him.

He just didn't have enough strength to do anything about it.

He'd almost finished his sermon; he could see that the few who'd bothered to listen were losing interest, so it was time to wrap things up. He tried to avoid looking at Irene during his sermons, because eye contact usually upset him so much that he'd lose his place and stumble over the words. But he couldn't resist, and as his eyes moved over the faithful they stopped at Irene. She listened intently. Maybe that was why he loved her—she always listened to his dull sermons.

Those eyes.... Even though she sat halfway back in the middle section of pews, her blue eyes still blazed at him. Father Ray's throat tightened, and he started to cough. *Idiot!* Why didn't he resist, because this is what always happened. He coughed and cleared his throat and said, "Excuse me. I guess my sermon was so moving I got all choked up," and the parishioners gave him polite chuckles. Irene smiled, and Father Ray's heart fluttered. She smiled at him. So beautiful.

He forced himself to look away from her, and he saw her boy, Itchy. Nice kid, he thought, although kind of odd about the whole Donner Party business. But being eleven allowed you to be a nerd. Irene's mother Jacqueline sat next to them, her bleached hair too poofy and casual for mass, but Father Ray let it pass. Anyone who could create something as delightful, as heavenly, as Irene Donner deserved respect and admiration. That Irene existed was the only thread Father Ray could hang on to that pointed toward the existence of God.

She was all he had left of his faith.

He rushed through the rest of the mass, using the shortest version of the Eucharistic prayer, because he wanted it to be over. He wanted to hurry outside and do the after mass meet-and-greet. Because then he'd get to speak to Irene. He'd get to see her close-up. He'd get to lock her eyes with his, see her beautiful honeyed hair wisp lightly in the October breeze, listen to the music of her voice, maybe even get a whiff of her skin's delicate perfume, those eyes, oh, those eyes, maybe she'd smile, of course she'd smile, she always gave Father Ray a smile—

He lived for after mass. His forced little chitchat with Irene would keep him going for another week. And torment him for another week. Sweet misery.

Father Ray supposed he was going through a mid-life crisis. He was forty-seven, a prime age for the mortality thoughts to lurk and make you do stupid things. He'd seen many a marriage break up because a late-forties spouse—usually the male—lost his mind and wanted to be eighteen again.

But Father Ray had never really been eighteen. All his life he'd yearned to be a priest. From the time he was in third grade collecting donations for pagan babies, he knew that the priestly life was for him. Women had tempted before, of course. Women like priests, especially rugged guys with thick hair like Father Ray. But until Irene Donner he'd never had problems resisting them.

Until Irene.

And Irene did nothing untoward. She was unfailingly polite, treated him with priestly respect, was the perfect little parishioner—but that was the point, wasn't it? The thought of him as anything other than a priest never crossed her mind, which made him all the crazier.

He'd arrived in Tamarack after her husband had deserted her, and it astonished him that any man could've left a woman like Irene. Father Ray ached with the desire to be the new man in her life, the one who could take care of her, help her raise Itchy, love her, share her bed, love her....

As he gave the final blessing, Father Ray's voice quavered with anticipation. In a few short minutes he'd be speaking to the only person who mattered anymore:

Irene Donner.

"'Morning, Father Ray," Irene said. She smiled pleasantly, then gave Itchy a mother's pinch. "Itchy..." she said, a hint of mom annoyance at the edges of her voice.

"'Morning, Father Ray," Itchy sniffled. He was dressed in his Sundays' best of stylish ultra-baggy pants and a giant puffy jacket. Irene made sure that Itchy dressed like his peers. She felt it was important that in spite of his skin problems he be like everyone else. The only downside was that he was so spindly and scrawny that he disappeared inside huge clothes like a rashy little stickman.

"Good morning, Itchy," Father Ray said. His voice cracked and he blushed red hot.

"Nice sermon, Father," Jacqueline added, although since she hadn't been listening it was pro-forma politeness. She wasn't all that impressed with Father Ray, and her Catholicism was the go to church on Sunday kind and forget about it the rest of the time.

"It's a beautiful morning, isn't it?" Irene said.

Father Ray gulped. She was so calm, so aware of the now and so blissfully ignorant of her irresistibility. "Yes. Yes it is. Fall is my favorite season."

"You said that about spring," Irene teased, and he glowed brighter red.

"Well, all God's seasons...." he sputtered, and Irene just laughed delightfully. Father Ray was drowning, and he knew he had to do something. He looked down at the perpetually scratching Itchy. "How's the research going, Itchy?"

Itchy lit up. "Sara and me found a new picture from Alder Creek!" he said excitedly, and then he launched into a long, boring eleven-year-old's description of the past week's Donner Party net surfing.

Jacqueline lit a cigarette and did a theatrical eye roll. "Don't encourage him, Padre," she said, blowing a stream of Marlboro fog in Father Ray's face. She roughly tousled Itchy's hair. "Itchy's obsessed."

"Obsession isn't necessarily a bad thing," Father Ray said, speaking to Jacqueline but looking at Irene.

"It's a sin, isn't it?" Jacqueline asked.

"Well, it can be, you see—"

"We should go, Father," Irene said. "We're keeping you from everybody else." A pair of hunched old ladies stood patiently behind them, waiting for their after-church flirt session with the handsome young priest. Old ladies loved Father Ray as much as he loved Irene.

Life wasn't fair.

"Certainly," Father Ray said, devastated that he was so stupid and boring that he couldn't keep Irene's interest.

"Have a nice week, Father," Irene said, and with that she was out of his life until next Sunday. Father Ray tried to be pleasant to his elderly admirers, but he wasn't listening to them. He watched Irene and Itchy and Jacqueline drive off in their battered old pickup, and, as usual, the emptiness of Irene's leaving left Father Ray feeling that he couldn't survive another seven days.

A week without seeing Irene Donner felt like death.

*   *   *

"That priest has a crush on you," Jacqueline said. Irene was busy making Sunday morning breakfast, but she'd burned the first batch of pancakes and now the singlewide stunk of their acrid, charred remains.

"He does not," Irene said, pouring more batter onto the skillet. "He's just shy."

"He's just horny," Jacqueline laughed, and Itchy looked up sharply from his latest Donner Party book.

"Father Ray likes Mom?" Itchy asked. He loved his mom and all, but the thought of any man actually...liking her—especially a priest—was too much. The only person who should like his mom was his long-gone dad.

"Mother," Irene glared. "Please don't say stuff like that around Itchy."

Jacqueline grinned. "Itchy knows what's going on in the world, don't you, darlin'?"

Itchy shrugged. He loved Gramma, but sometimes he didn't understand what she was talking about. She teased him as much as some of the scummy kids at school did.

"Just ignore her, Itchy. Father Ray is a good priest."

"No such thing," Jacqueline said.

"They why don't you go to Pastor Earle's church?" Irene snapped. The next batch of pancakes had already started to blacken.

Jacqueline worked on the crossword puzzle in the Sunday paper. "He's just as bad. The only thing worse than Catholics are bible-thumping pinheads like Earle and his bunch. I went to high school with Earle, I know his secrets."

Irene scraped the blackened pancake fragments out of the pan and poured more fresh batter in. Third time's a charm.

"You sound like an atheist sometimes, I swear," Irene said.

"I'm just skeptical, honey. You should be skeptical about everything. Especially anything men are involved with." Jacqueline looked over her paper at Itchy. "You're not gonna be like the rest of the men in the world when you grow up, are you Itchy?"

"I dunno."

"'Spose not. You'll be a Donner Party scholar, probably spend your life at some college library with musty books about cannibal pioneers."

"They weren't cannibals!" Itchy and Irene said in unison.

Jacqueline grinned. "Gotcha! You two are so predictable." Pleased with herself, she went back to her crossword.

Itchy thumbed through his book. Gramma tired him out with all her opinions and jokes. She constantly made fun of the Donners and it really bothered him. Just because she wasn't related to them didn't give her the right to accuse them of being cannibals. At least his mom understood; she was as proud of the Donners as Itchy was, even though she didn't have their blood running through her veins.

The book Itchy studied was a new one. Mrs. Frandsen at the library had ordered it from another library for him. It was a day-to-day account of the Donner Party trip, with lots of pictures and maps and quotes from the people who'd been there. It was a really good book, except for the parts that said the Donners ate people near the end. That never happened. It couldn't have. Itchy got so mad at all the books that accused the Donners of eating people. He'd even read that other Donner descendants—these were people who were *related* to him, for gosh sakes—say they understood why the Donners ate people. That they had to survive and all that junk. What a pack of lies. If they just would read Eliza Donner's book they'd know the cannibalism stuff wasn't true. Eliza was *there*, and if she said the Donners didn't eat anybody, that was good enough for Itchy.

A rotten muffler's roar growled up in front of the singlewide. "That'll be Stanley and Mart. Go let 'em in, Itchy," Jacqueline said. She was closer to the door than Itchy, but Jacqueline never interrupted her crossword puzzle working when a kid was in the house. It bugged Itchy that he was the automatic slave around grown-ups, but what could you do? They always had the power and used it. Even the nice ones. Itchy looked forward to being old enough someday to be able to boss kids around. It must be fun, he thought.

He opened the door and watched as Gramma's boyfriend Stan the Man helped Mart Lane out of the truck. Mart was a friend of Itchy's mom—and had been a friend of his dad, too, they told him. Mart was a really good guy; he always treated Itchy as if he was interesting and paid close attention to Itchy's Donner Party stories. Stan the Man Bent was the local Mr. Fixit/contractor/jack-of-all-trades; his beater pickup's bed always overflowed with junk and bizarre-looking tools whose uses Itchy could never figure out, and the smeary lettering on the truck's door read: "Stan the Man—Rome wasn't built in a day, but then, I wasn't on the job." Stan the Man was proud of his logo even though Jacqueline teased him unmercifully about it. He was a gangling, unattractive guy, all bobbing Adam's apple and bony elbows, and, at thirty-one, was old enough to be Jacqueline's son. Jacqueline had dated him on and off since he graduated from high school with Irene. "For shits and giggles," she always told Irene. "Besides, he fixes things for me," she added with a leer that grossed her daughter out. Stan the Man's loyalty to Jacqueline amazed everyone in town. Jacqueline could be a bossy handful, but Stan the Man put up with everything she dished out because he loved her the way a kicked dog loves his master. He never could convince her to love him back. He kept trying, though.

"Hey, Itchy," Stan the Man waved as he wheeled Mart up the driveway. Mart's wheelchair bounced and bucked in the soft gravel, and Stan the Man had to wrestle the chair like it was alive and fighting back. "Wish to hell Irene would let me pave this for her," Stan the Man grumbled.

Mart grinned. Stan the Man complained every Sunday when they came over for breakfast. It was one of their many rituals. After Mart had been crippled, Stan the Man took him in and looked after him. They'd been pals back in high school, and after graduation Mart had gone to work in the woods. His parents died, but he stayed in town, and when the accident happened Stan the Man stepped up, did the right thing, and helped his old friend out. Tamarack was tight-knit and looked after its own, so after all the Mart Lane fundraising dinners and carwashes and Stan the Man's generosity, Mart had turned out just fine.

Except he couldn't walk anymore.

Itchy had asked him once at a Sunday breakfast what had happened to him, and that was the only time that Mart hadn't been friendly. He suddenly clammed up, and didn't say a word the rest of the morning. Irene had scolded Itchy afterwards.

"Don't ask Mart about that again. It's not something he wants to talk about with...us."

"Why?"

"Because."

"Is it a big secret or something? How come I can't ask him?"

"Because I say so."

"But that's not a real reason!"

Irene said nothing more, but the way she glowered at Itchy warned him that he'd better keep his mouth shut around Mart. At least about the accident. By next Sunday all was forgotten, and Mart had been real nice to Itchy. They even played Monopoly after Irene's blackened pancakes ("Cajun style," Jacqueline teased) and too-pink sausage links.

Today, everything was fine. As Stan the Man wheeled Mart into Irene's singlewide, Irene leaned down and gave Mart his Sunday kiss on the cheek. Mart had known Irene since kindergarten, but she tended to treat him like an infirm, elderly uncle. She patted him, cooed feminine concern, but in the end—to Irene, anyway—Mart was a dear old friend, with the emphasis on *old*.

Which was too bad for Mart, because he, like Father Ray, was desperately in love with her. Always had been, even when they played tag in the first grade, when he'd shyly watch her from across the classroom in sixth grade, when he won the Tamarack junior logger championship in the ninth grade and gave her his ribbon, when he'd played football on Tamarack High's 1987 eight-man state champion team and she'd cheered him on, even...even when Red Donner blew into town and stole her heart.

And broke Mart's.

Mart first saw Red Donner in Pencil Pandola's bar, the Tamarack Slurp 'n' Burp. Pencil had run the bar since the late '50s, after he'd sawed off three fingers in the Tamarack mill and decided that working around buzzing saws wasn't for him. Tamarack's only other bar had burned down shortly before Pencil's accident, so, seeing a need, he borrowed a few thousand dollars from A. Jackson Flynn's dad—who was a firm believer in keeping his employees happily inebriated on Friday and Saturday nights—to open his own place. Tamarack without a bar was like a Catholic church without a crucifix...it just didn't make any sense.

Pencil—who'd gotten his nickname in high school after friends noticed the alarming thinness of his dick while in the P.E. showers—ran the Slurp 'n' Burp as Tamarack's cathedral of beer. He couldn't count the number of fights, love affairs, divorces, conceptions, and all manner of human behaviors that had occurred in or because of his beloved bar. Tamarack without Pencil's Slurp 'n' Burp was unimaginable.

And, on a chilly Saturday night in 1988, Red Donner walked in and changed a whole bunch of lives.

The Slurp 'n' Burp was jumping that night, the day after payday, when guys from the mill and the woods gathered to burn off money and steam. Loggers, even the old geezers in their forties, still had lots of energy at the end of a long week, and the Slurp 'n' Burp was the only place to get rid of it.

Mart was there with his pals, throwing back boilermakers and stealing glances at Irene. She was a regular on the weekends, as were most of Tamarack's single women, and on that night she was with her mom and Stan the Man. Even though Irene, Stan the Man and Mart were only nineteen, Pencil gladly served up the booze. Some of the town bluenoses like Pastor Earle had threatened to call the state and turn Pencil in for serving minors, but they thought better of it when a few anonymous calls warned them that if the Slurp 'n' Burp closed, they wouldn't be welcome in Tamarack anymore. They might even end up in bodily trouble, if they knew what that meant. So Pastor Earle backed off and instead held Friday night prayer sessions with his tiny flock. Pastor Earle had grown up with these people. He wasn't stupid.

Red Donner strolled in that night, his big boots clunking on the wooden floor, and even though the bar was a smoky, noisy, chaotic place, eyes immediately locked onto him. Strangers were always noted in Tamarack.

The first thing Mart noticed about Red was how big he was. He had a big man's swagger, and with a huge bushy beard, a massive head, huge muscles pushing against his shirt—Red Donner was one intimidating human being. To Mart's eyes he looked like the kind of guy who'd be hitting people before the night was out, punching poor losers into unconsciousness with his big, meaty fists.

Red strode up and leaned on the bar right next to Mart. He glanced Mart's way with a dismissive look, and with a deep, burly, manly-man's voice growled to Pencil Pandola, "Jack Daniel's. Leave the bottle." He tossed a twenty on the bar.

34

Mart and his pals watched silently as the huge stranger poured his Jack into a shot glass and downed shot after shot. Mart was as full of a nineteen-year-old's bluster and testosterone as any backwoods kid, but Red Donner scared him.

Red drank silently for a few minutes. When he spoke next, it was so softly that Mart almost couldn't hear him.

"Did it work?" Red asked.

"'Scuse me?" Mart said.

"Did it work? Everybody afraid of me?" Red looked over at Mart and grinned. And when Red smiled, Mart realized that as formidable-looking as Red Donner was, the minute he grinned the truth came out: Red Donner was a big, muscle-bound, goofy bullshitter.

"Scared the crap outa me," Mart grinned back.

"I love doin' that," Red said, and he poured Mart a shot. "Only problem is, sometimes some drunk meathead don't get the message and I gotta go *mano-a-mano* with him. Hate hurtin' people, but what can you do?" Red tossed back another shot, and the grin got even wider. "You believe that, son?"

"You look like you can hurt people."

"Looks are deceiving. I'm a fuckin' pussycat." Red held out his hand. "Red Donner."

Mart shook it and tried not to grimace as Red's huge hand crushed his. "Mart Lane."

"You a logger, Mart?"

"Yep."

"Me too. Best job in the fuckin' world, ain't it?"

Mart shrugged. "You looking for a job?"

"Heard there might be something. I been working down in Northern California, but the fuckin' tree huggers are stirrin' up so much trouble it's hard to keep workin'. Thought I'd give it a shot up here."

Mart told him that times weren't great, but a good man could usually hook up with a crew.

"Glad to hear it," Red said, looking around the bar. His eyes came to rest on Irene and didn't leave. "Well now. I think I might like it here."

Mart followed his gaze. "It's a good town," Mart said. "People are nice." Mart knew he sounded like a dope, but he wanted to keep Red talking—and not looking at Irene.

"How come nobody's dancin'?" Red asked. "Place like this should be jumpin'. 'Specially with all these pretty women sittin' around."

"Usually starts later," Mart said, and he knew the jealous lump in his stomach would keep him awake tonight. Mart was a sensitive soul, especially where Irene Weatherly was concerned. And as much as he'd taken an immediate liking to Red Donner, if this guy was going to hit on Irene there'd be trouble. Well, maybe not trouble, exactly. Mart was still afraid of him. He was big and older and Mart sensed a little craziness inside him. You could never tell with gigantic, happy-go-lucky bullshitters.

Red strode over to the jukebox, fed it, and the country twang began. He came back to the bar and poured himself and Mart another shot. "Let's see if that wakes 'em up."

"Where you from originally, Red?" Mart asked. He liked talking to the big man, even if he did have his eye on Irene. And maybe if Mart kept him occupied he wouldn't put the moves on her, although Mart doubted that anything could stop Red Donner from doing what he wanted to do.

"Sacramento," Red said. "Come from a long line of Donners that've been livin' there forever. You heard of the Donner Party?"

"Sure."

"Those're my people. Great-great-grandparents."

"No shit? I thought they all got eaten?"

"See, there's a goddamn misconception about that. Nobody ever gets the fuckin' story straight." Red proceeded to tell him the real Donner saga, at least in Red's opinion. "And the way I heard my old relatives tell it," Red finished up after he'd taken Mart through the Sierras with his ancestors, "the Donners were the only ones who didn't eat nobody. Some of *them* got eaten, though. After they passed on. But the Donners never had ass roasts or finger sandwiches," Red said, then he chuckled. "Ass roasts...sometimes I crack myself up." He threw back another shot. Red Donner had an amazing capacity for liquor; he'd already finished two-thirds of the bottle. Mart had a major buzz going, and he knew that if he didn't stop he'd soon be puking out in the parking lot.

And that just wouldn't do, because he wanted to make sure he got in a dance or two with Irene.

A few couples started dancing, and pretty soon the bar was really jumping. Red asked a couple of older women to dance, and he did a mean two-step. He had the natural ability that some big men possess to be both huge and oddly graceful.

He came back to the bar, sweaty and grinning, and poured himself another shot.

"Pretty good dancer for an old guy," Mart said.

Red grinned. "Fuckin' A, Bubba. Learned a long time ago that bein' a good dancer was the key to gettin' laid. Women love the shit. You dumb-ass kids oughta figure that out."

"I can dance okay," Mart protested.

"Let's see you, then," Red said. "Go ask that pretty little thing you been starin' at since I walked in here. Show me your shit."

Mart blushed and felt like an idiot. Was it so obvious that a big, drunk stranger could tell he loved Irene?

"Well...."

"Don't be a pussy. Get her started, then I'll show you how to do it."

Mart tossed down a shot and headed over to Irene's table. After all these years, she still made him nervous. Whenever he got around her, he stammered and bumbled and blushed like a fool. She always acted like she didn't notice, but that was only because she was so nice.

Another reason to love her.

"Hey, Irene. How 'bout a dance?" Mart asked. Stan the Man grinned like he always did when Mart acted dopey around Irene. He knew Mart's whole unrequited love story. So did Jacqueline. She invariably said something to humiliate Mart and make him feel like a third-grader with a crush on his teacher.

"You been in the sun, Mart? Lookin' kinda flushed," Jacqueline said with an evil grin. She sucked down Marlboro smoke and nudged Stan the Man in the ribs. She'd just started dating Stan the Man, and Stan the Man thought he'd died and gone to heaven. "You wouldn't believe the shit she does to me in bed," he bragged to Mart. Mart thought the whole older woman/younger guy business was tawdry, but at least Stan the Man was getting laid.

That was more than Mart could say.

His love for Irene was of the Virgin Mary variety, and Mart wasn't sure he could ever get past the worship-from-afar place he'd been stuck in since 1973.

"Forget them," Irene said brightly. She gave Mart a dazzling smile, the smile that always made his knees weak. She jumped up, took his hand, and they went to the crowded dance floor.

There was line dancing, two-stepping, all kinds of country-western bar stomping. Irene danced well, of course. It seemed to Mart that women just naturally knew how to do it. She led the way in a two-step, and Mart did his best. But even though Mart was lean and athletic, dancing never made much sense to his feet and they always got tangled up.

"You're doing good," Irene laughed encouragingly. Part of the reason his dancing sucked was that he couldn't take his eyes off of her. Her hair spun when she moved, sometimes touching his face, and her eyes, the smile...it was all to much for Mart. Irene Weatherly turned him into mush.

He was doing his best to two-step when he sensed something big behind him. He turned. Red Donner stood, grinning.

"Gonna let your buddy cut in?"

Mart hesitated. Time with Irene was precious, but Red was his new friend, and Mart was nothing if not polite, so he gallantly stepped aside. "Irene," he said, "this is Red Donner. He's new in town." That didn't seem like enough, so for some reason Mart added, "He's descended from the Donner Party people."

Irene smiled. "Really? I thought they all got eaten."

Red shook his big bear head sadly and sighed, "Oh Lord, gimme strength," and then he whirled Irene around the dance floor while Mart watched helplessly.

They were perfectly matched: delicate, beautiful Irene and larger than life Red. Their oppositeness complemented each other, and they danced perfectly. Mart understood now what Red had been talking about. A guy and woman dancing—the right way—it was like they were doing something intimate. It was a lot like sex.

Mart went back to the bar and finished Red's bottle of Jack Daniel's.

Red and Irene danced the rest of the night. And when Mart finally staggered outside, retching and gagging, the last thing he saw as he looked back inside the Slurp 'n' Burp was Red and Irene, alone together in a corner booth.

Red had Irene laughing, her eyes alive and sparkling. The big, blustery stranger was stealing her away from Mart.

Mart threw-up on the side of his rig, dropped his keys in the skittering autumn leaves, couldn't find them, and ended up staggering home.

"Hungry, Mart?" Irene asked as she loaded up his plate with pancake fragments. The third batch wasn't badly burned; they just weren't quite intact.

"You bet, Irene." He looked up at her and smiled. He marveled that she hadn't changed much since high school. She was thirty-one now, and having lived through the brief marriage to Red, raising Itchy alone, and being poor in Tamarack, Irene showed no wear and tear. She remained beautiful and apparently happy. Mart wished he could say the same about himself.

After the accident and the long convalescence, Mart's hair had thinned, his muscular frame shrunk, he'd turned sallow and pasty—if he'd ever hoped to win Irene, the accident ruined his chances forever.

All because of fucking Red Donner.

"Whatcha been up to this week, Mart?" Jacqueline asked. It was her standard Sunday breakfast question, one that Mart dreaded.

"Not much, Mrs. W," he said. He'd never quite gotten comfortable calling her "Jacqueline." She was old enough—just barely—to be his mom. And as far as Mart was concerned, you didn't call your mom by her first name.

"You workin' hard on the computer stuff?" Jacqueline asked.

"Yeah," Mart said. He'd signed up for an online university class in accounting. He hated it, but he needed to do something. He cashed a disability check each month, but he despised himself for living like crippled loser. If he got some kind of degree, maybe he could work and start feeling decent again.

"I'm so glad you're doing that," Irene said. "You won't leave Tamarack once you get smarter than the rest of us, will you?" Her voice, the smile she gave him when she teased "smarter than the rest of us"...it just killed him.

"You oughta do somethin' like that, Stanley," Jacqueline said, looking Stan the Man up and down with a disappointed frown.

"I'm just a workin' grunt. Mart's got the brains." He shoveled in pancake debris like a starving man. "Besides, you don't want me leaving town, do you?"

"Nah. Guess not. You're my boy-toy."

"Mom, please," Irene said disgustedly, gesturing to Itchy.

"What?" Itchy asked.

"Gramma's being weird again."

"Your momma's old for her age, Itch." Jacqueline speared one of Itchy's sausages from his plate. "You weren't gonna eat that, were you?"

"Gramma!"

"Jeez, everybody's pickin' on Jacqueline today. You wouldn't want me to starve like those old relatives of yours, would you?"

"Mother," Irene warned.

"Gramma!" Itchy said, annoyed. More Donner Party bashing was on the way. Itchy couldn't understand why his Gramma insisted on making fun of them.

"So sensitive," Jacqueline said.

Mart decided to rescue Itchy; he was looking a bit put-upon. "Hey Itch, after breakfast why don't you show me the latest."

"Sure!" Itchy said. His gramma-induced pout wafted away. Whenever an adult showed the slightest interest in his never-ending quest for Donner Party trivia, Itchy's spirits soared. It was the *one* thing he had over everybody else. He might get beat-up at school, he might get made fun of, or have to listen to cannibal jokes, he had to scratch his way through life with scaly, ugly, crusty patches, but Itchy Donner always had the ace in the hole:

He was descended from the heroic Donner Party. And he swore to himself he'd never let anybody forget it.

Mart listened politely as Itchy showed him the latest stuff he'd downloaded and printed at Sara's house, and then they thumbed through the new library book. Mart liked Itchy. He felt bad that the kid was so scaly and nasty looking, but Mart understood the feeling of being different. People in town were always nice to him—as most of them were to Itchy—but when you were crippled or disfigured or diseased people treated you differently. Mart couldn't stand condescension and pity. He was proud, a man, not a delicate little girl—and he hated being treated like one.

He knew that Itchy had a tough road ahead. Especially if he stayed a Donner Party nerd. It was one thing for a little kid to be obsessed by something—dinosaurs, baseball cards, computer games—but you had to let the kid stuff go when you grew up. Mart hoped the Donner Party curiosity would recede as Itchy aged. If not, he'd end up a sad, scaly spaz forever cornering unwilling victims with noisy blurts of, "Hey, look at what I just found out about Tamsen Donner!" And as much as Mart hated Itchy's father, he didn't want anything bad for Itchy. Because although Itchy was half-Red, he was also half-Irene. And the Irene part was what mattered. Mart saw more of Irene in Itchy than Red, thank God, and he hoped that would never change.

Sunday morning became Sunday afternoon. Jacqueline worked on her crossword puzzle and bantered with Stan the Man, who watched the Patriots and the Rams between spells of dozing off. Irene puttered, doing some laundry, sitting down to watch the football game, hanging around as Itchy and Mart played Scrabble (Mart got the word "cannibal" on a triple letter score and really teed Itchy off). Mart kept an eye on Irene at all times. To Mart, Sundays at Irene's was like being married. It wasn't real, it never would be, but that didn't matter.

It *felt* real.

Irene stood beside Mart, her hand on his shoulder, and studied his letter tiles. "Hmm," she said. "You could make 'blrgnrp'."

"Thanks a bunch." He tried to sound light and cheery, but her touch made him self-conscious. Had his voice just cracked?

"He made 'cannibal' on the triple word score!" Itchy complained. "'Cannibal'! Can you believe it?"

"Not everything is about the Donners, honey," Irene said. And she gave Mart's shoulder a squeeze.

He was about to speak when somebody knocked at the front door. Two heavy *bangs!*

"Jesus," Jacqueline said. "Sound like they're gonna knock it down."

Irene took her hand from Mart's shoulder and went to answer the door. Mart closed his eyes for a second. The touch, as always, was so sweet.

Irene grabbed the doorknob. She usually looked through the peephole, but this time she didn't. Maybe it was because everybody was over, and she felt safe. Maybe she forgot. She'd never know.

Because, she thought later, if she'd looked through the peephole first everything might've been different.

She opened the door.

And there stood Red Donner.

During a rest break, we children stretched our limbs and scampered off on frolics. We waded the creek, made mud pies, and gathered posies in the narrow glades between the cottonwood trees. The wild, free spirit of the plain prompted us to canter with the breeze playing through our hair.

Eliza Donner
July 2, 1846

Chapter Three

Irene stood, paralyzed.

Stan the Man sat up on the couch, muted the football game, and stared at the doorway. Jacqueline was unnaturally silent. Mart rolled his wheelchair away from the table, knocked the Scrabble game sideways and sent the letter tiles flying.

Itchy didn't recognize Red at first—he'd only seen a few blurry pictures—so he was the first to break the silence. "Who is it? How come everybody's acting so weird?"

Jacqueline shot him a sharp look and held up her hand. Irene didn't move. Red studied her for the longest time, and then a thin smile creased his face. "Miss me?" he asked.

Irene slammed the door.

"No reason to be that way, Irene," Red called from outside.

"Is that...my Dad?" Itchy asked.

The blood had drained out of Mart's face; his skin was transparent.

"Yeah," Mart whispered.

Nobody ever said much to Itchy about his dad. Irene would dutifully answer his questions—because Itchy *was* curious, after all—but she usually kept her answers short and sweet and squeezed any judgment out of her voice.

"How come he left?" Itchy had asked.

"Well, sometimes things don't work out between people."

"Did he leave because of me?"

Irene gave Itchy a reassuring hug. "Your father left because of other things that happened. I'm sure that if he'd stayed he would've loved you just as much as I do."

"How come he's never come back to see me?"

Irene hesitated. It was the only time Itchy could remember her saying anything negative about Red Donner. "Your father is...weak. He's afraid of problems. And I think he has a guilty conscience. I'm sure he thinks about you every day, and I'll bet he's sad that he can't be here to be your father and to love you. So I just have to make up for it and love you twice as much." Itchy liked what she said and that she hugged him so hard, but he still wondered about his dad. It seemed weird to him that the guy didn't want to meet him. After that, Itchy pretty much stopped asking about Red. Nobody ever gave him a straight answer, not even Gramma. She usually just lit up another cigarette and told him not to worry about it.

"Don't think he's goin' away, honey," Jacqueline said softly as Irene stood at the door. "Might as well let him in and see what he wants."

Irene still couldn't move. She swallowed hard.

"Honey?" Jacqueline said. "Let him in. Itchy should meet him."

This was all too strange for Itchy. Everybody was acting like Red was at the door waving an Uzi. Should they be afraid of him?

Irene finally reached out and slowly turned the knob. The door creaked open.

Red smiled. "Hello again."

"Hi...Red." Irene said his name with difficulty. "Was that you who called the other night?"

Red shrugged. But the guilty smile said, "Yes."

Itchy got up and slowly moved next to Irene. Red looked older than the pictures Itchy had seen. His big, bushy beard was speckled with gray, and his chin was snow white. His hair was graying too, and he looked grubby and dirty to Itchy, like he hadn't washed his clothes—or taken a shower—in a while.

The thing that amazed Itchy was how huge Red was. How could this be his father? Itchy was a puny runt, he couldn't believe he was related to the giant, bear-like guy standing in the doorway. It gave Itchy hope that maybe someday he'd be big and strong, too, and wouldn't have to take any more junk from the bullies of the world.

Red Donner looked past Irene and down at his son. The psoriasis was in a surly mood, and the patches on Itchy's cheeks and neck were particularly inflamed.

Red frowned. "Is this?—" he asked Irene.

"Itchy."

"Itchy?"

"Jacob George. But we call him Itchy."

"What's wrong with his face?"

Tears immediately flooded Itchy's eyes, and he tried to fight them back but couldn't. They spilled out onto his cheeks and Irene protectively grabbed his shoulders and pulled him to her.

"Damn you, Red!"

"Well, I just wondered—"

Itchy couldn't believe it. His own father finally meets him, and the first thing out of his mouth is a biting question just as mean as anything he had to put up with at school. He hated crying like a little baby, but the long-imagined reunion with his dad wasn't supposed to start this way.

"Hey, I'm sorry, okay? I'm not good with kids." Red reached out and touched Itchy's shaking shoulder. He squatted down to Itchy's level. Itchy turned from his mother's hug and faced his father. "Sorry, Itchy. I'm kinda stupid sometimes. But I'm sure your mom's told you that."

Itchy sniffed back snotty tears. His dad's face was so close, so real. But it seemed like a bad dream. Itchy gulped and resisted the urge to scratch at his flaming patches. They itched so much they hurt. But he didn't want to be a baby. Not in front of his dad, who seemed like the strongest man in the world.

"It's okay," Itchy said, so quietly that only Red heard him.

"Kids give you a load of crap about that stuff?" Red asked.

"Sometimes."

"You kick their asses when they do?"

"Red, please," Irene said.

"He should stand up for himself, Irene."

Red stood and smiled. "Helluva an entrance, huh?" He looked around the singlewide. "Hey, Jackie. Stan. Still together, huh?"

"*Jacqueline*," she corrected.

"Oh yeah, I forgot," Red said. He sighed.

"How you doin', Red?" Stan the Man asked.

Red shrugged. Then he saw Mart. It surprised Itchy that his father suddenly seemed smaller and weaker when he looked at Mart. It was as if Red had been punched in the stomach.

"Hey, Mart."

Mart said nothing.

"You doin' okay, buddy?"

"What do you think?" Mart snapped.

"Guess everybody's glad to see me," Red said.

"You want some coffee?" Irene asked.

"Sure."

Red plopped down on the worn easy chair opposite the couch. He sat across from Jacqueline and Stan the Man, and nobody said anything. Mart glowered from the kitchen table. He made no move to join them in the living room.

"You're smelling a little ripe, Red," Jacqueline said.

"Love you, too. Been on the road awhile. Had to hitchhike up here."

"You gonna stay?" Stan the Man asked.

"Don't know. Maybe. Depends." Red looked over at Mart. "Depends on a lot of things."

Itchy sat next to Jacqueline. He stared at his dad, trying to figure out what had just happened. If he was going to stay, did that mean he was moving in? Maybe it was good that his dad was back, but he wasn't sure. Nobody seemed very excited, and he wasn't all that positive that he'd be able to like this guy.

Irene poured coffee in the kitchen. Mart watched her. Her hands shook so badly that coffee sloshed onto the counter. She carefully wiped it up and put two level teaspoons of sugar in the mug. She passed by Mart and touched his shoulder.

"You okay?" she asked.

"Yeah. How about you?"

Irene smiled gamely. "I don't know."

He wheeled behind her out into the living room and stopped next to the couch. They all faced Red like a firing squad. Irene handed Red his coffee and retreated to their side. She squeezed in next to Itchy and her mother.

Nobody said anything as Red sipped his coffee. The only movement was Red's rhythmic sipping and Itchy's squirming. His back itched, and he had to scratch it or go crazy. Irene gently rubbed him as she always did when he was nervous and uncomfortable. It usually helped, but right now the situation was so weird that all the rubbing in the world wouldn't fix things.

"Good coffee," Red said. "Got the sugar just right, as always."

More silence. Stan the Man glanced at the silent football game, but resisted the urge to turn the sound back on

Jacqueline wasn't good with long silences. "So why'd you come back?" she asked.

"Thought it was time."

"Runnin' from the law?"

Red didn't take the bait; he just smiled. "I'm different now," Red said to Jacqueline as he looked at Irene. "Eleven years changes people."

"You're not born-again or anything, are you?"

"Nah, J.W. Same old Red, just a little improved, that's all. Did one of them twelve-step deals, gave up the old demon rum."

"That supposed to be reassuring?" Jacqueline asked.

Red gave Jacqueline a warm grin. "Sure have missed you." He stood and gestured to Irene. "Can I talk to you a minute?"

"I don't think we have anything to talk about, Red," she said.

"I think we do."

Itchy pressed against her, and she realized that, at least for Itchy's sake, she needed to be adult about this. She reluctantly followed Red outside. As she closed the door she gave Mart a friendly smile, but she could tell he was seething. She didn't blame him.

She faced Red with her arms folded against both him and the October chill. Red hung his head in that hangdog way that she knew so well.

"If there's a gooey Red Donner apology on the way, don't bother."

"Dunno if it's gooey or not, but I am sorry, Irene."

"For what?"

"Everything."

"I can't forgive you. Not after what you've done to us," she whispered. For years she'd imagined what she'd say if she ever saw Red again, but now the carefully memorized bitter words jammed in her throat. Her voice had vanished, and the best she could do was a raspy croak.

"Don't expect you to," he said. "But I've come back to try and fix things anyway."

"Then start with Itchy and Mart. It's too late for you and me."

Red shoved his hands in his pockets and looked down the street. The singlewide was perched on a hillside above Tamarack and had a commanding view of the town. It was beautiful now, with the golden red fall colors and clear air. Even the shacky houses and trailers looked good in the hard October light.

"You own this place?" Red asked.

"Yeah. I saved, and Mom helped. We wanted a real home for Itchy."

Red gazed out over Tamarack. "Where's that little house we used to live?"

"They tore it down after Itchy and I moved out. The county condemned it." Another sore spot. Red had gotten them tied into a lease on the nastiest, most ramshackle dump in a town filled with them. Pencil Pandola owned it, and Red swore that Pencil gave them a good deal, but Irene suspected that Pencil forced Red into a lease because his tab at the Slurp 'N' Burp was so high.

"Too bad," Red said. "Always liked that old house."

"It was a wreck, just like everything you ever had anything to do with. Why'd you have to come back, Red? We were doing fine."

Red sighed. "I fucked everything up, Irene. I fucked up bad. But I need to fix things. I need to get to know Itchy. Maybe even patch things up with Mart, if he'll let me. But most of all...I need to make things up with you."

"I already told you, that's not possible." Irene tried to be firm, but Red's woebegone contrition had thrown her off. She was too kindhearted to enjoy kicking him while he was down—even if he deserved it.

Red gave her his best impossible-to-resist smile. "Can't blame me for trying, can you? I never forgot you. And you're even more beautiful now than when I left."

"Stop it. You're pulling the old Red Donner con on me. I'm not nineteen anymore."

"It's no con. It's the truth. But I don't expect you to believe me right off the bat. That's why I'm gonna stay here until—"

"There won't be an 'us.' Ever."

"I'm gonna stay here until...." Red continued, then trailed off. Red's confused frown was a first—Irene couldn't remember him ever seeming so vulnerable. She had to be careful; Red was sneaky. *Don't forget what he's done*, she reminded herself.

"Until what?" Irene asked quietly.

"Until you dance with me again," he smiled.

She shook her head. This was going to be a nightmare. She turned and went back inside the singlewide. She prayed that Red wouldn't follow her.

But he did.

Sunday afternoon passed as a tense blur. Mart retreated to a far corner of the living room and pretended to watch the football game with Stan the Man. Jacqueline pretended to work her crossword puzzle, Irene pretended to be busy in the kitchen making Sunday supper—

And Itchy didn't know what to do. He was both fascinated and frightened by his father. Red sat silently, watching the football game and contentedly sipping an iced tea. Itchy sat on the floor and flipped through his Donner Party book, but for once he didn't really see the pictures. Too much tension, too much weirdness in his home. He wanted to talk to his father, but he didn't know what to say or how to start. He kept waiting for Red to do something, to act Dad-like, but all Red did was sigh and drink his coffee. Itchy had always wished his father would come back, he'd fantasized about it, but now that he had the reality wasn't all that special. His father was just a big stranger who nobody seemed to like.

The game was a blowout, and at the beginning of the fourth quarter, Red glanced down at Itchy.

"Whatcha readin'?" he asked.

Itchy hesitated. Red's gruffness made it sound like he was always mad. "Nothin'," Itchy said.

"Must be something, 'cause I can see it," Red said. His voice had an irritated edge to it, and Itchy realized he'd better not pull any pouty stuff with this guy or there'd be big trouble.

"It's about the Donner Party."

"You know we're related to them, don't you? Your mom tell you about that?" Red's voice was suddenly friendly.

"Yeah. She told me back when I was a kid."

Red smiled. "A kid? What the hell are you now?"

"I mean when I was a really little kid."

Jacqueline looked up from 48-across. "He's obsessed with those cannibal cousins of yours, Red. All he ever does is study 'em."

"They weren't cannibals!" Itchy complained.

"Nobody ever gets it right, do they, Itch?" Red chuckled.

"No! It makes me mad. The Donners never ate anybody. The Murphys, Keseburg, the Breens—"

"Shit, you been studyin'. Sounds like you know more about it than I do."

Red got down on the floor next to Itchy and peered at the book. Itchy pointed out the pictures he liked best—photos of Donner Lake and the Alder Creek campsites today. "Have you ever been there?" Itchy asked.

"Drove by it a bunch of times. You can see that big-ass memorial from the freeway."

"How come you never stopped?" Itchy asked, appalled. He couldn't imagine being close to where his ancestors met their infamy and not stopping. He dreamed of spending days at the Donner Memorial and Alder Creek, wandering the woods, breathing the air that Tamsen and Eliza and all the rest of them breathed, seeing the views their eyes saw, absorbing the place. It was part of him, in his blood.

"I was usually in a hurry, I guess. Always headed somewhere."

"Or away from somewhere," Jacqueline added.

Red ignored her. "Maybe we could go down there sometime, Itch. Check the place out. Light candles or somethin' for our dead relatives."

"Really?!"

"Sure. Why not?"

Itchy glanced over at his mother. She was peeling potatoes to boil for her usual Sunday supper of lumpy mashed spuds. Her expression was fiercely neutral. At least she wasn't screaming "No!", so Itchy figured that was a good sign. "Can I go, Mom?" he asked.

"We'll see."

Itchy hated the "We'll see" or "Maybe later" answers. They invariably meant "No."

"You and Itchy gonna hitchhike down there, Red?" Stan the Man asked. "Don't have a rig, do you?"

"Not yet. Soon as I start workin', though, that'll change."

"So you staying, then?" Jacqueline asked.

Red looked down at Itchy and smiled. "I believe I might," he said quietly.

Irene closed her eyes. Mart grimaced.

Red Donner was back to stay.

It didn't take long for things to seem routine.

Red showed up at Irene's singlewide every Sunday for breakfast, watched football, and stayed through supper. In a short time Red was as much a part of the weekly ritual as Stan the Man falling asleep on the couch or Jacqueline begging for help with her crossword puzzle. Red slowly got to know Itchy, and they spent a lot of time talking about the Donner Party.

"Did anybody ever tell you anything?" Itchy had asked. "I mean, like old relatives or something?"

"Yeah, my grandma told me some stories," Red said as he inhaled Irene's pancake fragments and runny eggs. Her food bill had risen noticeably with Red's Sunday visits, and she was considering charging him. His appetite—like everything else about him—was huge.

"What'd she tell you?" Itchy asked with wide, eager eyes.

"Well, you gotta remember, she heard this stuff from *her* grandmother, so you know how people get stuff screwed up," Red said, pancake debris clinging to his beard. "But she used to tell me when I was a little squirt about your age how she heard stories about the Donners eating leather straps. Said they tore apart some of the rescuer's snowshoes and ate the leather."

Jacqueline looked down at the burned breakfast mess on her plate. "Doesn't sound so bad to me," she said.

Irene threw her a glare. "You could always make breakfast yourself."

"Just kidding, darlin'," Jacqueline smiled sweetly. "You'll learn how to cook someday. I just know it."

"And she told me," Red continued, "that when the little Donner girls were headed down the mountain with the rescue party that they pulled pieces of leather from one of the guide's pants and ate 'em."

Itchy nodded seriously. He didn't have the heart to tell his dad that he'd read the same stories in some of the Donner Party books. This was different. It was eyewitness—four times removed. That made it better.

"Wooowww," Itchy said.

Irene watched Red as he and Itchy talked. He'd behaved so far since his return to Tamarack, and his presence seemed to be good for Itchy.

But with Red back Mart stopped coming by on Sundays, and Irene missed him. He was part of the ritual, her forever pal, and she hated the idea of him off sulking while Red happily stuffed his face and regaled Itchy with Donner trivia.

"I'll be back in a little while," Irene said, leaving Stan the Man dozing on the couch, Red and Itchy engaged in a serious discussion about the nutritional value of leather straps, and Jacqueline grousing that the crossword puzzle was full of stupid puns and no wonder she couldn't figure it out.

Irene drove over to the Slurp 'n' Burp. It wasn't noon yet, but a good-sized crowd had already started in on their Sunday football beer and peanut intake.

"Hey, Irene," Pencil Pandola said. His shaved bullet head glistened in the bar light. "I hear Red's back."

"He hasn't been in yet?"

"Nope. And he still owes me. He skipped out on a big tab. Tell him to get his ass in here and pay me off."

Irene sighed. She wasn't married to Red anymore, she didn't really want him around, but people already assumed that she had control over him. She'd never been able to make Red do anything when they were married—why would things be any different now?

"I'll tell him, Pencil. But I don't know what good it'll do. Is Mart here?"

Pencil gestured back toward the corner. Mart sat alone, his wheelchair backed into a shadowed recess behind the tables. He nursed a beer and watched the football game on the bigscreen TV.

"Hi," she said. She pulled up a chair up. Mart's lips tightened; he reminded her of Itchy when he was being a petulant snot. "We miss you on Sundays."

"Yeah." He took a Michelob sip. He couldn't look at her.

"If I could lock Red out I would, but he's Itchy's dad, so I kind of have to let him in...." It sounded wishy-washy and lame to her; she could only imagine how bad it sounded to Mart.

"Yeah, I know." He looked over at her. Her beauty always stunned him; his reaction to her never changed. "How's it going with Itchy?"

"Red's being decent so far. They talk about Donner stuff. You know how it is with Itchy. He misses you, though."

"Yeah. Kid needs his old man, I guess. Probably good they can Donner bond."

"I miss you too, Mart."

Mart set his beer down. His hands trembled, and he didn't want to waste good beer by dumping it on his lap.

"Would you consider coming back?" Irene asked.

"Not with him there."

"Would you do it for me? For Itchy?"

"It's Red, Irene, I mean, shit, I can't—"

Irene took his hand. "*I* need you there, Mart. I know how hard it is for you to be around him after...everything. It's hard for me, too. We've all suffered because of that goon."

"Some more than others."

"He's really trying with Itchy. And I think he wants to make things right with you. He just doesn't know how."

"It doesn't matter."

"It *does* matter if he messes up our lives again. And since you're not coming over anymore, that qualifies. We can't let him do that to us." Irene squeezed his hand. He looked into her eyes and couldn't look away. He was toast, and he knew it.

"Okay. You win," Mart said. "You always win."

"I know. I don't play fair." She smiled and let go of his hand. Already he missed her touch.

"Chicks...."

"Aren't we great? If you hurry there might be some leftover raw sausage and burned pancakes that Red hasn't devoured yet."

"How come you can't cook?"

"I can. I just don't like to show off. I wouldn't want people to think I'm too perfect."

I already do, he thought, disgusted with himself that he was like a lovesick junior-high-schooler. But as Irene pushed his wheelchair out to her truck and helped him in, Mart felt the lightness of relief. He might have to put up with asshole Red, but at least he'd be seeing Irene again.

Sometimes you had to make sacrifices.

My mother enthusiastically searched for botanical specimens. She delved into the ground, scraping out the crevices, and zealously gathered mosses, roots, and flowering plants. She made pencil and watercolor studies, having in view the book she planned to publish at the completion of our journey west.

Eliza Donner

July 14, 1846

Chapter Four

Itchy hated getting beat up.

Tamarack School, grades K-8, teemed with kids who enjoyed tormenting him. Sometimes Itchy wondered if his psoriasis was some kind of a green light that let grammar school punks know it was okay to smack him around.

Because it happened constantly.

Jason Bent was his biggest enemy. He was Stan the Man's second cousin, a grade ahead of Itchy, bigger, stronger, meaner—the perfect recipe for a grade school nemesis.

Jason had just tripped Itchy and sent him sprawling to the dirt. His new Donner Party library book splatted into a mud puddle, and his manila folder of printed-out Donner information fluttered into the wind, the sheets blowing like autumn leaves.

"Don't fall down," Jason taunted. He and a couple of his buddies laughed with gleeful nastiness. They reminded Itchy of hyenas.

Sara was with him, and as Itchy vainly tried to retrieve his papers and his dignity, she let the bullies have it. "You guys are mean! Jerks!" It didn't have the desired effect, though, because they just laughed and sauntered away, making sure to stomp and grind Itchy's papers into the dirt.

"Hey Itchy? Who you gonna eat for lunch today?!" Jason mocked as he went inside the dilapidated old school's front door.

"Are you okay?" Sara asked.

"Yeah. Fine." It was nice that Sara stood up for him, but it kind of bugged him, too. A geeky girl protecting him made him feel like an even bigger loser.

"Jason's such an idiot," she said.

"Forget it." He delicately rescued his Donner Party book from the puddle. Half the pages were wet and muddy, and Itchy's heart sunk. Now he'd probably have to ask his mom for money to pay for the damage when he took it back to the library. Stupid Jason Bent.

But even though his usual torturers were hard at work making his life miserable, at least some things had changed for the better recently. His dad was back and he had a new ally in town, one who understood how hard it was to be a Donner. Itchy needed allies.

He gathered up as many of the papers as he could find and he and Sara went inside for class.

Itchy fanned the pages of his wet Donner Party book as Mrs. Gronowick explained fractions. Itchy hated math, and he tuned out when numbers came up. Right now fixing the muddy book was more important than understanding the intricacies of fourths and thirds.

By the time recess came around, the book had started to dry and Itchy held out a faint hope that he might not have to pay for the damage after all.

"Wanna look at that book some more?" Sara asked.

"No. If I take it outside Jason and those guys will just mess it up again."

"Oh."

"I think I'll stay in here."

"Okay." Sara didn't have any friends other than Itchy, so if he didn't want to go outside and do something, she was stuck being alone. "Whatcha wanna do?" she asked.

"I dunno."

Mrs. Gronowick solved the problem by shooing them out. She didn't like kids staying in the classroom when they should be out in the fresh air.

Itchy left the book behind to dry, and he and Sara went outside. Their classmates did the usual recess thing—the little kids playing and squealing, the older ones in tight groups discussing important grammar school matters.

Itchy never saw the fist that smacked him in the ear and sent him to the ground. But before he heard a sound, he knew who it was.

"Your dad's an asshole," Jason Bent said.

Itchy rolled over and looked up. Jason glared down at him.

"You guys are gonna be in so much trouble, I'm telling!" Sara said as she ran off to get Mrs. Gronowick.

"He's a cannibal, huh?" Jason sneered.

"Shut up," Itchy said, rubbing his throbbing ear. "Just shut up."

"He's a drunk, too. He fucked up Mart Lane because he was drunk. Everybody thinks he's an asshole. Just like you are. Asshole. Cannibal asshole."

"Shut up!" Itchy threatened, and his squawky voice cracked. Jason and his pals just laughed at him.

"Gonna eat us?"

"Shut up!"

"Would your cannibal relatives eat you even though you have that rashy

61

shit all over you?"

Itchy snapped. He'd taken too much guff from these guys, especially Jason, and it was time to do something about it. It was one thing to make fun of him and his psoriasis, or insult his dad, but the Donner jokes, the Donner Party insults about cannibals—Itchy wasn't going to take it anymore.

He lunged at Jason Bent. He caught Jason by surprise, knocked him down, and got in a couple of weak punches before Mrs. Gronowick pulled him off. But even with Sara's eyewitness claim that Jason started it—and the obvious fact that Itchy wasn't a bully—Itchy was the one who got sent home. Which was just fine with Itchy. He could spend the rest of the day by himself, protected from bullying loudmouths who didn't care about the bravery of the Donners. He could look through his books and pictures, read the survivor's accounts for the millionth time, dream and pretend and transport himself back to January 1847. He could be with his ancestors, and maybe he could even help them. He fantasized about being at Alder Creek with Tamsen and George, he could comfort little Eliza and gather wood and maybe find food, shoot a deer or a bear, he could help them survive. If only he could go back, Itchy could be a hero, not the inflamed, itchy-skinned loser he was in the here and now.

Itchy spent the rest of the afternoon immersed in the past.

It was his favorite place.

"Did you start the fight?" Irene asked. She'd left work early after Mrs. Gronowick called and told her that Itchy had been sent home.

"No. Jason Bent did."

"Why?"

"I dunno. He makes fun of me. And he said Dad's a drunk. And he called us cannibals."

"Sticks and stones, Itchy."

"I know. It just makes me mad. People shouldn't say stuff they don't know anything about."

Irene cleared a place to sit on Itchy's bed. It was covered with his Donner Party documents and books.

"Anything new to look at?" she asked.

"No. I'm just reviewing stuff."

"You'll have everything memorized pretty soon."

"I already do," Itchy said proudly.

"Do you...." Irene hesitated. She wasn't sure she should ask, but she wanted to know. "Do you...like your father?"

"Sure. He's okay."

"What Jason Bent said about him, it might be kind of true. Your dad had trouble before with drinking and things."

Itchy shrugged. "It doesn't matter." He moved books and pictures around and rearranged them like a puzzle. "If Dad'll take me down to Alder Creek, can I go?"

"We'll see."

"Mom...."

"I said we'll see, Itchy. Your dad makes promises and sometimes he doesn't keep them."

"He'll keep this one."

Irene rubbed Itchy's back. "Even if he doesn't, maybe you and I will go down there someday. Okay?"

Itchy nodded. "It's just that he's a real Donner, he understands things. What it's like."

Itchy's words stung. Irene felt she was as much a Donner as Itchy. She was used to Itchy's undivided attention, and now she had to share him with Red—the *real Donner*. But she hid her hurt.

"Don't fight with Jason anymore. Just ignore him, okay?"

"I'll try."

Irene stood and looked down at Itchy. He'd grown recently. He was taller—although no heftier—and his face seemed different. Only eleven, and already she was losing him. Before she knew it, he'd be in high school, becoming a man, leaving her behind. And now that Red had reappeared, she feared that Itchy's leaving would only accelerate.

Irene went out to the kitchen and put water on for some tea. She stared at the kettle, waiting for it to boil. She began to cry. She wanted everything to stay the same—Itchy to always be eleven, she forever frozen at thirty-one, always cutting and styling with Jacqueline at the salon, Sundays with Mart and Jacqueline and Stan the Man—things had been perfect, why'd they have to change?

What Irene *didn't* want—and what she now had to put up with—was Red.

As the teakettle whistled, Irene sniffed back her tears and wiped her eyes. She needed to talk to somebody.

The day after Red got back into Tamarack he strolled into the Tamarack Logging and Milling Company's offices bellowing, "Action Jackson!"

A. Jackson Flynn was busy reviewing power costs with his mill foreman when Red Donner's voice boomed over the mill's shrieking saws. Red burst through the office door, grinning.

"How you doin', A. J.?" Red asked, pumping A. Jackson's hand so hard that it took all of A. Jackson's manly pride not to whimper.

"Fine, Red. Fine. Didn't think I'd be seeing you again."

"Yeah, decided to come back and try to un-fuck-up and get to know my rugrat. I hear he and your kid are best friends. Kinda ironic, ain't it?"

"They seem to like each other," A. Jackson said vaguely, trying not to grimace. He gestured to the foreman. "Give us a minute." A. Jackson waited until the foreman had closed the door, then said, "I suppose you want a job."

"The thought had crossed my mind," Red grinned. "Been on the road for awhile, it's time to start bringin' home some cash."

"Business is tough right now, Red."

"There's always room for a good faller, A.J. Nobody can put as much wood on the ground as fast as me. I'm the best. We both know that."

"Yeah, you're good when you want to be. It's just that when you left before...."

"Nobody's perfect. That's all history, anyway."

"Not to a lot of people in this town. You know how it is here, Red. Long memories. You seen Mart Lane?"

"I'm gonna work on that." Red paused, thinking. "Tell you what, you hire me on for half the goin' rate. I fuck up, you toss me, hasn't cost you much. Gimme a month to prove that old Red has changed for the better, then you pay me normal."

A. Jackson considered. Red Donner was a pain in the ass, he had some bad history, but he was as good a logger as A. Jackson had ever seen and he knew his way around the woods. And right now A. Jackson needed to save some bucks.

"We'll give it a shot," he said.

"All right." Red cuffed A. Jackson hard on the back. A. Jackson flinched. He didn't care for chummy blue-collar guys like Red pretending they were bar-room buddies.

"Planning on staying around this time?"

"Yeah. Itchy needs his old man. Too many women in his life so far. It's not good for him. Don't want him to end up a pussy."

"You and Irene getting back together?" It wasn't really any of A. Jackson's business, but since he was the mayor *and* owner of the town, he figured that in the end *everything* was his business. Whatever these people did affected his bottom line.

"Hard to say, A.J. You know women. I never been able to figure 'em out."

A. Jackson winced at the thought of Miriam, sitting at home this very moment sipping Merlot. "They're a puzzle," he agreed. Then he regretted it. He didn't like Red Donner, and he shouldn't be male-bonding with him. Keep it strictly business. "I'll let everybody know you're on board. Crew up tomorrow morning."

Red thanked him profusely and wandered off, whistling happily, yelling "Howdy" to old coworkers, and generally acting like he owned the place.

A. Jackson's doubts deepened. But it was too late now. He was a man of his word. Flynns stuck to their decisions, even if they were wrong. Besides, knowing Red Donner, something would eventually blow-up and he'd hit the road once again.

A. Jackson just hoped that nobody would get hurt like last time.

Father Ray hated writing sermons.

The parishioners didn't realize how much creativity it involved. Public speaking of any kind was tough—look how few politicians or famous people could do it well—and churning out a spiritually uplifting fifteen minutes every

Sunday had to be the most difficult public speaking of all. Father Ray admired guys like Pastor Earle who could quote scripture and scream fire and brimstone and get the crowd riled up, but that wasn't the Catholic—or Father Ray's—way.

It struck Father Ray as cheap theatrics, whipping people into an "Amen!" shouting frenzy, when what mattered were the philosophical and intellectual underpinnings of belief. God wasn't easy, or understandable, so you had to explore thoughtfully. You had to consider and study and think. Literal belief and yelling, "Can I have an Amen from the congregation!" weren't useful.

Of course, Father Ray might have had an easier time with his sermons if he wasn't so corrupted with doubt and disbelief, but that was *his* problem, not his congregation's. He had a job to do—to deliver the word of God and the teachings of the Church to these faithful people, and even if he was a faithless and disbelieving priest, he still needed to do what he was getting paid for. He likened it to somebody who hated their job, who didn't care if the company they worked for burned down, but who still showed up every day and did what was expected. Ministering was about a clock-punching work ethic. You didn't have to be a believer—you just needed to show up.

Not terribly inspiring, but it was the best he could do.

He thumbed through a well-worn joke book, searching for something clever and witty that might coax a smile from Irene Donner. He spent most of his sermon-writing time thinking of ways to impress her. It was *so* juvenile, and he knew it. Tough luck, though. Nothing he could do about it. He smiled to himself, because he knew he sounded just like some of his parishioners in confession: "But Father, I couldn't *help* it! Maybe the devil made me do it." Yep, the old devil excuse. Father Ray decided that his Irene infatuation must be the work of Satan. Nothing to be done. He was a victim.

He gave up looking through the book after a few minutes. None of the jokes seemed funny. Father Ray slouched at his cluttered desk and stared at the notepad lying in front of him. Scribbled ideas, words, phrases—he knew what it meant. This Sunday would be another in the long, inglorious line of crappy Father Ray sermons. He wasn't any good at this. Why in the world did he ever want to become a priest? Just because you're filled with faith and fervor doesn't mean you've got the talent to move others, to minister to their needs. He should've gone off to a contemplative monastery and spent his days praying and pulling weeds in the monk's orchard. Manual labor for God. He probably would've been good at that. At least in a monastery there wouldn't be women to tempt him away from love of the Lord and faith.

He should never have become a parish priest. It seemed so obvious now.

He turned up the space heater against the early November chill. His office and living area was a cramped little shack to the side of the church, and it was never comfortable. Frigid in the winter, sweltering in the summer. Just more punishment, he decided, for his faithlessness. He deserved it.

He almost didn't hear the light knock at his door. It was early evening, and the hard cold that descended on Tamarack was lit by a bright full moon. Father Ray had watched the moon rise over the nearby hills, hoping it would give him inspiration, but all it did was make him lonely. The freshening cold and impending winter always depressed him.

The knock sounded again, and Father Ray reluctantly went to answer it. He hoped it wasn't anything bad, like his being summoned to give last rights. Usually, nighttime visits were either that or troubled members of the flock seeking forgiveness or advice. He'd have to brush off whoever it was. He wasn't in the mood to be helpful and understanding. Not tonight.

When he opened the door and saw Irene Donner, smiling that smile that made him weak, it blew away his cold night's sermon-writing depression. Maybe things weren't so bad after all.

"Oh! Hello, Irene."

"Hi, Father. I hope I'm not catching you at a bad time?"

"It's not like priests have real lives or anything," he smiled, and she laughed. *Good, very good.* A clever comeback and for once he didn't sound like an idiot. "C'mon in."

He stood aside and let her pass. She was small and slight, so feminine, and her slender presence made him want to put his arms around her. The urge almost overpowered him, and he had to force himself to think of something, *anything*, other than holding her.

"Have a seat," he said. He pulled a worn chair over by his desk. She sat and smiled up at him.

"Are you sure it's okay to bother you?"

"It's not a bother, Irene. I promise. That's why I get the big bucks." It was light and flip, and Father Ray worried that he sounded mercenary and uncaring, so he quickly added, "It's always a pleasure. We're friends after all." He hoped whatever she wanted to talk about would take a long, long time, because he didn't want her to leave. He could spend all night sitting across from her. It beat sleeping—and it certainly beat writing a stupid sermon.

He sat down and willed himself into concerned priest-mode. "Would you like some coffee or something? I might even have a beer or two in the fridge...just don't tell anybody."

"No thanks. I need to ask you...well, I'm not sure."

He nodded and waited. He'd had enough encounters with troubled people over the years to know it was best to keep your mouth shut until you knew what they wanted. Mostly, parishioners just wanted to vent. Father Ray could usually help by listening and giving plain vanilla advice along with some prayer mumbo-jumbo. Catholics loved the supposed power of priests. As long as he could hide his disbelief, Father Ray figured he could still be effective.

"Anyway," Irene continued, "I suppose you heard my ex-husband is back."

"Yes." Father Ray had seen Red Donner in town a few times. He was less than impressed. Red struck him as a bullyboy bigmouth. He wondered how someone as delightful as Irene ever got together with a guy like that. "Is it difficult for you?" he asked.

"I'm glad he's back for Itchy. They seem to be getting along."

"That's good."

"They spend a lot of time talking about the Donner Party."

"Itchy's gonna be an expert someday."

"He already is," Irene said with a hint of motherly pride. She hesitated, and then looked at the floor. Father Ray studied her face. She was so small, so delicate. He couldn't believe he was the same species as Irene. He was so coarse and unrefined. Everything about Irene said delicacy. Beauty. And she was nice on top of it all. Why would God—if there was one—put people like Irene Donner on the planet to make the rest of us feel inadequate? he wondered. It's not that she let ego or self-absorption affect her. But by her very being she pointed out to people like Father Ray how imperfect they were. Not fair. Not fair at all.

"I'm worried, Father Ray."

"About what?"

"That I wish he was gone. That I don't want to share Itchy with him. It's so selfish, I know, Red's his father and he has every right to see him. I just can't get past...I just don't want to give Itchy to him. That's all. Is that a sin?"

"Of course not. It's perfectly understandable. Your ex-husband hasn't been here for Itchy's childhood, and now he wants to move back into his life. Into *your* life. I can understand how hard that is for you."

"But it's wrong."

"Not necessarily. You're human. You can't help what you feel."

Irene smiled tightly. "I thought that being a Catholic meant you're supposed to feel guilty all the time?"

"Well, yeah, that's the general rule. But then we feel guilty about feeling guilty and we talk to priests to make us feel less guilty about our guilt. It's a great system, huh?"

Irene laughed, and Father Ray laughed with her. This felt so nice. His mind raced for more ways to be clever.

"Red wants to take Itchy down to Tahoe. To the Donner Memorial. I think it'd kill me to let Itchy go anywhere with him."

"Don't give up all your mom rights because you feel guilty. Red needs to prove himself to you and Itchy. I wouldn't let him go until you're satisfied you can trust him. Are you at that point yet?"

"I probably never will be with Red, Father."

Father Ray wasn't sure how far he should venture into Irene's life, but since the talk was going so well he pressed on. "Did Red ever...abuse you?" he asked quietly.

"No," she said. "Nothing like that. It just started out so good, and then...." She gazed out the window. "It started so good...." she repeated.

"You dance great, Irene," Red shouted over the music. He'd just cut in on Mart, and Irene wasn't sure what to think of this big, grinning old guy with the happy feet.

"So do you."

Red spun her expertly and they moved in perfect rhythm. "I hope your friend Mart isn't mad at me for cutting in." He had a great smile, one filled with mischief and fun.

"It's just Mart. He doesn't mind."

"The boy spends a lot of time staring at you. Think he might be smitten."

Irene blushed. "He's just a good friend."

"Bet you got lots of friends in this town."

They danced the next three songs, and Red worked her hard. Most of the guys in Tamarack were lousy dancers, weak and indecisive. It was fun to be led by somebody who knew what they were doing. But it was tiring, too. Irene was sweaty and out of breath. Red didn't get tired; he just seemed energized and happy.

"Let's take a rest," she suggested.

"Surely."

They found a table in the corner behind the jukebox. Jacqueline caught Irene's eye and winked.

Red saw it. "Friend of yours?"

"My mom. She likes to embarrass me."

"No kiddin'? She have you when she was ten?"

"I'll tell her you said that. It'll make her day."

"I'm good with complements. So if I said something like 'Hey, do you work out?' would it be bad?"

"Only if you don't mind sounding like a lounge lizard."

"Wouldn't want to get into the sleaze zone," he grinned.

Irene watched Red as he went to the bar to get drinks. Big and strong and cute in a burly way, but at least ten years older than her. She wasn't sure about that. At least he was a new face, though, and that interested her. She'd known every guy in Tamarack for years, and nobody intrigued her anymore. You couldn't be raised with people from kindergarten and know all their secrets and still be interested in them when you grew up. It just wasn't possible.

Red came back with two pitchers of beer. "One for you and one for me."

"Planning on a big night?"

"I get thirsty. I'll help you finish yours if you can't."

He poured her a mug but drank his right from the pitcher. He wiped the foamy leftovers from his mustache and beard with his sleeve.

"You've got a lot of class," Irene said.

"I know it. Too much for this town, but what's a sophisticated guy like me gonna do? That's why I wanted to meet you. Seems like you might be a match for me in the class department."

"I'll take that as a complement. I guess."

"Got any men in your life, Irene?"

"Maybe. Got any in yours?"

Red hooted. "You're a wise-ass. I like that." He sucked down more of his pitcher. "Irene's a pretty name."

"I hate it. It makes me sound like I'm eighty."

"Nah, it's got class. Your momma picked good."

"She was watching an old Cary Grant movie when she was pregnant with me and she liked the actress in it. Her name was Irene something-or-other. Anyway, she had nice cheekbones, so my mom named me after her. My mom's kind of weird sometimes."

"Like your momma's style. It's good to do stuff for whacked-out reasons. Seems like she done a good job raisin' you, even with an old lady's name."

Irene smiled. The complement felt good. "So, are you really related to the Donner Party?"

"You betcha."

"Then you must be a vegetarian, right?"

"You disappoint me, Irene. You've fallen victim to the old stereotypes about my kin. Donners never ate nobody. Some of them got eaten, though."

Irene sipped her beer. The dancing had picked up, and the Slurp 'n' Burp was packed. She caught a glimpse of Mart and his friends at the bar. She smiled, but Mart didn't seem to see her. Or maybe he looked away. She couldn't tell.

"As soon as you're rested up, I think we oughta get back out there," Red said. "These folks around here might be nice, but none of them can two-step worth a shit."

Irene looked back at Red. His wild hair, big beard, sparkly bad boy eyes, the grin....

She drained her beer and pulled him to his feet. "Let's rock 'n' roll," she said, and they danced the night away.

It was a whirlwind.

Red Donner's force-of-nature personality grabbed hold of Irene, and she couldn't resist.

He came by each night, still grubby from his day crewing in the woods, but Irene didn't mind. There was something majestic and romantic about a guy who was so anxious to see you that he couldn't spare the time to clean up. Red brought her presents every day—bouquets of wildflowers he'd picked in the woods, or a pretty rock, sometimes just a pizza and beer—but always something.

"He's nothing if not persistent," Jacqueline commented to Irene. She wasn't wild about Red. Too noisy and pushy for her taste.

The thing about Red that got to Irene the most, though, wasn't the presents, or that he was older and so worldly-wise with his many tales. Irene fell in love with Red because he made her laugh.

Men had always treated Irene strangely. Guys acted like she was too beautiful to be human. She liked looking good, and she loved that men noticed her—it was just that she wanted to be treated like she was real, not a scary idealized fantasy. She wanted to be both a friend *and* a fantasy.

And Red Donner saw her that way. He *was* head-over-heels—but that didn't stop him from being rude and crude and goofy. He was the first guy she'd ever known who wasn't intimidated by her looks. She'd told him so after they'd been seeing each other a month.

"Yeah, sure, you're hot all right," Red said. "But that don't mean you're better than anybody else. Don't take offense. But it's always been my opinion that the real good-lookin' people don't work hard enough on what's inside. They don't need to. Stuff's too easy for 'em because of the way they look. Now you, you're different. You got the looks, but you also got a good brain and a nice heart. Good taste, too, 'cause you've hooked up with a stud like me."

"You've never had to worry about the good-looking part, I guess."

"Damn straight. That's why I'm so evolved. The perfect male. As long as you don't count the drinkin' and foul language."

When they made love, Irene insisted that Red clean up, because the romance of a grubby guy could only go so far. For Irene sex with Red was...okay. She'd had a few unsatisfactory, fumbling sexual encounters with locals, so Red was a pleasant change. He was patient and surprisingly gentle, although like most guys he lost his focus near the end and got a little too caught up in his own pleasure. But at least he tried.

They spent more and more time together. She seldom saw Mart anymore—the Sunday breakfasts were still in the future—but Red filled her days and nights so much that it didn't matter. Clingy old friends were easy to forget when somebody like Red Donner stormed into your life.

She began staying at Red's place, a small downstairs room he rented from another logger. Curiosity got the better of her one night and she asked Red if he'd ever been married.

"Nah, ain't been tempted, really. Lived with a few women here and there."

"Don't tell me about them." Irene decided that listening to his love history was a bad idea. They cuddled in his saggy bed. Red was so big he created a valley she naturally rolled into whether she wanted to or not.

"Well, now. Perfect little Irene Weatherly got some jealous bones in her tight little bod, huh?"

"No. I'm just not interested."

"Admit it, it's normal. Can't say as I'm thrilled that every guy in town is in love with you, either."

"That's not true."

"Bullshit. I seen the way they all act around you. Like a bunch lovesick puppies."

"No way!" Irene said. But the thought pleased her.

"You know," Red said, pulling her even closer, "it seems to me that I might need to do somethin' about this." Her head rested on his chest, nestled in a cushion of coarse hair. She'd always disliked hairy guys, but Red was an exception. What seemed gross on others became sexy on him.

"What do you need to do?"

"All these guys are a threat to little ol' Red Donner. I'm kinda sensitive."

"Right."

"What I'm thinkin', since I've got issues, is that maybe we oughta do something to calm my anxiety."

"What *are* you talking about?"

Red's smile faded and he became very serious. "Let's hook up. Permanent."

Irene sat up. The blanket fell away, leaving her breasts tantalizing close to Red. He had trouble keeping his eyes on her eyes.

"Like get married?" she asked.

"Sure. Why not?"

"I'm only nineteen."

Red leaned forward and kissed her breasts. "I'm thinkin' you're plenty old enough. Trust me on that."

She pushed him away, laughing yet uneasy. "I'm serious. I don't know...."

"Give it some thought. The thing you oughta know, the thing that matters, is that I love you. More than anything in the world. Can't help that. You stole my heart, Irene. Do an old geezer a favor and hitch up with him. It's the only thing that'd make me happy."

"You're not a geezer, you're only thirty-one."

"Is that a 'no'?"

"No! I mean yes. I don't know."

"Give it some thought. That's all I ask." Red pulled her close and kissed her gently. "I love you."

Two weeks later they borrowed Jacqueline's '67 F-100, drove down to Reno, and made it legal.

Being married didn't change things all that much.

Irene worked at the salon with Jacqueline five-and-a-half days a week. She was learning the mysteries of perms and trims by trial and error. She still screwed up occasionally, but Jacqueline was a patient teacher, and the customers remarkably forgiving. The main difference in her life now was that she went home to Red instead of Jacqueline. *Married.* Sometimes Irene couldn't believe it. Only grown-ups got married, and she didn't feel grown-up. Not yet.

But as always happens, they quickly fell into an old married couple's routine. Red rose before sunrise every workday, pulled on his heavy calk boots and chaps, grabbed his helmet and gloves, and with a quick kiss to the snoozing Irene headed off to the woods. Irene got up an hour later, went to the salon, and before she knew it another day had passed. Was this going to be her life for the next fifty years? she wondered.

She and Red still went dancing at the Slurp 'n' Burp Friday nights, but Red spent lots of other nights out drinking with his work buddies. He'd wander home long after dinnertime, long after Irene had tried to cook up something nice that she had to leave crusting over for him in the warm oven.

"Sorry, Irene," he'd say, contrite like a guilty little kid. "Just needed to unwind with the guys. You know how it is."

Irene would pout, and Red could usually coax her out of her grumpiness before bedtime. But a few days later the same thing would happen, and Irene began to wonder if Red was forgetting about her.

"It's the way men are, honey," Jacqueline told her. "'Specially loggers. They're like little kids—except ones that drink too much. I remember your daddy...." and Jacqueline launched into a long story about Bob Weatherly's boozing and carrying on. Irene politely listened, but she didn't think the way her dad behaved had anything to do with Red. Red was from a younger generation, he was more in tune to Irene and her needs. At least she'd thought so. But since they'd gotten married, he was turning into the basic Tamarack Man— a hard-working booze hound who took his wife for granted. Red had seemed so different at first. Had she made a mistake?

Everything changed the morning she told Red she was pregnant.

Red settled down and sat on the side of the bed, his face creased with a dopey grin. "Shit," he mumbled. "There's gonna be a fuckin' baby Red."

"There's a nice way to put it. Are you happy?"

"Fuck yeah!"

"Really?" Irene wasn't so sure about the idea herself.

"Well, yeah. That's the way God intended it, for people to breed."

"I thought you didn't believe in God?"

"Depends. I'm a situational religious kind of guy. Findin' out your wife's expecting makes you get all emotional and holy."

"You're neither, but that's okay. Are we ready to do this?"

And then Red surprised her. His eyes glistened. "I love you, Irene. Nothin' I want more than to be married to you forever and have a slew of rugrats."

She hugged him and cried, touched by his bumbling gruffness. Having his baby suddenly felt right, and as they hugged and kissed Irene thought that as long as she stayed with Red Donner she'd be safe.

At first, Red's excitement over fatherhood kicked him into overdrive. He leased Pencil's ratty house for his family-to-be, spent his off-work hours building a crib and refinishing a room for the baby, and was an exemplary pregnant dad. But as Irene's belly swelled and the months passed, Red gradually fell into his old nights-out-with-the-boys routine. He came home late, and he came home drunk.

Two months before the baby was due, Red's drinking and carousing had reached the point where people noticed. Boozing loggers were nothing new, but Red's drunken tirades at the Slurp 'n' Burp reached legendary proportions. He started fights, got tossed out by Pencil, got into more fights, drank until he puked—which, for Red, took an amazing amount—and spun wildly out of control. He got sloppy at work, too. Red was a faller, and if he messed up, his crew could be in danger. Showing up in the woods with a chainsaw and a hangover was a recipe for disaster.

At around the same time he began phoning Irene. After hours of tossing back shots at the Slurp 'n' Burp, he'd call to check and see if she was okay, or let her know he was on his way home, or sometimes, late at night, when he should've been cuddling his pregnant wife, he'd just dial her up and say nothing. Breathe. And creep Irene out.

"What's wrong with you?" she demanded the morning after one of his breather calls.

"Dunno," he mumbled.

"Is it me? Have I done something?"

"Dunno." He dragged out of bed and staggered into the bathroom.

"Tell me what's wrong!"

He stood at the bathroom door, head hung low, eyes red and droopy and angry. "You seein' somebody?"

"What are you talking about?"

"Sure that baby's mine?"

"Red?!"

He rubbed his shaggy hair. "Yeah, probably is. Just know this, Irene. Somebody else...touches you, I find out somethin' like that...they're fuckin' dead."

Irene was so dumbfounded she couldn't speak.

"Sounds like he was still drunk, honey," Jacqueline said when Irene told her the story.

"He just got up."

"From what Stanley tells me, your hubby puts away enough booze to stay permanently drunk." Jacqueline put her arm around her confused daughter. "Sorry, sweetie. Had my doubts about him from the start. But you just gotta buck up, have this baby, then maybe you can deal with Red. He don't hit you or anything, does he?"

"No."

"That's good. Be careful, okay? Guys like him drink too much, no tellin' what they'll do."

"I made a mistake, didn't I?"

"With men everything's a mistake. I'm no psychologist or nothing, but I'll tell you what I think: you havin' this baby makes him realize it's time to grow up. Got him scared to death. These big, strong mountain men are just little boys inside. He doesn't know whether to shit or wind his watch, so he gets drunk. Just between you and me, we'd be better off if we were lesbians." Jacqueline hugged Irene tight and squeezed a little laugh out of her.

But things stayed the same with Red. The marriage that had started with such promise had quickly faded away.

"And then the thing with Mart happened and he took off," Irene told Father Ray.

As she'd told him about Red hurt shadowed her voice. Father Ray wanted to hold her, to touch her, to show her that not all men were disgusting pigs like her drunken lout of an ex. But then, *he* was a disgusting pig too, because he wanted to hold her and love her and it was the ultimate betrayal of trust.

"So what should I do?" Irene asked.

Father Ray sighed. He didn't have the slightest idea. "Be patient," was all he could think of . "Pray for guidance."

Irene nodded as if his suggestions helped, and maybe they did. Just because he knew his advice—and he—were fraudulent, didn't mean that Irene noticed. She struck him as a truly faithful believer, one of those innocent souls who had the ability to trust, whose faith was childlike, even after life had punched her around. Things had always been so easy for Father Ray, yet he didn't have one-tenth the faith of Irene.

"I think," Father Ray said, deciding to offer more advice, "I think that you should be careful with Red. I'd hate for anything to happen to you. Or Itchy."

"I don't think Red would hurt us," she said. "He does seem...calmer than before. He's nicer. So far, anyway."

"I don't know if it's possible, but you might want to try to convince him to stop by. Who knows? At least I could get a read on him for you."

Irene stood. "Thanks, Father Ray. Maybe I'll do that."

He guided her to the door. If only he could come up with some reason for her to stay. He already dreaded the thought of being alone in the drafty little room after she left.

When she turned and surprised him with a hug, Father Ray couldn't breathe. He awkwardly patted her on the back.

"Thanks again, Father Ray. I really needed to talk tonight."

She pulled away and gave him a smile that melted him. What had Red Donner been thinking to have Irene as his wife and then desert her?

"If you need anything...." he said, his voice fading away in a wistful sigh.

"Thanks," Irene said, and she walked off into the cold November night.

Father Ray stood at the door for the longest time, watching her figure recede down the moonlit street.

The rest of Father Ray's night was cold and lonely and miserable, and his sermon never did get written.

My father and others deliberated over a new route to California. The proposition seemed so feasible, and after cool deliberation and discussion, a party was formed to take the new route. My father was elected captain of this company, and from that time on it was known as "The Donner Party."

Eliza Donner

July 19, 1846

Chapter Five

The widowmaker always came down the same way.

Over the years Mart had tried to remember it differently, to see it fall from other angles as if multiple cameras had recorded the scene, but he never could get a view in his mind that changed the reality. He tried to relive it with a different outcome, to imagine himself a tenth of a second quicker jumping away, a tenth of a second that would've changed everything. He saw Red screaming, he saw Red's big Stihl chainsaw drop to the ground, its blade kicking up duff before the safety shut it off, the *crack* and shriek of splitting wood, the cedar toppling sideways, snapping a huge snag's dead top, a mistake, the bleached snag plummeting, and Mart stuck, nowhere to run, nowhere to hide, not enough time, even if he had that tenth of a second he wanted so badly, so what? Where would he go?

Strangely, the accident never appeared in his dreams. And that made it worse, because he couldn't relegate it to nighttime's emptiness. The memory punched through all day long, and no matter how hard he tried to hold it back, here it came, unsettling, unwanted, impossible to banish. Brain chatter. An endless loop, replaying over and over. He'd gotten to the point where he could think about other things while the accident played in the background, like having the TV on while you talked on the phone. And Mart knew that thinking about it was a waste of time, that nothing would ever change. But it didn't matter. He couldn't control what his brain wanted to do. So he lived his life, eleven-plus years later, and constantly, *constantly*, thought about what happened. He tried to change the ending, but he never could.

He sat in his wheelchair on the small front porch of Stan the Man's house. They lived down the street from the mill, and all day long Mart listened to the saws' screaming and breathed the cloyingly sweet odor of smoldering slash. He pulled his Skoal can from his back pocket, pinched out a nice morning's snoose, and savored. Bad habit, and he'd probably end up with some kind of hideous jaw cancer, but who gave a shit? He was a gimp who couldn't fuck, he needed some vices. Dipping was pretty innocuous when you came right down to it.

Mart watched the world go by—such as it was in Tamarack. He enjoyed soaking up what little warmth the November sun offered. The snow would fly soon, and he'd be trapped inside until March. Old buddies waved and nodded as they drove by, and Mart realized he'd become one of the coots he and his friends used to make fun of—the over-the-hill, creaky-bodied ancients who sat around in their *Logger's World* suspenders and flannel shirts with nothing to do but shoot the shit about the pre- "tree-hugging liberal" good-old-days and wave to anybody who passed by.

Fucking Red Donner.

He should've known something bad—like the return of Red—would happen. The omens were there. So far, this was the first fall in his life that he hadn't gotten a buck—and that was just plain weird. He and Stan the Man went out a couple of times a week, but neither of them had filled their tags yet. Pretty sad when you couldn't shoot a deer around Tamarack. Mart wanted to get a bull elk this year, too, and he hoped he'd have a better chance later on. After the first snows he and Stan the Man would head out on Stan's ATV and see what they could turn up. But Mart had gotten to wondering if Red Donner's return had somehow ruined the hunting. Red had a giant negative cosmic influence, Mart decided. Had to be it.

Fucking Red Donner....

"Getting married. You believe that shit, Mar-teen?" Red had bragged so long ago. The night before he and Irene had decided to tie the knot. "Figured you oughta hear it from me instead of somebody else."

"Married? To Irene?" Mart paled. A gray dawn broke as he and Red bounced along a rutted road on their way to the logging deck. Mart swerved and almost plowed into a ditch for no reason other than shock.

"Yeah," Red said. "Careful with the drivin', bud. You know we been pretty close for awhile. Appreciate you introducing us, by the way."

"Sure," Mart said through clenched lips.

"See, the thing is, I don't want you to be pissed off over this."

"I'm not."

"I'm thinkin' you might be. You're a good kid, I like you, like workin' with you. Don't want you running me over with the skidder." Red smiled, but he watched Mart closely.

"You guys...in love?"

"Fuckin'-A Bubba. Like a goddamn movie. Wouldn't get married otherwise."

Mart sighed. *He who hesitates....* "I'm glad for you, Red."

"There's one other thing."

"What?"

"She's havin' a rugrat."

"Oh."

"Yeah, come as a surprise to me, too, but it's kinda okay. Just hope I don't fuck him up too much. Or her. Can you imagine a pig like me with a little girl? Shit...." Red smiled a dreamy smile.

They drove on in silence. Mart couldn't make his mouth form words. Too many jumbled thoughts, too much regret, too many should've-could'ves— this ought to be happening to him, not Red. He liked Red just fine, that wasn't the problem. Wasn't Red's fault. It was Mart's. Weak. Wussy boy. Waiting, waiting, waiting—for what? He'd fucking known Irene forever, he'd had plenty of chances. If only he'd gotten off his ass, Irene would be his.

Now he'd lost her forever.

"A baby, huh?" he finally said.

"Yeah."

"Congratulations, Red. Hope it all works out." And he *did* hope things worked out for them.

Sort of.

As the baby grew in Irene, though, Mart noticed Red getting weird. The boozing at the Slurp 'n' Burp became aggressive and nasty, and Red never seemed to want to go home. Mart couldn't understand that.

"Just celebratin' being a daddy," Red had grinned, waving the pool cue like a light saber before he smacked the six ball in the corner pocket.

"Irene doing okay?"

"Little moody, but I 'spose it's all those hormones roaring through her. Building a baby gotta be tough on your body."

"She pissed that you're here all the time?"

Red threw back another shot of Jack Daniel's, chalked his cue, and fixed Mart with a steely glare. "I don't know if that concerns you, Mart."

Mart shrugged it off. "Just wondered."

They played the rest of the game in silence. Red got plowed that night, and Pencil had to toss him out when he broke a pool cue over Mike Standly's head after an argument over who was the better faller.

Red won the argument, but only because Mike ended up unconscious.

After that, Mart had trouble sleeping. He couldn't eat. It might've been jealousy, but he didn't think so. He was worried that Irene was in trouble. Mart wanted to help her, only he didn't know how. She and the baby were Red's responsibility. Mart knew that it was none of business.

The night before the accident—and Mart had a hard time thinking of it *as* an accident—Red got drunker than usual. A Tuesday night, not much jumping at the Slurp 'n' Burp, but Red bellowed in his usual full drunken glory. Mart had come by—only because Red insisted—to shoot a couple of games. He wanted to get home. He decided he was spending too much time with Red—all day in the woods, then drinking and hanging out together after work. Even if Red didn't mention her, being with him stabbed Mart with Irene regrets—and he had plenty of those already.

Red easily won the first two games—the guy was the most amazing pool hustler Mart had ever seen. He could be falling-down drunk and still somehow summon up the coordination and reflexes to snuff anybody dumb enough to take him on.

"Need a ride?" Mart asked.

"Leavin' so early?" Red slurred. Pencil poured him another beer. Red liked to alternate between shots of anything strong—schnapps, whiskey, bourbon—and beer.

"Gotta work tomorrow, Red."

"So do I, but you don't see me pussying out. C'mon, 'nother game for the road."

"No thanks. I'm gonna roll."

Red shrugged and drained his mug. "Whatever you say." As Mart headed toward the door, Red called out across the bar, "How come you never did nothin' about her?"

Mart froze. "What?"

"You shoulda fought for her. Instead of lettin' me come along and snag her. You had your whole fuckin' life to get her before I showed up, you know."

Mart faced Red and slowly walked toward him. Pencil discretely stepped away.

"I don't know what you're talking about," Mart said.

"You coulda had a T-shirt made that said, 'I Love Irene' and it wouldn't have been any more obvious."

"I don't think—"

"Now I'm married to her. And I get to be a daddy. Coulda been you. Probably shoulda been."

"Shut up, Red."

"Never understood guys like you." Red slammed the mug down on the bar. Pencil didn't refill it. "Say the word, she probably woulda gone for you. Or maybe it woulda took a little work, but you coulda done it. So how come, if you love her as much as you do, you didn't do nothin'?"

"Shut the fuck up."

"I admit, I'm a charming mo-fo. Got some bullshit and stories. Ladies like that. But you. Young, good-looking kid. So much better for her than me. Shoulda been a man, Mar-teen. You'd like bein' trapped in fuckin' Tamarack with a pretty little wife and squally kid. You were born to be a lifer here."

Mart couldn't remember actually throwing the punch, but he'd never forget the surprised look on Red's face as he catapulted backwards to the floor. Mart's right caught Red's jaw perfectly, and Red flopped, rubber-limbed, like he'd been dropped from a second-story window. Before Red had a chance to recover, Mart jumped him, punching, swearing, the white-hot jealousy coming out with every *smack-thud* of fist to face. By the time Pencil pulled Mart off, Red was spitting up blood and rubbing at a rapidly swelling eye.

He was also laughing. "Seems that Mar-teen got some fire in his belly after all."

"Don't do nothing crazy, Red! Leave the kid be," Pencil warned, shielding the ready-for-more Mart.

"I ain't gonna do nothing." Red got up on wobbly feet. "I had it comin'. Pour me something strong to clear my head."

Mart tried to pull away from Pencil. He wanted another piece of Red.

"Get on home, Mart," Pencil said. "You proved your point."

Pencil heave-hoed Mart out the front door. Mart swung furiously at the cold night air. Nobody to punch, nobody to blame, nobody to save. Irene. Shit. Fucking Red was going to ruin her life. Mart hopped in his truck and headed to their place. He parked in front, chest heaving from fury. He had to save Irene. Had to protect her.

Red was going to ruin her life…. He had to do something.

But—

He didn't get out of his truck. He suddenly wasn't sure. Irene chose Red, not him. What if he charged inside, what if he told Irene, "I'm here to rescue you!" What would she say?

Probably laugh in his face.

Fuck. This wasn't his business. Irene might as well have been a movie star he'd loved from afar for as much sway as he held over her. He could make a fool of himself, but she had the final say. If she wanted to stay with Red-fucking-pig-Donner, then so be it. Wasn't Mart Lane's call.

Another cowardly failure. He hadn't pursued her when he should've, what right did he have to do something now? Red wasn't hurting her, not really. He just wasn't as interested as Mart thought he should be. As much as Mart would've been in his shoes.

Mart didn't get out of his truck. He sat there, hating himself for being so weak, but he couldn't—wouldn't—get involved. Irene made the choice, she had to live with it.

When the porch light clicked on, Mart gunned the engine and roared off down the street.

Irene peeked out the front door, puzzled. She recognized Mart's truck, and she expected to see Red get out and stagger to the door. But when Mart sped off and Red was nowhere to be seen, she didn't know what to think.

She meant to ask Mart the next day why he'd been there.

She never got the chance.

"This site is so cool!" Itchy said.

He expertly clicked the mouse of Sara's computer, popping from page to page of a picture-filled Donner Party website.

"It's a new one?" Sara asked.

"Yep. This lady's a college professor, she has some really good stuff." Itchy clicked to the Donner family section and read. Then his smile disappeared. "That's a lie!" he shouted at the screen.

"What?"

"She has that same old stuff about Tamsen eating...you know."

"Oh." *Here we go again,* Sara thought. Itchy needed to get real about his family's cannibalism. Everybody said they did it, so maybe he ought to just accept the truth.

"What's a lie, Itchy?" Miriam asked from the doorway. She slouched against the doorjamb, a glass of Merlot in her hand. She cradled it like something very valuable. Itchy thought she looked like she could fall asleep any second.

"Um, hi Mrs. Flynn. This website says that my family ate people. It isn't true."

"I see."

"Everybody only cares about cannibals. It makes me mad."

"Certainly it would," Miriam agreed. "How's your father?"

"Okay."

"He's working now, isn't he?"

"Yeah. For Mr. Flynn."

"Aahh. That's right. I guess he did mention it. Will your father be staying with your mother again?"

"I don't know."

"Would you like him to?"

Itchy squirmed. He just wanted to look at Donner stuff, not be interrogated about his parents.

Sara looked at her mother with pleading eyes. *"Mom...."*

"Would you like your father to live with you again, Itchy?" Miriam asked, this time more firmly.

"I guess. But I don't think he will."

"Why?"

"My mom kinda...hates him."

Miriam smiled and sipped her wine. She seemed pleased. "Why does she hate him?"

Itchy shrugged. "Um, 'cause he left, I think."

Sara knew this wasn't right, but she didn't know how to stop her mother's nosy questions.

Miriam continued, "Does your father still drink? I know he used to have a problem."

"Not anymore," Itchy replied. He glanced at Sara for help, but she just watched her mother with embarrassment.

"Does your mother have any boyfriends?" Miriam asked.

Itchy looked at Miriam with utter confusion. What in the world did she want from him? All he wanted to do was to Donner surf, not answer a bunch of pushy questions about his mom and dad. At first he wasn't going to say anything, but then something inside told him to put a stop to this. "Why don't you ask her yourself, Mrs. Flynn?"

Miriam's eyes widened a bit. "I think it's time to you went home, Itchy," she said coolly, and then she turned and headed off to the parlor.

"What'd I do?!" Itchy asked Sara.

"I dunno. My mom gets weird sometimes. She doesn't have anybody to talk to except me and Daddy, and she's kinda strange. I'm sorry, Itchy."

Itchy sadly gathered up his backpack. He really wanted to read more of the college professor's site—even if it was filled with the Tamsen cannibal lies.

"See you at school tomorrow," Sara told him at the door. She hated for

Itchy to leave. She liked watching him get so excited while he surfed her computer. Now all she had to look forward to was an afternoon alone and probably a fight between her parents when Daddy got home. "I'm really sorry about my mom. She likes to find out gossipy things about people. It's like a hobby."

"It's okay." Itchy slung his heavy backpack over his shoulder and disappointedly trudged off.

Itchy slowly meandered toward home, idly kicking at stones and gravel and crushed beer cans. The sweet smoke of woodstoves firing up for the evening settled over the valley. The sun dipped behind the mountains, and the night's chill instantly hit. Itchy's cheeks burned from the sudden cold. He never could understand why cold sometimes felt hot. Weird. Did Tamsen and all the rest of them feel hot when they were freezing to death? Another imponderable question. So many questions about the Donner Party. It seemed like the only thing that Itchy ever thought of was questions. He never came up with answers. Maybe when he got older. He hoped so.

"Hey, Itchy!"

Itchy turned to the voice. He'd been so deep in frozen/hot thought he hadn't paid any attention to where he was. Mart waved from the porch of Stan the Man's house.

"Hey, Mart."

"C'mon up. Want something to eat?"

"Yeah!" Itchy scrambled up the gravel drive.

Mart knew that something gross awaited Itchy for dinner. Irene may have been an angel from heaven, but her cooking sucked. And she insisted that Itchy eat healthy garbage like garbonzo beans and spinach. Mart felt bad for the kid. He remembered being perpetually hungry at Itchy's age, and health food just wasn't what a growing kid wanted. He needed cookies and Doritos and pizza—

good American food. Irene's one major flaw, as far as Mart was concerned, was a big one—no respect for guy food. He tried not to let it color his opinion of her, though. Even Irene couldn't be entirely perfect.

Itchy bounded up the stairs and clumped noisily on the wooden porch. "Whatcha got, Mart?"

"Skittles, dude. Stan the Man bought a big old bag last night to chase down our sausage-pepperoni pizza."

Itchy's eyes softened like a guy in love. The words "sausage-pepperoni" made him wistful. "That's so cool...."

Itchy held the door open while Mart rolled inside. The old house was a pad o' guys, unsullied by femininity of any type. Cluttered and slovenly, it smelled of dirty socks and mold. The only valuables were guy-toys: the large-screen TV that Mart bought with some of his insurance money, and a hot sur-round-sound system that Stan the Man found at a pawn shop in Seattle. They popped in noisy DVDs most nights when they weren't at the Slurp 'n' Burp, movies with lots of explosions and broken glass and breasts, and when they watched, enthralled—the walls shaking with thunderous DTS sound—all was right with the world.

Itchy followed Mart as he rolled into the kitchen. He grabbed the half-eaten bag of Skittles and tossed it to Itchy. Itchy gobbled them up like a starving man.

"Good, huh?" Mart smiled.

"The best. Thanks, Mart."

"What's your mom making you for dinner tonight? Some cruelty-free nuts and berries stuff?"

"Gramma's coming over. So's my dad. So she might make something sort of okay, maybe even hamburgers or spaghetti if we're lucky. I hope so."

The mention of Red put Mart on edge. "Why's he coming over? I thought Sundays were the only days he came by?"

"My mom invited him."

"Huh...." The familiar knot tightened in Mart's stomach.

"She talked to Father Ray and he told her she should be nicer to my dad. I think, anyway. She didn't tell me exactly, but I figure stuff out, you know?" Itchy scratched at the crimson scaly patch on his cheek.

"Want a Mountain Dew?"

"Sure!" Itchy eagerly opened the refrigerator, dug through the packed beer bottles and pizza boxes, and found a Dew. He popped the can and savored the forbidden nectar. "Can I have some cold pizza, too?"

"Sure."

Itchy gobbled a slice. "You and Stan the Man are sooo lucky. I wish I could live here."

"It's not as great as it looks, Itch. Trust me."

Itchy stuffed too much pizza in his mouth and had to wash it down, coughing and gagging, with a big slurp of Dew. But his beatific smile said he was in culinary heaven.

"Don't eat too much. Your mom'll kill me."

"I won't tell," Itchy grinned.

"Any new Donner stuff?"

Itchy went into his usual long-winded explanation of websites and books. Mart had listened to Itchy for so long that he'd started to feel like a Donner Party scholar himself. Too bad he couldn't make a living at it.

Mart made the appropriate noises as Itchy droned on, but he couldn't stop thinking about Red seeing Irene. He wanted to know why she'd invite Red over in the first place. That didn't seem right.

"Your mom say much about your dad being back?"

"Not really."

"Think she likes that he's here?"

"I dunno. How come everybody wants to know about them?"

Mart sighed. Now he felt like a dirtbag for pumping Itchy. "I guess people are just naturally nosy."

Itchy finished his pizza slice and asked, "What'd my dad do to you?"

"Your mom never told you?"

"Nobody ever tells me anything. They think I'm a stupid little kid."

"Well, you are, kinda," Mart said with a smile.

"Funny."

"Just kiddin', Itch. I'll tell you if you really wanna know."

Itchy rubbed at his rash and waited.

"He...put me in this chair," Mart said.

"How?"

"Cut down a tree. He screwed up, it took out an old snag that fell on me."

"Did he do it on purpose?"

Mart hesitated. *Did he?* "I don't think so. Probably just an accident. Maybe you should ask him sometime."

"Wow," Itchy said. This was a big deal, and he wasn't sure what to think.

"We got into a fight the night before. At Pencil's."

"About what?"

"Your mom."

"Why?"

"I...didn't think Red was treating her good."

"Why?"

"She was getting ready to have you, and Red was at the bar all the time. I thought he shoulda been home with Irene. So I told him so. He didn't like hearing it, though. So one thing led to another and I punched him out."

"*You* beat up my dad?" Itchy didn't think that was possible. Red was so huge and intimidating.

Mart smiled. "Well, he was drunk, so that probably made it easier. But yeah, I put him on the floor." Mart couldn't resist a little male puffery. He'd spent so long trapped on his ass in the fucking wheelchair he'd almost forgotten how good it felt to play the macho stud. Even if it was only in front of a scrawny eleven-year-old.

"So he cut down a tree on top of you because you beat him up?" Itchy asked, horrified.

"No, wasn't like that." Mart wheeled over to the refrigerator and grabbed a beer. "He kept drinking that night after I hit him. Pencil said afterwards he was there till closing and even more wasted than usual. Your old man could put away a lot of booze. You sure you want to hear all this?"

Itchy nodded and listened with wide eyes. Finally, some real, inside dirt about his dad. It felt kind of weird to hear about it, but since nobody in his family would tell him the truth he appreciated that Mart thought he could handle it. It wasn't like he didn't know about the world; how many eleven-year-olds were experts on something like the Donner Party, where people were at their best and worst, where they got eaten and starved and froze and all the rest. Itchy Donner was nothing if not sophisticated in the ways of the world. Sure was nice that Mart realized that.

"So the next morning we go to work," Mart continued, "we were working a cut up on Deadman Ridge. We usually rode together, but that morning, well, we weren't feelin' real social with each other, so we went separately. Your dad was faller, as usual. He's good at it, almost always puts the tree right where he wants it. I was bucking and running the skidder. Anyway, we hadn't said a word to each other all morning. Your dad wasn't talking to anybody, which was unusual, since he doesn't like to keep quiet."

"Yeah, I've noticed."

"But I couldn't tell that he might've still been drunk. It's hard to see with him, he doesn't act that much different. So he's cutting away, I'm standing a couple of tree lengths off to the side, where I thought I should've been safe, watching, burning up because I'm still so steamed at him. Next thing I know, this big-ass cedar is going cockeyed, snaps the top off an old snag and the widowmaker is coming down and I've got nowhere to go. Your dad's yelling, other guys are yelling, and all I see is that thing heading for me and I know I'm dead."

"Wow...."

"Yeah. Wow. So I try to jump out of the way, but there's nowhere to go, I turn away, running, something hits me square in the back, and the next thing I know I'm in a hospital bed in Seattle and I can't move my legs."

"What'd my dad say?"

"I never talked to him again. Until he showed up at your house last month. He told some of the other guys on the crew that it was an accident, that he might've screwed up because he had a lot to drink the night before and he was hungover and not thinking straight. Me, I think he was still drunk. I think I'm paralyzed because your old man was pissed-off and wasted and he screwed up with his cut and here I fucking am." He forced a smile. "Sorry for the language, Itch. I get kinda mad when I think about it."

"It's...okay." No wonder people weren't glad to see his dad, Itchy thought. After a lifetime in Tamarack, Itchy knew that if you messed up and let your logger brothers down, you were in big trouble. "He never said he was sorry?" Itchy asked.

"Sent me a postcard about six months later. Said he didn't mean it, that he felt bad. But it didn't do much for me. By then I was in rehab learning how to be a gimp. I wasn't feeling a whole lot of forgiveness. And your mom had you by then, and she didn't have a husband to help her. That's why a lot of people aren't real fond of your dad."

Itchy sipped his Dew and considered all that Mart had told him. Mart was the coolest, and Red had messed him up. Not to mention deserting his mom. *And* him. Itchy decided that he might have to rethink being friends with his dad.

"So that's the story. It's why I'm worried about your mom with him around. I know he claims he's not drinking anymore, and from what I hear he's doing a good job out in the woods, but nobody really trusts him, everybody keeps a close eye on him. I'd just hate for your mom to get hurt by him again. That's all." Mart hesitated. "She's one of my best friends. So are you, Itch."

Itchy smiled. He wasn't used to people other than his mom—and especially somebody old like Mart—saying nice things to him. "I think we're okay. My mom's nice to him, but I don't think she trusts him like she trusts you. But you know what? He said he might take me down to Alder Creek and the Donner memorial!"

"Oh yeah?"

"Yeah! And I could see where everything happened. Wouldn't that be cool?!" And then Itchy was off into Donner Party never-never land. Mart smiled. Itchy seldom ventured far from his past. Mart listened politely, although his mind was on Irene.

And Red.

*   *   *

Irene bustled in the kitchen, annoyed with herself over how nervous she felt.

A roast had been...crocking, is that a word? she wondered...in the crock pot all day, and now she busily peeled potatoes and carrots. She promised herself that this was going to be a good dinner, without anything charred or raw or icky. At least that was her plan. Cooking seemed to have it in for her. She tried her best, but somehow she always lost her focus in the middle of things and ended up with disastrous messes that looked like autopsy photos.

"Bless your heart. You just got too many things rattling around in that pretty little head of yours," Jacqueline told her. "I know you're smart as hell. Too smart to be a *hausfrau*, that's all. Nothin' wrong with that."

Irene didn't know whether to be flattered or angry, but since Jacqueline said it, she assumed that an insult was intended. Jacqueline enjoyed making her points passive/aggressive style.

Tonight Irene was giving reconciliation a chance. Her talk with Father Ray convinced her that if she was going to be a good person and a good Catholic— although she wasn't sure she could ever be either—then she needed to forgive Red. It would be hard, but she needed to try. Especially for Itchy's sake.

So tonight would be a...well, family evening was too strong. She decided to think of it as an *extended* family evening. Like those amicable divorces you read about in magazines, where the ex's are still friends and do things together with their kids, only they're not married anymore. Sophisticated. That's what Irene wanted to be. Reconciliation with Red would never happen, but at least they could be on civil terms. He'd been back over a month now, seemed to be working hard, hadn't been into Pencil's and hadn't been drunk—so maybe they could live in a sort of balance. See each other, share Itchy, but without the baggage of old hurts or new entanglements.

That's what she hoped.

Jacqueline wandered in at five, trailing Marlboro smoke and stories of her afternoon clients. She sat and watched Irene rush around the kitchen.

"You need any help, honey?" she asked after waiting long enough to be sure there wasn't much left to do.

"It's okay," Irene said with a touch of sarcasm.

"Smells good. Nothin's burning. Yet."

"Mom...."

"Joke, funny, ha-ha. Sheesh, kinda touchy." Jacqueline pulled a Bud from the refrigerator and popped it open. "How come you don't want Stanley or Mart here?"

"I want it to be a...family dinner."

"That's rich. Family with Red?"

"I'm trying, Mom. I want Itchy to feel like we're a real family."

"I thought we already were?"

"You know what I mean. With a father."

"If you consider Red a father. Me, I think that's stretching the term."

"He's been better."

"It's only been a month. Give him a chance, he'll fuck up again."

"Please don't cuss so much. You sound like—"

"Red?"

"—White trash."

Jacqueline grinned and held up her Bud in a toast. "White trash and proud of it, honey. Gotta be true to your roots."

Irene shook her head and smiled. There just was no way to rile Jacqueline up, no matter how hard she tried. Irene wished she could be more like her.

"So what else did that priest tell you?"

"Just to be careful with Red."

"Good advice. Maybe he's not as big a knucklehead as I thought."

"Mom, please. He's a priest."

"Whatever. Where's Itchy?"

"He called from Mart's. He's on his way."

Jacqueline stubbed out her Marlboro. "Red hasn't talked to Mart yet, has he?"

"I don't think so."

"If he's gonna stay in town he needs to take care of that."

"I'm not Red's keeper. He'll do what he does."

"You be careful with him, honey."

"I learn from my mistakes. Besides, it wasn't all bad. If it wasn't for Red I wouldn't have Itchy."

Itchy came crashing in the front door, noisy and big-footed, and immediately shed his jacket and backpack. He left both on the floor and came sniffing into the kitchen.

"My God, you're a noisy little shit. Give Gramma a hug," Jacqueline ordered. Itchy did as told and even gave Jacqueline a little smooch on the cheek.

"Hi, Gramma. What's for dinner?"

"Human garbage disposal," Jacqueline said. She glanced down at Itchy's feet. "You're like a puppy that needs to grow into his paws. Jeez, those boats of yours are big enough for somebody six-foot-six."

"He's gotten two sizes bigger in six months, his feet are costing me a fortune," Irene sighed as she grabbed her gangling bigfoot and pulled him to her. "I want a kiss, too."

"Mom—" Itchy protested. The Gramma kiss was one of those spur-of-

102

the-moment things. But he relented and gave his mom a quick peck. "When are we gonna eat?"

"When your dad gets here. Are you hungry?"

"Does a bear—" Jacqueline began.

"Mom!"

"'Does a bear' what?" Itchy asked.

"Never mind," Irene said. "Did you hang up your coat?"

"I think so."

"Liar. Go hang it up and put your backpack in your room."

Itchy thumped out and called back, "Mart wanted to know how come he wasn't invited for dinner."

Jacqueline gave Irene a raised eyebrow. "You should call him. He gets his feelings hurt easy."

"I will. Later." Irene had enough on her mind getting dinner ready for tonight. She'd talk to Mart. He'd understand. But right now Irene needed to be nice to Red. It mattered. To Itchy.

To Itchy, she told herself.

"I read that book you gave me, Itch," Red said as he dished up a third helping of mashed potatoes. The dinner had turned out amazingly well for an Irene Donner production. Things looked the way they were supposed to look, and even tasted the way they were supposed to taste. Nobody was more surprised than Irene.

"Wasn't it neat?!" Itchy said.

"Yeah. Except for the same old bullcrap about the Donners eating folks. That kinda pissed me off."

"Does every conversation in this house have to revolve around those damn cannibals?" Jacqueline groused, clanging her fork down on the plate. "Just once I'd like to eat a mouthful of beef without picturing it being some pioneer's thigh."

Irene smiled. This was kind of fun. She liked the banter. All in all an unexpectedly pleasant evening so far. And Red had cleaned himself up, too; he was tidy and had even trimmed his beard. He was on his best behavior, and she thought that he and Itchy definitely had a bond going.

"It has some great pictures in it, huh?" Itchy said, ignoring his Gramma.

"Yeah," Red said. "Lots of good stuff." He looked across the table at Irene. She smiled. He winked.

Jacqueline noticed and she wasn't pleased. "So Red," she said.

"Yeah, J.W.?"

"Isn't it about time you said something to Mart?"

Irene shot Jacqueline a killer glare.

"Funny you should mention that," Red said, not the least bit bothered. "I been thinkin' real hard about doin' somethin'. Old Mar-teen is the main reason I come back. Mar-teen and Itchy, that is." Red glanced down at Itchy and smiled.

Itchy asked, "Is it true you cut down a tree on top of Mart?"

"Who told you that?" Irene asked. Her good feeling had just gone up in smoke like one of her less successful cooking adventures.

"Mart did," Itchy said. *Uh-oh*, Itchy thought. He knew that tone of voice. He'd just stirred up big trouble.

"It's okay, Irene. The boy should know what happened. It's not like it's top-secret or nothin'."

"Did you do it on purpose?" Itchy asked quietly.

Red's voice softened. "No, Itchy. It was an accident. Mart think otherwise?"

"He said he wasn't sure. But he said he thought you were drunk."

Red slowly set his fork down. His shoulders drooped and his face, usually so exuberantly smiley, had no expression. Just weariness.

"I'll tell you what I'm gonna tell Mart, Itchy. I don't exactly know if I was drunk or not, to tell you the truth. Back in those days there wasn't much difference between me drunk or sober. Ask your mother," Red said, nodding toward Irene. "I screwed up bad back then, Itch. Left you and your mom, hurt Mart. It *was* an accident, but that don't matter much to him, I'm sure. I run off like a coward—which I was. So that's why I'm back. I don't drink no more, I want to make things up to all the people I let down. It's hard to forgive, I know. I've never been very good at it. But I suppose now's as good a time as any to tell you guys how sorry I am for bein' such an asshole. I can't ever make it up to you. So I'll just ask you to try and forgive me, if you can. And I'll try not to be such an asshole in the future. No guarantees, though." Red smiled ruefully.

Nobody said anything. Itchy stared at his plate, Jacqueline made an elaborate show of moving carrots around, and Irene—

Irene swallowed hard. Red locked her eyes with his.

"I'm sorry, Irene. You know that, don't you?"

She didn't say anything. She couldn't.

But she nodded and gave Red a tiny smile.

"Time to bury the fuckin' hatchet," Red said. He slammed a six-pack on the wooden porch.

Mart had been sitting outside, whiling away the day in his usual watching-the-world-go- by routine, when Red strode up with his six-pack of peace.

"Get the fuck outa here," Mart said. He started to roll himself back inside the house, but Red blocked his way.

"We *need* to bury the fuckin' hatchet, Mar-teen."

"Get drunk on your own, Red. You don't need me to help you."

"I don't drink no more. Brought these for you."

"Shove 'em up your ass!"

"Plenty of room for 'em, I suppose. Bein' that I'm such a huge asshole, I mean." Red waited for a response, but Mart stayed silent. "Guess you're not in the mood for jokes, huh?"

"Not for the last eleven years."

Red leaned against the front door. "I'm sorry, buddy."

"So what? Doesn't do me much good now, does it?"

"Itchy says you're not a hundred-percent sure it was an accident. I'm here to tell you it was. Don't think I was drunk, neither. I just fucked up, that's all. No excuse. But it's the truth."

"Yeah. Fine. Okay. Now take your beer and leave."

Red grabbed a five-gallon plastic bucket from Stan the Man's debris pile of junk on the porch, flipped it over, and sat down. "You ever try to do anything about Irene?"

"What do you mean?"

"After I left."

Mart held his arms out and gestured to his chair. "Yeah, right Red. Like she's gonna want a crippled loser."

"Give her some credit. She's no airhead."

"Just get out of here, okay? I'll put up with you on Sundays, but other than that I don't want anything to do with you."

"It was an accident, Mart. An *accident*. I took off like a fuckin' chickenshit 'cause of what happened to you and Irene bein' pregnant. I'm sorry. But it won't do no good to fuckin' brood about it the rest of your life."

Mart lurched forward in the wheelchair and knocked Red off the bucket. He swung uselessly at Red, but he couldn't get close, he couldn't get out of the chair, he couldn't smash fucking Red Donner in the face, and oh, he wanted to so bad, he wanted to kill the fuck.

But Mart couldn't do anything but make airswings. Red stood and slowly backed away, shaking his head.

"Gotta let it go, Mar-teen. I ain't gonna give up on you."

"Get the fuck outa here!"

Red slowly headed back to the street. "I got some plans for us. Maybe even some fun, who knows. I'll talk to you about it on Sunday."

"Fuck you!"

He took one last look back at Mart, gave him a friendly wave, and he was gone.

Mart grabbed the six-pack and threw it into the street.

And then he rolled back inside.

To be alone.

The tedious delays and high altitude wrought distressing changes. Thence our course lay through a wilderness of rugged peaks and rockbound canyons until a heavily obstructed gulch confronted us. We believed it would lead to the Utah River Valley. We had been thirty days reaching that point, which we had hoped to make in ten.

Eliza Donner

August 15, 1846

Chapter Six

Winter came early to Tamarack that year, with howling gales that whipped crushing snowfalls into monstrous sculpted drifts. By Thanksgiving the berms lining the streets made them into bobsled runs, and it was easier to get around by snowmobile than beefy four-by-fours. The days stayed frigid, the thermometer never nudging 32 degrees. A terrible winter lay ahead, and already the Tamarack townies were grumbling and crabby. March seemed an eternity away, and with their luck the thaw would probably hold off until April. Happy Thanksgiving.

But not everyone found the weather depressing. Conditions were perfect, Itchy decided, to experience how it *really* felt to be a Donner.

Because Itchy Donner was going to starve himself.

Well, not starve, exactly. He wanted to go without eating for awhile to get a real taste—maybe "taste" wasn't the best word—of what Tamsen and George and Eliza and all the rest of them had gone through. Since he lived in a semi-warm singlewide and went to school in a heated classroom, the experiment wouldn't be exact, but a growling stomach and miserable cold weather outside would at least give him an inkling of understanding.

108

"Whatcha think?" he asked Sara after he'd told her his plan. They were killing time at the library, thumbing through magazines while they waited their turn at the computer. They now spent their afternoons camped out at the library, since Sara's mom had made it obvious that Itchy shouldn't come around anymore. It was a major pain, because they had to wait in line to use the only web-connected computer, and the librarian always kicked them off after twenty minutes. Donner Party surfing needed to be done casually, wandering from site to site without stupid time limits. Itchy couldn't find new things so quickly, and inevitably, just as he was zeroing in on something interesting, he'd get booted from the computer and have to get in line again. Most vexing.

"How come you want to starve?" Sara asked.

"Because. That way I can be like them."

"Does that mean you're gonna eat people, too?"

"The Donners never—"

"I know, I know," Sara grinned. She liked teasing Itchy.

Itchy scratched at his cheek. The psoriasis had flared up lately and was really bugging him. Maybe if he stopped eating for awhile it'd go away. Psoriasis had to eat too, didn't it?

"I wish I could go to Alder Creek," Itchy said.

"And starve?"

"No. Well, maybe I'd like to go there when I'm really hungry. In the winter. It'd be so much like the way it was for them."

"You're weird, Itchy."

"Wouldn't it be cool to be there during a blizzard or something? And see the same stuff that they saw?"

"I guess."

"My dad said he'd take me down there."

"When?"

"I dunno. But I'm gonna go."

"Can I come?"

"Sure. If your parents will let you."

Sara considered. Would Daddy say yes? Probably not, but then again, he was so busy with work lately he'd probably never notice she was gone. And her mom? Well, if Sara sneaked out during the wine hour she could get away with it. It'd be fun—in a weird sort of way—to see the places where all those people died. Maybe they'd even find some bones!

"Can I starve with you?" Sara asked as the idea popped into her head and suddenly seemed to make good sense.

"You really want to?"

"Yeah! I mean, I know almost as much about the Donners as you do, we should do stuff like this together."

Itchy was touched. For a girl, Sara was okay. She was about the only one—other than his mom and dad—who had any idea of what it was like to be a Donner.

"Okay! Let's start at dinner tonight," Itchy said.

"We don't eat anything, right?"

"Right. Will your parents let you?"

"They won't even notice. How about your mom? She kinda watches you close, doesn't she?"

Itchy nodded. "I'm gonna have to be sneaky."

"How long will we do it?"

"Um, until we're starving."

"How long does *that* take?"

"Well, it took Tamsen and them a couple of months. But they had stuff to chew on like leather straps and they ate their dogs and made this kinda gluey stew stuff out of boiling oxhides. Do you have any oxhides we could boil?"

"I don't think so."

"We'll just have to pretend."

"When will we eat again?"

Itchy rubbed his rash. Deep in thought. Good question. "When we understand," he finally said.

"Understand what?"

"Understand what they went through. We'll know."

And they both hurried home that night, excited at the prospect of starving.

Just like the Donner Party.

Sara's Donner fast lasted until the next morning. She made it through dinner—that was easy because her mom didn't bother to make anything and all they had in the refrigerator was wilted spinach—but by morning she was *truly* starving and couldn't stand it anymore. She devoured two bowls of Lucky Charms and went off to school crushed by miserable guilt over her faithless betrayal of Itchy.

Itchy stayed more dedicated to the cause. He managed to fool Irene at dinnertime, elaborately moving his food around the plate in intricate patterns and then hurriedly taking it to the kitchen when her head was turned. He scraped the uneaten meal into the garbage disposal. Irene didn't have a clue.

He slept fitfully, his stomach gnawing in protest, but it was okay. He savored the sensation his ancestors had felt, and already his kinship with them overpowered any hunger pangs. To be a Donner, a *true* Donner, you had to be hungry and uncomfortable. It was the only way to understand.

The next morning Itchy easily deceived Irene. As she rushed around getting ready for work, she didn't notice as he carefully poured his Wheaties and milk, clanked the appropriate spoon-against-bowl sounds, and then just as carefully dumped the sodden mess into the garbage disposal to join last night's dinner.

"Did you remember your lunch?" she called out as Itchy grabbed his backpack to head off to school.

"Yeah, Mom. 'Bye."

"Love you, honey," Irene said, and Itchy grunted an indecipherable reply.

He tossed his PB&J and Granny Smith apple into the garbage can and hurried down the street, his stomach growling, proud and excited at his genuine starving Donner-ness.

At recess, Itchy and Sara huddled together on a pine-shrouded bench at the corner of the schoolyard to compare starvation notes. Jason Bent yelled some insult about "nerds," but Itchy didn't care and ignored him. Since he got no response, Jason lost interest in the traditional morning Itchy torment session and instead spent recess tossing a football around with his pals. Itchy usually took teasing hard, spending long hours sulking and plotting imaginary revenge, but this morning was different. He was too excited about starving to let Jason Bent bother him.

"My mom made me eat breakfast this morning," Sara lied. Her face reddened in shame at her weakness, but if Itchy noticed he didn't let on.

"Oh," he said.

"Are you still...starving?"

"Yeah. It's great! My mom doesn't know. But I already feel like Tamsen must've felt."

Sara listened raptly. Itchy was so strong and determined. If only she could be more like him. But she realized that he came from incredibly strong pioneer stock; the people in his past had been tough, had suffered, and the ones who survived passed down their survival traits to Itchy. That was why he could starve so easily. Sara's ancestors had been rich people who always had things easy. They didn't know how to suffer—not like the Donners. It made her envious, but it wasn't her fault she was so weak. It was Mommy and Daddy's fault.

"Tomorrow's Thanksgiving. How are you gonna not eat then?" she asked.

"There'll be lots of people there, I bet they won't notice. And my mom's cooking isn't so good, so it makes it easier."

"Too bad you don't have a dog you could feed under the table."

Itchy nodded seriously. "I wonder if somebody has a dog I could borrow for the day?"

"Forget about the dog. It's dumb. What are you going to do about tonight?" Sara asked.

"I'll think of something." Itchy rubbed his face. It might've been wishful thinking, but the patch didn't itch as much as usual.

By the time he got home the hunger pangs had lessened, but his head felt spinny and dizzy. Gloppy dinner muck bubbled on the stove, some nasty Irene health concoction that smelled vaguely of vegetables and dirty sneakers.

"I think I'm sick," Itchy said, figuring that a mystery illness would be the easiest way out of eating.

Irene's hand immediately clamped onto his forehead. "Do you have a fever?" she asked. "You don't feel warm." She studied his face. "You do look a little pale, though."

"Maybe I better just go to my room," Itchy suggested helpfully. "I don't think I feel like eating."

Irene hugged him. "Poor baby. You go lie down, I'll bring in some water, maybe some saltines, okay?"

"Okay," he said. He trudged off to his room, dragging his feet so he had that "Boy, am I ever sick" body language. Moms always fell for that.

He pulled on his pajamas, grabbed his latest Donner Party library book, and hopped into bed, looking forward to a night of starvation and deep Donner study. Maybe he should open the window later and let the cold night air blow in. Not exactly Alder Creek in January 1847, but as close as he could get.

Irene bustled in moments later, lugging an old mineral-encrusted vaporizer. "I'll just set this up, honey."

"I don't think I have a cold, Mom."

"Better safe than sorry. The air's awfully dry."

"I think I just have a stomach ache."

Irene plugged in the vaporizer and fiddled with the lid. "Maybe I should put some Vapo-Rub in, too."

"Mom—"

"How about some Pepto Bismal? Do you feel nauseated?" Irene sat on the edge of his bed and felt his forehead again.

"It's okay," Itchy said. His mom was awfully nice, even if she turned kind of geeky whenever he got sick. His conscience nudged at him though, lying to her and all. But she wouldn't understand his need to starve, so this was the best way. It saved her feelings, and anyway, she got to be all Mom-ish toward him, which seemed to make her so happy.

"Does your psoriasis hurt more than usual or anything?" Irene asked. She knew that it wasn't usually a life-threatening disease, but sometimes, lying awake late at night, her darkest fears surfaced and she'd worry that Itchy's condition would turn into something horrible like leprosy or cancer. Irrational, she knew, but she couldn't help it.

"It's okay," Itchy answered. "Don't worry, okay? I just don't feel real good, but it's nothing bad."

Irene gave him a kiss. "My brave little man."

"Mom!" He hated it when she got all dorky and emotional for no reason. What was the deal with girls, anyway?

She kissed him again, jiggled the vaporizer one last time, and said, "Call me if you need anything, okay?"

"Okay."

She closed the door and left Itchy alone. Cool. Just what he wanted.

The vaporizer began to hiss and spit, and Itchy settled in to read his book. Unfortunately, this wasn't a particularly good Donner book, and as he thumbed through it he found nothing he didn't already know. The usual stories, and some lies about Donner cannibalism, so after a few minutes of disappointed skimming he set it aside. He'd reached a point where he knew as much as any of these guys who wrote these books—sometimes more. He had a few more on order from the library, but Itchy didn't hold out much hope for new information. What else could he do? He'd work on getting his dad to take him down to Alder Creek, but until that happened, what new things—other than starving—could he do to understand his ancestors?

The vaporizer's clogged nozzle didn't make much steam; it just shot sizzling hot water droplets like a mini-geyser. He got up and unplugged it. Vaporizers. *Sheesh.* Like the Donners had vaporizers when they camped at Alder Creek. A rotten old oxhide held up with poles, leaky and stinky and cold, a smoky fire—that was it. And most of them survived. Starving, too. He had it so easy. Life in a singlewide in Tamarack, Idaho was living like a king compared to Tamsen and George's and Eliza's miserable Alder Creek camp.

Itchy opened the window. He gazed out into the November night, so still and clear, so cold. The frigid air poured into his room, and now, suddenly, he got a sense, just a tiny sense, of...back then. Cold. Hungry.

He picked up the book and thumbed through it again. Nothing new. His eyes stopped on one paragraph. The story about Tamsen's journal, the one everybody who survived the ordeal talked about. Tamsen Donner wanted to open a girls' school in California. She was a smart lady, and she spent a lot of her time on the ill-fated journey west writing a journal—her botany studies, and her daily report on the trip. But her journal had never been found. Itchy considered. What if Tamsen's journal showed up some day? Wouldn't that be cool?! Great-great-great Gramma Tamsen Donner, *her* version of the story, of what happened. If only they could find it. Was the journal sitting in somebody's attic somewhere, quietly moldering away into dust?

Itchy sighed.

And then he wondered.... What if somebody else on the trip scribbled down what Tamsen said? The real Donner family story, without all the lies and mistakes that people later added. Wouldn't that be....

Itchy smiled. He grabbed a yellow pad from his desk, a pencil, and he started writing.

The Unknown Story of the Donner Party as told to Itchy Donner
by his Great-great-great Gramma Tamsen in her Lost Journal

By Itchy Donner, her Great-great-great Grandson

Great-great-great Gramma Tamsen said that the Donners never ate anybody. She said that Keseburg, and the Breens, and the Murphys, and lots of the other people ate people. But not the Donners. I believe her.

She said that it was cold at night. She had to take care of Great-great-great Grandpa George. He hurt his hand fixing a broken wagon wheel. He was cutting wood and the ax slipped. That was back before they got up in the mountains. His hand didn't heal. When they got stuck at Alder Creek, Great-great-great Grandpa George got sick. Pretty soon after they were stuck he was so sick he couldn't help out with anything. He just stayed in the ox-hide tent because he was so sick.

Tamsen...

Itchy stopped writing. Maybe he shouldn't be doing this. After all, he was just making stuff up, pretending that he knew what Tamsen wrote. Even though they were related, it *was* a hundred and fifty years later, and did he really have the right to put words in Tamsen's mouth? It might be okay since she was dead, but she had to be watching from up in heaven, and he didn't want to make her mad. He'd meet her someday after he died and went to heaven too, he figured, and then she could tell him the whole story.

But she probably wouldn't mind if he wrote some things down just for his own satisfaction. He'd write what he thought happened; knowing as much as he knew about the Donner Party—which was a lot—he'd guess at what Tamsen would've said. He'd never show anybody, he'd just do it for himself. Tamsen would understand. Maybe someday they'd laugh about it together. Maybe she'd help him, like ghosts help people out sometimes.

Why not?

Tamsen had to decide what to do about the kids. The first rescue party came, and she wanted her kids to go. But she didn't want to leave George. He was too sick. She knew he was going to die. If she stayed, she'd probably die, too. But she wouldn't leave him. She loved him too much.

Itchy stopped writing. Wow. Those words didn't come from him. Not really. *She loved him too much.* That's not something he would write on his own. Not without somebody helping.

It had to be Tamsen! Tamsen's ghost was talking through him. He shivered, and not from the cold November air. If ever there was proof of his special Donner-ness, this was it. He figured he better stop for now, until he thought about this some more and decided what else to do. Starving and freezing had brought Great-great-great Gramma Tamsen into his life, her reality was sneaking into his head.

Itchy leaned back against his pillow and smiled.

So far, starving was everything he'd hoped it would be, and more.

More cooking. For somebody who hated to cook, who wasn't any good at it, it seemed to Irene that all she ever did was cook.

It was Thanksgiving morning, the turkey roasted in the oven, spattering occasionally and filling the singlewide with that wonderful smell—the thick, delicious scent of holiday good times. Irene missed the good old days when she was young, when Jacqueline made the holiday dinners and Irene got to goof off and just eat. But the second Itchy was born, Jacqueline decided that Irene, being all grown-up, should inherit the holiday chores. Now, Jacqueline and Stan the Man showed up like honored guests, Jacqueline poked subtle and not-so-subtle digs at Irene's cooking prowess, and Irene got to spend the day slaving away in the kitchen.

Irene stood at the sink, peeling potatoes. Always peeling. Why didn't she just buy instant mashed and make her life easier? She had to prepare lots of everything for today, twice the amount she usually cooked for Thanksgiving, since Red would be here.

Red.

How do you deal with something like this? Irene didn't have a clue. She'd come to terms with being alone, with raising Itchy as a single parent, and then *knockknockknock*, Red's at the door and everything changes.

She'd kept her jealousy in check at sharing Itchy, although sometimes, when Red and Itchy were deep in discussion about the nature of Donnerhood, she couldn't help but pout and feel left out. *She'd* been the one to instill Donner pride in Itchy, she'd been the one to encourage him to study his ancestors, and then along comes Red-go-lately to nose in between them and make her an afterthought to her own son.

Okay, she thought, maybe that was over the top, but she couldn't help the way Red made her feel. She had to remind herself what Father Ray had said— be wary of Red, but don't get in the way of his being a father to Itchy. She couldn't interfere. It wasn't right. It was a sin. Just keep an eye on Red and make sure he didn't do anything to hurt Itchy, because Itchy was such a vulnerable kid. She'd die to protect him.

If only he didn't have to grow up.

Her thoughts made her peel the potatoes roughly, smacking at them with the peeler like they were trying to escape and needed to be whacked into submission.

"How come you're hitting the potatoes?" Itchy asked.

Irene jumped. She hadn't heard him come into the kitchen. "Are you feeling better?"

"Sort of. I don't know if I'll want to eat, though." He gave her a theatrical *sigh* to really sell it.

"Even turkey and all the trimmings?"

His stomach ached and growled with hunger, and the tantalizing smell of roasting turkey didn't help matters. "I dunno."

"You take it easy today. Gramma and Stan and Mart will be here in a little while."

"When's Dad coming?"

An innocent question, but the very sound of it bothered Irene. *"Dad."* Such a strange word coming from Itchy. "He...I'm not sure."

"But he's coming, right?"

"He said he would. Your father never passes up a free meal," Irene said, and then immediately regretted it. *Stop being such a bitch!*

"Good. I've got some stuff to show him."

"About the Donner Party?"

"Yeah."

Itchy wandered off and Irene was left alone again in the kitchen, smacking potatoes and feeling sorry for herself.

"Bring me an ashtray, would you, honey?" Jacqueline asked. She and Stan the Man lounged in their customary spots on the couch. A football game blared on the TV, and Stan the Man had already nodded off for his pre-dinner snooze. Sometimes Jacqueline accused Stan the Man of acting more like a retired geezer than a young-buck thirty-one-year-old.

Mart and Itchy played Scrabble, and Mart clicked his tiles around desperately trying to make a word out of three a's and four r's. Itchy tried to concentrate, but his stomach wouldn't let him.

"Itchy?" Jacqueline asked. "Did you hear what I said?" The ash on the end of her cigarette had grown to an alarming length and she needed an ashtray right now.

"Go ahead, Itchy, this is gonna take me awhile," Mart said.

Itchy stood and swayed. Stars flickered before his eyes and he almost fell over.

"You okay?" Mart asked.

"Yeah. I've been kinda sick." He found an ashtray and got it to Jacqueline just in time for the ash to drop.

"Thanks, honey. You seem a little more out of it than usual. Been studyin' your pioneers too much?"

"I dunno. I guess." His brain didn't seem to be working right. His thoughts got scrambled, and the only one he could keep track of was overwhelming hunger. He went back to the table as Mart gave up his turn to get new tiles.

Thanksgiving Day at Irene's passed just like any Sunday, except more food awaited them. Irene hid out in the kitchen, even though everything was pretty much ready to go. She didn't know why. The people she loved were out in the living room, but she couldn't force herself to go out there. Not right now.

She opened a bottle of cheap Chardonnay—nobody in her family knew or cared much about wine—and poured herself a tumbler. As she drank it up, Mart rolled into the kitchen.

"Hey, you need help?" he asked.

Irene set the glass down with a sheepish, guilty smile. "Nope, everything's fine. How's the game?"

"Itchy's whippin' my butt. Kid's way too smart for me," Mart smiled. He found Irene especially fetching today, her long hair carelessly swept up and held with a big plastic clip, lots of strays—Mart loved strays—and a cheap but nice dress. No matter what, she always looked classy and beautiful to Mart.

"No Red yet?" she asked.

"Nope." The sound of Red's name wiped the smile off his face. "He came by my place the other day."

"Really?"

"Brought a six-pack and apologies."

"What'd you do?"

"Told him to shove it up his ass."

Irene tried not to smile but one leaked out anyway. "And I suppose he just shrugged it off."

"You know Red," Mart said. "Nothin' bothers him."

"That's the problem."

"Itchy's looking kind of green. Has he got the flu or something?"

"I don't know. I'm starting to get worried about him—"

Two big *bangs* at the door, and the conversation stopped.

Red's boomy voice shook the singlewide. "Hey, hey, hey, Itchy my man, happy T-Giving!"

Irene held up the Chardonnay bottle to Mart. "Want some?" she asked. "I think we'll need it."

Mart took the bottle and drank straight from it. "Three or four more and I might even be able to put up with him."

Irene held up her tumbler in a toast. "Cheers, Mart. Happy Thanksgiving." She leaned over and gave him a little kiss.

As usual, Mart's insides turned to Jell-O. He took a long gulp from the Chardonnay bottle and then they went out to join the others and celebrate Thanksgiving as one, big pretend happy family.

"Damn, Irene, I never woulda left if you'd cooked like this before," Red grinned. He was on his third plateload—or was it four?—and showed now signs of slowing down. Irene didn't respond. How could she to a weird, left-handed compliment like that?

Jacqueline watched him and frowned. "You know, Red, when you get the big metabolism slowdown that hits everybody sooner or later, you're gonna turn into the Goodyear blimp."

"Won't happen, J.W. I got a lot of energy. Besides, that cheap sumbitch A. Jackson's got me puttin' so much wood on the ground I never get a chance to catch my breath. Must be burnin' a million calories a day."

"Word is he's goin' out of business. Think it's true?" Stan the Man asked Red between mouthfuls of turkey.

"Probably. Nothin's forever. He's so desperate he's got us cuttin' twigs we wouldn't have peed on twenty years ago. What can you do, though? Between the enviros and the feds and the fact that we basically cut everything down that was worth a shit in the last hundred years, there's not much left. Gotta Zen out, Stanley. Learned that down in California, you gotta be Buddhist about life, take what comes, don't fight it."

"You're a Buddhist now?" Jacqueline asked.

"I belong to the First United Congregational Church of Red Donner, J.W. I'm kinda ecumenical."

"Uh-huh. Did you know that about your old man, Itchy?" Jacqueline asked.

Itchy stared at his plate. He'd taken tiny portions and now busily moved the food around, fantasizing about how good it would taste. Starving was killing him. It was one thing to starve when you didn't have anything to eat; it was a whole lot harder when food stared you in the face every way you turned.

"I don't know what you're talking about, Gramma," Itchy said.

"Are you still feeling bad, honey?" Irene asked.

Itchy nodded.

Red, sitting next to Itchy, gave him a manly slap on the back that almost put Itchy's face into his plate. "Kinda scrawny, Itch. Eat up. Don't want to be a ninety-eight pound weakling all your life, do you?"

"Red—" Irene warned.

"Boy needs to eat, Irene. Too many Donners starved already, ain't that right, Itch?" The food on Itchy's plate moved before his eyes, but he hadn't touched it. He blinked, trying to make the food stay put, but the turkey slice jumped from one side of the plate to the other, and then the jellied cranberry sauce slithered toward him like it wanted to attack, and then the stuffing glob quivered, ready to pounce.

"I don't feel so good," Itchy whispered.

"Honey?" Irene reached across the table, but it was too late because Itchy's eyes rolled back in his head and he keeled over, landing like a feather in Red's lap.

Irene panicked. Red carried him to the living room couch and laid him down, Jacqueline splashed a glass of cold water on Itchy's forehead, Stan the Man offered to drive him down to the clinic in Elk Creek—and Mart rolled around on the perimeter of the action.

"Itchy, ohmyGod, Itchy!" Whispers of hysteria lurked on the edge of Irene's voice.

"He's comin' 'round, Irene. Calm down," Red said.

Itchy's eyes fluttered open, and he wiped his face. "How come I'm all wet?"

"Your gramma threw water on you," Red said quietly. He gently touched

Itchy's forehead and smoothed back his wet hair. "How you doin', buddy?"

"Okay. I guess."

Irene knelt next to the couch and touched Itchy's cheek. Her small, delicate hand and Red's huge, rough hand cradled their son's head. "Sweetie? Where do you feel bad?"

"Um...." Itchy hesitated. "I think I know what's wrong with me."

"What?" Irene asked. "Is it the psoriasis?"

"Uh-uh. I'm starving."

She and Red looked at each other, completely puzzled. "Don't get you, Itchy," Red said.

"I wanted to see what it felt like to be a real Donner," Itchy said earnestly.

"Oh, for Christ's sake!" Jacqueline said. "This is what happens when you fill the kid's head with all that gloomy Donner nonsense. C'mon, Stanley and Mart, let's us normal people finish our dinner and let these Donner psychos deal with their nutcase issues."

Stan the Man eagerly went back to the table with Jacqueline, but Mart stayed on in the living room to watch.

"Why would you do that?!" Irene demanded. "Why would you want to starve yourself?"

"To see what they went through," Itchy answered. Now, all of a sudden, he felt like a dope. He looked at Red, hoping for a better response, but Red's expression stayed impassive.

Red continued to gently stroke Itchy's wet hair and watched his son with a bemused smile. "You had us worried, Itchy. Got your mom all upset on Thanksgiving. That ain't real cool."

"I know," Itchy said. Irene glared at him, and his eyes filled with guilty tears.

"I can't believe—" Irene began, but Red held up his hand.

"Give the boy a break, Irene. He feels bad enough as it is."

Irene stood. Mart watched in awe; she suddenly looked like Lara Croft getting ready to kick some ass.

"Can I talk to you please?" she said through clenched teeth to Red.

Red made an "Oh-oh, I'm in trouble" face to Itchy, then followed Irene out the front door. She spun on him the minute he closed it.

"Don't tell me what to do with my son! If I want to be mad at him, I'll be mad at him! Don't you fucking think I know him, that I love him more than anything in the world? You come strolling in here after eleven years, after you *abandoned* him, and me, and you think you've got the right to tell me how to raise him!? Who the fuck do you think you are?"

"Never heard you cuss before. Must really be pissed."

"No shit, idiot! Don't ever come between me and my son again!"

"Yeah, I'm sorry. You're right. I'm an asshole, I got no right."

"No, you don't," Irene sputtered. Red's hangdog apology deflated her fury. "You can...be his dad, you *are* his dad, but don't think you've got parent rights. Not like a real parent. Not like me."

"Okay."

Irene folded her arms against the cold. "Okay," she said.

"But you think it might help if I had a little talk with him? Man to man, you know."

"I don't know, Red. I just don't want him to hurt himself. This Donner stuff is getting out of hand."

"It ain't easy being a Donner, Irene. We got a legacy. Itchy feels it more

126

than most, I think."

"He's just a little boy," Irene said, and now the tears started.

Red slowly, carefully, moved toward her. He hugged her.

She didn't resist.

"He'll be okay, Irene."

"I just want him to be safe."

"He will be. I promise I'll help."

"Just don't help too much," she said, and a little laugh escaped through her tears.

"Yeah, well, the new improved Red Donner is kinda saint-like, you know? I'm like a big-ass Mother Teresa with a beard."

"A saint is one thing you'll never be."

Red pulled away from her. He looked her in the eye and smiled, then gently smoothed one of her errant stray hairs. "I'm never gonna convince you I'm not an asshole, am I?"

"No."

"I appreciate you lettin' me hang around. I know it's hard."

"Itchy...needs you."

"What do you need?"

They stood close. The day was brilliantly clear; the sun reflected off the snow and brightened Tamarack, making the little town seem much more appealing than it really was. Smoke curled out of chimneys, but no one walked the streets. The mill was silent. The only thing that quieted Tamarack down was a holiday.

Irene took a step back from Red. She gazed out over the view. "It's pretty today."

"You know, I figured when I got back you'd have been living with some-body."

"Nope."

"How come?"

"Hasn't been anybody."

"What about Mart?"

"He's just a good friend."

"Not that it's any of my business," Red added. "Just seems that somebody as smart and nice and pretty as you woulda hooked up by now."

"Hasn't worked out that way. Anyway, you've been gone too long to be asking me about this kind of stuff. We should go back in."

"You get lonesome, Irene?"

"I have Itchy. He's all that matters."

"He's gonna grow up and leave some day. I don't see him as a Tamarack kinda guy. Anyway, this town's gonna fold sooner rather than later."

"I just have to see what happens. Zen out, like you said."

"Shit, I'm an idiot, don't be listenin' to me." Red paused. "You're still so young, you're...what, twenty-nine?"

"Thirty-one. Thanks for keeping track."

Red grinned. "What can I say, I'm losin' my memory. Somebody as young as you oughta get—"

"It's not your concern, okay?" Irene snapped. "The only thing you should worry about is Itchy. I'll take care of me."

"Sure. Can't help carin' about you, though."

Neither said anything more, and the awkward moment grew. Finally, Irene said, "Let's go finish dinner," and they went back inside.

Itchy sat at the table, apparently recovered, because now he voraciously devoured a plate overflowing with Thanksgiving plenty. Everybody else ate, although Mart watched closely as Irene and Red sat down.

"Glad you two finished your spat. Hate to see a nice holiday ruined by fightin'," Jacqueline said.

"Are you feeling okay?" Irene asked Itchy. He nodded but didn't say anything. He couldn't. His mouth was too full.

"Seems like the starvation boy is recovering nicely," Jacqueline said. "Why didn't you tell him he's related to Bill Gates instead of those dead cannibals, that way he'd spend his time doing something useful."

"Grmmma!" Itchy protested, but he couldn't get the words out through the turkey and stuffing.

"Don't let her get you riled up, Itchy," Irene said. She shook her head and gave him a smile. "What a bonehead. You had me scared."

Itchy shrugged and shoveled yet another forkful of mashed potatoes into his already overstuffed mouth.

"You realize he'll be barfing all that up shortly," Jacqueline pointed out.

"Can you pass the stuffing, please?" Stan the Man asked.

Jacqueline couldn't hide her astonishment. "My God Stanley, you eat like got a goddamn tapeworm."

"You make me burn a lot of calories, Sugar."

"There goes my appetite," Red said. Even Mart laughed.

"Save room for dessert, everybody," Irene said amidst the laughter.

Stan the Man chowed down as Jacqueline clucked teasing disapproval, Itchy stuffed himself, Mart silently finished and carefully set his silverware on the plate, and Red and Irene watched their son—and each other.

Irene sipped her cheap Chardonnay and surveyed the table. Her family— such as it was. She could do worse, she decided. Maybe, in spite of Itchy's starvation experiment—and Red's presence—Thanksgiving wouldn't turn out so bad after all.

"Itchy!" Red whispered. Irene had just served everybody slices of mincemeat pie.

"What?"

"Don't this stuff look like boogers?"

Itchy giggled. "Sort of."

"We're having booger pie for dessert!" Red chortled.

Itchy's giggles turned uncontrollable. Stan the Man caught the infection and his explosive laughter and bobbing Adam's apple infected even dour Mart.

"Booger pie!" Itchy screamed as his laughter convulsed him into a boneless Gumby boy.

Irene and Jacqueline watched the jabbering maniacs with complete mystification. "Must be a guy thing," Irene said. "It's really good pie."

"Don't let 'em bother you, honey," Jacqueline said. "I can understand Itchy acting like an eleven-year-old...the rest of 'em, it's just plain pathetic." She smacked Stan the Man upside the head, but he just laughed all the harder.

"Okay, okay, real funny," Irene said. "Stop it, just eat your pie."

"BOOGER PIE!" Itchy screamed, and Irene gave up. Her table was surrounded with a bunch of immature bozos.

But she couldn't resist smiling.

There had never been this much laughter in her home before.

*   *   *

"I got an idea," Red said. Everybody was crammed into the kitchen helping with clean-up. Irene washed, Red rinsed, Mart and Jacqueline dried, and Stan the Man and Itchy put away. Very efficient, surprisingly organized. But not enough room—especially with Mart's wheelchair—and collisions were inevitable.

Jacqueline handed a plate to Itchy. "You know, Red, those words frighten me."

"You gotta think outside the box, J.W. That's what A. Jackson keeps sayin'. Bullshit buzzwords, huh?"

"So what's your idea?" Stan the Man asked.

"Well, Stanley, seems to me it's time for some winnin' amongst this bunch. Seems to me you all been a little mopey in the last few years."

"How would you know?" Jacqueline asked.

"Good point, J.W. Just a sense I got. So what I'm thinkin' is this: Team Donner/Weatherly/Bent/Lane kicks some Tamarack butt."

Stan the Man put a glass in the wrong cupboard and Itchy tapped him on the back and pointed to the right place. "Oh, thanks, Itch. Whatcha talkin' about, Red?"

"Logger Days."

"Anybody seen my lighter?" Jacqueline asked. She was too vain to wear reading glasses, and small items tended to vanish easily. Itchy retrieved it from the counter and gave it to her. Jacqueline rewarded him with a rough hair tousle. "Thanks, darlin'. What about Logger Days, Red? You got some dumb-ass scheme?"

"You betcha. 'Dumb-ass' is my middle name."

"Amen to that." Jacqueline fired up a Marlboro Light.

"See, what I'm thinkin' is this: we got seven months until Logger Days, we start trainin' right now and win us some events."

"The only event I ever enter is beer-drinking," Jacqueline said.

"That's gonna change this year, J.W. I'm thinkin' you and Stanley oughta enter the Jack 'n' Jill double buck. Stanley's young and strong and you're meaner than hell, you'd be a great team. Me and Irene could team up, too."

Irene added more hot water to the sink. A greasy scum floated on the surface, and she couldn't get the detergent to foam. "I'm not strong enough for that, Red."

"Got seven months to buff up, Irene. Be good for you. Don't wanna get flabby and old, do you?"

Irene shot him a look. But he just grinned back at her.

"What about me?" Itchy asked.

"It's obvious, ain't it Itchy? You're the perfect age, you should be goin' for the Wimp o' the Woods."

"We tried to get him to do it last year," Jacqueline said. "He was a little *too* wimpy."

"This time it'll be different," Red replied. "His old man will teach him the finer points so he can win."

"You will?" Itchy said.

He seemed excited, which amazed Irene. "I thought you hated that kind of stuff?"

"Well, nobody ever said they'd help me before. I didn't want to do it and get creamed and look stupid."

Red nodded. "Might be a good chance to go after that cousin of Stanley's that gives you so much grief."

"Jason's been champ for the last two years," Stan the Man nodded. "Should be loyal to the family, but he *is* a little jerk. Be nice to see somebody take him down a notch."

"There you go, Itch, give you all the incentive you need."

Nobody said anything for a moment. Just the sounds of dishwashing, rinsing, drying, the clink of plates being put away.

Red's idea must've taken root, because everybody was quietly considering.

Irene glanced at Mart. He rubbed plates with the dishtowel, his eyes downcast. He hadn't said much today, and except for his momentary booger pie laughter, he'd stayed pretty glum. Red leaned against the counter and looked down at Mart. "Here's the wildest-ass idea I got. I want to win the men's double buck. Me and Mart."

"Just one problem with that, Red," Mart said quietly.

"And what would that be, Mar-teen?"

"What do you think?"

"So what? It's not like I'm sayin' you oughta enter the pole climbing. You're still stronger than shit, I can see that. We build up them big old manly biceps a little more and you and me could do good. We just gotta work on technique, that's all."

"It'd never work. Anyway, I don't want to do anything with you." Mart folded the towel, set it down on the counter and rolled out into the living room.

"You really oughta think about what you're saying before you open your big mouth," Jacqueline said.

"He'll come around."

Irene handed Red the last plate and rinsed out the sink. She looked at Itchy. He flicked at his scaly patches. She could read Itchy's every mood, and Red's idea had him excited. At least it wasn't anything connected to Donnermania, and right now, after the starvation nonsense, that seemed like a good thing.

"I think we should do it," she said.

Red grinned. "All right, I knew you'd want to. See, Irene's got the competitive fires burnin'."

"I just think it'd be fun, that's all. I don't care if we win or come in last."

"You're too ladylike to say it, that's okay, I understand. Inside you're a seething cauldron of ass-whuppin' competition."

"Whatever, Red. If you keep talking like that, then forget it."

"Let's do it, Jacqueline," Stan the Man said.

"I ain't that physical."

"Sure you are," Stan the Man said with a lascivious eyebrow arch.

"That's twice you brought that kinda stuff up today, Stanley," Red said. "Knock it off, you're grossin' me out."

Jacqueline sneered at Red. "Give your sexy ex-mama-in-law some respect, you dirtbag. 'Spose I don't have a choice, do I? Stanley'll just find some tight-bodied little twenty-year-old if I don't help him, won't you, Stanley?"

"You never know."

"All right, then," Red said. "We're all agreed. Logger Days next year belongs to us!"

"What about Mart?" Irene asked.

"I'll convince him."

"Good luck," Jacqueline said.

"When do we start training, Dad?" Itchy asked.

"You gotta promise me one thing, Itch."

"What?"

"You gotta be serious about it. You gotta want it bad, you gotta live to be Wimp o' the Woods."

"I will."

"Jesus," Jacqueline said. "You sound like Knute Rockne."

"You gonna win, Itchy?" Red asked.

"Yeah."

"I CAN'T HEAR YOU!"

"I'M GONNA WIN! I'M GONNA BE WIMP O' THE WOODS!"

"All right, little man. That's the spirit."

"I'm gonna spend the next seven months rollin' my eyes at you bozos," Jacqueline said.

"Ready to start trainin', Itchy?" Red asked.

"YESSIR!"

"Then let's rock 'n' roll!" Red picked Itchy up and carried him out under one arm like a piece of firewood.

"Sure was a hell of a lot quieter around here before he came back," Jacqueline said. She put her arm around Stan the Man. "What kinda training you have in mind, punkin'?" she asked as she licked Stan the Man's ear.

Irene escaped into the living room before things got any more disgusting. Mart sat at the front window, gazing outside like a trapped cat longing to hunt birds. Itchy balanced on an ice-covered post while Red tried to push him off. They both laughed like little kids.

Irene didn't say anything to Mart. She looked past him out through the window, at her ex-husband and their son.

She smiled.

Things seemed...right.

She hoped it would last.

A bewildering guide board, flecked with bits of white paper, showed that a notice which had recently been pasted and tacked theron had since been stripped off in irregular bits. Mother knelt and searched for fragments of paper, which she fit together with the scraps on the board. The patchwork brought out the following foreboding words: "2 days—2 nights—hard driving—cross—desert—reach water." Mother and the other emigrants gazed at the board's message, and then at the dreary waste beyond.

Eliza Donner

August 28, 1846

Chapter Seven

The Tamarack Logging and Milling Company's cash flow had dwindled to the point where bankruptcy loomed.

The usual winter slowdown was expected, and A. Jackson still had a few crews—Red Donner's among them—putting timber on the ground down at lower elevations, but the upcoming spring looked to be positively catastrophic.

A. Jackson had bid on some prime Forest Service second growth, but enviros in Seattle had filed ESA suits over salmon habitat, and the chances of getting in to cut the timber appeared bleak. Unless he could find some large private tracts—which was iffy anymore, especially since he was up against the big boys like Boise and Weyerhauser—A. Jackson feared his business, the Flynn family legacy of over a hundred years, would implode.

And it would be all A. Jackson's fault.

Christmas had been especially dreary this year. Miriam had sulked and pouted and drifted in a continual Merlot haze, and even Sara, A. Jackson's reason for living, had been mopey. She'd decided to punish A. Jackson because he'd forbidden her to hang around Itchy Donner after he overheard Red telling

Itchy's starvation story.

"So the little dipshit passes out cold as a cucumber at Thanksgiving dinner," Red had told a couple of his buddies in the mill. A. Jackson wandered by and stopped to listen.

"He wanted to starve?" A. Jackson asked.

"Just a little bit. Said he wanted to understand what the real Donner Party felt like. Ain't he somethin'? His mother was fit to be tied."

A. Jackson shook his head, glad that he didn't have to worry about such idiocy from *his* precious daughter.

"Guess your own kid got a little more on the ball than my rugrat," Red continued. "He says she gave up after only one day."

A. Jackson didn't say anything. He forced a smile and left Red to tell his stories.

When he got home that night, A. Jackson confronted Sara. She tearfully confessed that since Itchy was her best friend, and since she was *really* interested in the Donner Party, she'd wanted to starve with him and find out what the Donners experienced.

A. Jackson disgustedly forbade her from seeing Itchy after that—and she punished him from then on, giving only cursory answers and sullen stares.

Between his alcoholic wife and pouting daughter—and now his collapsing livelihood—A. Jackson Flynn's life had bottomed out.

He sat in his office, clicking the computer mouse, bouncing from spreadsheet to spreadsheet, hoping the numbers would change. They didn't.

He wouldn't say anything. Not yet. But he couldn't deny the facts, the truth of his failure.

By the end of next summer, unless some unforeseen miracle happened, the Tamarack Logging and Milling Company would be no more.

And Tamarack the town would go down with it.

The brief January thaw fooled no one, but its Chinook winds were welcomed by all. Although Tamarack had turned into a giant slurpee, its snow a dirty mush, temperatures in the high 30s felt like summertime. In Tamarack, you took what you could get.

Half the loggers and millworkers were on their usual winter layoffs, and the few who continued to work—like Red—envied those who didn't. Even though Red and his crew were cutting down in White Pine valley, it was still miserable and required an hour's drive each way. White Pine was low enough that they could work in the light snow and not be mudded out, but winter logging was nasty and cold and even more dangerous than usual. Cashing an unemployment check didn't seem like such a bad idea.

Christmas had passed uneventfully for Red and his not-so-ex family. On Christmas day Red got cleaned up and went to church with Irene and Itchy and Jacqueline and Stan the Man. Stan the Man wasn't Catholic, but when Jacqueline insisted—and she *always* insisted on Christmas and Easter—he'd tag along and try to stay awake during the unfathomable, interminable rituals.

Mart never went to church with them. He used to be a Catholic, but after the accident he'd drifted away. Irene tried to convince him to come back, because even though she sometimes had doubts about God, she figured going to church was good afterlife insurance. But Mart wouldn't budge. He couldn't believe in God anymore, not after what had happened.

Red had never been religious in the organized sense. When he and Irene had gotten married he went to church a few times, but he never wanted to commit.

"If it works for you, great," he'd told her. "Me, I'm more of a natural kinda guy. My church is the woods."

"The ones you cut down?"

"Well, yeah, I guess. But see, after I cut 'em down, they grow back. That's the fuckin' miracle of life, man. Proves to me there's a big fella up there lookin' after us."

"Why don't you just admit you'd rather sit home and watch football and drink beer?"

"Buuusted," he grinned. "Gimme the *Cliff's Notes* on the padre's sermon when you get back, huh?"

This Christmas, though, Irene thought Red seemed more interested.

He showed up Christmas morning looking halfway decent. With his hair slicked down and his wild beard trimmed, Red Donner looked al-most...respectable.

"Aren't you pretty," Jacqueline told him. "Wish you'd let me or Irene cut that mess of hair, though. We could do good things with that natural curl you got."

"You'd make me look like a fag, J.W. I seen what you guys do to good-lookin' studs like me"

Jacqueline glared a look of red-hot withering scorn that only an ex-mother-in-law can muster. "Red," she said slowly, "I think you got manhood issues. You sure you're not latent? I seen stories about guys like you on *Maury Povich*."

"Merry Christmas to you, too," Red shrugged. He put two wrapped gifts—one large, one small—under Irene's scraggly Christmas tree.

"Either of those for me?" Jacqueline asked.

"Nah, I'm just sendin' you a big check. Where's Itchy?"

Itchy came stomping out from his bedroom at the sound of his name. Irene had just finished slicking down his hair, and she had him dressed up in a tie and ill-fitting coat.

140

"Merry Christmas, Itch!" Red said.

"Thanks, Dad. You too."

"Take a look under the tree, buddy. Looks to me like ol' Santa Red brung you something."

Itchy eagerly grabbed the big package and ripped it open.

"Cool!" Itchy grinned. It was a newly-published book about—what else?—the Donner Party. "I read about this one on the web!" Itchy quickly leafed through it, pausing at pictures, savoring its newness.

"Glad you're excited. Thought you'd like it. Check this out." Red took the book and flipped to a picture of wagon ruts through a forest. "This is up near Donner Lake, and there's still ruts there from the pioneers. Cool, huh? When we go down there we'll check it out."

"Cool!"

"'Cool, cool, cool'," Jacqueline muttered. "You two are a real pair. 'Cool' isn't the word that comes to mind to describe you."

Irene watched from the hallway. Red and Itchy pored over the book, Red nodding seriously as Itchy explained the history behind every photo. Watching them together, sharing their Donner blood, their connection...Irene's breath caught, that strange feeling of almost-excitement—or was it fear? Love?—that you got sometimes when an emotion hit you from out of nowhere. Seeing Red and Itchy—friends, father and son, Donner Party buddies—made her tear up. Disgusted with herself—all she ever did was weep anymore, was she turning into a complete weenie?—she went to them and peered over Itchy's shoulder.

"Look at the cool book Dad gave me!" Itchy said.

"Pretty neat. That was nice, Red."

"I'm a beautiful guy, what can I say?" He pointed at the small present under the tree. "Go ahead and open it, Irene. It ain't much, but I think you might like it."

"You didn't need to get me anything. I didn't get you a present."

"Don't deserve one. I been naughty." Red grinned. "Open it up."

Irene unwrapped the package and opened the little white box. She frowned. Inside was a small, smooth rock. "A rock?"

"Found it down in White Pine valley."

Irene took it out and studied it. At first it seemed nothing more than a rounded river pebble, worn shiny and smooth by millennia of melting snow. But as she gazed at it, turning it over in her hands, the light caught something.

"See it yet?" Red asked.

"What is it?"

"Hold it just right and look real close," he said, smiling.

Irene held the stone near her eyes. She carefully moved it, and a glimmer, a tracing became visible as the light hit it at the right angle.

"There you go," Red said. "Ain't that somethin'?"

Irene gazed at the stone, transfixed. A tiny fern leaf was etched on its surface, so delicate it looked as if it might crumble and slide off to float weightlessly like dust specks in the air. It looked like someone with a microscopic engraver had spent countless hours carving mere atoms from the stone to make the outline, a gauzy, lacy, beautiful picture of something from the distant past.

"Is it a fossil?" Itchy asked, peering at it through the crook in Irene's arm.

"Yep. Little bitty fern leaf from way back when."

"It's beautiful, Red," Irene said softly.

"I seen it and I thought of you. Remember how I used to bring you stuff I found out in the woods? This is the prettiest thing I ever found, I think."

"Thank you," Irene said. "I feel really bad I didn't get you anything."

"Oh, that don't matter."

"It's not like he bought you a new pickup, for God's sake. You get all emotional like you're in the menopause," Jacqueline muttered. A rotten muffler rumbled out front, and a couple of horn honks sounded. "That'll be Stanley. If you're done boo-hooin' about a rock, let's get goin'. We don't want to be late for mass or we'll have to stand."

Irene carefully set the stone down on the kitchen table, and Red helped her on with her coat.

"You look real nice today, Irene. Merry Christmas." Red held the door open for her, and they packed into Stan the Man's beat-up crewcab for the short ride to church.

Irene didn't say anything. She just listened while Itchy chattered about his cool new book, Jacqueline chastised Stan the Man for not wearing a tie, and Red tossed in occasional gooney comments.

She knew that if she opened her mouth she'd cry.

Father Ray couldn't concentrate on saying Christmas mass because Red Donner sat a few pews away with Irene and Itchy, staring back at him with a smug, bored smile on his grubby barfly's face. As he elevated the chalice for the consecration, Father Ray's thoughts weren't on bread and wine becoming the body and blood of Jesus, but on what a miserable prick Red Donner was.

Irene deserved so much better than this guy. Father Ray still couldn't believe that Red Donner could've abandoned her. And not a word, nothing, for eleven long years. Irene left to raise her odd little son, only her white-trash mother to help.

Ungrateful prick.

Father Ray toughed it out and made it through mass—barely—and the only good part was handing Irene the communion wafer and watching as she placed it in her mouth, gave him a shy, heart-melting smile, and walked back to the pew.

God, she was so beautiful. Father Ray's mouth went dry, and he couldn't even sing *Joy to the World* at the end of mass. Too beguiled by Irene, and too angry with her grubby ex.

Merry Christmas.

"This is Itchy's father, Father," Irene said at the meet 'n' greet after mass, giggling slightly at the dueling "fathers." "Red Donner, I mean."

"Hey, Padre, nice to meet you." Red gripped Father Ray's hand with his usual death-crush handshake.

"Hello," Father Ray said, forcing a smile. "I've heard a lot about you."

"Probably nothin' good, I bet."

Father Ray shrugged.

"It's okay, Padre, whatever they say is true. I'm the guy you priests warn everybody about."

"Oh."

Jacqueline lit up. Long masses without a cigarette were brutal for her. "Don't waste your energy listening to Red, Father. He just likes the sound of his own voice."

"Well then, Merry Christmas to you all," Father Ray said.

Irene stood with her arm around Itchy's shoulder. "Merry Christmas, Father Ray," she said, smiling and looking impossibly beautiful. Father Ray knew he couldn't speak coherently, so he just nodded.

He watched them pile into Stan the Man's truck and drive off.

Then he spent the rest of Christmas day alone and miserable.

"Breathe out!" Red ordered. "You hold it in, you ain't gonna get the benefit, you might have a stroke or something. Breathe, go, go, go! You got it, little more, little more!"

Irene grunted and groaned as she tried to lift the weights back up. Red had her doing bench presses, and in the two months he'd been coaching her she'd doubled the weight. Her upper arms had tightened and now she had the beginnings of nice biceps.

"You got it! Go!"

She gasped, pushed, and locked her elbows straight. Red helped her guide the barbell back into the rack.

"All right! Personal best, you are one buff bitch!"

Irene sat up on the bench, sweat rolling down her forehead. Stan the Man kept an old weight set in his basement, and she and Red had been meeting three nights a week for workouts. At first she thought the whole idea of training for Logger Days was pretty stupid, but now, in mid-February, as her muscles and confidence grew, it didn't seem like such a bad idea. If nothing else, Red's mission to take the top prizes would whip her into shape, and she couldn't complain about that.

"How come I never see *you* working out?" Irene asked as she toweled off the sweat.

"Don't need to. I'm a natural athlete."

"Uh-huh."

"Hey, I'm doin' this shit all day long in the woods. Last thing I need is to work out."

"I suppose," she said. "When do we start cutting things?"

"The term is 'bucking'."

"Whatever."

"When you get stronger."

"Do I have to take steroids?"

"Wouldn't hurt. Do you mind growing a dick to help us win?"

"Sure. Then at least one of us would have one."

"Ooooh, you're turning mean just like your momma. Start smokin' like a chimney and sayin' the 'F' word a bunch and you'll be a clone of her."

Irene stood and slowly stretched. Even in baggy sweats and ratty old T-shirt she looked great.

"Stop leering," she said.

"What would make you think I'm leerin'?"

"It's the testosterone stench in the room."

"Shit. Can't get away with nothing. Can't blame me for admirin' you, though. You look nice."

"Thank you. And stop looking. You're supposed to help me train, that's it."

Red sighed. "You gonna punish me forever, aren't you?"

"Why shouldn't I? It's fun. Besides, you already had once chance with me. That's all you get. Now we're strictly ex's. In training." She came out of the stretch and faced him. "Got it?"

"Yes, dear."

"Good. Go up and be nice to Mart while I finish."

Red grabbed a pair of twenty-five pound dumbbells and dutifully trudged upstairs. "Time to turn on the charm," he said.

Irene smiled. She'd never admit it to Red, but this was fun.

Mart hated the nights Red and Irene came over. He loved seeing Irene, but Red, well, that was another matter.

He'd slowly gotten used to Red being back. Seeing the asshole every Sunday at Irene's and now three nights a week here had desensitized him a little. The blazing hatred had dulled to a low-grade ache, but seeing Red, hearing his voice, listening to his gleeful bullshit—it still burrowed under Mart's skin like nasty little bugs. And Red's hovering around Irene...that only added to the irritation.

He'd gotten to the point where he'd grudgingly talk to Red if he had to, but he wouldn't go out of his way to be chummy. Red kept needling him good-naturedly, trying to rekindle the old buddy days of yore, as if nothing had happened, as if Red hadn't fucked up and put Mart in a wheelchair. Mart stayed icily distant, but if Red noticed he never let on.

The toughest part about Red and Irene coming over all the time was listening to them down in the basement. They laughed a lot. Mart usually popped in a noisy DVD, something with lots of explosions that he could crank up on the surround sound, but Red's bellowing and the *clanks* of the weights floated up through the floorboards, grating on Mart like a constant insult.

Stan the Man was gone again for another night at Jacqueline's and some elder-sex. Stan the Man had started staying with Jacqueline most nights, so Mart had the place to himself. Not that it was so great being alone all the time; he missed Stan the Man's low-key, good-natured company. Mart had reached the stage where he realized he needed to make changes in his life. Sitting around day after day, pretending to be working on training himself for something new but really doing nothing—Mart had started to become a recluse. He knew he was slipping away from the real world, the world where getting up in the morning meant something, where you dealt with people, worked, put up with the good and bad, and lived.

Mart wasn't so sure he was alive anymore.

He'd lost interest in the movie—was it *Die Hard 1* or *2*? he couldn't remember—when Red stomped up from the basement carrying a couple of dumbbells.

"Hey Mar-teen, turn that horseshit off. I need to talk to you."

Mart reluctantly clicked the DVD to pause. He hadn't been paying attention to the movie, but it still annoyed him that Red assumed what he had to say was more important. The world revolves around Red Donner, as always.

"What?" Mart asked.

Red set the dumbbells down, one on either side of Mart's chair.

"If we're gonna have a shot at the double-buck, you need to start workin' out."

"I'm not doing it. I already told you that."

"I talked to A. Jackson about us entering. He's runnin' the show, as usual. Anyways, he said no problem as long as we don't do nothin' that gives us an unfair advantage."

"How many times do I need to say 'No'?"

Red sighed and sat heavily on the couch. "I ever tell you 'bout my brother?"

"No."

"He's a college professor. Does research into high-level math stuff, I can't even begin to understand what he does. Can you believe that? Somebody related to old white-trash Red a snooty genius professor. Anyways, he's a couple years younger, never had much use for me."

"Don't blame him."

"Yeah, I 'spose. Weird how he turned out, though. Our parents were like me, kinda uneducated, working stiffs, they both drank too much. Hated rich people, I remember my old man bitchin' and moaning about 'College-educated idiots' and all that. Then my brother Jimmy turns out to be a genius. He's up on the roof starin' into the sky having deep thoughts about the nature of the universe while our folks are drinkin' Pabst Blue Ribbon and watchin' *Hee Haw*. And I'm like them, so they understand me. They don't understand Jimmy."

"Why would I care?"

"Well, Mar-teen, the way I see it, we all got choices in life. My bro' coulda given up, coulda rolled over and been another loser Donner. But he knew he was special, and he didn't let my parents or me drag him down. Soon as he could he was outa there, he got scholarships, worked his ass off, made some-thin' of himself. He's a little too proud for my taste, but I suppose he's earned it. The thing I've just got around to realizing, though, is that it took guts for him to do what he did. He was brave. When I ran outa here after the accident, it took me eleven years to find some guts. Eleven years to realize I couldn't be a fuckin' pansy-ass coward runaway."

Mart folded his arms and waited. Red always took the elliptical path to his conversational destination.

"Comin' back here was hard. Irene hates me, you hate me, never knew Itchy, so I didn't know what I was comin' back to. And I'm still not sure if it'll work out. You never know if you can fix things you've fucked up. But you gotta take little steps, you know? You get in a hole, you gotta try and climb out. Might fall on your ass, but you still gotta try. Little brother Jimmy understood that—maybe because he was a genius. He knew he had to get the hell outa the rathole Donner family. I figured out I needed to come back here and try to patch shit up. And you, Mar-teen...whataya you 'spose you need to do?"

"Win the fucking double-buck with you, right?"

"Little steps, buddy."

"Only I can't walk, asshole."

Irene came up the stairs. "I don't need a ride home," she told Red. "I'll jog." She touched Mart lightly on the shoulder. "See you Sunday?"

"Sure."

"Okay. 'Bye." With a wave she was gone.

Red stood to leave. "Start climbin' outa the hole, Mart," he said with a sad smile, and then he left.

Mart sat for a long time, the frozen image of Bruce Willis staring back at him from the large screen. *Yipee-ki-yay, motherfucker.* Bruce would've said that as he kicked Red Donner's ass.

Mart glanced down at the dumbbells on the floor. Moments passed. He reached down and picked them up. Surprisingly heavy, yet only twenty-five pounds.

He curled them a couple of times.

Didn't feel so bad. Maybe he'd do a few sets....

Yippee-ki-yay, motherfucker.

Itchy missed Sara.

He didn't realize how important she was to him until her dad got mad about the starvation thing and kept them apart.

Itchy missed their web-surfing for new Donner Party sites, he missed the long afternoon discussions about whether Keseburg really murdered Tamsen or not—basically, he just missed being with her. They still talked at school during recess and lunch, so at least it wasn't a complete cutoff. But Itchy missed the lazy hours after school, when they leisurely hunted through Donner Party minutiae and rode the time machine to his family's past.

Itchy was whiling away another lonely afternoon at the library, waiting his turn at the computer. Some noisy junior high-schoolers had been surfing porn sites for the last fifteen minutes, smirky and giggling while the glum librarian scowled at them. Itchy hung back, pretending to do homework while he peeked over their shoulders at the ever-changing parade of naked ladies. Very interesting, he thought, at least until one turned up who looked vaguely like his mom. That grossed him out so he stopped looking.

The librarian booted them when their twenty minutes were up, and Itchy took his place at the keyboard. He had a surfing strategy written down, because that was the only way he could use his time efficiently. He'd started mouse clicking away and had just come across some good stuff when Red strode in, still wearing his muddy calks and smelling of sweat and the woods.

"Hey Itchy!" he said way too loud for the library. The librarian threw him a glare.

"Hey, Dad."

"Knocked off early today, figured I'd find you here. Let's head out, we got stuff to do."

"But I'm just getting started," Itchy protested. Sometimes his dad got in the way of serious research.

"It ain't goin' nowhere. C'mon."

Itchy reluctantly gave up his spot at the computer and followed Red out.

"How you doin' today?" Red asked the librarian.

She nodded and said through tight lips, "Fine."

"What a ray of sunshine," Red said as he and Itchy got outside. "She's like one of them crabby librarian cliches you see in old movies."

"Yeah." Itchy didn't know what he was talking about, but that was nothing new. Adults spent a lot of time yammering about things he neither cared about nor understood. Maybe someday he'd be in the loop, but he doubted it. It seemed that what interested him didn't interest other people, and vice-versa.

"You do them exercises I was showin' you last week?"

"Yeah," Itchy said. Red had him doing jumping jacks, pushups, and chinups. Itchy could only make his spindly arms do one pushup and half a chin-up, although yesterday he swore he'd gotten an inch higher in the chin-up than the day before. "I'm really sore," he complained.

"That's a good sign. Shows you're buildin' up. Your momma's been bellyachin' about how sore she is, too. Between the two of you, I'm gonna make you like those WWF guys. Maybe you could make it a career, 'Double-I, Itch and Irene, mom and son tag-team ass-kickers of the World Wrestling Federation.' Whatcha think?"

"I guess," Itchy said. Yet again he had no idea what his noisy dad was on about.

They walked together through town, Red chattering about his Logger Day dreams, Itchy only half-listening. Itchy liked the idea of winning the Wimp o' the Woods contest, and he thought it would be pretty cool if his mom and dad could win the Jack 'n' Jill double buck, but it wasn't the most important thing in his life.

Going to Alder Creek was. The Donner Party. Great-great-great Gramma Tamsen. Those things *really* mattered.

"I'm thinkin' we'll do some balance work today," Red said as they climbed the hill to Irene's singlewide. It hadn't snowed much recently, but the weather had stayed nasty cold and the snow had crusted over solidly. Treacherous ice slicks lay in wait for the unaware, and in the last three weeks two Tamarackers had broken legs to show for their carelessness.

"Hey Dad?"

"Yeah?"

"When can we go to Alder Creek?"

"One of these days, buddy. Maybe in the fall."

"Really?"

"Don't worry, Itch. I'll get you down there. I promise."

"Cool!"

They got to the singlewide, gingerly sidestepping icy patches along the way with the seasoned grace of veteran cold-weather dwellers. Irene hadn't gotten home from the salon yet, so Itchy quickly dumped his backpack inside, turned on the heat, and came back out for his Wimp o' the Woods training. A few weeks ago Red had dragged an old log up and dumped it in the front yard. Irene wasn't thrilled, but Red convinced her it was necessary in order to get Itchy ready for the big contest. Itchy watched his huge, muscle-bound dad balance delicately on the log, almost dancing along its icy surface. Sometimes Red's gracefulness astounded Itchy. Itchy didn't understand how a huge guy in giant, Frankenstein-sized boots could tiptoe along an icy log and not look the least bit off-balance or scared.

"I'm amazing, huh?" Red said.

"How do you do that?"

"Practice. And natural ability, of course. Don't want to brag or nothin', but I'm naturally good at a lot of things."

"Oh."

"So are you."

"No I'm not," Itchy said. "Jason Bent says I throw like a girl."

"Jason Bent's a wanker. You'll kick his ass. Besides, I seen lots of girls who got arms like Randy Johnson. Anyway, the physical crap ain't everything."

"Sometimes it seems like it is."

"Yeah, maybe. But you're smarter 'n' shit. In the end, that's the big deal. All this stuff about sports and athletics, that's just window dressing."

"What's 'window dressing'?"

Red did a delicate pirouette on the log and faced Itchy. "Fuck if I know. It just means stuff that don't really matter. See Itch, you got your brain, all that Donner Party research you done, it's made you smart. You know how to think. Most people don't. Maybe Jason Bent can toss a football in a nice tight spiral, maybe he can throw a runner out at home from center field, but I'd be willing to bet he don't know how to think. Probably never will, neither."

"If that stuff doesn't matter, how come we want to win Logger Days so bad?"

"To show the assholes," Red grinned. "I said the athletic stuff isn't the *most* important thing in the world. I didn't say it don't matter at all."

Once again the ways of the world confused Itchy. The answers adults gave him for things always came up a little short in the making-sense department.

"It's like the revenge of the nerds," Red explained. "Lotta people in this jerkwater town look down their noses at us. Dunno why, except maybe for the fact they don't like me all that much. So if we can show 'em we're good enough to whup their asses, that means somethin'. Even if it's something kinda unimportant in the scheme of things like Logger Days. Know what I mean?"

"But how come we care?" Itchy asked. "If we're happy being us, isn't that all that matters?"

Red stopped walking along the log. He peered down at his earnest, skinny little son. "You know, Itch, I believe you're right. Maybe we shouldn't give a shit and just do it for fun. Whatcha say?"

"Okay."

"So if Jason Bent whups you, it don't matter. 'Specially if your little girlfriend Sara's watchin'."

"Well," Itchy hesitated. "It *would* be nice to beat him at something. And she's not my girlfriend."

"Uh-huh. Climb on up." He reached down and pulled Itchy up on the log. Itchy immediately lost his balance, and Red had to grab him and hold him upright. "Okay, get your bearings. Don't think so hard. You're worryin' 'bout how skinny the log is, and once you start thinkin' about it your dead. Just stand on it like you're standin' on the ground. It ain't no different."

"Okay," Itchy said. He swallowed hard and concentrated, imagining the log was just a wide piece of wood on the ground. Gradually, he stopped wavering and was able to stand still.

"See," Red said. "It's all in your head."

"Yeah," Itchy smiled.

"Now, take a couple of steps."

Itchy hesitantly stepped forward, but he started to lose his balance and flailed his arms. He almost slipped off, but recovered. Red urged him on, and Itchy stepped forward again, this time with less weaving.

"Good. Now, close your eyes."

"Dad!"

"Just stand still, get your balance feeling right, and then close 'em. It'll be okay."

Itchy took a deep breath, got comfortable, then closed his eyes. He didn't let the thought intrude that he stood on a slippery log. Just pretend it's ground, just pretend it's—

Red shoved him in the chest. Itchy's eyes popped open, his arms waved wildly, and he flew off the log and crashed into the crusty snow with a *thunk!*

"Why'd you do that?!"

"You gotta expect the unexpected, Itch. You gotta be able to recover when somethin' weird happens."

"But you pushed me!"

"So what do you do now?"

Itchy got up and brushed off the snow. He glared up at his grinning father. "I'm going inside," he said with a snitty petulance in his voice.

"Wrong answer."

"What?"

"So what do you do now?" Red asked again. His smile faded away. Itchy said nothing, and they stared each other down. "Make the right choice, buddy. Don't want to be a wussy little faggot all your life, do you? No son of mine is gonna be like that, I can guarantee you."

Itchy felt tears forming. He hated the way he cried so easily. Like a little girl. He fought them back. He wasn't going to cry in front of his dad, no way. He sniffed. *Be tough*, he told himself. Be a...Donner.

A Donner. Yeah, of course. Be like them, like Tamsen and George, don't be a wimp. Do you think they cried when things got terrible, when they were scared and starving and eating leather and dying? Don't be a loser. A fag. Live up to the Donner name. Don't let this guy—even if he is Dad, even if he's a Donner, too—push you around.

"You ain't gonna cry, are you?" Red taunted. "Cryin' ain't gonna do you no good."

"I'm not crying!" Itchy said, his voice cracking.

"Make a choice, Itchy. Do the right thing."

Itchy slowly climbed back up on the log. He almost fell off again, but he regained his balance. He faced Red. He said nothing.

And then, he suddenly jumped forward and shoved Red as hard as he could, pounding with both hands into Red's massive chest. Red flailed wildly at the unexpected attack, and he flipped backwards off the log and into the snow. Itchy barely stayed on, but he managed to get his balance. He looked down at his shocked father.

"'Expect the unexpected,'" he said.

Red sat up in the snow and shook his head. And then he began to laugh. Big, hooting, Red Donner laughs that carried into the cold wind and echoed down the street.

"All right, Itchy 'Hardass' Donner, whups his old man...*yee-fuckin'-haw*!" Red clapped his hands.

It took Itchy a few seconds, but then he smiled, too. Winning felt good.

Real good.

The Unknown Story of the Donner Party as told to Itchy Donner
by his Great-great-great Gramma Tamsen in her Lost Journal

By Itchy Donner, her Great-great-great Grandson

Chapter Two

I started telling the story in the wrong place before, when Great-great-great Gramma Tamsen (I'll just call her 4G Tamsen since it's easier to write) and 4G George were almost dead. I need to go back to earlier, when stuff was better. They weren't always so afraid. They thought that going to California would be great. They thought that when they got there, everything would be okay. They had a farm in Illinois, and it was okay. 4G George was a good farmer and stuff, and he made a lot of money, but he wanted to go places. People are like that. Like my Dad. He doesn't like to stay in one place too long, I don't think. He must be like 4G George. Except to my Dad 4G George is really 3G George.

But anyway, all the people in the Donner Party wanted to move. That's the way people were back then. They thought things would always be better someplace else. I haven't really thought about it, but maybe things would be better for me if I was someplace else, too. Tamarack's okay, but we don't have cable TV and it's hard to get on the internet and there's a lot of grouchy poor people here. I think they work too hard and don't get enough money.

Maybe that's the way it was back in 1846 when the 4G's left for California.

So their trip started good. 4G Tamsen wrote a letter to her sister at the beginning, and she sounded really excited about going. She must have started writing her Lost Journal by then, and I'll bet this is what she would've said:

It's pretty here. There are lots of birds and plants and animals I haven't seen before. It's hard to travel in a wagon—we don't even travel in the wagon really, we walk beside it—and sometimes we see Indians. The children think they're cool (Itchy Donner note: 4G Tamsen wouldn't have said "cool," but that's what she meant), but sometimes they scare me. They ride along the wagon train, or behind it, and they want presents. They never threaten us, but I think they might hurt us if we made them mad. I tell George to be careful. He's always careful. George is a good man and a good husband. He's strong and honest and a good father to the girls. He was married before—so was I—and he had three other daughters that I'm raising as my own. I love them like they were my own. When we get to California and I start my girls' school they all want to help. It's pretty out here on the plains, but not as pretty as it will be in California. Eliza, the littlest one, is very excited. So am I.

Itchy stopped writing and looked out his bedroom window. It rattled ominously as the cold wind pounded it. A fierce storm had blown in that afternoon right after he'd pushed his dad off the log. Itchy wondered if God was trying to say something like, "Thou shalt not hit thy Father." Or maybe, "Thou art strong, Itchy Donner. Way to go." Itchy had weird thoughts sometimes.

But it did seem biblical. Red was still sitting in the snow, laughing, when a sudden gale howled through Tamarack and a hard, biting snow pelted them, driving them inside the singlewide. Red decided to make the best use of their time, and he made Itchy do jumping jacks and pushups while he raided Irene's refrigerator—but he kept on laughing and congratulating Itchy for being so tough.

"And then the little shit knocks my fat ass off the log!" Red told Irene when she got home.

"He did what?" Irene asked, horrified.

"You betcha. He sucker-wopped me, just like he's gonna need to do to win the Wimp o' the Woods."

Irene turned to Itchy. "You hit your father?"

Itchy smiled proudly. "Well, kinda, but not really."

"Wasn't like that, Irene. I was tryin' to teach him to be aggressive."

"I don't know if I like this," she said.

Red gestured to Itchy. "Why don't you go study in your room for awhile. Work on some Donner stuff or something. I need to talk to your mom."

Itchy started to object, but Red shot him a no-nonsense back-off look. He hated being treated like a kid, but in truth he'd probably be bored by whatever they were going to talk about anyway. He just wished *he* could make the choice instead of being bossed around all the time.

After Itchy left, Red faced Irene. "You can't protect the kid forever. He needs to toughen up."

"He's only eleven."

"And he's already way behind as far as I'm concerned. Don't it bother you that Jason Bent and those other little snotballs treat him like a doormat?"

"It's not that bad."

"It *is* that bad. Let's face it, the kid's probably never gonna be no athlete, he's always gonna have to put up with people givin' him grief about that skin condition shit he's got, and he's smart, so that makes him a target."

"So what's your plan? Teach him to be a bully?"

"Irene, he ain't never gonna bully nobody. It ain't his nature. I'm just tryin' to teach him to hold his own, 'cause you know as well as me that the world is full of ass-kickin' motherfuckers, aggressive pieces of shit that like nothin' better than pushin' 'round faggy little weaklings. The boy's gonna have a tough life as it is—shit, we all do—so why not help him out, teach him to stand up for himself? No harm in that, is there?"

"I want him to be kind."

Red sighed. "Kind is great. Real nice. Don't kick puppies and kittens, give money to poor people, sure, wonderful. But kind don't mean being a punching bag. That's weak. That's just being...."

"A girl?"

"I didn't say that!"

"It's what you meant."

"Women don't ever understand what it's like," Red complained. "You don't have the same pressure we do."

"No, we have more. We get to put up with idiot men along with back-stabbing women and every kind of treachery and betrayal there is. Don't tell me that women are weak, Red. That's just bullshit."

"Okay, okay, okay. Jeez, you've gotten impossible to argue with."

"That's because I'm not a nineteen-year-old airhead anymore."

Red flopped on the couch and held up his hands. "What, you a liberated woman or something now?"

"I've just gotten tough. You helped me get that way. Isn't that what you want?"

"Tough, yeah. Mean, no."

"Quit whining. You sound like a girl."

"I ain't smart enough to fight with you no more."

"You never were."

"Yeah. I'm just a blowhard when you come right down to it," he said wearily. Then he grinned. "But ain't I handsome?"

Irene smiled. "Maybe when you were young."

Red flinched and clutched his chest. "Oh, man, she's killin' me."

Irene sat down next to him. "I don't mind if you teach Itchy things, and I don't even mind if you try to make him tougher. I suppose he needs it. But remember something: he's sweet and sensitive and he hasn't had you around for the first eleven years of his life, so you need to take it slow. He idolizes you and everything you say and do. So think about what you say to him and what you show him. Because every bit of stupid loudmouth baloney that comes out of you affects him. You're a lot more important than you think. So use your head for once. You've got one chance with him. Be careful. That's all I'm asking, Red. Please be careful."

Red didn't say anything for a long time. The refrigerator clicked on and wheezed in the kitchen, and the energy-saver fluorescent lights buzzed.

"Guess it's kinda like bein' a family, huh?" he said.

"Like it or not."

"Never thought I'd do this, you know?"

"What? Be an adult?"

"Yeah. After I took off I...I dunno. I didn't think I'd ever be part of things."

"You have a son. He needs you. He wants to love you."

"No shit?"

"Yeah, Red, that's what kids do. They love their parents."

"Never much cared for mine."

"Be different. Love Itchy. He *needs* you."

Red nodded slowly. "I'll try, Irene."

The Unknown Story...etc.

Chapter Two

(Continued)

We have lost time. It's taking us longer than we thought to get to California. We've just gotten through a terrible mountain range. The man Hastings said it was a shortcut, but he lied. We had to cut through terrible trees and brush, and it took us so much longer. The girls are doing fine, but I think they're tired. It's not fun anymore, and it's so much work, and....

Itchy stopped writing. It was hard pretending to be somebody else and writing their thoughts. He knew the story inside out, he knew what happened every day of the journey, every mile they traveled, every spot they camped. But that wasn't enough to really get inside Tamsen's head and understand. He was just guessing, and he wondered if that was wrong.

He reread his story. *Tamsen's* story. What her *Lost Journal* might say.

Hmmm. Maybe it's not so bad, he thought. Kinda caught the flavor of the story. Maybe....

The girls. He read the words. Wait a second. Girls. Tamsen and George only had daughters. That didn't make any sense. If Tamsen and George were Itchy's great-great-greats, and *his* last name was Donner, how could they have only had girls?

He quickly rummaged through his reams of research. The genealogies, the family trees. None went past the third generation after the original pioneers, and there was nobody, *nobody,* on Tamsen and George's side whose last name was Donner.

Because the girls had all married and taken their husband's names.

Itchy frowned. What happened?

"Dad?" Itchy asked.

Red lounged on the couch, staring blankly into space. Irene fussed in the kitchen, frying up some hamburger. Red hadn't asked to stay; he just assumed he was welcome for dinner. Irene didn't say anything to dissuade him.

"Yeah, Itch?"

"I was wondering about something."

"What?"

"Well, if we're related to Tamsen and George and they only had daughters, how come our last name is Donner?"

"Yeah, I wondered about that, too," Red said. "Asked my Gramma 'bout it when I was a little older than you. She said her old man changed his name to Donner because he was so proud of the family. Must've been 'round the turn of the century. Lotta stuff was written about the Donners in 1897, she said, since it was the fifty-year mark after what happened to 'em."

"Oh. That makes sense."

"Yeah, guess her old man was kinda like you. All proud of bein' a Donner. And he wanted the world to know who he was."

Itchy nodded. Then he frowned. "But wait a second. If your Gramma's *dad* changed his name to Donner, wouldn't she have ended up as whatever the last name was of the guy *she* married?"

"Nah. My Gramma was one tough old bitch. She was so proud of bein' a Donner she kept her name when she got married. Made the old man promise that any kids they had would have to be Donners too. She was way ahead of her time. A women's libber. Kinda like your mother."

"I heard that!" Irene called out from the kitchen.

"Not that there's anything wrong with it," Red added quickly.

"Wow," Itchy said. "Our family's really something."

"Yeah, Itch, they are. 'Specially you."

"Why?"

"'Cause you're carryin' it on. All the Donner stuff, I mean. Me, I'm interested in it and all, I read some books. But you, you're an expert. Guy like you will discover stuff, make sure the world knows the true story."

Itchy tried not to show his pride. But his dad telling him, well, how special he was...*that* was special. Pride. Being a Donner. It all went together.

"Let's eat," Irene said. "I guess you'll be staying?" she asked Red.

"If you insist."

She resisted the urge to sneer and eye-roll him and they all sat down for dinner. Together. Itchy chattered about the glory of Donner-dom.

Irene listened. This was starting to feel normal and comfortable. She and Red and Itchy.

Mom, dad, child. Home.

Family.

She couldn't shake the feeling that no matter how hard she fought it, Red, Irene, and Itchy Donner *were* a family....

We followed dimly marked wagon tracks. After two days and two nights of continuous travel, over a waste of alkali and sand, we were still surrounded as far as the eye could see by fearful desolation. The water casks were empty, and a pitiless sun was turning its burning rays upon the glaring earth. Disappointment intensified our burning thirst, and my good mother gave the suffering children wee lumps of sugar, moistened with a drop of peppermint, and later put a flattened bullet in each child's mouth to engage its attention and help keep the salivary glands in action.

Eliza Donner

September 9, 1846

Chapter Eight

Winter dragged on as it always does in Tamarack, sputtering away in reluctant fits and starts—miserable late-season storms followed by teasingly mild spring days. By the end of April most Tamarackers, disgusted by the unfulfilled promise of spring, had begun to get surly. It happened every year. Unemployed loggers needed money, everybody was fed up with mud and gloom, and the primal need for spring's rebirth made people twitchy.

Pencil Pandola swore that the Slurp 'n' Burp had more fights this time of year than any other, including the darkest, dreariest days of January. Something about the sap rising, was how he put it.

On this late April day, Mart sat alone at a table nursing a Bud. It was only three-o'clock in the afternoon, and a few hardcore earlybirds besides Mart had gotten a head start on the evening's drinking. The Slurp 'n' Burp was as dreary and depressing as the weather.

Pencil noticed Mart slouched over his beer, alone and unhappy. He wandered over to Mart's table and pulled up a chair.

"How you doin', buddy?"

166

"Okay, Pencil."

"Shitty time of year."

"Yep."

"Anything new?"

"No."

Pencil rubbed his shiny scalp. He'd kept his head shaved ever since he got out of the Marines, through longhair fashions and short. At the moment he was back in style. Not that it mattered a whole lot to a geezer bartender in a backwoods place like Tamarack.

"Red's been runnin' his mouth off about you."

"I know."

"Says him and you gonna win the double-buck this year."

"Red's full of shit."

"Yeah, that he is. I been surprised he hasn't come in to drink since he's been back. Paid the money he owed me from when he was here before, but that's about it. He really off the bottle?"

"Seems like it. He's still an asshole, though. Just a sober one."

Pencil leaned back against the chair. It squeaked in protest at his bulk. His triple chins shook slightly as he scratched his bulbous nose. "People been wonderin' 'bout him and Irene. They back together?"

"Why don't you ask them?" Mart jerked the mug to his mouth and swallowed the last of his beer.

"Need a refill?"

"No."

"Don't get bent out of shape. People just wonder, that's all. It's a small town, people talk."

"They aren't gonna get remarried or anything," Mart said. "Red comes around to be with Itchy. Irene just puts up with him."

"The kid needs a father. That's good. Better than I would've expected from Red."

Red, Red, Red. Mart was sick of hearing about Red. Things had been so much better before he'd come back. Mart massaged his bicep. He'd been secretly working out since Red suggested he bulk up, although he didn't know why. He had no intention of doing the double-buck. Getting back in shape just seemed like a good idea.

"Lotta dicks in this world," Pencil said.

"Uh-huh."

"More than a few of 'em in this town."

"Uh-huh."

"The thing of it is, sometimes even the biggest dicks change."

"No lectures, okay Pencil?"

Pencil coughed wetly. All the years of smoking unfiltered Camels had left him with gooey lungs, and it wouldn't be long before he'd be coughing up blood and dragging an oxygen bottle around. "Okay. Like to see you and Red give the double-buck a shot, though. When I was in the Corps we didn't make excuses for nothing. You just did things whether you were afraid or not."

"I'm not afraid, Pencil. It's not like I think I couldn't do it. It's just fucking Red."

"Give it a shot, son. Be good for you. If your old man was still around he'd tell you the same thing."

Pencil lumbered back behind the bar. Mart stared into the disappearing foam scum at the bottom of his mug. Everybody was on him about the fucking double-buck like it was the most important thing in the world. When the local bartender busybodies up your ass, you know people have got way too much time on their hands.

But as Mart sulked, he also considered. Maybe he *should* do it just so people would shut the fuck up. It might be worth it. As long as Red understood they weren't buddies and didn't pull any of that chummy pal bullshit. Okay, he'd train. Maybe Irene would be impressed. He'd see more of her, probably. That's not all bad, he thought.

If he could tolerate Red for a few months, do the Logger Days thing, make everybody happy, so be it.

Fuck 'em.

"Okay," Mart said.

"Okay what?" Red asked.

They were lazing away another Sunday afternoon at Irene's. Mart and Red watched an NBA game, but Irene's rickety antenna only brought in a blurry, ghost-filled image. It was good enough. Stan the Man snored on the couch, Jacqueline bitched about the bad puns in the crossword, Irene bounced around doing chores, and Itchy was in his room busily scribbling Tamsen's pretend journal—Sundays at Irene's were nothing if not predictable.

"Okay I'll do the double-buck with you."

Jacqueline glanced up from her crossword. Stan the Man *blurgle-snorted* to semi-wakefulness, and Irene peeked out from the kitchen.

"Good," Red said. "Think we'll do well. You been workin' out?"

"A little."

"Why the change of mind?" Jacqueline asked.

"I got tired of people bugging me about it. Red's got the whole town talking."

"Me?" Red said, feigning innocence.

"I'm glad, Mart," Irene said.

"It's not that big of a deal."

Red clicked off the TV. "Gimme a few minutes, Mar-teen. I gotta show you something."

He hurried outside and went into Irene's dilapidated storage shed.

"You gonna be able to put up with that bozo?" Jacqueline asked.

"I figure it's time off in Purgatory."

"You're not Catholic anymore, Mart. Don't need to worry about that stuff."

Stan the Man rubbed his eyes and sat up. "You and Red can practice all you want. Me and Sonny Gould gonna kick your asses."

"My God, ten seconds after they decide to do it and the trash talk starts," Jacqueline moaned.

"Bullshit, Stan. You wusses are toast," Mart said.

"Don't *bring* that shit in here," Stan the Man said. "You guys are losers with a capital L-O."

Itchy wandered out from his room. "How come Stan and Mart are fighting, Mom?"

"They're just being stupid. Mart's gonna do the double-buck with your dad."

"Cool!" Itchy said.

"And we're gonna stomp everybody. Stan the Man especially," Mart added.

"No way. You dudes are fags," said Stan the Man.

"All right," Jacqueline interrupted. "Stop acting like idiots. Jesus, I seen more maturity in a preschool."

Red poked his head in the front door. "C'mon outside everybody."

They followed him out into the muddy yard.

"Gather 'round, little children. This," Red said proudly as he gestured to an odd-looking wooden contraption, "is the Donner-matic Buckmaster Wheel-chair Adapter 5000."

Jacqueline put her arm around Stan the Man. "You started drinkin' again, haven't you, Red?"

"I'm just high on havin' you as my ex-mom-in-law, Jackie O. Now, I want you all to look closely at this little beauty."

"What is it?" Mart asked.

"This, Mar-teen, is our ticket to the double-buck crown."

"Looks like somethin' a retard made," Stan the Man mumbled.

"Takes one to know one," Red shot back. "C'mere, Mart, let's show these wads how we're gonna be victorious."

Mart wheeled through the mushy grass to Red. Red hammered long spikes into the ends of the star-shaped two-by-four base to hold it to the ground. A spring-loaded platform was attached to the frame.

"Is that the guts from a chair?" Mart asked.

"Yep. Pencil sold me his old La-Z-Boy for fifteen bucks, so I ripped it apart and used the swivel/recliner part for this bad boy." Red giggled happily. "This is gonna be so fuckin' cool."

"Hurry up, Red. It's cold out here," Jacqueline complained. She clung tightly to Stan the Man. "Keep me warm, honey."

Irene watched with a bemused smile. Red gently wheeled Mart up onto the platform. The wheels slid perfectly into wooden rails.

"How'd you get this thing to fit so good?" Mart asked.

"I had Itchy measure your chair one day while you were watchin' T.V. Sneaky little shit's good, huh?"

Itchy grinned, the proud co-conspirator. Red bolted Mart's chair to the platform with a pair of U-bolts on each wheel. Once he had it tightened up, he gave Mart's chair a push and a twist. His chair rocked back and forth and swiveled perfectly, firmly attached to the frame and the ground.

"No give, you'll be able to get some leverage. This baby's gonna fly, Mar-teen. Just one more thing we gotta try." Red skipped back into the shed like a little kid fetching a favorite toy.

"He's gotta be on drugs," Jacqueline said.

Mart rocked back and forth and swiveled, getting used to the feeling of moving in unfamiliar ways. Red stomped out of the shed lugging a wobbly, double-handled six-and-a-half foot crosscut saw.

"Okay, let's see how it feels. I didn't know we'd be doin' this today or I woulda set up a log to cut. We'll just have to pretend."

Mart grabbed one end of the long, vicious-looking saw, Red the other.

"On my count, Mar-teen. Ready?"

Mart nodded. Took a breath.

"One...two...three," and then Red pulled his end. Mart's chair pivoted perfectly toward Red. Mart pulled on the saw, and the chair swiveled back and reclined slightly. Then back toward Red, they worked on the rhythm, slowly at first, then faster, back and forth, back and forth. Mart quickly got the feel of using his upper body to push and pull the saw and control the movement of the chair.

"Wow," Itchy said. "That thing works pretty good."

Irene watched them. Red grinned huge as he and Mart quickened the pace, working as a team to cut an imaginary log. Irene could see Mart's sudden determination, the serious jaw-clench as he and Red sawed, their movements already in sync.

"Oh yeah baby!" Red said.

"Looks like Red and Mart might have something here, Stanley," said Jacqueline. "You gonna be man enough to beat 'em?"

Stan the Man frowned but made the best of it. "Yeah. Sure. They don't have the mental toughness we got."

"Uh-huh."

Red and Mart stopped sawing, both already out of breath. "We gonna need to work on conditioning, Mar-teen. How's the thing feel? You gonna be able to get enough leverage to pull? Without legs and all, I mean."

"I think I might," Mart said, sounding surprised. "It'll take some practice, but it might work, Red."

"Fuckin'-A Bubba, you bet your ass it's gonna work." Red turned to Irene and flashed Jack Nicholson eyebrows. "Pretty cool, huh? Didn't know your ex- was such a mechanical genius, did you?"

"'Genius' might be a little extreme."

"You're a beautiful woman, Irene, but envy don't suit you."

Red put the saw back in the shed, and the rest of the group wandered into the singlewide. Mart sat, bolted to Red's invention, rocking back and forth and pivoting left and right.

When Red came back from the shed Mart was all alone. The clouds had broken, and the bright sunlight quickly warmed the air.

"Finally feels like spring, don't it?" Red said as he unbolted Mart from the frame.

"Yeah." Being alone with Red felt strange. It had that forced sense, like every word needed to be considered; normal conversation was impossible.

"Glad you changed your mind," Red said.

"Could be fun."

Red finished unbolting him and wheeled Mart back onto the grass. "I'll set up a log next week, we'll start workin' on our technique." Red pushed Mart up onto the porch. He opened the front door. "We a team, buddy?" he asked. He held out his hand. A sudden breeze bathed them with its delicate warmth. The slight hiss and click of awakening bugs floated down from the trees.

Mart hesitated, then shook Red's hand. The words, when they came out, were almost inaudible. "Yeah, Red. We're a team."

"I'm pretty sure you're too young for Alzheimer's," Jacqueline said. "But maybe you oughta get tested anyways."

Irene had lost track of time and left Muriel Denny's perm solution on too long, and now her scalp was on fire and her hair had a weird, greenish tint.

"We can fix it. Can't we?" Irene asked. Muriel had been pretty understanding, all things considered.

"I'll take care of it, honey," Jacqueline said with a sigh.

Later, during lunch, Jacqueline scolded her as they ate their microwaved Weight Watchers entrees. "We don't make all that much money, do we, honey?"

"Mom...."

"And we gotta keep our customers happy. Even if they're people we've known all our lives. We screw up their hair, they'll start driving down to Elk Creek or do it themselves."

"I know. It's not that bad."

"I don't know what's got into you lately. You act like you're a dreamy little kid who's someplace else all the time. Hell, you're startin' to remind me of Itchy. Somethin' on your mind?"

Irene stirred her gelatinous beef-with-mushrooms-in-burgundy-wine-sauce. It tasted like something nasty she would've cooked up on a Sunday afternoon, except with less fat.

"I don't know. I'm...confused."

"'Bout what?"

"Red."

"Oh, Jesus H. Christ. What in the world is wrong with you, girl?"

"I don't know."

"You're not thinkin' about getting back together with that lunkhead, are you?"

Irene tossed her remaining lunch into the trash. She'd lost her appetite. "No."

"That's the weakest 'No' I ever heard. How could you even consider something that stupid? I know you got brains, use 'em, for Christ's sake."

"It's not that easy."

"What the hell needs to be easy? He's no good, Irene. Yeah, he's stopped drinkin' for the time being, he's been good to Itchy and Mart, great, so get him a birthday card and fix him dinner once in a while. You don't owe him more than that."

"He's changed so much," Irene said. The words tasted strange. Saying positive things about Red didn't come naturally.

"Honey," Jacqueline said with the sure pronouncement of one who knows all about everything, "people don't ever change, really. They might nibble 'round the edges, make little minor corrections and such, but inside, the main part of 'em, that doesn't ever change. I'm not sayin' Red's Hitler or anything, but deep down inside, he's not a good man. He's weak. He's selfish. You got any idea what he was up to for the eleven years he was gone?"

"He hasn't really said."

"Think there might've been a few women in his life? He could have more kids out there. Who knows what he's hidin'? To say nothing of the time before he came into your life the first time. The thing about men like Red is that they got secrets. And they lie. Men are liars. And Red's one of the biggest." Jacqueline shook her head. "And let's face it, you've been like a nun ever since he left. I know you're lonesome, that you need a man. It's just that Red isn't the one. Don't look to him for anything just because it's the easy way."

Irene stood and gazed out the salon's smeary, flyspecked front window. Itchy was supposed to clean up the salon every Thursday after school—she paid him three dollars to sweep and clean the windows and the bathroom. She'd have to point out that if he wanted to keep earning money he needed to do a better job. Typical Itchy. Probably dreaming of starving Donners instead of spraying a little Windex.

"It's just that watching him with Mart. That got to me, Mom. He's been so nice—"

"He oughta be nice to Mart, he crippled the poor kid!"

"That's the point. He's sorry for everything stupid or mean or thoughtless he's done."

"It's easy to feel guilty after the fact. If he had any sense he wouldn't have screwed up in the first place."

"And Itchy. He's changed Itchy's life."

Jacqueline went to Irene and put her arm around her shoulder. She pulled her daughter close to her. "Goddamnit, Irene, I love you so much it tears me up inside sometimes. You know how it feels, you're the same way about Itchy. Now, I'll admit, Red's done some good since he's come back with Itchy and all. I don't fault him for that. But I don't want to see you hurt again. And I *won't* let it happen. I stood by once before when he sucker-punched you. It's not gonna happen again. I'm in full momma-protect mode this time."

Irene tilted her head against her mother's shoulder. Like a little girl.

"Be careful, honey," Jacqueline said. "That's all I'm sayin'. Don't fall back into the old trap just because he seems different. You'll be sorry if you do."

"I...like that he's back."

"Leave it at that."

"I'm not sure I can."

Jacqueline said nothing more. She held Irene tightly, stroking her hair, until their one-o'clock appointments showed up.

Miriam Flynn was seriously bored.

The afternoon Merlot had turned into mid-morning Merlot, but still it didn't help. Tamarack and A. Jackson's creepy old mansion were closing in on her, and she wasn't sure how much longer she could take it.

A. Jackson now spent most of his time trying to save the family business, and Miriam knew things weren't going well. He never confided in her anymore, but she wasn't an idiot. She could tell by A. Jackson's moods and his growing desperation that their livelihood wouldn't last much longer. What would she do when the money vanished and she wasn't the queen of this nasty little town anymore?

The potential trouble didn't really interest her all that much, however. Boredom. That's all she could muster.

She tried to stay interested in Sara—you had to at least make the effort with your own child—but even then Miriam had trouble. She couldn't remember what was going on in Sara's life, what she studied at school, or who her friends were—did she even have any? Whatever happened to Itchy Donner? He hadn't been around in ages.

Miriam sipped her wine. Glanced at the clock. Three-thirty. Was that when Sara got home from school? Maybe. Sometime in the afternoon.

A short while later—or was it longer?—Sara came in lugging her huge backpack. Miriam looked at her curiously, like she was studying a stranger, or something odd she'd never seen before.

"Why do you carry so much stuff around with you?" she asked.

"It's for school," Sara replied.

"Oh."

Sara started climbing the stairs to her room. Miriam watched. The gloomy old house always reminded her of one of those haunted mansions in movies, where ghosts thumped in the attic and faraway screams sounded at odd hours. Sara's small little body ascending the huge stairway...it looked odd. Creepy.

"Sara?" Miriam asked.

"Yeah?" Sara stopped and looked down at her mother.

"How come Itchy never comes over anymore?"

"Because you and Daddy said he couldn't."

"Why would we do that?"

"Because of the starving thing last Thanksgiving. Don't you remember?"

Miriam frowned. She knew she shouldn't, because lines had begun etching themselves into her forehead, but it was a hard habit to break. Anyway, she'd get botoxed one of these days and take care of them. "Starving?"

"Don't you remember?" Sara asked, exasperated.

Miriam sipped the last of her wine. Time to pour just one more *eensie* glass before dinner. "You need friends. Invite him over."

"But Daddy'll be mad."

"No he won't. And even if he is, he'll get over it."

Sara hurried upstairs. Miriam sat in the living room, pursing her lips. A bit numb, but not quite enough. One more glass should take care of that, she thought. Starving? What *was* Sara talking about? It sounded vaguely familiar, but Miriam couldn't quite put all the pieces together. Whatever. Itchy was odd and off-putting, but Miriam remembered that Sara always seemed to enjoy his company. Good. Her little daughter, homely and shy as she was, needed contact with people—even goofy, rashy ones like Itchy Donner. Maybe next week Miriam would start working on Sara's future. Teach her how to put on makeup, show her the ways of being a woman.

Sure. Next week. That'd stop the boredom for awhile. She should be a better mother.

Next week.

"'Eliza has been a very good little girl,'" Itchy read. "'She obeys and helps me as much as a child that small can. All our daughters help us. It's a good thing, because there is much work to do. We have to try and keep clean. It's hard traveling and keeping clean.'"

"Do you really think Tamsen would write about housework stuff?" Sara asked. "That seems kinda weird to me."

"But it was important!" Itchy protested. They were in Sara's room, and Itchy had been catching her up on his attempts to reconstruct *Tamsen's Lost Journal*. They'd already spent an hour on the computer—so much nicer than fighting the goons at the library for a spot—and now they were back into their old pattern of batting Donner ideas around before Itchy had to go home for dinner. He hadn't been to Sara's in months, but it felt exactly the same as always. Itchy didn't trust Sara's parents, though...her mom seemed weird and he was afraid of her dad, so he figured he'd better sneak out before her dad got home, just in case. Why look for trouble?

"But would she write about it?" Sara continued. "I mean, it's a hundred and fifty years ago, she's all excited about going to this new place, but she's kinda scared, too, and she's telling the story of what's happening and the plants she's seeing and the school she wants to start and all that. Would she talk about washing socks?"

"That's not what she—*I*—said!"

"Yeah, but that's what it sounds like."

Itchy hated to admit it, but maybe Sara was right. He'd been having a little trouble lately with *Tamsen's Lost Journal*. At first it seemed easy, like maybe somebody (Tamsen in heaven?) was helping him. Now, though, writing every word was just hard work. Nothing came easily or felt right.

"I think you need help," Sara said.

"Maybe. But from who?"

"Me!"

"I dunno...."

"Tamsen was a lady, I'm a girl. I know things you don't. Let's write it together!"

"What kind of things do you know?"

"Girl things. Secrets."

Itchy had always suspected that girls knew about things they didn't tell guys. He'd heard his dad complain how women always seemed to know secret

180

stuff that guys didn't understand. He hated to give up his sole authorship—well, with Tamsen—of *Tamsen's Lost Journal*, but Sara was right. He needed help.

"Okay," he told her. "We'll try."

Sara smiled. Then they began work—together—on *Tamsen's Lost Journal*.

The Unknown Story of the Donner Party as told to Itchy Donner
by his Great-great-great Gramma Tamsen in her Lost Journal

By Itchy Donner, her Great-great-great Grandson

(And Sara Flynn, Itchy Donner's friend)

Chapter Three

I am afraid for my children. We're crossing a great salt desert, we're weeks behind where we should be, we're tired and scared and we don't have enough water.

We walk all day and all night. We can't stop because we have to get across the desert and get to water. The cattle are dying. The children are so afraid and so tired. I'm afraid for my children, and the other children too. I'm so afraid I haven't even looked around at the animals and birds. It's the desert but there's still birds flying around (Itchy Donner note: I don't know if this is true but Sara thinks so) and I see animal tracks sometimes. When we get to water I'll write about it. But right now all I can think about is how thirsty I am and how worried I am for the children.

"She sure worries about her kids a lot," Itchy said.

Sara stopped typing and gave him a long look. "Of course she does, Itchy. That's what mothers do."

"If you say so."

"She'll be happy when they get out of the desert, right?" Sara asked.

"Sure. But still scared, because Tamsen's smart and she knows they're way behind. And she'll be mad that they waste time looking for the Reeds' lost cattle. We'll have to put that in. Tamsen gets mad sometimes. She's not perfect."

"Okay."

Sara *taptaptapped* at the keyboard, much faster and more accurately than Itchy could. As they talked about and negotiated the words, Itchy felt his control over *Tamsen's Lost Journal* slipping away, but it was okay. Doing it with Sara was fun, and she helped him see things he wouldn't have noticed by himself.

They finished the chapter about crossing the desert, and Itchy was happy with the result. It felt more real—maybe because every word hadn't come out of his head, or maybe because Sara could pretend to be Tamsen better—Itchy wasn't sure which. But in the end it didn't matter, because the *Lost Journal* was getting written. That's all that mattered.

Itchy was still in Sara's room when A. Jackson arrived home. He'd forgotten his plan to sneak out, so when A. Jackson popped his head in the door to say hello to Sara, Sara immediately started making excuses.

"Mommy said Itchy could come over!"

A. Jackson gave Itchy a bland look. Itchy was positive he was in big trouble.

"You been eating regularly, Itchy?" A. Jackson asked.

"Yessir."

"No more of that weird Donner Party 'see what it feels like to starve' business?"

"I still study it a lot, Mr. Flynn. That's all, though."

"But nothing...strange?" he asked mildly. A. Jackson didn't seem angry or irritated. Just slightly distracted.

182

"My mom and dad made me promise not to get too, um, involved in stuff. Like starving."

"Or camping in snowbanks for the winter?"

Itchy didn't really understand what he was talking about—he assumed it was a lame joke about the Donners—but he smiled and nodded. Seemed like the best thing to do.

"Good. I suppose you two can be friends if you don't go off into weirdness." A. Jackson stared into the half distance. He seemed far away. "Nice talking to you, Itchy."

"Yessir."

A. Jackson left. Itchy turned to Sara. "How come he wasn't mad?"

Sara shrugged. "I dunno. Both of my parents are weird." Sara printed out the *Lost Journal* chapter for Itchy. "Wanna work on it some more tomorrow after school?"

"Sure."

Sara handed Itchy the printed sheets. She leaned toward him—he thought she was reaching for something—and she quickly kissed his non-rashy cheek. Itchy gazed at her with astonishment.

"What was that for?"

"Um...." Sara blushed and giggled. "I'm glad you're back."

"Oh." Itchy was utterly dumbfounded. He didn't know what to do or say, so he just burbled and bumbled, stuffed the chapter in his backpack and mumbled, "Okay, see you tomorrow then."

As he walked home, Itchy's brain buzzed with a thousand thoughts and images. For once his usual preoccupation with all things Donner Party had been blasted away, replaced with the reliving of Sara's little peck on the cheek.

A girl—someone besides his mom or gramma—had actually *kissed* Itchy

Donner! This was big—even if it *was* only Sara. It meant that maybe he wasn't so gross after all. Itchy had always figured—when he thought about it, which wasn't often—that he'd be alone forever. It just seemed like girls would never like him. He was a nerd, after all. He realized that. And he had the stupid psoriasis, which even grossed him out. The possibility of being liked didn't seem realistic.

But Sara Flynn had just kissed him! And she said she was glad he was back. Like she'd missed him or something! Unbelievable. Sometimes you just couldn't figure life out.

By the time Itchy got home—he didn't even remember walking—Irene was busily frying up some hamburger. This was great! Instead of the usual disgusting healthy stuff, tonight was going to be regular food. This day had been too good to be true.

"Hi sweetie," she said as he came in and plonked his backpack on the kitchen table. "Did you have a good day?"

"It was great!" he said. "Sara's mom said I could come over again, so we used her computer and worked on *Tamsen's Lost Journal.*" He almost added, "And then Sara kissed me!" but he decided at the last second to leave that out. His mom would get all weird if she knew.

"Well, I'm glad. Gimme a hug."

Itchy usually found his mom's "gimme a hug" ritual annoying, but tonight he didn't mind. He felt like hugging the whole world.

Because a girl kissed him today.

Dinner was a blur. For once things tasted good—fried burgers and over-microwaved baked potatoes that mushed nicely—but Itchy couldn't concentrate on the food. Irene chattered on about things, but Itchy didn't listen. She made fun of him a couple of times for being so out of it, but he knew that she thought his far-away-ness was because of his usual Donner preoccupation. If

184

only she knew the real reason, he thought.

Red dropped by later to give Irene a ride over to Mart's for their workout. Itchy was dialed-in enough to notice that his father had recently been taking better care of himself, showing up showered and groomed instead of dirty and smelly like he used to. He acted differently, too, kind of goofy and giggly. He talked too loud—well, even louder, because he'd always been noisy—and even when he talked to Itchy his eyes stayed fixed on Irene. Itchy wondered if his dad had a crush on his mom. The way he acted reminded Itchy of the way he'd seen kids at school act around girls they liked. The way he'd probably be acting now that Sara had kissed him.

"What's up, Itch?" Red said as he swept into the singlewide. Whenever Red came in he filled up the room, like he was bigger than real life, or that the singlewide was made for a race of three-quarter-sized people.

"Hi, Dad. Me and Sara are working on *Tamsen's Lost Journal.* Together."

"Got yourself a co-writer, huh? Good idea. Get somebody else's brain workin' on it, probably turn out better. Plus you get a little romantic action, too." Red threw Itchy an elbow nudge that almost knocked him over.

Irene came out in baggy sweats, no makeup, casually clipped back hair— looking absolutely, irresistibly cute. Red stared at her.

"Well," Itchy said, fighting to hold back the words but losing. "Sara's maybe kinda like my girlfriend. Sort of."

Both Red and Irene turned and stared at him. "What do you mean?" Irene asked.

Itchy blushed flame-red, and now he wished he'd kept his mouth shut. "Well," he said, his high voice squeaking even higher than usual, "Sara kind of...kissed me today."

Neither Red nor Irene said anything for a long, long moment. Itchy watched them closely. Had they stopped breathing? Then, Red's face broke into a huge, astonished grin.

"Sumbitch! Itchy 'Studmuffin' Donner, ain't you somethin'! Chip off the old block."

"Did you...kiss her back?" Irene asked, horrified yet fascinated.

"Mom! It wasn't like that."

"Give him a break, Irene. A manly man like Itch don't kiss 'n' tell." Red slapped Itchy hard on the shoulder. "You and me'll discuss it later, you little stallion."

"Sara kissed you?" Irene asked softly. "She's your girlfriend?"

Itchy shrugged. The blush faded. Now he felt stupid. But proud, too. A strange combination. Maybe, just maybe, his parents would take him a little more seriously. The way his mom stared at him made him think he'd earned some new respect.

"Well, if you can keep the little ladies away," Red told him, "I want you to work out some tonight. Pushups, chin-ups, you know the drill. Can't be the Wimp o' the Woods unless you get a little stronger. 'Course, with a girlfriend and all now, maybe you'll get a little more exercise." Red winked at him and smiled knowingly.

"Stop it, Red," Irene said, but with a smile. She kissed Itchy on the top of the head. "Behave while we're gone."

"What else would I do?"

"What your mom means is don't let no women in while we're over at Mart's."

Red winked at him again and he and Irene left. Itchy went into his room and reread the third chapter of *Tamsen's Lost Journal.* At least he tried to. But he couldn't concentrate.

He kept thinking about the kiss.

*   *   *

Irene had to slam the truck's door three times to get it to latch. Red had bought an old beater Chevy four-by-four from one of Stan the Man's cousins, and every part of it was rusting, creaky, dying, or dead. Red turned the key and the worn engine ground sadly before finally catching with a sputtery, unhappy growl.

He yanked the sticky shifter into reverse, but before he backed away from the singlewide he looked over at Irene.

They exchanged no words, but they simultaneously burst out in laughter. Hard, impossible-to-stop laughter. Irene held her hand to her mouth.

"Oh...my...God!" Red finally sputtered. "A girlfriend? Dunno 'bout you, but I feel like I'm a fuckin' million years old."

Irene tried to stop laughing. "It's mean, Red, we shouldn't make fun of him, but—" She couldn't go on.

Red hooted, "Itchy's got a *girlfriend? She kissed him?!*"

They lost it and laughed until they were exhausted. Red finally brushed the tears from his cheeks and backed the truck down the steep hill to the road.

"God," Irene sighed. "You think *you* feel old...I can't believe I'm going to have to deal with girlfriends and all the other growing-up stuff."

"Quit complaining. At least you still look like you're nineteen. People treat me like I already got my fuckin' AARP card."

"I wonder if Sara's dad knows?"

"This is too good to be true. A.J. will fuckin' lose his mind. I *love* this kid, it's like he's got the natural Donner instinct of how to piss off snooty dildoes."

Irene was silent for a moment. Then she looked over at Red. "You love Itchy?"

"Well...yeah. 'Course. He's my rugrat."

"Do you *really* love him?"

"Yeah, I love him. 'Specially since I've got to know him and all, well, you know. He's lovable. I ain't real good at the love stuff, you know that. But anyway, yeah, I love Itch."

"Have you told him?"

"Guys don't do that. It's faggy."

"God, you sound like a redneck idiot. Telling your son you love him is normal."

"Yeah. Maybe. I 'spose it is. Never heard it from my old man, though. Or my mom, either."

"That's no reason for you to make their mistakes."

"He knows we're pals. All the Logger Days training and stuff. Talkin' 'bout the Donner Party. That's how you show it. Don't necessarily need to come right out and say things."

"It wouldn't hurt to tell him. He might not be as perceptive as you think. He's just a kid."

"How come I just keep gettin' older and dumber and you don't ever change? Stay beautiful and nice and...perfect."

"I'm not perfect," she replied. But a blush crept up her neck.

"Yeah, you pretty much are. Got the right outlook on the world. Know how to deal with people, even assholes like me. I admire you, Irene. You got your shit together."

"You always put things so poetically."

"It's a gift. You got a good heart. You done a good job with Itchy. I just hope I don't fuck things up with him."

188

"You're doing fine, except maybe for all the cussing. He loves being with you."

"Yeah, maybe. But once the novelty wears off he'll see me like the rest of the world does. He'll hit his teens and realize I'm just another dickhead old man. Always happens with boys."

"Itchy isn't like most other kids. I think he'll be different."

They rolled up to Stan the Man's house. Red shut off the engine, but it sputtered and bucked a few seconds after he pulled out the key. "Feels weird, don't it?"

"What?"

"Talkin' 'bout Itchy like this. Feels like we're still married, like we're doin' normal family stuff."

Irene began to speak, then stopped. Better to say nothing, she decided.

Tamsen's Lost Journal

(Me and Sara decided to shorten the title so it's less typing)

Chapter Four

It's September already. We're so far behind where we should be. I see birds flying south already, and that scares me. (Itchy Donner note: Sara wasn't sure what kind of birds they would be, so we'll have to look that up. Maybe geese or ducks.) Mr. Reed has made many enemies in the party because of his personality. He's very uppity and acts like he's better than everybody else, even though he had to abandon a lot of his stuff and his cattle have died and it was his idea to use Hasting's Cutoff and now we're really late because of that. My husband George doesn't complain though. George is a good man. But I don't like Mr. Reed. I don't like Mr. Keseberg either. He hits his wife and he's grouchy. It's too bad we're stuck together with a bunch of people we don't really know or like, but that's the way it is on a wagon train.

If it was just us Donners it would be much better. But things will be okay, I'm sure. I can't wait to get to California and start my girls' school. But I'm going to be very tired, so I'll have to rest for awhile. Little Eliza doesn't ever seem to get tired. She's so cute and happy. No matter what. She doesn't complain, even when there isn't enough water or the weather is bad or I'm scared. She never is. She makes me feel safe, even though she's a little girl and I'm her mother.

Itchy sat next to Sara and read the words on her computer screen. As he read, he momentarily forgot how weird it felt to be with her. All the time they'd been friends he'd never really thought about her before, never really considered that she was a...girl. Now, everything had changed.

When he saw her at school his heart beat faster, his scaly patches flared, his mouth got dry and his stomach fluttered. She acted like nothing had changed, though. Great, Itchy thought, I have to feel all weird and nervous and she's fine. Typical. Nothing was ever easy for Itchy Donner.

She didn't mention the kiss—nor did she try it again. They settled into a pattern of recess friends and after school web surfers and *Tamsen's Lost Journal* authors.

"This is really good," Itchy told her. "It's like you can read her mind."

Sara proudly said, "Thanks. But you did a lot of it, too."

"It seems real. That's important."

"It's gonna be hard to do the end."

"You mean when they die?"

"Yeah. It'll be sad."

Itchy nodded gravely. "But we have to tell all of Tamsen's story. Even the gross stuff. *Especially* the gross stuff."

"Will you say that Keseberg killed her?" Itchy and Sara had engaged in long conversations about the various theories of Tamsen Donner's demise. Some sources claimed that Keseberg murdered and ate her; others went with Keseberg's claim that she froze in a creek first and *then* he ate her.

"I dunno," Itchy said. "I haven't decided yet."

They silently looked at the words on the screen. Sara traced the last sentence with her finger. "Even though they've been dead forever it's like they're our friends, huh?"

Itchy nodded. "I know them better than anybody else. Even better than my mom and my dad and my gramma. Even you."

"You're so lucky, Itchy."

"I know."

"I mean to be related to all these famous guys...."

"Yeah. It's pretty cool."

"My relatives are boring."

"But rich," Itchy added. "And you kinda own Tamarack."

"That doesn't matter. Nobody in my family were...heroes."

"It's okay, Sara. Not everybody can have famous heroes for great-great-great grandparents. I'm just extra lucky," Itchy said. Strangely, though, right now he didn't feel all that lucky. He didn't know why. Maybe because Sara was sad and he didn't know how to make her feel better.

Sara's bad mood vanished as quickly as it appeared, however, leaving Itchy confused. She went back to being chirpy and chattery in a matter of seconds. Itchy was beginning to realize he'd never understand girls.

"Where do we go next with the *Lost Journal?*" she asked.

"Well, they have to get across Nevada, and the Ruby Mountains. Then Mr. Reed kills John Snyder in the argument and gets banished, then George

Donner hurts himself, and—"

"We've got a long ways to go."

"Just like the Donner Party," Itchy said seriously.

Sara laughed. Then she did it again. Leaned over and gave Itchy a kiss on the cheek. Itchy froze. Should he kiss her back? Maybe, but where, how? On the lips? The thought of that made him a little squeamish. So he clumsily lurched toward her and gave her a glancing lipsmack on her cheek. Couldn't really call it a kiss; it was more of a slobbery smooch like a big dog gives you when he's glad to see you. Sara giggled, but didn't seem to mind.

"What should we write next?" she asked.

Itchy had a hard time coming out of his mutual kiss daze. He mumbled, "Ummm...maybe something about the Indians that follow them for stuff. And maybe how...." Itchy couldn't think straight. He gulped. *Kisses*....

"We'll just start writing and see what happens," Sara suggested. She began to tap the keys.

Itchy tried—he really tried—to focus. To concentrate. But he couldn't.

Sara Flynn was the first thing in Itchy's young life that could distract him and take his mind off the Donner Party.

What amazed him was that he didn't mind.

Anguish and dismay now filled all hearts. Husbands bowed their heads, appalled at the situation of their families. Some cursed Hastings for his false statements and for his broken pledge of a safe shortcut. They cursed him for his misrepresentation of the distance across this cruel desert, traversing which had wrought such suffering and loss. Mothers in tearless agony clasped their children to their bosoms, with the old, old cry, "Father, Thy will, not mine, be done." It was plain we must proceed regardless of the fearful outlook.

Eliza Donner

September 18, 1846

Chapter Nine

The missalettes fluttered in unison, the prayers and gospel readings going unread as the pages moved the warm air like dozens of butterfly wings. But their cooling power was limited by Our Lady of the Woods' cramped stuffiness. Air came inside the church to die, and the early summer sun beating down on the metal roof heated the church far faster than puny, makeshift fans could cool it.

Father Ray tried to keep his sermons short on days like these, but he was torn. Not because he felt his message was important, but because he wanted to maximize his Irene Donner time.

She sat in her usual spot, about halfway back, with Itchy and her mother. As he preached to his disinterested congregation, his eyes kept stopping on Irene. She listened attentively and seemed to smile slightly every time he looked at her. She wore one of those thin cotton dresses, flowery and flattering, the kind that looked so absolutely wonderful on a thin woman. As Father Ray preached, his mind wandered, and he pictured Irene Donner silhouetted against the summer sun, her body's outline plainly visible beneath the clingy cotton.

Father Ray's forehead popped beads of nerve sweat. He bumbled through the rest of his sermon—had he mentioned that next Sunday was the diocesan donation drive?—and, as usual, he sputtered to a dull, unsatisfactory conclusion.

After mass Irene and Itchy and Jacqueline left without doing the howdy-hi grip 'n' grin with Father Ray. He was bitterly disappointed. Now he had to wait another whole week to see her.

Unless....

It was important to stay in touch with the flock. Drop in and see how the parishioners were doing. Part of the ministry and all. Maybe sometime this week, maybe one evening, Father Ray would drop in on Irene Donner. Unannounced. Say hello, have a cup of coffee—Irene wouldn't mind, she was polite and sociable—maybe even bless her house, discuss her no-account ex-husband, whatever she wanted.

Excellent. Good idea.

Father Ray could hardly wait.

"Something's wrong," Mart complained. "I can't get the feeling that I'm moving right. Not enough leverage or something." Sweat rolled down Mart's face. It was a warm night, and mosquitoes and biting flies buzzed annoyingly around his head. He and Red had been practicing for over an hour, and as the light faded and the bats came out to fill up on springtime bugs, Mart's frustration grew. They'd been honing their double-buck technique, cutting pieces—called cookies—off the end of a log that Red had set up in Irene's yard.

Itchy was their official timer and sprayed WD-40 on the big crosscut saw while they worked. So far their best time cutting the twenty-inch log was thirty-two seconds—at least twelve seconds too slow. No way they'd even get in the top ten if they didn't pick up the pace.

"Can you tell what the problem is?" Red asked, hot and sweaty and annoyed that his invention wasn't working as well as he'd hoped.

"Uh-uh. Just doesn't feel right."

Itchy crouched down and looked at the pivoting La-Z-Boy guts on Red's contraption. "I think it's too loose," Itchy said.

"Whataya mean?" Red asked.

"It looks like when Mart pulls on the saw the chair spins backward too fast. And when you pull it, I dunno, it just looks weird. Like it's too easy or something."

"That don't help any. This pisses me off. I know this is a good idea." Red stared at the mechanism, rubbing his beard as he pondered.

"No, I think Itchy's right," Mart said. "It's the leverage thing. Since there's not much resistance going either way, I can't get any pressure going. It's like I'm just spinning. It feels like I don't have legs. You gotta be able to brace against the ground, you know?"

Red thought for a moment. "Okay," he said. He hurried into Irene's shed and came out with a toolbox. He fiddled with a socket wrench, tightening up and banging on the old recliner's mechanism.

"Now," he said, grabbing Mart's wheelchair and trying to pivot it. "It's stiffer 'n' shit, I can hardly move it. You think that'll help?"

"One way to find out," Mart said.

Mart grabbed his end of the saw, Red grabbed his. Itchy took his place at the log, WD-40 spray can ready in one hand, stopwatch in the other.

"Ready?" he asked.

"Let's rock 'n' roll," Red said.

"GO!"

Red groaned and grunted, the saw bit into the log, woodchips and sawdust flew, Mart pulled, back and forth, Itchy sprayed the saw with each pass, and they sawed in perfect rhythm. This time, with the stiffened wheelchair pivot, each cut ripped deeper, more efficiently.

The saw sliced through the bottom of the log, the cookie hit the ground, and Itchy clicked the stopwatch.

"Fuck, that was ten times harder!" Red gasped.

"No shit," Mart said, red-faced, veins pulsing in his neck and forehead. "Good thing I'm strapped into this fucker, 'cause I'd fall down otherwise." Mart didn't cuss much, so Itchy knew he must really be tired. Every other word out of his dad's mouth was something nasty, so Itchy didn't pay much attention to him. But Mart swearing, that was unusual.

"You guys wanna know the time?" Itchy asked with the world's biggest grin.

Red grimaced through his gasps, "Better be an improvement."

"Twenty-three seconds!"

Red grinned at Mart. "Fuckin' A Bubba! I think we might have it."

"You sure about the time, Itchy?" Mart asked.

"Yep. You guys are awesome!"

Since the twilight was fading and the mosquitoes extra-ravenous, they decided to end on an up note. Itchy ran inside to tell Irene the good news while Red unbolted Mart's chair from the stand.

"Feels like we got a chance now," Red said.

"Stan the Man's getting worried," Mart remarked. "We got him psyched. It's easy to freak him out. I think he's a little intimidated by you."

"He oughta be. Just 'cause he's doin' Jackie-O don't make him tough enough to beat us in the double-buck." Red rolled Mart off the stand. "Glad you're doin' this, Mar-teen."

In the dim light Mart couldn't clearly see Red's face, but Red's voice had a gooey, let's-hold-hands-and-sing-*We Are the World* feeling that Mart didn't care for. "It's just a little fun, Red. Nothing more. Doesn't change anything."

"Yeah, I know. I ain't tryin' to be your therapy guy or nothin'. Just musing."

"Irene in shape yet?"

"She's gettin' there. What she don't have in strength she makes up for in mean."

Red pushed Mart across the bumpy grass to the singlewide's front door. As Red opened the door, a tiny car drove up the driveway and ground to a stop in the loose gravel.

"Who's that?" Red asked.

"I think it's the priest's car." There had been much comment in town over Father Ray's old convertible MG. In Tamarack you were judged by your ride, and if it wasn't a big four-by—preferably a Dodge—you didn't get much respect. A little sports car, no matter how cool, just didn't fit. Especially when a priest owned it.

"'Evening," Father Ray said as he climbed out.

"Hey, Padre," Red said "Warm out tonight, huh? Just right for that little toy you got there."

"Yes, yes it is," Father Ray answered. His voice wavered nervously.

"What brings you to where the rich folks live, Padre?" Red asked.

"I, uh, like to drop in on my...the church members. Say hello, you know."

"Trollin' for cash?"

"Well, no, of course—"

"Just jerkin' your chain," Red grinned. "Irene don't have any money anyway."

Father Ray forced a smile. He didn't move from the MG's door, and Red and Mart waited silently for him to do or say something.

Red finally asked, "You comin' in or what?"

"Yes. Of course." He walked stiffly toward them. When he got to them, still with that uncomfortable forced smile, he shook Mart's hand. "How are you?"

"Fine."

"Me and Mar-teen are workin' out, gonna do the men's double-buck for Logger Days."

"Really?"

"Yep. You competin' in anything, Padre?"

"I don't think so."

"You know, seems to me they used to have a tug o' war between the Catholics and the Protestants way back when. Maybe you and Pastor Earle oughta start that up again. Show them crazy Baptists they're pussies compared to ass-kickin' Catholics. Can you bring some nuns in? Ain't nothin' tougher than a crabby old nun."

"I think I'd prefer—"

"I'll have to ask ol' Pastor Earle 'bout that," Red said, cutting off Father Ray. "Be good for the town. Tamarack needs a few more grudges, don't you think?"

Father Ray sputtered, "Well, no, I don't think...."

Red opened the front door and gestured him inside. "After you, Padre." Father Ray nodded and went in. Red looked down at Mart and whispered, "I love fuckin' with guys like him."

"You're gonna do hard time in hell, Red," Mart smiled.

Itchy was excitedly telling Irene about Red and Mart's double-buck glory. When Itchy came in she'd been reading a two-month-old *Time* magazine she'd brought home from the salon. Irene liked to keep informed—even belatedly—about the world. She worried that life in isolated Tamarack might make her ignorant. Itchy's insatiable curiosity about the Donner Party was a constant reminder to Irene: you had to keep using your brain and never stop wondering about the world. Another reason to love Itchy. He taught her all kinds of things, even though he was blissfully unaware of it.

"Oh! Father Ray," Irene said, surprised and a little bewildered. She quickly stood and set aside the magazine.

"Hey, Father," Itchy said.

"The Padre come by to say 'hi,'" Red told them.

"That's nice."

"I hope I'm not catching you at a bad time, Irene," Father Ray said. His voice wavered again and cracked on the word "bad."

"Not at all, Father."

"He swore he ain't lookin' for money. I asked," Red added helpfully. Father Ray swallowed loudly but didn't—or wouldn't—look at Red.

"Would you like something to drink? Coffee or beer or something?" Irene asked.

"A beer would be great," Father Ray said. Red caught Mart's eye and raised an eyebrow.

"You guys want something?" Irene asked them.

"Nah," Red said. "We're gonna take off. You wanna come along, Itch? Might have some real food in my fridge you can scarf." On Irene's nasty glare Red grinned, "Just kiddin' beautiful."

After they left, Father Ray stood awkwardly, waiting in the living room while Irene rummaged around in the kitchen. He tried to slow his breathing. *Control, control.* Maybe this wasn't such a good idea. He'd gotten what he wanted—being alone with Irene Donner. Now what? Instead of exhilaration and excitement, guilt and fear gnawed at his guts. Priest. What a joke. Love-sick doofus, more like it. Don't be afraid, he told himself. She's a sweet, pretty, nice woman. Just...visit. Do what you said you're here to do. There's nothing wrong with the parish priest dropping in on his flock. *Yeah, right.* Especially ones he's crazy about. Real nice.

Good thing he didn't really believe in God or sin anymore.

When Irene came out with a beer and a smile Father Ray had begun to settle down.

"Thanks," he said. She had thoughtfully poured the beer into a mug. He sipped it, but couldn't place the brand. Thin, though, probably something cheap and no-name. Bless her heart. No money, buying cheap beer, but still she generously offered him what little she had.

"Would you like to sit down?" she asked. Father Ray sat on the couch and Irene took a place across from him in the old chair. He looked around the singlewide. Threadbare carpet, saggy furniture with shiny spots on the uphol-stery from long years of wear, everything about this place said "poor." And yet Irene exuded class. If you took her out of this old trailer, out of Tamarack, you'd think she was a cultured rich woman, all style and grace. Amazing, he thought. Irene Donner's natural class could overcome anything.

"How've you been, Irene? We haven't had a chance to talk much lately."

"I'm good, Father Ray. I think things are better than I expected they'd be. With Red and Itchy, I mean."

"So they're getting along okay?"

"Better than okay. They're pals. Red's got him training for Wimp o' the

Woods. And they're always talking about their Donner Party stuff."

"And how about you?"

"I'm...fine."

"Really?" He couldn't resist probing. Being a priest came in handy when you wanted to get to know as much as possible about a woman.

"Well," she hesitated. "You know. Things are always complicated."

"How so?"

"I don't know about Red. And me."

Father Ray paused. He wanted to keep *her* nervous and off-balance for a change. Cruel, he knew, but he couldn't stop. "Would you like to talk about it?" he asked softly.

"I'm not sure—"

"You can speak freely to me about anything that troubles you. That's what I'm here for. To help."

Irene smiled. Her gaze, so direct, so trusting...it killed him. He wanted to hold her. Touch her. Kiss her.

Kiss her. Kiss. *Kiss*. He tried to banish the forbidden thought, but once the word got loose in his mind he couldn't make it go away.

"Thank you, Father Ray. I guess I should talk about it."

"Go ahead." *Kiss!*

"Well, it's kind of weird with Red," she began. "When he came back I wanted him to leave. I was so mad about everything he'd done—or hadn't done. But he's changed a lot, and he's stopped drinking. And, I dunno, maybe it's because I'm older, but he seems better now. He loves Itchy, he's trying to be a good father. He's even been trying to make up with Mart. I don't know if that'll ever work out, but at least he's trying. I guess I'm trying to forgive him.

It's hard, but in a strange way it's getting easier, too."

Father Ray didn't like the direction this was headed. He wanted Irene to say that she was miserable, that Red Donner was Satan, that she needed a real man, a gentle, loving man to rescue her from her life. A man like Father Ray. He had to warn her, to pull her back. He had to save her from the Red Donner trap.

"Are you sure that you're doing the right thing, Irene?"

"What do you mean?"

"A man like Red," he said, his voice calm and reasonable, "often reverts to his old ways. It's hard for me to say this, because it goes against what the Church teaches, but I've seen so many cases where a...troubled person tries to change, and even does for a time, only to eventually slide back down where they were and drag good people with them. I'd hate for that to happen to you. And Itchy."

"How can you say that? Doesn't everything the Church teach basically boil down to forgiveness? Isn't that why people go to confession? Isn't that what you preach every Sunday?"

"Of course, but you have to be realistic," he said. His voice trailed off weakly. He'd blown it. He was no good at this. Irene was too sharp, and he wasn't clever enough to manipulate her. *Idiot!*

"I don't think being realistic means giving up on people, Father Ray."

"No, that's not what I meant. Just be careful, that's all."

"Thanks for worrying," she said. "I'll be fine."

"Are you getting back together with Red?"

"I doubt it."

Father Ray finished his thin, warm beer. This had been a miserable, stupid idea. What had he been thinking? He stood. "Well, I'd best be going. Other

202

people to see and all."

Irene led him to the door. "Thanks for coming by, Father."

And as they stood there, Irene so close, the sensation that hit Father Ray was unlike anything he'd ever felt before. He'd never had such a strong, overwhelming pull toward another person. Her eyes. He couldn't.... Weakness. His knees wouldn't hold him, his breathing stopped, he—

Had to go. Quickly. Or—

Irene smiled. He couldn't, wouldn't, this *couldn't* happen, he had to make himself leave, but he couldn't move, frozen, then—

He grabbed Irene, pulled her to him, kissed her roughly, the touch of her lips, every dream he'd ever had, every fantasy, kiss her, kiss her hard, *is she kissing back?!*

Irene shoved him away with surprising strength. Hard enough to knock him against the front door.

"What the hell are you doing?!"

"I'm...I'm sorry," he mumbled, grabbing for the doorknob. He had to get away. Quickly.

Irene wiped her mouth as if he'd covered her with slime; he flung open the door. He scurried into the night like a bug. He hopped into his MG, fired it up, and sprayed a roostertail of gravel as he floored it—backwards—down the driveway. He spun onto the road and his taillights disappeared into the night....

Irene stood at the door for a long time. The shock faded. So did the anger. Sadness was the only thing left. The poor guy—he was lost, confused, a mess. Jacqueline had been right about his crush on her. Why couldn't she see it? Stupid naïve Irene, oblivious to the obvious, as usual. How many other important things didn't she notice?

When she and Red had gotten married, everybody knew that it was a mistake—except her. Was letting Red back into her and Itchy's life another catastrophe in the making? And Father Ray, how could she have missed the signs? Sure, he puppy-dogged her, she saw how nervous he was around her, but she thought it was kind of cute. It never occurred to her that it might be a problem. How could she have known that Father Ray's infatuation was so...real? She decided to tell no one what had happened. Some things needed to stay secret. She'd continue as usual, she'd go to mass, go to communion, but not look Father Ray in the eye, and *definitely* not chat after mass. She'd never mention what happened—or let him mention it—again.

She stayed outside and gazed into the starry night sky until Red dropped Itchy off. Red gave her a honk and a friendly wave and drove away. Red. He was starting to seem like the most normal and dependable thing in her world. Did what he needed to do, worked hard, tried to fix his mistakes, was fun to be around and never mopey—okay, kind of loud and crude, but that was part of his charm. Irene caught herself smiling. She never thought that Red could make her smile again. Strange.

"Hey, Mom," Itchy said as he bounded to the door. The toe of his gigantic high-top imitation Nike caught on an invisible seam and he stumbled. Preteen clumsiness had started to plague him. Red had laughed about it, telling Irene, "He's just gotta grow into them goddamn huge feet. Must be like walkin' around on skis all the time."

"Hi, honey," Irene said to Itchy.

"What'd Father Ray want?"

"Nothing. Just talk."

"How come you're standing outside?"

"Just waiting for you, sweetie." He tried to slither by, but she caught him and held on. He squirmed. "Not so fast. Cost you a hug." Itchy knew resistance was futile, so he gave her a half-hearted hug back. "Did your dad feed you something nasty?" she asked.

"Um...."

"Don't even bother trying to protect him."

"Maybe some Pringles. And maybe a Mountain Dew."

"'Maybe'?"

Itchy grinned a con-man's grin. "I'm not saying exactly."

"That sounds like something your father would say."

"He's teaching me to be Red-like. That's what he calls it."

"Wonderful. Like one of him isn't enough."

"He says we're gonna win all the stuff we enter in Logger Days. Do you think so?"

"Winning isn't everything, Itchy."

"But do you think we have a chance?"

"We might."

"Dad says you're stronger than shit."

"Itchy!"

"Well, that's what he says!"

"You don't need to repeat it. Your father's mostly a good guy but he has a filthy mouth."

Irene rubbed Itchy's shoulder. The psoriasis patch on his cheek was in a semi-dormant phase, barley visible. "Your skin looks good."

"It's been okay," Itchy said vaguely. He hated talking about the stuff. Every time it came up it reminded him that he was different from everybody else, and *that* he didn't need.

"Don't cuss," Irene told him. "Cussing makes people sound stupid."

"Dad doesn't sound stupid. He just sounds like...Dad."

"Whatever. I don't want to hear you using bad language. It's bad enough that Gramma and your father and everybody else in the world cusses. Don't you start, too. You're too good for that."

Itchy shrugged. This was another odd rule that made no sense—everybody does it, so don't do it. He wiggled free of Irene's grasp and he and his titanic shoes clomped off to his room.

Irene closed the front door. She stood for a long time, thinking. Father Ray. Another problem. How come things couldn't go along without complications? Red's return had floored her, but at least it seemed to be turning out okay. Better than okay. But there was no way this Father Ray thing could end well. An embarrassment, an irritation, and—she hated to use the word—but guilt, that was part of it, too. How to deal with it? Silence. Bury it. Forget what happened. Avoid the guy.

She sighed. Always something.

At least she could count on Itchy. The only surprises up his sleeve were Donner Party things, and as long as he didn't do something stupid like trying to starve, she could live with it. Itchy was a constant in her life.

And, it amazed her to think of it, so was Red....

Tamsen's Lost Journal

Chapter Five

Tamsen's Lost Journal (as written by Itchy Donner and Sara Flynn) is what Tamsen would've told us about the trip if we could talk to her. We just wanted to remind you what you're reading. We're pretty sure this is what she would've said if her Lost Journal hadn't been lost. Anyway, we're getting close to the Sierra part of the story, but that part gets really gory and sad. We just wanted to warn you. It's rated PG-13 or maybe even R. So it's pretty gross. So we'll go back to listening to Tamsen. She was there. And she can tell the story better than anybody else....

Reed was banished from the party today. He got into an argument with John Snyder over something stupid, and instead of just arguing or fighting Reed shot and killed him. Some (especially Keseberg) wanted to hang Mr. Reed on the spot, but my husband and some of the other good men in the party decided banishment was the best idea. I feel sorry for Reed's wife and children, because now they're alone without a man to take care of them, but that's the way it has to be.

We're getting closer to the mountains, but I'm afraid of how late in the year it is. We already have frost in the mornings, and the light is changing (Itchy Donner note: Sara had the idea about the light changing. I never really noticed it, but she says in the fall the shadows get longer and stuff. Sara's good at noticing stuff.) If only we can get over the mountains quickly and into California, then all our dreams will come true. The trail has been very hard, we're all so tired. I'm sick of the dirt and the Indians and the arguing and all the trouble of trying to be a family while you're moving all the time. I sure hope we get over the mountains fast. I'm sick of this. Really sick.

Itchy read the latest installment that he and Sara had written. He thought it was good. Really good. Working together had been the best idea ever. When he didn't have ideas, Sara did—and vice-versa. They were a good team. And then there was the kissing part. Every day now, after they finished working at Sara's computer, she'd kiss him or he'd kiss her when he was ready to leave. It felt so grown-up, like the husband going off to work and kissing his wife good-bye. They didn't giggle about it anymore, and Itchy wasn't embarrassed or shy. They just kissed each other—usually on the cheek, but sometimes they brushed lips, although Itchy wasn't sure he liked that. It seemed kind of unsanitary.

Sara's parents left them alone. Mrs. Flynn didn't say much other than "hello" and "goodbye"—and sometimes not even that. She hid out in her dark parlor, sipping wine, sometimes muttering to herself or having angry imaginary conversations.

"I think my mom drinks too much," Sara had told Itchy. "My dad tells her she does. But then they fight and sometimes she cries and sometimes Daddy yells at her." Itchy felt bad for Sara and gave her a kiss. That seemed to help. Sara also told him that her dad said they might have to move away from Tamarack. Itchy was appalled.

"No!" He'd said too loudly; it came out like a bark.

"He wasn't sure. But I don't think his business is doing too good."

"That means we'll all be in trouble," Itchy said. "My dad said he thinks things are going bad for your dad, too. He said he didn't think Tamarack would last too much longer. But you wouldn't really move, would you?"

"I hope not, Itchy. But that's why we need to finish *Tamsen's Lost Journal*."

"I don't want you to move," Itchy said. He leaned over and kissed her cheek.

"I don't want to, either," she replied. And then she leaned over and kissed *his* cheek. She was always careful to kiss the non-psoriasis side. They went back to working on the *Lost Journal* after that, but Itchy had felt bad ever since.

Sara Flynn was his best friend. Maybe, just maybe, he thought, she might even be his girlfriend. Okay, he was only eleven—almost twelve—and it was kind of early to be thinking about things like that, but he wondered if maybe someday he and Sara might get married. Marriage didn't seem to work too good for a lot of people—like his mom and dad, and Sara's parents. And there were lots of single-parent families in Tamarack. But Itchy realized that if you found the right person then it might work. Look at Gramma and Stan the Man. They weren't married, but they acted like they were, and they were best friends.

They always hung out together, Gramma always insulted Stan the Man—which, Itchy knew from personal experience, meant that she liked you. And even his parents...Itchy had noticed that his dad seemed to really like being around his mom. And she was starting to act like she didn't hate him, either. So there was hope, he decided. People could stay together and like each other. Sara might be *his* person. The thought was pleasant. And those kisses.... He sure looked forward to those kisses.

At night he prayed that Sara wouldn't leave. Itchy didn't think much about God and all the things Father Ray talked about at church. Irene had made half-hearted efforts to teach him the Catholic stuff, but Itchy wasn't really interested. God and heaven and hell were too far away. It was like all the sins and warnings they talked about didn't apply to him. He preferred to spend his time thinking about and studying the Donners. And Sara. Much more interesting than worrying about Jesus and sins. But when the occasion arose, Itchy could pray with the best of them—if he really wanted or needed something, that is. And he *really* wanted Sara to stay, so he prayed hard.

Sara was right about one thing: they needed to finish *Tamsen's Lost Journal* quickly. Just in case the worst happened and Sara had to leave. Because, Itchy realized, nothing was more important than the Donner Party. Nothing.

Not even Sara.

"Sometimes I'm so goddamn romantic I make myself horny," Red announced as flopped in a plastic chair and idly thumbed through an ancient *Cosmopolitan*.

"Well a statement like that surely proves it," Jacqueline grumbled. As she counted and stacked the salon's daily haul of checks, charge receipts and cash, Jacqueline muttered and shook her head. "We're not makin' as much money as we used to. Not that we ever made all that much to begin with."

Irene busily rinsed out the sinks and organized the combs and curlers for tomorrow. She was beat. All day breathing stinking perm solution and hunched over trimming, clipping, combing—maybe it wasn't as tough as logging, but it wiped her out anyway. It amazed her that Red always had so much energy when he worked so incredibly hard. She realized that deep down inside she was a weenie.

"Anybody gonna ask me why I'm so goddamn romantic?" Red asked. "Jesus, you Weatherly women aren't very damn curious."

"It's because you're a boring bozo," Jacqueline said.

"J.W., you are truly a ray of sunshine. I can see why Stanley loves you so much."

"How come you're here? Are you sniffing around for a free dinner?" Irene asked.

"Always thinkin' the worst about ol' Red. Sad, Irene, really sad. I'm gonna surprise you, ex-wifey. I'm gonna treat you to a night on the town."

Jacqueline snorted, "In Tamarack?"

"Even better. I'm gonna take your lovely daughter out to dinner and a little dancing down in Elk Creek."

"Woo, bigtime. Sure you can afford it, Red?" Jacqueline asked. "Elk Creek, that's like goin' to Paris or something."

"Best I can do on short notice, J.W."

"I'm pretty tired, Red," Irene said.

"No excuses. I already told Itchy to hang out with J.W., so alls you gotta do is hop in my rig and we're on our way."

"Did you plan on checking with me?" Jacqueline asked.

"Just did. You don't mind, do you?"

Jacqueline grunted.

Red shot Irene a fifty-cent grin. "Ready to rock 'n' roll whenever you are."

She was going to say no.

But then she said yes.

The town of Elk Creek was a fifteen-minute drive from Tamarack, along a winding road that dropped precipitously through Skookum Canyon. Irene loved the drive, because the steep road forced you to go slow and there were gorgeous views at every turn. They had never logged in the steep canyon, and the old growth cedar and firs' beauty rivaled any mountain scene in the world. Red had to slow down a couple of times to let deer cross the road, and at one meadow clearing he stopped and pointed out a bald eagle circling lazily in the warm evening air. The long twilight's golden light bathed the trees.

"Nice evening to come down here," he said. "'Course, it's always pretty. Lucky to live where we do, huh?"

Irene nodded. She was suddenly so relaxed she thought she might drift off.

"You hungry?" Red asked.

"Sure."

"Then we'll just have to pig out."

They were headed to Elk Creek's only restaurant, an old hunting lodge. Elk Creek was a smaller town than Tamarack, and although plenty of loggers and millworkers lived there, it existed mostly for hunters, fishermen, and other outdoorsy types who took advantage of its woods and water. Being closer to the main highway and a bit more touristy, Elk Creek had more amenities than Tamarack did, like a bus stop and few more shops and stores.

The lodge was quiet, and Red and Irene sat at a nice table by the window overlooking Elk Lake. Red ordered a bottle of wine, and as they sipped they both looked out at the water. The light lingered, a dusky glow over the mountaintops that reflected on the lake's still, burnished surface.

"See that?" Red said, pointing to the far lakeshore. "Looks like a cow moose and her calf."

Irene squinted. From the distance they looked like a couple of horses as they moved through the reed-choked shallows. "You've got better eyes than me," she said.

"Just notice things. I been outside more. Get a sense for movement." He held up his wineglass. "Toast?"

She held hers up and looked at him uncertainly; with Red you never knew what he might say.

"To you and me and Itchy. We're doin' pretty okay, don't you think?"

She clinked glasses. "I'm glad you're back."

"Shouldn't have ever left. Glad you're big enough to let me hang around."

"You've been good for Itchy. But you already know that."

Red paused and watched the moose. "How 'bout you, Irene? I been good for you?" She didn't say anything. "I'll take that as a 'yes,'" Red said as he swirled his wine. "I ain't leavin' again. No matter what might happen, I'm always gonna be there for Itchy."

"I'm...glad, Red."

"I can be there for you, too, if you'd like."

"Red—"

"Just so you know. No pressure or nothin'."

"We should just leave things the way they are."

"Why? See, the thing is, since I come back I realized, well, I realized that I never stopped lovin' you. Nothin' I can do about it. It's like a disease."

212

"Thanks. I guess."

"You know what I mean. I'll do whatever you want. You want me to back off, I'll back off. But I thought you oughta know how I feel."

"We're just friends, Red. After you left I didn't think we could ever be friends again, but now it's happened. It can't be anything more. We're Itchy's divorced parents, we can be friendly, we can even go out for a big night once in a while in Elk Creek. But we can't go back to where we used to be."

He poured Irene more wine. "Fair enough. One thing, though. Didn't hear you say in that nice little speech that you don't love me no more. Just tell me that, I'll shut up about it."

"C'mon, Red."

"Need to hear the words, Irene. I'm a concrete kinda guy. Don't do real good with between the lines stuff."

Irene kept her voice steady. Quietly, she lied, "I don't love you anymore."

"Okay then," he said, unfazed. "Don't eat too much, now, 'cause I don't want you gettin' all flabby right before the competition."

It amazed her that Red could shrug things off so easily. Did he know she was lying? The thought worried her, because then he'd have power over her again, and she didn't want that to happen.

The dinner was pleasant, and they stayed for hours, talking, laughing, enjoying each other's company. Red was convivial and amusing, gentlemanly, gracious—on his best first date behavior, with the exception of his usual profanity-laced language. Irene was so used to him that she didn't notice all the "fucks" and other swear words that inevitably punctuated every sentence. That was just Red being Red.

They never got around to dancing that night; instead they talked about everything from Itchy's various Donner Party obsessions to Red's conviction that Bigfoot really did exist. "I seen piles o' shit in the woods that had to come from somethin' unhuman," he told her. She just laughed.

When they drove back to Tamarack, Red switched off the headlights and drove by moonlight. Irene was scared, but Red pointed out that the full moon was so bright it didn't matter. And he was right. It was eerie and beautiful.

Back at Jacqueline's to pick up Itchy, Red leaned over and gave Irene a little kiss. "That wasn't nothin' more than a good friend's kiss. Kinda like what you'd give to a big old fat-ass aunt or somethin'."

"God, you're a sweet-talker."

"Yep. I know what women like to hear."

Irene surprised him with a kiss back. Just a tiny one. "That's a good friend's kiss, too, like what you'd give to a disgusting old perv uncle."

Red laughed, then honked. Itchy came charging out, Jacqueline waved from the doorway, and Red drove his family home.

"HIT ME AGAIN!" Red screamed.

Itchy pounded his father with the ratty old pillow, but Red didn't budge. Itchy swung so hard he almost flew off the log, but he regained his balance and tried again. The pillow bounced harmlessly off Red's chest.

"C'mon, Itch, do it like you mean it!"

"I'm trying!"

"Try harder!"

They balanced on the log Red had set up in Irene's yard. Logger Days was only a week away, and Red had Itchy working brutal two-a-days in preparation. So far Itchy had only succeeded in knocking his father off the log once, which, considering how scrawny Itchy was compared to Red, seemed to Itchy like a pretty good average.

"HIT ME!"

Itchy swung the pillow as hard as he could, but he didn't have much muscle behind it and it biffed off of Red like a little puff of air. He disgustedly yanked the pillow away from Itchy, *whapped* him hard on the side of the head with it and sent him flying. Itchy crashed to the grass with a *thump*, and even though he felt like crying, he held it back. He knew better than to cry around Red.

"That's what that little prick Jason Bent's gonna do to you unless you get tough, Itchy," Red said, hopping off the log. He grabbed Itchy's hand and pulled him up. "Is that what you want?"

"No."

"Then you gotta get the killer instinct. You were just patty-cakin' me up there. Gotta go for the fuckin' kill. Remember that first day, how pissed off you were at me, and you knocked my fat ass into the snow?"

"Yeah."

"Get the feeling back. Gonna need it if you wanna win." Red roughly put his arm around Itchy's bony shoulders. "Don't get pouty on me. Just tryin' to help you out."

"I know."

"All right, then. Tell you what, you been workin' hard, let's spend the rest of the day goofin'."

"Wanna look at some new Donner books?" Itchy asked, brightening.

"Let's give the dead relatives a rest for the day," Red said. "It's nice out, a beautiful Saturday, I'm thinkin' we oughta do some fishin'."

"I've never been fishing."

"Jesus, you been livin' around women too long. They ain't raised you right. Boy your age oughta be out plinkin' in these streams all the time. Fishin' it is, then."

They went by Stan the Man's place and borrowed a couple of rods, swung by the salon to let Irene know what was up, and then headed out into the back-country on a rutted Forest Service road. Red bought a bag of nacho Doritos and a handful of Slim Jims before they left town, and Itchy gobbled the garbage food contentedly as they bounced through the forest.

"Good shit, huh?" Red asked.

"I wish Mom would buy this kind of stuff."

"Yeah. She's got some weird-ass ideas. Vegetables and healthy shit....jeez, what's she thinkin'?" He looked down at Itchy, grinning, and they both laughed.

"Where we going, Dad?" Itchy asked. He liked saying "Dad."

"I seen a little creek out here a ways. Some of the boys in the crew told me it was full of cutthroat. Now since you never been fishin', you don't know what a cut looks like. Pretty little things. They don't get real big seein' as how there ain't that much feed in these little creeks, but they're always hungry and they like to fight. Got a real pretty little red slash by their gills...that's why they call 'em cutthroats."

"Oh...." Itchy wasn't sure about this. It seemed kind of stupid to catch fish—unless you really needed them for food. "The Donners tried to fish when they were trapped," he said, pleased that he'd found a Donner connection to going fishing.

"They have any luck?" Red asked. "Guess not," he said, answering his own question. "Wouldn't have starved otherwise."

"They tried, but the fish weren't biting...and there was all the ice, too."

"Yeah, fish kinda hibernate. Trout 'specially. Only way to survive when it's colder 'n' shit. Too bad our relatives couldn't have curled up and slept through that nasty-ass winter, huh?"

Itchy nodded like it was a serious suggestion. They bounced along for awhile, and Itchy watched the passing trees. The road narrowed, and branches scraped against the sides of Red's truck.

"Hey, Dad?"

"Yeah, Itch?"

"Did you leave 'cause of me?"

"Nah. Your mom tell you that?"

"No. She never said much bad about you. I just wondered, that's all."

"What scares you the most, Itch?"

"I dunno."

"C'mon. Be honest. Gotta be something that scares the shit outa you."

Itchy paused, considering. "Um...I dunno. Not being a Donner."

"Lots of people ain't Donners and they do just fine. Be serious. What scares you more than anything?"

Itchy paused for a long time, thinking hard. Slowly, he said, "Something happening to Mom."

"Yeah. Makes sense. Your momma's one of the best people on this earth. She loves you more than anything, and I can see why that'd scare you if something happened to her." Red paused. "I get scared of stuff too, Itch. I know it don't seem like it, bein' as how I'm so big and noisy and all. But that's just my bullshit shell. Some stuff scares the shit outa me. And when I fucked up and hurt Mart, and your mom was gonna have you, well, I got scared. Real scared. Drinkin' too much, a loser fuck-up, I didn't think I could be a dad or a husband or a friend to Mart or nothin'. Scared shitless was what I was. Probably the

217

same feeling you have about somethin' happening to your mom. You know the feeling when you get scared, you got big old birds flapping around in your gut, you don't think you can do nothin', maybe you're even afraid of dyin'. Whatver. I was scared and I was stupid, so instead of bein' a man, I ran off. Like a cockroach. Worst thing I ever done desertin' you and your mom and Mart. Wish sometimes I was more flexible, 'cause if I was I'd kick my own ass."

Itchy giggled at the thought of his dad kicking his own butt. He chewed off the end of a Slim Jim and savored the satisfying smear of greasy fat on his lips.

"You ain't mad that I left, are you?" Red asked.

"Uh-uh," Itchy said, crunching a handful of Doritos.

"Good thing about kids," Red said. "Don't hold grudges. Too bad we grow outa that."

They reached the unnamed creek twenty minutes later, and Red parked his wheezing rig in a small clearing. They gathered their gear—Itchy made sure the Doritos and Slim Jims came along—and hiked down the creek.

"It smells good here," Itchy said. He liked the woods' odor, the spicy-sweet smell of bark and sap and duff. The little creek splashed and wandered, disappearing beneath mossy fallen logs and carving through granite crevices.

"You're lucky to live here, Itch. I wouldn't wanna work nowhere else," Red said. "Always feel like shit when I can't be out here. Growin' up in a shithole like Sacramento I never got to enjoy this when I was a rugrat. Best thing I ever did was quit school, wander into the mountains and become a logger."

They scrambled through brush and hopped over fallen logs and limbs, finally coming to a wide spot where the water slowed.

"This looks like a good place," Itchy said.

Red smiled, "See, you got a good eye. Natural born fisherman."

Red showed him how to tie the hook on the line, how to decide how much split-shot to clip on, how to stick the squishy salmon eggs on the treble hook. Itchy watched in awe. There wasn't anything his father didn't know.

Red worked with him on casting. Itchy had a hard time getting the hang of it, either splatting the hook right at his feet or snagging it behind himself in the bushes. Red patiently worked with him until he finally began to understand.

"We gotta work on that eye-hand coordination thing with you. Your mom's a great lady, but there's some things she ain't taken care of, like teachin' you how to be a boy. Anybody ever play catch with you? Throw a football or Frisbee or anything like that?"

"No." Itchy felt stupid. His dad was being nice, but Itchy knew his clumsy oafishness irritated Red. It irritated Itchy, too, because he had to take crap from coordinated sports-type guys like Jason Bent. Even though Itchy knew that the sports stuff wasn't important in the long-range scheme of things, it mattered. It mattered because if you were a klutz you ended up a target, and there was nothing fun about that.

"Well," Red said, "it's a good thing I come back. I'll get you ready to face all them mofo's out there."

"Okay," Itchy said. It was good to have a dad.

Itchy finally got a decent cast, and his salmon egg-laden hook slowly sunk to the bottom of the slow running creek. Red effortlessly tossed his out, and they sat together on the bank and waited. Neither said anything; they just lounged and ate Doritos.

They idly swatted away marauding mosquitoes, and the distant *thwakthwakthwak* of a woodpecker echoed through the woods. Red spotted a great horned owl perched far above, peering at them with the haughty air of a hungry cat.

"Every time one of them things stares me down it makes me feel like prey," Red said. "You imagine how a mouse must feel when it sees that thing swoopin' in on him?"

"Dead," Itchy said, and Red laughed.

The setting was great; the fishing wasn't. Neither got any bites—except for mosquitoes—and Red suggested they move further along the creek.

They pulled up their lines and hiked on. As they walked, the roar of falling water got louder. Red stopped and listened. "There's a falls up here a ways I think, nice little pool at the bottom. We'll see if there's any fish there."

They hiked on, but as they got closer to the falls, they heard laughs and screams and splashes.

"There's somebody there," Itchy said.

"Ain't gonna do much for the fishin'," Red grumbled.

When they reached the top of the falls, Red stopped and peered down. A big grin crept over his face. "Itch, c'mere. Check this out!"

Itchy moved to Red's side and looked down over the rocks. Below them, a half-dozen high school kids—three guys and three girls—laughed and hooted as they splashed and frolicked in the shallow pool.

"Looks to me like we got us a bunch of skinny-dippers," Red grinned.

"Wooww...." Itchy said. He didn't much care about the guys, but he found the three naked girls *very* interesting. He recognized them all from around Tamarack...he'd seen the girls before, but they looked a whole lot different without their clothes on. They kept climbing out of the pool onto the surrounding rocks and jumping back in. They sure seemed to be having a lot of fun. Itchy envied the guys. Wow...naked girls. Itchy gulped.

"Girls got nice tight little bods, huh?" Red said. "You old enough to appreciate them yet?"

"Yeah." Itchy's voice was raspy and hoarse.

"Glad to hear you're not a fag. I'm feelin' a little ripe myself. Whataya say we join 'em?"

"You mean...?"

"Let's get naked," Red said with a huge smile.

Itchy followed him down a steep path alongside the falls. The teenagers spotted them, and although they weren't hooting and hollering quite as much, nobody made a move to put their clothes back on. Itchy kept tripping because he couldn't keep his eyes on the trail; he kept stealing glances at the girls.

"Hiya!" Red greeted as he and Itchy got down to the pool.

"Hey, Mr. Donner," one of the guys said. He was buzz-cutted and muscular.

"Jesus H. Christ, Mr. Donner's some old fart I don't know. Call me Red. You a Bent?" Red asked, squinting at the kid.

"Yessir," the kid replied. "Stan's cousin."

"Shit, everybody in Tamarack's Stan's cousin. You Bents fuck more than any people I ever heard of." The girls giggled and the guys laughed. "Mind if we join you?"

"Sure," the Bent kid said.

Red quickly peeled off his clothes. Itchy had never seen his dad naked before, and he was amazed at how hairy he was. He was huge and muscular, and his giant biceps and weightlifter's chest put the high school guys to shame. Itchy was particularly impressed by the enormity of his dad's dick—at least compared to his own. Incredible...Itchy wondered if he'd ever be that big. He sure hoped so.

He looked at the girls. They watched as Red stripped, and Itchy could tell they were as impressed by Red's hugeness as he was.

"Let's go, Itch. You ain't jumpin' in all dressed, are you?"

Itchy reluctantly got undressed, but it sure felt weird to be getting naked in front of strangers—especially girls. Red hopped into the pool, and his huge splash soaked Itchy. The teenagers went back to splashing and hollering, and nobody paid Itchy any attention. Good. It made getting naked easier.

As soon as he had his clothes off he jumped in, and the chill water took his breath away for a moment. Red splashed him, laughing, and pretty soon a huge water fight broke out. One of the girls, a particularly cute blonde, paddled over to Itchy and splashed him in the face.

"Gotcha!" she giggled.

Itchy splashed her back, but he couldn't take his eyes off her breasts, which were tantalizingly visible right beneath the surface of the crystal clear water.

They swam and splashed, climbed the rocks and leapt in, and had a great time. Pretty soon Itchy wasn't so obsessed by the girls' nakedness—although he studied them whenever he got the chance.

They finally tired and their skin pruned. He and Red climbed out, shook off the water as best they could, and pulled on their clothes. The friendly teens waved goodbye, and Itchy and Red hiked further down along the creek.

"Fun, huh?" Red said.

"Yeah!"

"Them naked little cuties sure a lot more fun than fishin'." Red's smile faded and he got serious for a moment. "Probably best not to tell your mother we been skinny-dippin' with a bunch of teenagers. Don't know that she'd appreciate it."

"Okay," Itchy answered. He hadn't planned on telling his mom. He knew she'd freak out. It's the kind of thing moms freaked out about.

They spent the rest of the day fishing, without a bite. But the swimming and hiking had been great, and by the time they trudged back to Red's truck Itchy was exhausted—exhausted in that good way, where you're wiped out but it's because you've had such a great time. Itchy drifted off to sleep as they drove back to Tamarack. He dreamt of naked girls and cutthroat trout and riding in the truck with Dad.

It had been one of the best days of Itchy's life.

New troubles soon beset us. Uncle Jacob was giving the finishing touches to a new axle, when the chisel he was using slipped from his grasp, and its keen edge struck and made a serious wound across the back of father's hand. The crippled hand was carefully dressed, and to quiet uncle's fears father made light of the accident, declaring we had weightier matters for consideration than cuts and bruises. The consequences of that accident, however, were far more wide-reaching than could have been anticipated.

Eliza Donner
October 27, 1846

Chapter Ten

Chirping birds awakened Itchy at four in the morning, and no matter how hard he tried, he couldn't get back to sleep.

But it wasn't the birds that kept him awake. It was the hollow-stomach excitement of the day ahead. Today was the Fourth of July, and in a few short hours the Tamarack Logger Days celebration would begin. Today would be the day that the proud and glorious Donner family would finally show everybody in Tamarack their superiority—or so Itchy hoped.

Red's boot camp training continued right up until yesterday, and Itchy had finally reached the point where he could occasionally knock his dad off the log. He'd learned that if he managed to get Red off-balance with a flurry of alternating pillow *whomps* on the side of the head—rather than brute strength—he could get him to fall. And that's what he'd need to do to beat Jason Bent. Since Jason was a whole lot smaller than Red, it seemed to Itchy that he ought to be able to win. That was the theory, anyway.

Itchy got up as soon as dim light filtered through his window, and he hungrily devoured two heaping bowls of corn flakes and Wheat Chex. His mom wouldn't buy decent cereal, like Cocoa Puffs or Froot Loops, so Itchy had to be

224

satisfied with bland, boring, non-sugared junk. It really bugged him that his mom cared so much about health. Good thing he had Mart and Dad to sneak him real food once in a while.

Irene straggled out to the kitchen a short time later, still in her sack-like nightgown, rubbing sleep out of her eyes and yawning. Itchy looked at her and giggled.

"What?" she mumbled as she tried to get the coffee maker going.

"You have pillow head."

"Hmmm...." she said. "Looks pretty, huh?"

Itchy just pointed and laughed. She managed to start the coffee, then she quickly turned and grabbed him. "I've got morning breath, too. Want some?"

"Gross! Lemme go!" He squirmed out of her grasp.

"Teach you to make fun of me."

"When are we going?"

"Where?"

"To Logger Days!"

"It doesn't start till eleven."

"But we should get there early. Dad said we need to get together ahead of time for his pep-talk."

"I can hardly wait. I wonder how many times he'll use the f-word?"

"Hurry up and get ready!"

"It's only six-thirty, Itchy. Relax. Go outside and practice or something."

"Mom! It's important. We can't be late."

Irene looked at Itchy. Maybe it was her imagination, but lately he seemed bigger and stronger. All of Red's outdoor training sessions had given Itchy's skin a nice, healthy tan, and the blotchy psoriasis had almost completely disap-peared. He'd probably never be handsome, but Itchy was slowly blooming, she thought. Before too long his voice would drop, the whiskers would appear, and he'd be on his way. She'd have a man in the house. Amazing.

"Why are you staring at me?" he asked.

"Nothing. I just feel old."

"Grown-ups never make any sense," Itchy sighed. Itchy swore to himself he'd never be like them.

Irene reached over and wiped a milk dribble off of his chin. "No matter how you do today," she told him, "I want you to know I'm really proud of you. Of the way you and your dad have gotten ready for this. Just remember, it's all in fun, okay? Win or lose."

"But we're gonna win!"

"Okay, Itchy."

"So when are we going?"

"Ten-thirty."

"What if we're late?"

"It's not like there's gonna be gridlock. This isn't Seattle."

Itchy gave her a mopey frown, but if she noticed she didn't say anything. "I'm gonna go see if Mart and Dad are ready yet."

"I'm sure they'll be thrilled to see you."

Itchy clomped out the front door. "See you later!"

"Don't eat any junk food!" Irene warned, but he pretended not to hear.

Irene poured a cup of coffee and sipped it. Everything felt right for once. Itchy was growing up and out of the things that had worried her so much—his itchy skin and scrawniness—and Red was turning into a good father.

She went into her bedroom and pulled off the nightgown. She stood, clad only in panties, and studied herself in the mirror. Not bad, she thought. A little pooch, but nothing serious. Most women her age with kids were much flabbier, so she was way ahead of the game. She held her arms up and flexed. Nice biceps, no saggy arm skin. She hated saggy arms. Her boobs still looked perky, but that was the beauty of A-cups. She might be puny, but she'd never have to deal with "big old dangling jugs," as Jacqueline so delicately put it. And her skin still looked young. That was important. No blotches or leathery wrinkles. All-in-all, Irene Donner was looking good.

Only one problem: she didn't have anybody to look good for.

She sat down on the edge of her bed with a sad sigh. The loneliness was an ache she couldn't ignore. Jacqueline was right, she'd been like a nun the last eleven years. It wasn't normal. She'd acted like a martyr, ignoring herself for the good of Itchy. It was time to think about Irene Donner for a change. She needed someone of her own.

Another man....

Red.

No. No way. It'd be a disaster. There I go again, she thought. Blasting away a perfectly nice day with dumb thoughts.

Red.

It all came back to Red, no matter what she did.

And then another thought showed up, uninvited and unwelcome. Father Ray. She'd probably see him today. Great, wonderful. *Adios*, good feelings. She took a deep, cleansing breath. She'd read somewhere that people don't deep-breathe enough. Maybe that'd help. She took another, then another.

All it did was make her lightheaded.

Whatever, she thought. This is stupid. Just take life as it comes and live.

She showered and felt better.

As she got dressed, though, one thought, one word, kept popping up like a refrain:

Red.

Father Ray's misery had reached the point where suicide thoughts bounced around inside his head.

Extreme, the ultimate sin, the worst way to cut yourself off from God, but who gives a shit because there is no God and no heaven and no hell, just nothing. That's the way Father Ray felt. Now. Since....

The kiss.

The stupid, fucking kiss. Could he have been a bigger idiot, could he possibly have made a bigger ass out of himself? Nope. Not possible.

That night after he'd—what to call it? It wasn't really a kiss, he decided, it was more of an assault—he sped off into the night. He drove for hours, down out of the mountains, raced through the rolling wheat fields, through small farm towns, he drove and drove, the MG screaming as he pushed it to its limits, and finally, when he was too exhausted and sore to go any farther, he stopped. He'd gotten as far as the Snake River when he pulled off the road into a gravel overlook. Dawn smudged the eastern horizon, and he gazed at the river, far below, a black ribbon winding through basalt cliffs. He could end it so easily, he thought, pull a *Thelma and Louise*, floor the MG and fly off into the sky, he should've, but—

As with all things Father Ray, he didn't have the guts. If he'd quit being a priest, if he'd pursued Irene Donner like a normal man, then, *then* he might've had a chance with her. But to grab her, to lie, to make up a bogus reason to be alone with her...he was like a sick, fucking predator.

Father Ray sat at the overlook for most of the next day. He slept awhile, got out and peed, and finally left when hunger and thirst overwhelmed guilt. He slowly drove back to Tamarack, dead inside. Should've been dead, period. But no, he didn't have the guts for that.

He fell back into the rhythms of being Mr. Backwater Small Town Parish Priest. Irene showed up the following Sunday as usual, with Itchy and Jacqueline, but she wouldn't look at him. When she came to communion, she got in the other line and took the host from Leonard, the lay minister. She didn't smile at any of Father Ray's lame jokes, and after mass she vanished without so much as a glance.

He toyed with the idea of some sort of apology, maybe a note or phone call. But he didn't know what to say, and he didn't know that anything he said could fix the mess he'd made. At least before, his unrequited love provided some fantasy value, a hopeless hope that someday he'd be with Irene Donner. Now he'd never have a chance.

So Father Ray stewed, wishing he had the balls to kill himself. But as a true, world-class weakling, he knew he'd never do the right thing. He'd just bumble along, fuck up, and ruin his life. He'd quit eventually, because his weakness and lack of faith would become too obvious. Somebody (the bishop, would he ever notice?) would push him out for his own—and the church's—good. Until then, though, Father Ray was content to just exist in a hazy fog of guilt.

The thing that puzzled Father Ray at first was why his anger burned so hot toward Red Donner. The loudmouth hadn't really done anything, but then Father Ray decided that Red's reappearance had forced his hand, made him take the ill-fated lunge for Irene. Yeah, this whole mess wasn't really Father Ray's fault. It was that fucker Red Donner.

Asshole.

Father Ray smiled to himself. What a crock. Red Donner had nothing to do with his troubles.

But what the hell. He'd blame him anyway.

"You're fuckin' toast," Stan the Man said to Mart.

Mart was reading the sports page and shot back an obligatory, "Loser," with a smile.

"Fags."

Mart set the paper down. Stan the Man was really fired up. His brand new wifebeater T-shirt showed off his bulging biceps and tattoos, and even Mart had to admit that with the shirt and glowering thousand-yard stare, Stan the Man looked pretty intimidating. "If I didn't know you were such a wuss I'd be worried, Stan. But you spend so much time between Jacqueline's legs you got no stamina. Me 'n' Red gonna smear you and Sonny."

"No way. Prepare to have your ass whipped, weenie." And with that Stan the Man took off for Jacqueline's. He told Mart that Jacqueline wanted a quickie before the games began. Mart just shook his head disgustedly; Stan the Man was a good guy, but he didn't deserve *that* much sex. Some things just weren't fair.

The phone rang and Mart wheeled over to answer it.

"Hi," Irene said.

"Hey. You ready for the big day?"

"I guess. Itchy's bouncing off the walls. He'll probably be coming by your place to drive you crazy. But better you than me."

"I'll feed him good if I see him."

"Don't you dare!"

"Yeah, something with lots of fat and sugar. Maybe I'll just let him have a bowl of lard covered with syrup."

"Between you and Red I'll never get him back."

"Somebody's got to teach him how to be a disgusting pig. You weren't doing a good job."

"You sound like Red. You've been around him too much."

"He rubs off on you," Mart said. He didn't know if he liked being compared to Red. Actually, he was *sure* he didn't like it.

"I'm glad you guys are working things out," Irene said.

"Yeah. We're okay."

A long awkward silence opened between them. They'd entered the Red zone, and going there always caused discomfort.

Irene finally said, "I just called to wish you good luck."

"Thanks. You too. Red's psycho about winning. It's just more of a fun thing for me," Mart lied.

A *bang* sounded at the front door, followed by Itchy's nasally voice. "Hey Mart! You home?"

Irene laughed, "Sounds like you've got company. Don't say I didn't warn you. Make him leave if he's too much of a pest."

"Itchy's the coolest. We'll bond. We can spend hours making fun of you."

"Hey!"

"See you. Gotta go." Mart hung up smiling. A phone call from Irene made his day.

"Hey Mart!" Itchy yelled.

"C'mon in, Itch."

Itchy stomped in, grinning and out of breath. "Are you ready yet?"

"Almost Itch. You hungry?"

"Yeah!"

"Stan the Man bought a couple of cans of Beefaroni last week. It's kinda early, but are you up for some?"

"Sure!"

Mart rolled into the kitchen followed closely by Itchy. "Your old man's coming by to pick me up later. Wanna wait around for him?"

"I was gonna go to his house, but if you've got food...."

Mart smiled. The perpetually hungry kid cracked him up.

Every Fourth of July A. Jackson presided over Logger Days like a benevolent king, but this year would be different. He knew it would be the last. Sometime this summer, maybe late August, he'd announce the closure of the Tamarack Logging and Milling Company. A proud, century-plus-old company—and its town—would wither away. And A. Jackson couldn't do a thing about it.

As always on the morning of the Fourth, A. Jackson strolled through Tamarack City Park inspecting the Logger Days setup. Logger Days was a reflection of the Flynn family, and this year—especially this year—he wanted everything perfect.

"You ready to roll, Pencil?" he asked as a sweaty and panting Pencil Pandola lugged kegs to the beer booth.

"You bet, A.J. Gonna be a scorcher."

A. Jackson wandered on. A statue of old Patrick Flynn stood in the center of the shady park, and A. Jackson had made sure to have all the birdshit sprayed off of old Patrick's bronze shoulders. Dignity mattered.

A. Jackson sat down on a bench and watched as the park came to life. Logging truck drivers, eager to show off their newly polished rigs, carefully pulled into the equipment display area and parked next to a couple of huge skidders. Some old-time chainsaws were sitting on display on enormous split logs. The tug-o-war area that would pit Protestants vs. Catholics was ready. The dunk tank—A. Jackson would probably give in this year and be a target, even though it was undignified   was being filled up by volunteer high schoolers. Kids from the Junior Loggers Club set up the timber sports competition areas: the double-buck logs, the axe-throw, Jack 'n' Jill race, the Bull and Bullette and Wimp o' the Woods log. Pastor Earle's bunch had the "If You Died Today Would You Go to Heaven?" booth set up, complete with aborted fetus pictures and ominous scripture quotations.

A. Jackson watched and tried to fight off the sadness. His town would soon be gone. Tamarack, Idaho would be a museum, a ghost town, a deserted relic of a forgotten past.

And what would he do? Maybe open a tiny mill someplace, or run his own gyppo outfit. Who knew? He wasn't as hardcore as the lifer loggers, the Red Donner-type of guys who'd die if they weren't cutting trees, but A. Jackson still had the timber life in his blood. He'd find something.

White smoke puffed from the barbecues as they fired up and curled lazily into the trees. A. Jackson breathed deeply of the old familiar smell. Summer smoke, the promise of good times and heat, charred burgers and hot dogs, laughter, too much beer and sunburned foreheads, fireworks...Logger Days.

Tamarack. His town.

Forget about the future for a few hours, he thought. Just enjoy today.

"LET'S KICK SOME ASS!" Red shouted from his pick-up as he rolled up to Mart's place.

Itchy, led by his giant feet, charged out with his skinny arms waving wildly. "Yeah, kick some ass!" he shouted, but the intimidating fury lost something with Itchy's squeaky voice.

"Don't let your momma hear you say that," Red grinned. Mart rolled out, and Red helped him into the truck and put his chair in the back.

"Ready, Mar-teen?"

"Itchy's got me pumped," Mart said. "He's been here for hours."

"Good. Eye of the tiger, Itch."

"We're gonna kick some ass!" Itchy cried.

They drove to the park, Itchy chattering the whole way. For the first time that Mart could remember, though, Itchy didn't once mention the Donner Party.

Jacqueline and Irene were already there when they arrived, working on their first hot dogs of the day. Irene made an exception to her anti-junk food rule for Logger Days; it was the one day of the year when she'd happily gorge on anything deep-fried, barbecued or heavily sugared.

"Hey ladies, don't you look good," Red said after he and Mart found them by Pencil's beer booth. "Don't be eatin' too much now, Irene. Don't want you hurling it all up while we're winnin' the Jack 'n' Jill."

Irene didn't say anything because her mouth was too full. Jacqueline had troweled on the makeup that morning, and she'd had Irene put fresh highlights in her hair. To Jacqueline, good grooming was the most important part of being at any public event.

"You look like you're goin' to the prom, J.W.," Red told her. "Don't plan on sweatin' much, do you?"

"A little hygiene wouldn't kill you," Jacqueline sniffed. Stan the Man wandered over with two cups of beer. "Take Stanley, here. He knows that women like cleanliness."

"That's just 'cause he's whipped," Red said.

"Here you go, hon," Stan the Man said as he handed Jacqueline her beer.

"'Hon'?" Red said.

"Stanley knows how to treat a woman. You oughta take lessons."

"Where's Itchy?" Irene asked.

Red pointed across the park. "He seen his little girlfriend when we got here and took off after her like she was in heat."

Stan the Man frowned. "Itchy's got a girlfriend?"

"Yep. A. Jackson's little squirt." Red gave Stan the Man a wink and an elbow in the ribs. "But don't worry. I gave him a rubber just in case."

The hot dog suddenly didn't feel so good in Irene's stomach. "That's not funny."

Red threw an arm around her shoulder. "Oh, c'mon, I'm just goofin'. Don't go gettin' all offended."

"We're used to it," Jacqueline said.

"I'm starvin', want another dog?" Red asked Irene.

She shook her head. Red headed off in search of food, and Jacqueline and Stan the Man wandered away to browse the craft booths.

"Buy you a beer?" Irene asked Mart.

"Sure."

They sat together and sipped their beers, watching visitors fill the park. Lots of locals wore "Earth First—We'll log the rest of the planets later" T-shirts. A country-western band fired up in the gazebo, and the cheatin'-heart twang echoed through the valley.

Red strolled back a little later, happily stuffing a hotdog into his mouth. He smiled at Mart and said, "Blrrrnpfrodfgdrfo."

"No thanks," Mart answered, assuming Red had offered something. Red plopped on the bench next to Irene. Mart felt like a third wheel, so he took off. "I'm gonna go check out the action."

"Don't be late for the double-buck!" Red said, spitting out flecky bun chunks. Mart waved and rolled into the crowd. Red contentedly inhaled his second hotdog, and Irene sipped her beer. Red looked over at her. "Nice when we don't feel like we gotta talk all the time, huh? Like bein' married again."

"Silence is always good when you're around," she smiled.

"Damn, you're feisty. Channel some of that estrogen rage into the double-buck."

Father Ray wandered by, nibbling on a cotton candy. He glanced at Irene and then quickly averted his eyes. Red watched him for a moment and said, "Can't say as I care for that priest."

Irene tossed out the rest of her beer. The hot dog had really turned against her now; it sat like a brick in her stomach. "Why?" she asked. How come everybody else could see the guy was a loser and she was so blind?

"Just a feelin'. He's shifty. Don't strike me as very holy. 'Course, aren't very many of them who are, in my opinion. Plus, I seen the way he stares at you, all moony. Like he's got a case of lovesickness."

Irene sat silently for a moment, and then some strange compulsion made her blurt, "He...kissed me."

Red nodded, seemingly unperturbed. "Is that so?" He scratched his beard as if deep in thought. "You kiss him back?"

"No!"

"He just swoop in and do the old kiss 'n' run?"

"Basically," Irene said miserably. "It was that night he dropped by for no reason."

"Sounds to me like he had a reason, all right."

"You know what I mean."

"Want me to kick his ass? I'll stand up for you if you'd like."

"No!"

Red chuckled. "Yeah, didn't figure you'd let me protect your virtue. Can't blame him for wantin' to kiss you, but I don't much care for his technique. You gonna rat him out to the bigshots?"

"I don't think so."

"You should. He might pull that shit on somebody not as strong as you and cause all kinds of hell. Your choice, though."

"Maybe. I don't know. I'd rather just forget about it."

"Want somethin' else? 'Nother beer, nachos?" Red asked. He was his usual conversational self, as if Irene hadn't just confided her big, deep, dark secret. His calm amazed her sometimes.

"No thanks." Irene paused. "It's nice being able to talk to you about things."

Red shrugged and yawned. "Yeah, well, fuck-ups like me, we done every stupid thing there is to do, so we end up soundin' like we got wisdom. Besides, I told you before, I owe you. If a dumb bullshitter like me listenin' makes you feel better, great."

She studied his profile as he gazed impassively at the passers-by and tapped his fingers to the beat of the country music. If she didn't already know his goofball good nature, he'd probably terrify her. Set him on a Harley hog with a leather jacket and he'd blend right in with any scary meth-addled felon biker on the road.

Itchy ran up with Sara, both carrying little fishbowls with sad-looking, raggedy goldfish swaying listlessly in the cloudy water. "Look what we won!" Itchy said.

"Ain't really big enough to filet out," Red said. "More appetizer size, don't you think, Irene?"

"They're not to eat!" Sara said, horrified.

"You mean them little things is 'sposed to be pets?"

"Well, yeah!"

"He's just messing with you, Sara," Itchy told her. "That's the way my dad is."

Red grinned at Sara. "Itch has his old man pegged, that's for sure. You two ain't been off smoochin' somewhere, have you?"

Itchy flared crimson, but Sara threw Red's jokester's grin right back at him. "Maybe," she said. "But I won't tell."

"Well now," Red laughed. "Watch out for this one, Itchy. She's trouble. Gonna be a heart-breaker."

A. Jackson's voice rumbled over the loudspeakers after the band finished *Jesus and Momma Always Loved Me*. "It's time for the first event of this year's Logger Days! We need the Jack 'n' Jill double buck teams at the competition site!"

"That's us." Red grabbed Irene's hand and pulled her to her feet. "Your momma and daddy gonna compete?" he asked Sara.

Sara's expression darkened. "No. My mom couldn't make it this year. She's...busy."

"Sorry to hear that. C'mon then, cheer us on."

"Okay!" Sara said. She and Itchy—and their dying goldfish—followed along after Red and Irene.

A big crowd had gathered at the roped-off event area, and Red and Irene joined the five other Jack 'n' Jill teams.

"Here, hold him," Itchy said to Sara as he handed her his goldfish. "I have to lube their saw."

"Really?" Sara said with awe, as if spraying WD-40 was a magnificent honor.

Jacqueline and Stan the Man waited with the other pairs. Jacqueline waved to friends in the crowd and grinned like a Rose Parade queen. Stan the Man twitched nervously.

"You're lookin' a little peaked there, Stanley," Red said.

"Just worry about yourself."

Red leaned close and whispered, "J.W. gonna cut off your booty calls if you lose?"

"Fuck you, Red," Stan the Man glared.

"Puts a lot of pressure on a young man," Red continued. "Old bastard like me, don't matter 'cause I ain't gettin' any to begin with. But you, wouldn't wanna be in your boots."

"What kind of bullshit is he fillin' your head with, Stanley?" Jacqueline demanded.

"Just wishin' him good luck, J.W.," Red smiled sweetly. "Hope you don't break a nail or nothin'."

"Would you please shut him up?" Jacqueline said to Irene.

"Nothing I can do about him, Mom. The best way to quiet him down would be to win. But that's not going to happen," she added with a sugary-fake smile.

"My own daughter," Jacqueline grumbled. "Don't ever have kids, Stanley. They'll turn against you every time."

Stan the Man grunted but he wasn't listening. He was too busy stretching and rubbing his biceps.

"Okay," A. Jackson said, his voice screeching over the speakers' noisy feedback. "Let's get started. First up, Bobby and Joni Bent!"

More of Stan the Man's seemingly endless supply of cousins, Bobby and Joni took after the log like it was going to kill them, they grunted and groaned and sliced off the cookie in twenty-eight seconds. The crowd cheered, but Red leaned over to Irene and said, "Won't finish in the top three."

The next two teams went, and the best time was 25.8. Then it was Stan the Man and Jacqueline's turn. Itchy was also their official lube man, and as they took their spots on either side of the log Itchy leaned in close with the spray can in one hand and the wedge in the other.

"Keep that thing slippery, darlin'," Jacqueline told him. "We'll do the rest."

"Okay, Gramma."

Stan the Man took a nervous deep breath. Jacqueline told him, "Relax, Stanley, you tighten up too much it'll slow us down. I don't wanna have to do *all* the work."

A. Jackson hovered nearby. "Contestants ready?" he asked. They nodded. "Timer ready?" Pastor Earle, the official timekeeper, nodded. A. Jackson said, "One, two...Go!"

Wood chips instantly flew, Itchy sprayed the blade, the crowd cheered, Jacqueline suddenly became the Terminator Log-sawing Gramma, grimly determined, leading the team, Stan the Man was only along for the ride, Itchy sprayed, once the saw was deep in the log Itchy slammed the wedge into the kerf to keep the slot open—

"Jesus...." Red said. "Your momma's a goddamn beast. I never knew she was so fuckin' strong."

"Neither did I," Irene said, amazed. They watched Jacqueline and Stan the Man slice through the log like it was butter. The cookie hit the ground, Stan the Man dropped his end of the saw, Jacqueline's grim competitor's game face became a huge smile.

"New leaders," A. Jackson announced. "Jacqueline Weatherly and Stan Bent, 23.8 seconds!" A wild cheer from the crowd, and Jacqueline demurely bowed.

Stan the Man fist-pumped and pointed at Red. "Beat that!" he taunted.

"I plan to, Stanley," Red said, suddenly sounding less sure of himself.

Jacqueline hugged Itchy. "Good job, honey. Couldn't have done it without you."

"Thanks, Gramma."

"Remember, now, if by some chance you don't oil up your momma's blade quite so good I might treat you to a new Donner book or something."

"Gramma!" Itchy said, horrified.

"Just kiddin'."

The next two teams didn't come close to Jacqueline and Stan the Man's time, so it was up to Red and Irene.

"Last up, Red and Irene Donner," A. Jackson announced. Mart rolled to the front of the crowd to see. Father Ray watched all by himself from way in the back.

"Give us as good as you give your gramma and Stanley, Itch."

"You bet, Dad," Itchy said, taking up his position.

The second A. Jackson said, "Go!" the teeth bit into the wood, chips flew,

Itchy sprayed, and Red and Irene, their movements automatic, rhythmically sawed back and forth, Itchy screamed, "GOGOGO!" as he sprayed the blade, he popped the wedge into the kerf, Red gasped and the cut deepened, deeper, almost through, the cookie dropped—

"Twenty-four seconds!" A. Jackson announced. "Close but not quite good enough, Red. Ladies and gentlemen, Jacqueline Weatherly and Stan Bent are the new Tamarack Logger Days Jack 'n' Jill double buck champions!"

Stan the Man hugged Jacqueline and lifted her off her feet while she hooted and hollered.

"We gave it a good shot," Red said, chest heaving. "Two-tenths of a second, shit, that ain't off by much."

Itchy clumsily patted Irene on the back. "It's okay, Mom," he said. "Maybe because Gramma's so old she was destined to win or something."

"Make sure you tell her that," Irene smiled, hunched over to catch her breath.

"Are you disappointed?" Itchy asked. He worried that his mom would feel bad about herself. All the years of being kicked around had left him exquisitely aware of other people's feelings.

"No," she said. "It was fun. And we couldn't have done it without you," she added, doing her part to pump up *his* self-esteem.

"I really thought you'd win," Itchy said. "I mean, I'm glad for Gramma and Stan, but I feel bad for you guys."

"They just beat us, Itch," Red told him. "Happens. Part of life. Good thing is there's still more events to go."

Jacqueline and Stan the Man walked over; Jacqueline clutched their cheap trophy triumphantly. "The sexy old lady's still got some tricks up her sleeve, huh?" Jacqueline said.

"Congrats, J.W. Always knew you were a tough old broad. Just didn't realize how tough," Red said.

"Got an announcement," Jacqueline said as she fired up a cigarette. "You wanna tell 'em Stanley?"

Stan the Man shrugged and shuffled. He stared at the ground and mumbled something unintelligible.

"Oh for God's sake," Jacqueline said. "Stanley's a little shy. Anyhoo, I told him that if we won this thing, I'd give in and let him marry me."

Nobody said anything; there was too much shock in the air. Sara had wandered back and she stood with Itchy. One of the goldfish floated belly up in the bowl. She handed that one to Itchy and smiled ruefully.

It took Irene a moment to shake off the shock, then she grinned. "Well...that's great, Mom. And Stan, congratulations."

Stan the Man blushed and shrugged sheepishly. Surprisingly, Red didn't mouth off; he just smiled and shook Stan the Man's hand, then he hugged Jacqueline.

Itchy frowned and looked up at Stan the Man. "Does that mean I get to call you 'Grandpa'?"

Stan the Man ripped off his sunglasses and blinked in a wild panic. "No! It's okay, Itchy. I'm just Stan. Forever. You know?"

"Okay," Itchy said. He didn't understand why Stan the Man got so upset. Everybody else was laughing, and Itchy felt kind of bad that he'd brought it up.

"How you feel 'bout havin' a new step-daddy?" Red asked Irene.

"Um, great."

"All right, you had enough fun at our expense," Jacqueline said. "Remember who kicked your butts in the double-buck."

"You just marryin' her so you can get them senior citizen discounts, Stanley?" Red asked. "You'll like earlybird dinners."

"C'mon, Stanley," Jacqueline said. "We won't get any respect from these clowns."

They wandered off, hand in hand, like a couple of high-schoolers in love.

"Cute, ain't they?" Red said.

Irene watched them. "It won't really change much. They were already basically married anyway. I'm glad for her."

"Makes me kinda sad," Red said.

"How come?" Itchy asked.

"Well Itch, seein' them makes me realize somethin'. You're young, so you don't know it yet, but people, we got the need to pair off. Just like the ducks and geese do, the whole mate-for-life thing. What we all want is for somebody to be in our life forever. Huh, Irene?"

She nodded but didn't say anything. Mart watched her closely.

"I think I know what you mean," Itchy said. He looked down at his dead goldfish. Sara stood close, their shoulders touching. Itchy usually didn't like people getting too close to him, but with Sara it was different. Her touch felt good. "Tamsen Donner knew that," Itchy continued. "She wouldn't leave George, even though she knew he was gonna die and she could've been rescued. It's like that, huh?"

"Yep," Red said. "You hook up with somebody, you decide they're more important than you are. Look at Stanley. He's a goof, but he'd take a bullet for your gramma."

"But it doesn't always work out that way, does it Red?" Irene said quietly.

Red sighed. "Not always. No." The little group went silent as the crowd swirled around them. Red nibbled at his lip, deep in thought.

Mart watched Irene. She looked awfully sad. "Jeez," Mart said. "You guys are depressing. We're up in ten minutes, Red. You gonna stop moping about existence and go kick some ass?"

Red brightened. "I believe you're right, Mar-teen. That's the attitude. We'll ponder the meaning of life some other time. Let's whup those mofo's!" He high-fived Mart and they headed off back into the double-buck area. "C'mon, Itch. One more lube job for you. This time I'll make you proud."

Itchy handed his dead goldfish to Sara. "You can keep him," he told her.

Red and Mart were up first since it took a few minutes to get Mart's wheelchair contraption in place. A huge crowd gathered; the men's double-buck was the premiere event, and all the locals wanted to see how Mart would do.

A. Jackson went through a long-winded introduction—too much smarmy stuff about Mart's brave comeback for Mart's taste—but once A. Jackson shut up and Mart had the saw handle in his grasp everything felt right. When they got the signal and started cutting, Mart became a machine, dimly aware of Red on the other side of the log, of Itchy spraying the blade and screaming encouragement, of the crowd's roar. Just a machine, back and forth, stay in rhythm, work with Red, don't fight the log, just cut, saw, slice, one-two-three, not even tired, just cut, cut, cut....

And before he realized it, they were done. Sound came back, cheers, A. Jackson shouted, "Nineteen point one!" Red clapped Mart hard on the back, Itchy bounced up and down, Irene ran over and hugged him.

"Ain't nobody gonna beat *that* fuckin' time!" Red gloated.

And he was right. None of the other teams could break twenty seconds. Stan the Man and Sonny Gould came in third. Mart basked in the glory as he accepted congrats from all his old buddies.

And Irene kissed him—on the cheek, of course. But it was better than nothing.

The best part, though, the thing that changed everything, was something that nobody could ever understand. Because by winning the double-buck, by being out in the world again, Mart realized something important:

He was still alive.

The Catholics scored a quick, decisive victory in the tug-o-war. Pastor Earle's pre-contest prayers went unanswered, although after the loss he and his followers formed a prayer circle to ask almighty Jesus to forgive the Catholics for their antichrist-popish beliefs and deliver them to born-again salvation. Irene and Red sat out the tug-o-war, figuring that it was best to have nothing to do with Father Ray. "I'm still tempted to kick his ass," Red told her. Father Ray suffered nasty rope burns on his hands during the tug-o-war and left Logger Days early to tend his wounds.

The Wimp o' the Woods competition was next, to be followed by the Bull o' the Woods grand finale. Red hadn't placed in the axe throw ("Dumb-ass event," he snorted. "Ain't no reason to be throwin' axes in the woods unless you're a fuckin' Indian tryin' to kill somebody."), and he hadn't entered the pole climb, chopping or chainsaw contests. He wanted to save his energy for the Bull o' the Woods.

Itchy nervously waited his turn on the log. The Wimp contest was single elimination, and the kids drew numbers for their turns. Itchy was number seven out of seven. "Great draw, Itch," Red told him. "That way the weaklings are out of your way. Don't have to waste a bunch of energy smacking pansies off the log. You end up at the finish, and you win big. Couldn't ask for more." Itchy had his doubts. He wasn't so sure that *he* wasn't one of the pansies his dad made fun of.

Sara stood with him as they watched the early rounds. Jason Bent had drawn number two, and he easily dispatched every poor kid who came up—as expected. A. Jackson made the kids wear boxer's headgear, even though they only smacked each other with floppy pillows, because two years ago Spencer Weatherly—a distant cousin of Itchy's—had chipped a tooth when he got knocked off the log and Spencer's mom demanded that A. Jackson pay to fix it. That pissed A. Jackson off, so ever since he made the parents sign waivers and forced the kids to wear headgear. You never could be too careful in the liability-mad U.S. of A., A. Jackson decided.

"You can beat Jason," Sara said as Jason walloped another victim into the sawdust pit beneath the log. "He's not so tough."

"I guess," Itchy said. All the months of Red's training had helped his confidence, but watching Jason—he seemed so big and strong—scared Itchy. Jason was mean. Mean helped a lot in things like this.

Red wandered over with Irene and rubbed Itchy's shoulders. "You're almost up, buddy. Ready to take him out?"

Itchy nodded but said nothing. His stomach flip-flopped like something big inside was trying to get out.

"Don't be scared, sweetie," Irene said. "You'll do fine. Remember, it's just for fun."

Trevor Duncan, Jason's latest victim, didn't appear to be having all that much fun. As he pulled off his headgear, he cried big, snotty tears. Jason towered above him on the log, sneering down disdainfully.

"Trevor's a baby," Sara told Itchy. "You'll do okay."

Itchy nodded. Now the doubtful regrets started. Why in the world had he let his dad talk him into this? He was happy spending all his time doing Donner research...he should've stuck with that. That's what he was good at, not this athletic stuff, not fighting, not trying to be mean and aggressive. He'd made a terrible mistake. Now he was about to be publicly humiliated by a bully who hated him. What had he been thinking?

"I don't think I want to do this," Itchy said.

"Hey now, don't be gettin' cold feet," Red warned, a hint of threat in his voice. "You're ready, Itch. You can take this kid. Shit, you've knocked my fat ass off the log, you think this little bastard's tougher than me?"

"No," Itchy said. The telltale heat crept up his neck. He'd be blushing red-hot shame in a few seconds.

"Good," Red said. "Don't never be afraid of another human being. Nobody's better than you are. Nobody."

"You don't have to do it if you don't want to, honey," Irene said. Red shot her a silent glare.

Strangely, his mom's giving him permission to quit blew Itchy's doubts away. *Of course* he'd compete, and he'd beat stupid Jason Bent, too. He glanced at Sara, then his mom.

"I'm gonna win," Itchy said with steely determination.

Red nodded proudly. "Now that's the spirit. No quit in my boy."

They watched Jason finish off another sacrificial victim, and then it was Itchy's turn. Red helped Itchy pull on the headgear, still wet with previous contestants' tears and sweat, and handed him his battle pillow. "Feel good? Got the eye of the tiger?"

Itchy nodded. "Yep."

Red leaned in close and whispered. "Kick his ass, Itch. Whup the little fuck. You know you can do it."

"Okay."

"Ready, Itchy?" A. Jackson asked.

"Uh-huh."

"Climb on up, then."

Itchy hopped onto the log and faced Jason. Jason said nothing, he just gave Itchy a smirky sneer, one that Itchy had seen a million times—usually right before Jason beat him up or made fun of the Donner Party.

"Remember, guys," A. Jackson told them, "keep it clean, no hitting below the belt, and you can't touch each other with anything other than the pillow. Got it?"

"Yessir," Jason said.

"Okay," Itchy nodded.

Itchy looked around. He was used to balancing on a log—all the practice sessions with his dad had prepared him for that feeling—but being in front of a crowd, that bothered him. He'd gone through his short life trying to remain invisible, and now all these people were staring at him. It felt weird.

"Good luck!" Sara called out. Itchy smiled at her. His mom watched with a forced, worried grin, and Red gave him a big double thumbs-up. Mart clapped, and Jacqueline and Stan the Man cheered him on. Stan the Man told Jacqueline that he felt a little guilty rooting against his own blood, but she warned him he'd better be on Itchy's side or she'd call off the wedding.

Itchy turned back to Jason. The Wimp o' the Woods pillow fight final match was about to begin.

A. Jackson called out, "Go!"

Itchy wasn't ready when Jason charged. Red never came at him that fast, he usually let Itchy be the aggressor. Before Itchy could react, Jason was pummeling his head. Itchy flinched and crouched.

"Fight back!" Red shouted.

Jason smacked at Itchy, and staying low was the only thing that kept Itchy on the log. Jason couldn't get enough pillow momentum to knock him off.

Itchy didn't know what to do. If he stood up Jason would surely win, but he couldn't stay crouched forever. Jason thumped Itchy's head, and even with the headgear Itchy's ears rang and the world spun.

"FIGHT BACK!" Red screamed.

"Go, Itchy!" Sara yelled.

Irene watched, her hand over her mouth. Her little baby was getting beat up in public and she couldn't do a thing about it. She wanted to throw up.

Itchy didn't know what to do, Jason wouldn't stop hitting him, he couldn't move, maybe he should just take a dive into the sawdust pit and get it over with before Jason knocked his head off—

But then....

Jason hesitated. He'd lost his grip on his pillow from thwacking Itchy so hard, and in that moment Itchy acted. He jumped up, and as Jason regripped his pillow, Itchy swung. He caught Jason in the stomach and knocked him backward on the log.

"YEAH, YEAH, YEAH, GO GET HIM!" Red screamed. "EYE OF THE TIGER!"

Now Itchy had the advantage. He swung his pillow hard, smacking Jason in the stomach over and over, just like he did with his dad. He knew that if he could get Jason to think every hit was headed to his stomach he could fool him with a surprise whack to the head and nail him. Jason swung wildly, his pillow *swooshing* harmlessly in front of Itchy's face, and Itchy kept thumping Jason's stomach. Jason gasped, and Itchy gut slammed him so hard that Jason's breath poofed out of him and left him frozen. He stood momentarily helpless before Itchy's onslaught.

Itchy hesitated. He had him. He *had* Jason Bent right where he wanted him. Jason's eyes widened. He knew he was beaten, too. Every slight, every insult, every playground beating...Itchy could get even now. Revenge would be his.

But still he hesitated. Even after all the crap he'd taken from Jason Bent, he felt bad for the guy. Itchy knew what it was like to get whupped, he knew the rotten feeling of being a doormat. Itchy had lots of empathy for the loser's role.

So when he swung as hard as he could at Jason's head, when Jason ducked but not in time, when Itchy's pillow *thunked* satisfyingly against Jason's temple and Jason flew gracefully off the log and dropped, slow motion, into the sawdust pit—Itchy felt sort of bad for the guy.

But not that bad.

The crowd erupted in a deafening roar, hoots and hollers and cheers, Red hopped onto the log, pulled off Itchy's headgear, hoisted Itchy onto his huge shoulders and pranced along the log screaming, "LADIES AND GENTLE-MEN, THE NEW WIMP O' THE WOODS, MR. ITCHY DONNER!"

Itchy fist-pumped and the crowd cheered, Sara jumped up and down and the remaining live goldfish splashed out of the jar and flopped into the grass. He was immediately squashed flat. Irene tried not cry but did anyway, and Itchy....

Itchy savored. He looked down at Jason Bent, far below, he watched as he slowly got up, his dad helping him take off his headgear, and neither of them looked up at Itchy riding triumphantly on Red's shoulders.

Oh, Itchy savored. This was the best. The cheers, his dad proud, his mom crying, his—well, Sara was *kind of* his girlfriend—his girlfriend cheering for him. Life could never get any better than this, unless he somehow got into a time machine and went back to 1846 to be with his Donner Party ancestors.

Red lowered Itchy from his shoulders, and they both hopped to the ground. "Good sport time. Shake his hand, Itchy," Red said, and Itchy reluctantly shook hands with Jason.

"Nice...." Itchy was about to say "Game," but it wasn't really a game. He didn't know what to call it, so he just let "Nice" hang out there all by itself.

Jason didn't answer, but Itchy saw tears glistening in his eyes. Forget about pity, Itchy thought, just remember all the times Jason had messed with him. It worked. Seeing those tears...ah, sweet revenge. Jason shuffled off with his dad.

"Are you okay?" Irene asked as she hugged Itchy.

"I won, Mom. Of course I'm okay."

"He was hitting you pretty hard."

"Can't hurt a little Donner stud, Irene," Red grinned. "He's got a rock hard head, just like his old man."

"Amen to that," Jacqueline said. "Congrats, honey. Way to waste that little shit."

"Mom!" Irene said.

"Nothing wrong with teaching a Bent a thing or two. Ain't that right, Stanley?"

Stan the Man wasn't sure how to take that, so he just said, "Nice going, Itch."

"You da man, Itchy," Mart added.

Itchy had never been the center of adulation before, and he blushed and shuffled and stared at the ground. "Thanks, everybody." He looked up at Red. "Thanks for teaching me how to win, Dad."

Red rubbed Itchy's shoulders. "You won it all by yourself, son," he said, but his voice cracked just a bit. Irene was the only one who noticed it.

"Buy you a chili dog, champ?" Jacqueline asked.

"Sure!"

Sara leaned over to Itchy and gave him a little kiss on the cheek. "Congratulations, Itchy."

Itchy's face glowed bright red. The grown-ups all smiled, although Irene was pretty sure that the tiny flutter in her chest was her heart breaking.

"You know," Jacqueline said, "maybe when me and Stanley tie the knot we could have a double wedding with Itchy and Sara. Whatcha all think?"

Itchy's face burned brighter, and everybody had a good laugh at his and Sara's expense.

Except Irene. She didn't think it was all that funny.

Red was a killing machine.

Every poor sap who came up against him in the Bull o' the Woods competition was quickly eliminated and sent flying to the loser's pit—usually with a single, vicious Red Donner punch. Red possessed an incredibly strong and nasty right hook, and even though they wore headgear, several of Red's victims spat blood and had wiggly teeth after he'd finished with them.

The Bull o' the Woods was contested just like the Wimp o' the Woods— except with boxing gloves instead of pillows. Red mowed through all comers with almost no resistance, and when A. Jackson officially proclaimed him Bull o' the Woods, the applause was tepid. Itchy screamed, "YAY, DAD!" but that was about it.

"Seems you don't have as many fans as Itchy, Red," Jacqueline remarked after Red hopped off the log and joined them.

"Yeah, well. I made it look too easy. Crowds like it when things are close."

Irene said, "Congratulations, Red."

"Thanks. First ever father/son combo winners, at least that's what A.J.

told me. Pretty cool, huh? Next year you and me win the double-buck, Irene, and we'll be the ultimate hard-ass redneck logger family."

The word "family" hit Irene funny, like a mild electric shock. She didn't comment.

They spent the rest of the day wandering among the booths and eating way more garbage food than was wise. Itchy and Sara came and went, but, thankfully, won no more goldfish. Mart tagged along with Red and Irene most of the time. He felt strangely calm, almost as if he wasn't excess baggage. Odd. And when he saw Red shyly take hold of Irene's hand—and Irene not pull it away—Mart wasn't all that bothered. He couldn't figure out why at first. But as the day wore on, he realized something that both cheered and saddened him. Irene was happy again. Mart couldn't blame Red for wanting her back. Mart, of all people, could understand that. And this time, Red seemed to have his act together, he seemed to be doing everything mostly right. He'd become a good father to Itchy, and he treated Irene with respect. As much as Mart wished that Irene was his, seeing that she was happy—really happy—well, how could he complain?

Twilight darkened to night, and they waited for the fireworks to begin. Mart knew it was time to leave them alone. "Think I'll roll on down a little closer for a better view," Mart said. Neither Red nor Irene tried to stop him.

As he pushed away Red said, "Had fun today, Mar-teen."

"It was a good day." He hesitated, and the next word came out clumsily. "Thanks."

"You bet, buddy," Red smiled. Mart rolled away into the darkness. "Think he might finally be comin' outa that bad mood that's been troublin' him," Red told Irene.

"Thanks to you."

"Maybe. Seein' as how I fucked him up in the first place, it's the least I can do."

Irene leaned against Red's shoulder. They sat on a knoll at the back of the park beneath a stand of aspens. They looked out over the Logger Days booths and downtown Tamarack. "I'm glad you came back," she said.

"Me too."

"You'll really stay this time?"

"Not goin' nowhere. Wherever you and Itchy are, so am I." Red put his arm around her shoulders and held her tightly. "Seems like you're finally gettin' used to me hangin' around again."

"You're not quite as disgusting as you used to be."

"You're such a sweet talkin' little thing."

"I'm taking a big chance."

"I won't let you down this time."

The first skyrocket launched with a *pop*, its glittering trail buzzing into the night sky. Red and Irene watched it explode, a glittery flower of red and white. Red leaned over and gently kissed Irene's hair.

She looked up at him, the skyrocket's fading light reflected in his eyes. "I'm not sure—" she whispered.

Red kissed her. Tentative at first, but then they pulled together, tighter, she needed somebody, and Red, he was better now, not the old Red, she wanted him back, and maybe, maybe, she still loved him.

They kissed, more skyrockets exploded, and Red pulled away, laughing, "It's kinda like a movie, huh? Ain't the skyrockets supposed to explode right when you're havin' a big-ass orgasm?"

"Stop it," she laughed. "Only you can make a nice romantic moment gross."

"It's a gift." He paused. "I love you, Irene. Lemme be your old man again. And Itchy's dad."

They kissed. And the skyrockets exploded above....

"Your parents are making out," Sara said.

"I know, I can see it," Itchy snapped. It really bugged him when Sara stated the obvious.

"It's so romantic. Are they going to get married again?"

"I dunno." He watched as his parents kissed under the aspen trees, each new skyrocket lighting them in a strobe flash of different colors.

"It looks like they're having a lot of fun," Sara sighed. "I wish my parents loved each other like that. They don't ever kiss."

Itchy had been hunting for his parents to bum more popcorn money when Sara spotted them kissing. It was sort of okay, Itchy thought. He wanted them to be together, but this seemed a little cheesy to him. Kissing in the park on the Fourth of July. Kind of...high school.

"Itchy?" Sara asked.

"Yeah?"

"Never mind."

"What?"

Sara paused. Then she grabbed Itchy and planted a big kiss on his lips. She started to pull away, but then she went back for more and kept on kissing, even though he squirmed and resisted. Something about the moment, the sultry Fourth of July heat, the skyrockets exploding, seeing Itchy's parents making out...Sara was overwhelmed.

Itchy relaxed, and then he kissed back. This wasn't so bad, he decided. It was more than not so bad. Nice. Really nice. Wimp o' the Woods, Jason Bent defeated, his dad victorious, his parents maybe back together, Sara kissing him—

The best Fourth of July/Logger Days in the history of Tamarack. The world.

Or at least in the life of Itchy Donner.

Mart spotted Itchy and Sara kissing. He grinned. If A. Jackson only knew, he'd go completely apeshit. The thought warmed Mart.

And then, in a skyrocket's momentary flash, he saw Red and Irene locked in a world class romantic clinch. He looked away. *Remember*, he told himself, *all that matters is Irene*. As long as she's happy....

He turned his head to the sky, gazing at the showery embers, flinching as the booms echoed through Tamarack's tight valley, the shuddery, body-shaking *thuds* like an angry summer thunderstorm.

Mart stared into the sky long after the fireworks ended, as the stars popped out in the impossibly clear canopy of the mountain night.

He didn't look Red and Irene's way again.

Up and up we toiled until we reached an altitude of six thousand feet, when the intense cold drive us into camp in Alder Creek Valley. A piercing wind was driving storm clouds toward us, and those who understood the threatening aspect realized that twenty-one persons, eight of them helpless children, were there at the mercy of the pitiless storm-king. The snow was falling faster. It made pictures for Georgia and me upon the branches of big and little trees; it gathered in a ridge beside us; it nestled in piles upon our buffalo robe. Everything was cold, damp, and dreary, until our tired mother built the fire, prepared our supper, and sent us to bed, each with a lump of sugar as comforter.

Eliza Donner

November 4, 1846

Chapter Eleven

Itchy held the thick sheaf of paper in his hands and flipped through its satisfying bulk. He and Sara had written so much, and he was really, really proud of what they'd done so far. It read just as he'd hoped, like Tamsen herself had written it. And who knows, Itchy thought, maybe she had.

Tamsen's Lost Journal

Chapter 10

We're trapped now. A sudden snowstorm buried us, and we had to build shelters next to some big trees by a small creek. We didn't even have time to build cabins. We're just living in huts made out of branches covered with oxhides. I'm so worried about George. He doesn't say much, but I know his hand is bothering him. It's all swollen and ugly-looking, and he feels like he has a fever. I don't know what we'll do. The few animals we have won't live very long, and the ones that have already died are buried in the deep snow. We're not sure we can even find them. We heard the rest of the party is camped down by a large lake a few miles away. We'll never make it down there now, and maybe that's just as good. Everybody

has been arguing for the last few weeks, and the Donner family will be better off if we stay
with our own kin. The children don't understand what a bad state we're in. If we don't get
out of here soon, we'll have nothing to eat. I wish we'd never left Illinois. We were safe there
on our farm. We didn't need to do this. I don't say anything to George, but I think he
knows that I'm mad. I'm afraid I'll never be able to start my school, and all my studies of the
plants along the trail won't matter. Our only hope is that the snow stops and we can escape
over the mountains, or maybe somebody will come and rescue us. I'm very scared. I don't care
about me, but I don't want anything to happen to the children.

Itchy sniffed back tears and rubbed his eyes. This part always choked him up. Sara had written most of it—with a little help from him—and he was starting to wonder if Tamsen was inside Sara somehow, like a ghost that sneaks into your head and takes over. In movies ghosts were usually bad, but in this case being possessed by a nice, great-great-great Gramma ghost was perfect. They were hearing Tamsen's story. That's all Itchy had ever wanted.

"Hey Itch!" Red called out from the living room. "C'mon, *Monday Night Football's* on!"

"Okay, Dad." Since Red had moved in with them, he and Itchy spent a lot of time watching sports. Red had mounted a big TV antenna up in the trees and they got two new fuzzy channels—which meant even more games to watch. Now that fall was here and football season in full swing, Red and Itchy watched every game they could possibly see.

"Hurry up, you'll miss the kickoff!" Red said.

Itchy carefully stacked and straightened the Tamsen manuscript and reverently placed it in his desk drawer. They still had to write the final chapter about how Tamsen died, and Itchy didn't know how to approach it. Sara wanted to make it lurid like a TV show, with Keseberg chasing Tamsen down in the snow, hacking her up, and eating her. Itchy thought it might be best to go with the theory that Tamsen accidentally fell into a stream and froze. It was a tough call, though, because Sara could be awfully persuasive. And since Tamsen seemed to be talking through her, maybe they should go the way she wanted. He wasn't sure. He'd ask his dad—he had opinions on everything.

He went out into the living room. Red sprawled on the saggy couch, crunching noisily on pizza-flavored Pringles. With Red spending lots of quality time on the couch it had sagged to the point that nobody else dared sit on it anymore. Its squashed springs and cushions had become carnivorous and would swallow up unsuspecting victims.

Irene sat at the dining room table, scribbling on her bank statement and tapping on a calculator. Since Red had come back they'd pooled resources, but Red had a bad habit of writing checks and not telling her, so trying to balance the checking account was an impossible, irritating chore.

"Who's playing?" Itchy asked.

"Saints and the Steelers. Gonna be a good one."

"Oh. Hey, Dad?"

"Yeah?"

"Do you think that Tamsen got murdered by Keseberg?"

"Dunno Itch. You're the expert."

"Yeah. I just wondered what you thought."

Red stared at a Budweiser commercial on the tube. "Well, the way I see it, it don't much matter."

"Why?"

"You always said she wasn't goin' nowhere since her hubby was dyin', right?"

"Yeah."

"Well, she was toast no matter what happened. So if ol' Keseberg offed her, he did her a favor. If he didn't, well, then she just suffered longer. Either way, she was dead."

Itchy didn't like how harsh that sounded, even though it was true. "But it's worse to be murdered than to just die, isn't it?"

"Dead is dead. Myself, if I had to make the choice between starvin' and freezin' or havin' somebody whack me, I think I'd take the whackin', myself."

"Hmmm," Itchy nodded. He had a point. Maybe Sara was right, too. The only thing that bothered Itchy, though, was that Keseberg had sworn to Eliza Donner thirty years later that he didn't kill Tamsen, and Eliza believed him. She forgave him for whatever he might've done, and if Eliza could find it in her heart to forgive him, maybe Itchy shouldn't accuse the guy of being a crazed killer.

He'd have to think about it. But not for too long, since they had to hurry up and quickly finish *Tamsen's Lost Journal.*

Because Sara was moving away.

At the beginning of September, A. Jackson Flynn announced that the Tamarack Logging and Milling Company would close after the first of the year. He blamed the usual suspects—enviros, the feds, subsidized foreign logs—as he tearfully told a solemn assembly of Tamarack employees gathered at the high school gym how sorry he was that he'd let them down.

"I tried, I really tried to make it work," he said. "But the numbers just aren't there anymore. I'm so sorry." He fought to hold back tears. Afterwards, the people who'd just learned that they would lose their jobs actually comforted him. A. Jackson had never felt worse in his life. These good folks who'd soon be without work patted *him* on the back and told him not to worry, that everything would be okay.

Fall had been a nightmare of planning the mill's closure, of finishing the last few cuts on some leases he'd landed over the summer, and of getting ready for the bankruptcy sale. Most of the cutting crews had been laid off already, and the mill was down to a quarter of its full staff. Tamarack was in its death throes.

A. Jackson's wife Miriam had moved back to Seattle the day after he announced the business's failure. She packed her bags, flounced out with an airy wave and last words of, "Hurry up and come to Seattle!" and left Sara and her bewildered father behind. A. Jackson hadn't talked to her in weeks, but as soon as he finished liquidating the company he planned to go to Seattle with Sara and try to put his family back together again. Maybe he'd force Miriam into rehab. He wasn't sure yet what he'd do. If anything.

"Your mom's really gone?" Itchy had asked when Sara told him.

"Yeah," she said. "But it's okay."

"Really?"

"Maybe she'll get better there. She didn't really like it here."

"But *you* don't want to leave, do you?" Itchy asked. He'd been devastated when Sara told him that she'd be moving. They kissed a lot while they worked on *Tamsen's Lost Journal,* and Itchy really liked it.

Sara had shrugged off Itchy's question. "I don't really have a choice," she said in a small voice. "I have to go with Daddy."

"But...." Itchy wasn't sure how to put it. "Won't...you miss me?"

"We can send email," she told him, trying to sound cheerful. It didn't work. They both sat silently for a long while after that.

Itchy didn't bring it up again. If they pretended that nothing was going to happen, the time they had left together would be okay. They had to finish *Tamsen's Lost Journal.* Itchy needed Sara to be Tamsen's voice, and when they finished, then—and only then—would he let himself believe that Sara was really leaving.

"Did you write a check for twenty-eight dollars?" Irene asked Red. She'd just snapped off a pencil lead and Itchy thought she sounded surly.

Red glanced at her from the saggy couch. "I think so. Mighta been for that winterizing stuff I bought at the hardware store."

"Do you have the receipt? It'd make this a whole lot easier."

Red arched his eyebrows at Itchy. He climbed out of the couch and went to Irene. He leaned over her from behind and wrapped his arms around her shoulders. "Watch and learn, Itch. This is what they call a teachin' moment. Now your momma here, she's feelin' a bit annoyed with me."

"That's an understatement," said Irene.

"So, what's a Donner do in this situation?"

Itchy scratched at his psoriasis patch. "Find the receipt she wants?"

"Itchy, Itchy, Itchy. You got so much to learn. See, I got no idea where that receipt is. Probably pitched it. That ain't the point, though. 'Cause right now, your momma's pissed. So I gotta get her mind off the fact that she's wantin' to smack me."

"Will you please go away and let me figure this out?" Irene sighed.

"So," Red continued, "I gotta come up with a clever misdirection play."

"Like in football?" Itchy asked.

"Abso-damn-lutely. Just like a fake handoff to the fullback up the middle, then the QB drops back and tosses a nice little floater to the tight end who snuck out behind the linebackers. Gotta get the D goin' one way, then you head back 'nother."

"Okay...." Itchy said slowly. "How do you fake out Mom?"

"I normally like to use my natural charm," Red said. "But right now, she's on to me, so I can't be real subtle."

"You don't even know what the word means," Irene said.

"So," Red nodded, "I gotta be more direct." He paused. Irene waited. Itchy watched. Then, Red smothered Irene with wet, sloppy kisses. "Cover her up with big ol' smooches like this!" Irene tried to fight off the slobbery smooch attack, but Red overwhelmed her. They both started giggling. Itchy wondered if he should leave the room.

"You guys are weird," Itchy said.

Irene finally fought Red off. "Go watch your dumb football game and leave me alone."

Red came back and flopped on the couch. "See? Works every time."

Itchy liked having his dad living with them. It felt safe. His parents argued sometimes—mostly because Irene got mad at Red for saying stupid things—but most of the time they seemed to get along okay. The only problem that Itchy could see was that the singlewide was too small for all of them. But nobody was sure how long they'd be there anyway.

A. Jackson had kept Red's crew working, and Red figured he could hang on until after New Years. Then.... Nobody knew what lay ahead. Irene noticed that business in the salon was down, and pretty soon money would be even tighter than usual. Everybody in town was in the same boat. In the two months since A. Jackson's announcement, uncertainty had become a daily part of everyone's lives.

"Probably gonna have to hit the road," Red told Irene and Itchy recently. "I'm hopin' as a family," he added. Irene hadn't said anything.

Itchy tried to take it in stride. He liked Tamarack, but if they had to leave, then they had to leave. He was more upset that Sara would be gone before him. He secretly hoped that maybe they'd end up in Seattle, and he could still see Sara. But there weren't trees to cut in Seattle—although there *was* hair to cut—

264

so Itchy didn't know if they'd go there. Whatever. Just like the brave Donner pioneers, Itchy would have to be flexible. Good thing he was a Donner. Having Donner blood made dealing with uncertainty so much easier.

Itchy and Red watched the football game and ate sandwiches in front of the tube for dinner. Irene finally gave up on the checking account and joined them.

"Mom's coming over later," said Irene. "She's got more wedding plans."

Jacqueline had been making a big production out of her and Stan the Man's wedding. They were getting married in two weeks—though not in the Catholic Church, since, in a weak moment, Irene had told Jacqueline what happened with Father Ray. Itchy overheard, and when he incredulously blurted, "Father Ray *kissed* you?" Jacqueline had threatened to slap him like a red-headed stepchild and Irene got right in his face and growled, "This is private, and it stays private. You don't tell anybody. Is that clear?" His mother's steely tone scared Itchy into obedient silence. But he still couldn't believe that Father Ray would do something like that. It was just so gross.

Jacqueline was furious about Father Ray's indiscretion, and she fired off a venomous letter to the archbishop about he'd done—but she didn't tell Irene. Jacqueline wasn't going to let a nasty priest get away with kissing her beautiful daughter.

So, for the wedding, Jacqueline asked Pastor Earle to perform the ceremony. He was willing—although Jacqueline warned him not to go into full bible-thumper mode and to keep his mouth shut about the evils of Catholicism. He'd reluctantly agreed, but Jacqueline suspected he'd get fire-and-brimestoney anyway. Jacqueline's main interest wasn't the wedding ceremony; it was the reception. She'd rented the Slurp 'n' Burp from Pencil and she was going to throw a bash the town would never forget. They were getting married the week after Thanksgiving, and Jacqueline wanted the reception to be both for her wedding and for Tamarack. "Like a wake," was how she put it. "Everybody gets plastered, cries a little, then feels better after the hangover wears off."

"Only one problem I can see, J. W.," Red had commented.

"What?"

"Poor ol' Stanley's nightmare has just begun."

Jacqueline flipped Red off. "Dunno why you put up with a smart ass like him," she grumbled to Irene.

Irene was excited for her mom's wedding, but Tamarack's dying took a lot of the pleasure out of it. It broke her heart. The poor, scruffy little town, always an iffy survivor at best, was finally finished. Tamarack was inside her. It shaped her entire life, her character, her friends, Tamarack had thrown her and Red together—twice—Tamarack had given her Itchy, and Mart. She couldn't imagine not being part of it anymore.

She knew every street, every house, she'd watched kids and trees grow up in front yards, she knew everybody's business and they knew hers. How could she live anywhere else? Irene had to face the truth. It was time to move on. Grieve, mourn, but get over it. She hadn't gotten to the get-over part yet, and she wasn't sure she ever could.

She watched the football game with Red and Itchy, but her mind wandered. Worries. Concerns. Red looked over at her.

"Stop worryin' so much," he said, reading her mind.

"I wasn't."

"Sure you were. I know the look. Take shit a day at a time, Irene. We'll be fine. We're all together, that's what matters."

She couldn't shake the doubts. Red went back to watching the game, and Itchy stared at the TV but Irene could tell he was thinking about other things, too—probably Sara or the Donner Party or both. When the phone rang neither Red nor Itchy made a move, so she got up to answer it.

"Hello?"

A prissy, precise man's voice asked, "May I speak to Red Donner, please?"

"Just a minute." Irene took the phone over to Red. "For you."

Red muted the TV. "'lo?" He waited, listening. "Well, fuckin' A, Jimbo, how the hell are you? Get my birthday card?"

Itchy looked at Irene and whispered, "Who's 'Jimbo'?" Irene shrugged.

Red got up and went to the kitchen, chatting animatedly. When he came back, a big smile covered his face.

"Who was that, Dad?"

"Your Uncle Jimmy," Red said. "I sent him a b-day card a few weeks back. Felt kinda bad, ain't talked to him in ages. Anyway, he wants to get together for turkey day. Told him to come on up. He don't mind drivin' all over hell. Hope it's okay," he added quickly, looking at Irene.

"It's fine, Red. I'd like to meet him."

"Is this the guy who's the college professor?" asked Itchy.

"Yep. Jimbo's the evolutionary throwback to somethin' better in our family. The rest of us—you excluded, of course, Itch—are dumbshit white-trash crackers. Jimmy's a whole 'nother animal. Be good to see him again."

"Does he know a lot about the Donner Party?" Itchy asked. The idea of talking over their ancestors with a real college professor relative had Itchy's juices flowing.

"Well, there's a problem with that," Red said, rubbing his beard.

"What?"

"I'm gonna have to ask you a favor, Itch. See, Jimmy's kinda...well, he ain't real proud of the family's past. He took a bunch of shit 'bout it when we were kids, and he'd rather not have nothin' to do with it. Gets pissed if the subject is brought up."

"But how could he not be proud!" The thought was unimaginable to Itchy.

"Just the way he is. Anyway, like I said, if you could just keep quiet 'bout all the Donner stuff while he's here, so much the better. Ain't seen Jimmy in a long time, and I'd like it to be a friendly visit. Got your promise?"

"I guess," Itchy said. What a disappointment. Another Donner relative and he couldn't show him his best stuff? What was wrong with people?

"Where's he live?" Irene asked.

"Down in Berkeley. He's drivin' up, said he'd just swing by on T-giving and then head out."

"He's welcome to stay," Irene said.

"Ain't Jimmy's way. He's kind of a loner. He don't like bein' 'round people all that much. I suspect he'll just pop in for grub, then hit the road. Be nice to see him, though. You guys won't believe he's related to somebody like me."

They settled in and watched the football game. Itchy wasn't paying close attention. He couldn't. His mind worked over *Tamsen's Lost Journal* and the vague, nibbling disappointment over his uncle's lack of Donner interest. Unbelievable. Maybe he'd get a chance to change Uncle Jimmy's mind. Maybe he'd be able to convince him how important it was to care about your past, about famous ancestors.

Even though his dad warned him to keep quiet, Itchy didn't think that was right. Uncle Jimmy needed to be converted, to be brought over to pride in the glorious Donner family.

And Itchy Donner was just the guy to do it.

The Wednesday before Thanksgiving had always been a busy day in the salon, with local women wanting to look good for family gatherings and the holiday. But this year was different.

Only a couple of women had made appointments—and one of those canceled—so Irene and Jacqueline had lots of free time. Jacqueline chain-smoked and thumbed well-worn issues of *Glamour* while Irene cleaned imaginary specks off the mirrors.

"You rub them any harder you gonna take the reflection right off," Jacqueline said.

"I need to keep busy."

"Gonna get an ulcer, honey. Stop worryin', everything will be okay."

"How can you say that?"

Jacqueline peered over the top of her magazine and sighed. "Honey, life throws stuff at us. You just roll with it. Doesn't do any good to worry. Tamarack's goin' down. That's no surprise. We just have to deal with it. I wasn't gonna tell you this till later, but I 'spose you oughta know. Me and Stanley will be moving on after the first of the year."

"Where?" Irene asked. Her stomach felt hollow.

"Maybe L.A. Or Vegas. Growing like crazy down there. I can cut hair anyplace, and Stanley can work construction or drive a truck. And we won't have to put up with snow anymore."

"But it's not...Tamarack." Irene's eyes teared up. She hadn't realized how important Tamarack was to her until the reality of its demise hit.

"Yeah, well, that ain't necessarily a bad thing. We been in this inbred little town too long. I don't think it's done us any good. Don't you think Itchy'd be better off in a real city, with a decent school? Get his mind off all the gloomy-gus Donner garbage. Maybe he'd blossom if he wasn't stuck in a redneck backwater like this."

Irene shook her head. How come nobody loved Tamarack the way she did? Everybody acted like it was disposable, just a place to hang your hat for awhile—a few years, or decades—until something better came along.

"It's home," she finally said, quietly.

"Irene," Jacqueline said, setting down her magazine. "It may be cornball, but it's the truth: home is where you make it. You got a family now, even though I'm not all that thrilled you let Red back into your bed, but that's your business. But you got him and Itchy, that's all that counts. Don't matter where you live."

"But I won't...." Irene paused as she sniffled tears and wiped her eyes.

"There go the waterworks," Jacqueline smiled. She hugged her daughter. "Sure are an emotional little thing. You must get that from your daddy."

"I'll...miss you," Irene finally managed.

"Yeah, honey, I'll miss you too. That makes it hard. But we gotta live our lives. We got phones, email, whatever. It's not like we're gonna move and not leave a forwarding address."

"It's just...I don't want things to change. I want everything to stay the same."

"I don't want wrinkles or saggy boobs either, but I got 'em. It happens. Can't stop time. Itchy's gonna grow up, Red's gonna get older and dumber, and even you, you're gonna turn into one of those cute little skinny old ladies the rest of us are so jealous of...it just happens, honey. Don't be afraid. Just ride with it."

Irene hugged Jacqueline hard. She wouldn't let go. Jacqueline gently stroked her hair and murmured, "Everything'll be all right." Irene truly wanted to believe her.

But she couldn't.

*   *   *

Thanksgiving Day dawned bright and clear and unusually warm for Tamarack. A few leaves still clung stubbornly to the trees, and so far the frosts had been light. Scraggly tomato plants stood upright in gardens, only partially turned to slime by cold nights. Droopy sunflowers, their seeds long since plucked clean by hungry birds, leaned crookedly as if impatient for the first snows to knock them down.

Hunting had been good so far this year, with most hunters easily filling their tags. Red got a nice bull elk up by Ice Creek, and now Irene's freezer was packed with meat for the next year. Red tried to persuade Itchy to come along on the hunt, but Itchy had passed. Even though his Donner Party ancestors hunted, Itchy didn't like the unnecessary meanness of shooting something pretty like an elk or deer. Besides, in 1846 they didn't have grocery stores, so they had to kill things. Itchy figured there wasn't any reason to do it now.

Irene was up early Thanksgiving morning, making mincemeat pies (she'd made Red promise not to call it "Booger Pie" this year), and for once cooking didn't seem like an irritating chore. Maybe it was because this might be the last Thanksgiving they'd all have together for a long time, or maybe the visit by Red's brother inspired her—she wasn't sure. But this morning, rolling out pie-crust and getting the turkey ready, Irene was happier than she'd been in a long time. Yesterday's worries had temporarily receded. The people she loved most in the world would be here today, they'd eat, laugh, drink, good times would flow, and, at least for a day, everything would be all right. She'd forget about Tamarack dying, about moving, about being apart from her mom and her town, she'd just enjoy.

Red wandered out from the bedroom, sleepy-eyed, wearing only boxers and scratching at his butt. "Mornin' beautiful," he said. He pulled her hair back and gave her a light kiss on the back of her neck. "Man, I love kissin' that spot." He poured himself a mug of coffee and yawned. "Need help with anything?"

"Nope. Just relax. Today's my show. Carve the turkey and clean up the mess and it'll be perfect."

"Bitchin'."

"Is Itchy awake?"

"Uh-uh. Dreamin' 'bout Sara and dead Donners, I suppose."

"Will he like your brother?"

"Sure. I guess. Jimmy's a little odd, but then so's Itchy. They might bond pretty good." Red watched Irene roll out dough. The morning light spilled through the kitchen window, and a small cloud of sparkly flour swirled around her.

"Damn, you're pretty," he said.

She looked over at him and smiled. "Wish I could say the same about you. Go take a shower."

He kissed her on his way out, and she contentedly worked at the counter. Her sadness and doubts of yesterday seemed far away. At this moment everything felt so right. So safe.

Like nothing could ever go wrong.

"Hey, Mar-teen! Happy turkey day!" Red slammed Mart on the back as Stan the Man rolled him in. "Stanley, J.W.," Red nodded as they followed. Red even gave Jacqueline a kiss on the cheek.

"What the hell was that for?" demanded Jacqueline.

"Just a little love-smack for my ex-momma-in-law."

Jacqueline regarded him suspiciously. "You lookin' to borrow money or something?"

"Jeez, J.W., you got serious trust issues. I'm almost your son-in-law again. Oughta be nicer to me."

Jacqueline *harumphed* and went into the kitchen to say hello to Irene. Itchy rushed out from his bedroom. "Is Uncle Jimmy here?"

"Nope," Red said. "Just your gramma and Mart and Stanley."

"Oh. Hey," Itchy nodded to Mart and Stan the Man.

Mart smiled. "Aren't we good enough for you, Itch? Set up the Scrabble board, let's rock 'n' roll."

"Okay." Itchy went to get the game.

Stan the Man clicked on the T.V. and plopped down on the couch. He'd be snoring shortly. Mart rolled to the kitchen table. He called, "Hey" to Irene and she popped out and gave him a quick howdy and a kiss. Then she disappeared back into the kitchen to peel potatoes while Jacqueline smoked and supervised—but didn't offer to help.

"Here, buddy." Red handed Mart a beer.

"Thanks." Mart sipped contentedly. Since the summertime, he'd slowly gotten used to Red and Irene being together again. He still came by for Sunday dinners, and the situation felt...okay. "When you done working, Red?" he asked.

"A.J.'s got two more small leases we're cuttin' down by White Pine, then that's it. Probably January."

"That sucks."

"Ain't the end of the world, Mar-teen." Red sipped his iced tea. "I always been of the opinion that change is good. People get locked into the same ol' same ol' and they get soft and fucked up."

Mart nodded. He knew all about that. Itchy came back and they set up the Scrabble board.

"You want to play, Dad?" he asked.

"Ain't smart enough. Only words I know with more than three letters are nasty."

Mart and Itchy drew their tiles and the game began. Red watched, kibitzing occasionally, while the rich smells of Thanksgiving drifted out of the kitchen. "Don't smell nothin' burnin' yet," Red whispered to Itchy and Mart so Irene wouldn't hear. "That's a good sign."

Itchy paid scant attention to the Scrabble game. He listened intently for the sound of Uncle Jimmy's car.

He couldn't wait until there was a new Donner in the house.

Father Ray threw back another shot of Scotch. He'd picked up three bottles of Cutty down at the state liquor store last week, and he was already halfway through the last one. Another lonely, bitter holiday faced him. At least it would probably be his last in this miserable little town, he thought. Good. Fuck this place. And all the losers in it.

He'd said mass this morning in a thick, boozy haze, but he couldn't remember what he'd preached during the sermon. Didn't much matter. Nobody ever listened to him anyway. He'd gotten a couple of invites for Thanksgiving dinner from old lady parishioners, but he'd gruffly said, "No thanks." He preferred spending the day alone. With Scotch.

He glanced at the letter on his desk. It sat amidst other debris, business he hadn't tended to, things left undone, problems left to fester. He didn't care. The one letter was the only thing that mattered at the moment.

Because Father Ray was in big trouble.

It was a letter from the bishop. A complaint had been made, an allegation. Sexual in nature. With all the dirty priests and lousy press the church was get-

274

ting lately, every archdiocese in the country suddenly had zero tolerance for little boo-boos. It wasn't like he grabbed some altar boy's dick, he thought. So he'd kissed a woman. She was an adult. Unmarried. But a letter of complaint had gotten to the bishop. From her mother. That chain-smoking bitch Jacqueline Weatherly. Cunt.

Father Ray splashed another shot into his glass. Shouldn't think such nasty thoughts about people, how un-Christian could he get? Couldn't help it, though. Because that's what she was. At least Irene Donner hadn't complained. And maybe a second-hand complaint from somebody like Jacqueline wouldn't carry any weight. Anyway, being called on the carpet wasn't the worst thing in the world. They wouldn't kick him out. Probably just transfer him someplace else, which was fine and dandy, thank you very much. A wrist-slap from the bishop, maybe a forced letter of apology, and that would be it. And would it matter all that much if they booted him out of the priesthood? He was an imposter anyhow. But it was a job. He didn't need to worry about supporting himself in the real world as long as he was a priest. Fuck it. Whatever.

Maybe he'd pray about it.

Father Ray spat out a bitter laugh. Pray. Yeah, right. Get right on that.

He picked up the letter and read it again. Dry, dusty Church legalese. "Please appear at the chancery offices on Monday, November 30, nine a.m...." Fine. Okay. He'd leave Saturday afternoon just so crabby old Father Feeney would have to come up from St. Catherine's to cover his Sunday masses. Good. Father Feeney was a lot holier than him, probably never tried to kiss one of the faithful. Let him tend to their souls. Father Ray would take a leisurely drive down to Boise, push the MG around the twisty roads, enjoy the trip.

His last Thanksgiving in Tamarack. He held up his glass in a silent toast, then downed the Scotch.

Give thanks. Hallelujah! Praise the Lord. Have another drink!

Father Ray poured the rest of the bottle and wondered if Pencil Pandola would be opening up the Slurp 'n' Burp later on today even though it was a holiday....

Father Ray was going to need more Scotch. Lots more Scotch.

"That's him?" Itchy whispered to Red.

"Yep. Jimmy Donner in all his glory."

They watched as Uncle Jimmy climbed out of his silver BMW. Itchy had never seen such an expensive car before. Everybody in Tamarack—except Father Ray—drove pickups, and most of them were old beaters. But this car gleamed exotically. Like it was from another universe. Itchy had never seen anything like it.

And he'd never seen anybody quite like Uncle Jimmy, either.

Itchy expected Uncle Jimmy to bear some resemblance to Red, but there was none. Where Red was big and burly, Uncle Jimmy was slight and stooped. He was bald on top, but the fringe of remaining hair on the sides had been left uncut—and, it looked to Itchy, unwashed—for years. It dangled in greasy strands down to Uncle Jimmy's shoulders. When he looked at them his eyes darted nervously, as if he expected Red and Itchy to pull guns. He seemed much older than Red, and his twitchy mouth movements, furtive and frightened, gave him the look of an escaped mental patient. A sudden, horrid thought occurred to Itchy: what if he had Uncle Jimmy's genes and not his dad's? He'd never have a chance to grow up cooler than the scrawny, rashy runt he was now. He gulped. Too terrible to contemplate.

"Jimbo! How is you, bro'?!" Red charged forward and gave his shaky brother a spine-crushing hug.

"Uh, fine, Red. Good, good to see you," replied Uncle Jimmy, his voice whispery and feminine. He pulled away from Red and squeezed a weak grin.

His front teeth were brown and rotten looking, soft and cheesy and disgusting. Itchy gulped again. He'd have to make sure he didn't eat Thanksgiving dinner sitting across from Uncle Jimmy, because those teeth would completely kill his appetite. Unlike last year, when Itchy was in his Donner starvation test mode, this year he was hungry and planning to pig out.

"Is this your...son?" Uncle Jimmy asked, an odd, sing-songy inflection in his voice. He glanced at Itchy and then at the ground. Itchy noticed that Uncle Jimmy had trouble making eye contact. It was like he had a guilty conscience about something.

"Yep. This is Itchy Donner, the reigning Wimp o' the Woods and one hardass little mofo."

Uncle Jimmy nodded, smiling nervously, and gave Itchy a limp, fishy handshake. "My pleasure, nephew," he said.

"Hi," Itchy replied. He quickly let go of Uncle Jimmy's soft, clammy hand. This guy gave him the creeps.

"'Course, Itchy ain't his real name. That's...shit, I always forget," Red grinned.

"Jacob," Itchy reminded him. "Like the—"

Red cut him off. "That's right. Jacob. I think Itchy's a whole lot more distinctive, don't you, Jimbo?"

"Indeed."

Irene came out, wiping her hands on a dishtowel. She brushed back some stray hairs, and a fine kitchen sweat gave her face a healthy, glowing sheen. "Hello. I'm Irene. Your ex-sister-in-law. Sort of ex- now, I suppose."

Uncle Jimmy blushed as he shook her hand. "I see," he said. His eyes stayed on her face only a second, then he was staring at his shoes again. "I'm...Jimmy Donner."

"It's nice to meet you. I'm glad you came up to visit," she said.

"Yes. Indeed."

Irene exchanged glances with Red, who just smiled and shrugged. "Well," Irene said. "Come on in, we'll introduce you to everybody else. We'll be eating soon."

Red put his big arm around his frightened brother's shoulders and led him inside. Itchy stayed outside for a few minutes examining the BMW. His uncle seemed like a weirdo, but at least he had a cool car. Itchy guessed that since Uncle Jimmy was a math professor being weird came with the territory. He'd never known anybody in school who was good at math that wasn't a little on the creepy side.

Red made the intros, (he had to wake up Stan the Man), and Uncle Jimmy settled on the saggy couch and nursed a beer. Jacqueline had given up badgering Irene in the kitchen and sat in the living room with them. She studied Uncle Jimmy like he was an emissary from another planet.

"You're a professor, huh?" she asked.

"Yes. Yes I am."

"Down at Berserkley? With all those radicals and crazies?"

"Well, yes, there are some odd people there. That's the nature of a world class university." Although he never made eye contact, Uncle Jimmy sounded a bit snippy and arrogant.

"Uh-huh," Jacqueline said. "Mind if I smoke?"

"Not at all, no indeed."

Itchy had gone back to the Scrabble game with Mart, but he watched and listened as Jacqueline interrogated his odd uncle. Red just sat by, seeming to enjoy the spectacle. Itchy noticed that uncomfortable social moments never bothered his father; he seemed to find them vastly entertaining. Stan the Man had muted the T.V., but he still watched the silent football game. Stan the Man wasn't much of a talker.

"What I don't understand," Jacqueline continued, sucking in Marlboro smoke, "is why Red's got the I.Q. of a toilet seat and you're a math genius. How's something like that happen?"

Red chortled heartily at the insult. "God love you, J.W. Ain't she the sweetest thing your ever seen, Jimmy?"

Uncle Jimmy smiled wanly. "I think perhaps in answer to your question," he said seriously, "that the nature of intelligence can be distilled to probability. And equations." Then Uncle Jimmy went off into an incomprehensible flight of fancy regarding various mathematical theories. Uncle Jimmy was still talking by the time Jacqueline had finished her cigarette, and she was completely lost and bored so she excused herself to go help Irene in the kitchen.

Uncle Jimmy sputtered to a conclusion and then seemed to retreat inside himself to mull over his latest thoughts. Red looked over at Stan the Man.

"You get all that, Stanley?"

"Huh?" Stan the Man said, staring at the T.V.

"How 'bout you, Itch?"

"Um, not really."

"Guess I'm not the only clueless one, then," Red said. "So Jimbo, got any ladies in your life?"

"Not at the moment, no, Red. I certainly don't."

"How come?"

Uncle Jimmy squirmed uncomfortably. "Well, I don't really know."

"Yeah. Know how it is. Hard to figure women. Been scratching my head when it comes to them all my life."

"Yet you're with Irene, is that correct?"

"Yeah. Till she wises up and throws my dumb ass out." Red laughed and punched Uncle Jimmy in the shoulder. Uncle Jimmy flinched and his lips twitched in an unsuccessful attempt to smile.

Itchy watched his dad and uncle. Uncle Jimmy seemed to be afraid of Red. Itchy wondered if Red used to beat him up when they were kids. Itchy could see how Red might've tormented him. He liked his dad, but even Itchy realized that he was a bully sometimes.

Red chatted amiably with Uncle Jimmy while Itchy and Mart played Scrabble, Stan the Man stared, glassy-eyed, at the football game, and Irene and Jacqueline bustled around out in the kitchen. Uncle Jimmy finished his fourth beer and seemed less twitchy; by the time dinner was ready he was almost at ease.

Irene and Jacqueline brought out plates of food: the usual mashed potatoes (no lumps this time; Irene was finally getting the hang of it), gravy, rolls—all the usual fixings. Red took the ceremonial spot at the head of the table and prepared to carve the turkey.

"Before we dig in, I just wanna say a few things and get 'em off my chest. I ain't usually real eloquent, but lemme tell you this: today, this Thanksgiving is the best one of my life. I'm with my family, everybody who counts, and Jimmy's here, that's great, everybody's healthy and happy, J.W. and Stanley are gettin' hitched, and who knows, maybe me and Irene will try it again...Itchy's the reigning Wimp o' the Woods...it don't get any better than it is right now. So before I cut open this big ol' bird, I just wanna thank all you guys. Thanks for givin' me another shot, thanks for lettin' me come back...." Red paused. He continued, but very quietly. "Most of all, thanks for lettin' me...love you."

The table was completely silent. Itchy broke the tension by saying, "Hurry up and carve the turkey, Dad. I'm starving."

Red laughed. "My man Itchy's got his priorities straight. Enough of the gooey stuff, let's eat!"

He carved up the turkey, plates filled, and pretty soon Itchy agreed with his dad—it *was* the best Thanksgiving ever. Lots of good food, fun and laughter, and, Itchy realized, what really mattered most of all....

His family.

As Irene cut the mincemeat pie, Red exchanged a guilty smile with Itchy. Irene noticed.

"Red," she warned.

"What? I didn't say nothing!"

"Oh for God's sake," Jacqueline sighed. "Do we have to go through this again this year?"

Uncle Jimmy daintily dabbed at his mouth with his napkin. He folded the napkin with geometric precision and placed it on the table. "Excuse me, but what is everyone talking about?" he asked. He'd loosened up considerably during dinner and now made occasional eye contact. Itchy was beginning to like him—but those rotten teeth still made him queasy.

"Your no-good brother called this 'booger pie' last year, and your bozo nephew and, I hate to say, every male at this table thought it was the cleverest thing they ever heard," said Jacqueline. Itchy was giggling hard, and Red tried to stifle his laughter without much success. Mart and Stan the Man were being a bit more grown-up this year and hadn't slipped into guffaws. Yet.

"I see," Uncle Jimmy smiled. "Red has always enjoyed scatological humor."

"Whatever the hell that is," Red nodded. "Jimbo never had the fine appreciation for booger and fart jokes like me. Guess he's not quite as evolved."

Itchy ate his mincemeat pie—he wasn't crazy about the taste, but as long as he didn't look too closely at the filling it was okay—and he watched his uncle. Uncle Jimmy wasn't quite so nervous now; he listened to the conversations, joined in occasionally, and even smiled at Itchy a few times when their eyes met. Itchy decided to strike.

It was time to convert Uncle Jimmy to Donner pride.

"Hey, Uncle Jimmy?" he asked.

"Yes?"

"How come you don't like to talk about the Donners?"

Red clanged his fork down and shot Itchy a fierce glare. "Drop it, Itchy."

"Well, but," Itchy pressed on. "We're all related. And it's important!"

Irene was about to speak, to gently chide Itchy about being polite, but before she had the chance Red stood and stared Itchy down. When he spoke, his voice was quiet and steely. Much scarier than if he'd been yelling. "Let's go outside and have a little talk, Itch."

"I'm afraid I don't understand the question, Itchy," Uncle Jimmy said, oblivious to his brother's anger. The holiday good times dissipated like mist.

"Never mind, Jimmy. This is between me and my boy. Outside. Now." Red jerked his thumb at the door and moved toward it, expecting Itchy to follow.

Only Itchy didn't.

"But Dad! Uncle Jimmy should be proud of the Donner Party!"

Uncle Jimmy stared at Itchy, and his face twitched oddly with bewilderment. "Why would I be proud of them?"

"Because! Because they're...because we're part of them, we wouldn't be here if they weren't so tough, if—"

Uncle Jimmy's eyebrows furrowed. Confused.

And then he began to laugh.

Red stopped in mid-stride, and his shoulders drooped. He turned back to the table, his expression odd. Irene was astonished. She'd didn't recognize it at first, because she'd never seen it before.

Red was ashamed.

She turned to Uncle Jimmy, who still giggled as if he'd heard a truly funny joke. As he smiled his lips pulled back and exposed those dirty, diseased teeth.

Itchy couldn't understand what in the world was going on. Why was Uncle Jimmy laughing at him? And why was his dad standing absolutely still, looking almost...scared?

"What's so funny?" asked Itchy. He felt like an idiot. He had the same sick sensation he got at school when bullies made fun of him or the Donner Party. How could Uncle Jimmy *not* understand?

"It's very amusing," Uncle Jimmy said. "An amusing joke. Very amusing, indeed."

"What's a joke?" Itchy asked.

Red said wearily, "Let it go, Itch."

Irene was beginning to realize. "Oh my God, Red—"

"What?!" Itchy cried.

Uncle Jimmy frowned at Red. "Why does Itchy think—?"

"Because that's what I told everybody."

"That we're related to the Donner Party?"

Red nodded. He didn't move.

"How could you?..." Irene whispered.

Red shrugged. "Didn't mean nobody any harm."

"For Christ's sake!" Jacqueline snapped. "I *told* you, Irene! I told you to cut him loose! Why didn't you listen—"

"Be quiet, Mother." Irene reached out to Itchy. "Honey, this doesn't mean that, that you...." Irene stopped talking. She didn't know what to say.

Itchy's head spun, dizzy, was he going to throw-up? His face tingled, he couldn't feel his hands, his eyes darted between Uncle Jimmy's rotten teeth, his furious gramma, his mom's almost-crying frown, Mart staring at the table, Stan the Man moving food around his plate, and—

Red.

Itchy locked his eyes onto his father, who suddenly seemed smaller, shrunken. Beaten.

"Dad?" Itchy pleaded in a high voice.

Red looked away. "I'm sorry, buddy."

Uncle Jimmy nervously cleared his throat. "It's very possible, actually, that we might be related to, um, the Donner Party. Mathematically speaking, the odds are such that with that family name perhaps we have a connection some ways back. You never know. So many generations have passed. I could re-search it when I get back to the university, and then maybe we could know for sure."

Silence. Irene touched Itchy's arm. He jerked it away.

"Honey...."

Itchy sat, frozen. *Not really a Donner?* It couldn't be true. No. Not possi-ble. Somebody was wrong. A mistake. Uncle Jimmy didn't know what he was talking about.

"I *am* a Donner," Itchy insisted. "Tamsen is my great-great-great Grand-mother." He looked around the table, pleading for support. "She...I know that I'm...we're related, I know I am!" Tears burned his eyes. Red still wouldn't look at him. *"I am a Donner! I know it!"*

Irene again tried to take his hand, but Itchy pushed away from the table. He knocked his chair over. "I *am* a Donner," he said softly, crying. And then he ran into his room and slammed the door.

Uncle Jimmy blinked his eyes as if he had sand caught underneath the lids. "I'm so very sorry. I didn't know...."

"It's okay," Irene said, her voice flat. "It isn't your fault." She went to Red. He hadn't moved. "Why would you lie about something like that?"

Red shrugged stupidly. "Dunno. You know how it is with me and the truth sometimes."

"Nice going, idiot!" Jacqueline said. "How you plan to make it up to that little kid in there? His whole life has been set up around your big old whopper 'bout your cannibal cousins, now he's got nothin' to believe in. What're you gonna do about it?"

"I don't know, J.W."

"You better think of something," Irene told him.

Jacqueline said, "I told you you shouldn't have let him come back."

"Maybe we oughta leave," suggested Stan the Man.

"You're almost family, Stanley. Family don't run out when things get ugly," Jacqueline reminded him.

Irene ignored them and glared at Red. *"What're you going to do?"*

Red finally looked her in the eye. "Can't do a whole hell of a lot, can I? He'll get over it in time. Part of growin' up is when you realize your parents are assholes." He chuckled bitterly, but nobody smiled.

"God damn you, Red," Irene said, getting close enough to his face that little spit droplets hit him along with her words. *"God damn you!"* You come back after eleven years, you stroll in here with your stupid lies, how many other lies have you told? Is it a lie when you claim to love us?"

"No, that's true, I wouldn't lie—"

"*'I'm kin to the Donner Party, wanna hear about my ancestors?'* I can't believe I was stupid enough to fall for it. Is *anything* about you true? How could you keep up a lie like that for so long? Don't you have any decency? And to keep lying, to let Itchy get so caught up in it. How could you? *How could you?!*"

Red shoved his hands in his pockets like a giant twelve-year-old getting chewed out for not doing his chores. "It was...just a little innocent bullshit. Didn't know that you woulda told Itchy 'bout it and then raise him to make a big deal outa it, shit, it was just bar talk back when we met. When I come back and seen how into it he was, I couldn't very well tell him he wasn't related to those people, could I?"

"Don't you dare try to pin it on me, you asshole! I wanted him to be proud of something, to have something to believe in since his father deserted him. And then you come back and encourage him even more? Buy him books, talk about it all like it was true?! What the hell were you thinking?"

"Same thing as you, Irene. The boy needed somethin' to be proud of."

"And now he's got nothing," Irene said. "Get out. Get out of our lives, get the fuck out of my house, get out, *GET FUCKING OUT!*"

Irene spun away from him and stormed back to Itchy's room. She knocked on the door, forced her voice to be calm and quiet, and gently said, "Itchy, can I come in and talk?" but there was no response.

In the living room, Jacqueline said, "You heard her, Red. Beat it."

Mart wheeled away from the table and over to Red. He glared up at him. "You lying motherfucker."

"I'm...sorry Mart. Sorry everybody," Red sighed. "You're all right about me. I *am* an asshole. Nothin' I can do about it. C'mon, Jimmy. It's best we leave."

Uncle Jimmy shook his head. "I'm sorry I came here, Red. I'm sorry I exposed your lie. But nothing's changed with you, has it? It's always the same."

"What?"

"Trouble. Everything's always trouble with you." Uncle Jimmy nodded toward Jacqueline. "Give your daughter my apologies. And thank you for your hospitality."

"You bet," Jacqueline said.

"And say goodbye to Itchy for me. I hope he'll be all right."

"He's scrawny but he's tough. He'll come out okay with some time."

Uncle Jimmy shook hands all around, and then he and Red left.

Mart seethed. "Can you believe that asshole?" he said to no one in particular.

They began to clean up the dinner mess.

Nobody said anything.

Irene waited outside Itchy's door for half an hour. She heard his deep, wet snorts inside, the convulsive tears and murmurs. She couldn't take it anymore; she pushed open the door and went in.

Itchy lay curled on his bed in the dark.

Irene sat next down to him and stroked his hair. "He's gone, honey."

"Dad?" he sniffed.

"Yes."

"What about Uncle Jimmy?"

"He's gone, too."

"Will...they be back?"

Irene hesitated. "I...don't think so."

Itchy slowly sat up. His eyes were puffy and red, and teary snot glistened on his upper lip. "Dad doesn't have to leave forever, does he?"

"I don't want him to stay with us anymore," Irene said. The finality of the statement stung. "We have to leave Tamarack anyway. I'm not sure what's going to happen. But he won't be coming with us."

"It wasn't really a lie," Itchy said. He roughly wiped his eyes. The psoriasis patch was red and scaly; it looked to Irene like it had gotten worse in the last half-hour.

"What wasn't a lie? Being related to the Donner Party?" she asked.

Itchy nodded. "He didn't know for sure. But I'm sure. I *am* related to them. He just thought he was lying, but he was really right."

Irene gently cupped Itchy's face in her hands. She kissed his forehead, and for once he didn't resist. "Would it really matter all that much," she asked, "if you were just plain old Itchy Donner? If your ancestors were just me and your father and other regular people going all the way back? Nobody famous?"

"It'd be okay, I guess," Itchy said slowly. "But it's better that Tamsen is my great-great-great Gramma. And that I'm related to Eliza and George and Elitha and Georgia and all the rest of them. Because being a real Donner is the best thing in the world."

Irene's hands slowly dropped from her son's face. She could force the issue, she could make him understand that he'd have to let go of the lie. But what was the point? Did it hurt to let him pretend for awhile longer? Without Red feeding the lie, and with the knowledge—even if he wasn't ready to accept it yet—that Itchy's only connection to the Donner Party was the same last name, the fixation would slowly slip away. And Irene knew she had to share some of the blame. She'd bought Red's con and spent way too much time filling Itchy's head with tales of his bogus ancestors. If only she hadn't been so gullible, if she hadn't swallowed Red's line of B.S., if she hadn't said anything about it as Itchy grew up—they wouldn't be in this mess now. This was all Red's fault—but Irene had made it worse and she couldn't expect Itchy to dump everything he believed—everything she'd *helped* him believe—in a few minutes. She'd have to give him time.

"I'll never lie to you," she promised.

"I know." Itchy hugged her. "Can I go over to Sara's?"

"It's Thanksgiving, they're probably—"

"It's just Sara and her dad. I think she's lonesome."

"All right, I suppose. Only you have to help clean up here first." She smoothed back Itchy's mussed hair. "You're okay then?"

He nodded and sniffled. Irene wanted to hug him, she wanted to hold him, to reassure him, to undo the damage Red had done. But he seemed to be all right, and Irene knew—as much as she hated to admit it—that he needed to deal with this on his own. She fought back every mom instinct she had. Time to give him space.

"Come out and help when you're ready," she said, and then she left him alone.

Itchy sat on his bed for a long time. He listened to the muffled conversation out in the kitchen, the clanging and banging of clean-up. He'd go out in a minute. Then he'd go over to Sara's. He really needed to see Sara tonight. She'd help make things better.

He picked up the copy of *Tamsen's Lost Journal*. They needed to finish it quickly. Forget about all this stupid junk that happened tonight, he told himself. That was the adults fighting and fussing; it didn't affect Itchy. His dad and uncle—and everybody else—was wrong. He obviously *was* related to the Donner Party. No doubt about it. Whatever all this stuff was about lies, well, it didn't matter. His dad had lied, but the lie turned out to be true! That was the amazing part. It was too bad his mom was so angry, and that she kicked his dad out, but maybe that would work out okay in the end. He'd think about it later. Right now, only *Tamsen's Lost Journal* mattered. And for the ending, for the final chapters, Itchy realized that something important was missing. There was no way they could write it without firsthand knowledge. He had to understand what Alder Creek felt like. What it looked like. Smelled like.

Itchy Donner decided then and there what he had to do:

He was going to Alder Creek.

Red watched the BMW's taillights fade and disappear into the distance. Jimmy had said nothing as he climbed in his car and drove away. Just a sad, knowing shake of the head at Red. And then he was gone.

Red leaned against his beater pickup. The sun had set and a late November chill settled over Tamarack. Red had nowhere to go. He figured he could probably crash at somebody's place and sleep in their basement or garage. He hated to go knocking on doors on Thanksgiving night, but he'd deal with it later. If worse came to worst, he'd sleep in his rig.

What to do now? He climbed in the truck and drove down into town. He was surprised to see light spilling out of the Slurp 'n' Burp. Good old Pencil. Always open for his loyal customers. Red decided to wander in, maybe shoot a game of pool if somebody wanted to, hang out. Be among, well, not friends exactly, but not enemies, either.

Irene would get over her hissy fit. Couldn't really blame her for being pissed. But women, jeez, always getting fired up over little things. And Itchy. He'd be okay, too, Red decided. Probably best that he found out about the

Donner lie. Focus him on other things. The kid needed to move on.

Red walked past the priest's MG parked on the street. Well now, isn't that interesting? he thought. He pushed open the Slurp 'n' Burp's front door and went inside.

Dark and almost empty. A couple of notorious local boozers sat at the bar, Pencil parked on a stool watching CNN, and the priest. That was it. What was the asshole priest's name? Red couldn't remember. But the priest was off by himself at a dark corner table, slurping up a drink and staring at the floor.

"Hey, Red," Pencil said. "Happy Thanksgiving." He coughed his wet cough and scratched at a crusty scab on his bald head.

"You too, Pencil. Glad to see you're open today."

"Gotta make a buck."

Red hesitated. "Jack. Leave the bottle."

Pencil slowly set a glass in front of Red. He grabbed a bottle of Jack Daniel's and hovered it above the glass. "Sure 'bout this?"

"Just pour, Pencil."

"You're the boss. A little surprised, that's all." Pencil splashed the Jack in the glass.

"It's a holiday, time to celebrate." Red held the glass in front of him and studied it. A pretty, amber liquid. It looked so harmless. He swallowed; his mouth was bone dry. It'd been so long. Hesitation. Shouldn't do it. Just say no. But sometimes—and now was one of those sometimes—you needed a little help from old friends. And Jack was his oldest and dearest friend.

The first sip burned his lips and tongue. The second and third gulps felt just fine. It got better and better.

And when it finally kicked in, when the beautiful numbness hit his brain, Red knew that his old friend was just what the doctor ordered. How long it

291

took him to reach his old Red-ness, well, he didn't know. But he knew he'd arrived back at an old familiar place when he found himself shouting, *"Priest!"* and charging toward Father Ray.

Father Ray noticed when Red came in the bar, but he'd been so wrapped up in his own pouty drinking that he didn't care. He was *so* over Irene Donner now. Didn't care about her—or her family—anymore and couldn't understand why he ever did. Nope. It was already distant, like a high school crush. He wondered what had gotten into him, how he could let himself get so besotted with a skinny little woman. Sure, she was cute, she had nice hair and eyes and skin, but so what? There wasn't anything really special about her. He'd been bored, he decided. Trapped in this little chickenshit town, bored with being a priest, not all that hip about God anymore, so why not be infatuated with a cute little parishioner? Father Ray forgave himself. Good old self-absolution. Say three *Hail Marys* and a couple of *Our Fathers* and you're good to go. He hadn't done anything wrong, really. Yeah, swiped a kiss but so fucking what? No reason to make a federal case out of it. History. Irene Donner was history.

So when he looked up through bleary, Cutty-drooped eyes, when Red Donner stomped across the bar toward him like a bull going after the cape, Father Ray was rather surprised. As far as he was concerned, the whole Irene Donner thing was over. Apparently, however, Red Donner didn't feel the same way.

"Priest!" he screamed again, face flushed and eyes wide. Father Ray was alarmed, but also fascinated by the angry man. He *did* resemble a bull.

"Call me Father Ray," he said. He smiled. Bad idea, but he couldn't help it. God bless Cutty Sark.

"Fuck you, asshole, you hit on my wife!"

"Ex-wife, isn't it?"

Pencil hurried from behind the bar. "Red, let it go!"

Red ignored him. He towered over Father Ray, panting, glaring, clenching his fists. "You fuckin' little shitwad...I shoulda kicked your ass the minute I heard 'bout it."

Father Ray sighed. He knew what was coming, there wasn't a thing in the world he could do about it, so why not go out in a blaze of glory? He said with a grin, "Go to hell, you white trash piece of shit."

When the first punch landed and slammed Father Ray's head against the wall it was almost a relief. As the other blows peppered his body—stomach, face, oooh, even one to the balls, as Father Ray crumpled to the floor, he was secretly glad that Red Donner had decided to spend Thanksgiving night drunk and mean. The pain—and Father Ray didn't feel all that much because of the booze—was oh-so-sweet. So deserved. He wanted to say, "Hit me again!" but his mouth was full of blood and he couldn't make it move anymore. Oh well. Red seemed to be doing okay without his encouragement. As he slipped into darkness he wanted to thank Red. He wanted to shake his hand.

Thanks for the memories, pal. Thanks for making me feel alive again.

It'd been a long time.

The snow bank was not high enough to keep out a little sunbeam that stole down and made a bright spot upon our floor. I sat down under it, held it on my lap, passed my hand up and down its brightness, and found I could break its ray in two. I fancied that it moved when I did, for it warmed the top of my head, kissed first one cheek and then the other, and seemed to run up and down my arm. Finally I gathered up a piece of it in my apron and ran to my mother. Great was my surprise when I carefully opened the folds and found that I had nothing to show, and the sunbeam I had left seemed shorter. I watched it creep back slowly outside and disappear....

Eliza Donner
December 18, 1846

Chapter Twelve

Sara's fingers moved so quickly over the keyboard that Itchy swore they weren't touching the keys. But the *clickclickclick* and numbers and letters appearing on the screen proved otherwise.

"This will be easy," Sara said smugly. She loved showing off her computer proficiency.

"Will your dad be mad?"

"By the time he finds out, it won't matter. Anyway, since Mommy left he lets me do whatever I want. I think he feels guilty." Sara stopped typing and looked over at Itchy. "Do you think it's true?"

"What?"

"That you're not really related to them." Sara had wanted to ask him ever since he came over and told her what happened with his uncle, but she'd hesitated. With her skeptical nature she figured that Itchy's uncle was probably right, but she wanted to be supportive of Itchy so she hadn't said anything.

Until now.

"No way," he said. "Of course I'm related to them. How else would I know everything that I know...anyway, I'm sure of it. Sometimes you're just sure of things. That's all."

Sara nodded. "Okay." She decided not to press it. She looked back at the screen. "It's only two-hundred and eighty dollars each way. It says it takes twenty-three and a half hours. And you'll have to ask the driver to stop at Truckee, 'cause it's a place they usually just drive by."

"Okay," Itchy nodded. "It's a lot of money, though." He added it up in his head...over five-hundred dollars total! It seemed like a fortune.

Sara held up her father's VISA card. "Not when you have one of these," she grinned. She had borrowed the card from A. Jackson's wallet while he watched T.V. in the living room. "Want me to go ahead and book it for you?"

Itchy paused. This was a huge step. The idea of running away, of somehow getting down to Elk Creek where the bus stopped, of riding alone all the way down to Truckee—well, it was kind of scary.

"I'm not sure," he said, scratching at his scaly patch. It itched so much it hurt.

"We need to finish *Tamsen's Lost Journal* don't we?"

"Yeah."

"And you think you need to see Alder Creek before we can do it?"

"Yeah."

"Want me to come with you?" she asked.

It was a nice thought, but.... "I think I need to go alone," he said. "You understand?"

Sara pouted but nodded. "So you want me to reserve the tickets?"

Itchy exhaled deeply. This was big. Really big. His mom would be furious. But she'd understand. After he got back he'd explain it all to her and then she'd forgive him. Maybe. She'd have to understand. And his dad? He didn't know what was happening there. For all he knew, Red Donner was out of his life forever, just like before.

"Do it," he said. "Round trip, don't forget."

Sara peered at the bus schedule. "You'll have to be there eight hours before you can come back. Will that be enough time?"

Itchy considered. He'd need to go to the main memorial at Donner Lake, then somehow get up to Alder Creek. He didn't need to look at a map; he knew every inch of the area's topography in his head.

"The bus drops me off in Truckee, I walk to the memorial, that's a couple of miles, then I walk back up to Alder Creek, that's six miles...I don't think eight hours is enough time. Better make it for the next day."

"Where will you sleep?"

"I dunno. I'll find someplace."

Sara looked at Itchy with admiration. "You're so brave, Itchy."

Itchy shrugged. "It's because I'm a Donner. If they could camp there for months during the winter then I should be able to survive one stupid night." His bravado masked his fear, but he didn't want Sara to know. Tamsen and the rest of them were a lot tougher than he was. He hoped he wasn't too much of a weenie to pull this off.

"Do you have any money?" Sara asked. "For food and stuff."

"Thirteen dollars and seventy-two cents. It's all I have saved."

"I'll take some out of Daddy's wallet. I saw some twenty dollar bills when I borrowed his credit card."

"Are you sure this is okay?"

Sara clicked the mouse and ordered Itchy's bus tickets. She turned and smiled. "I'd do anything for you, Itchy. You know that."

Itchy blushed. Sara was the best. He wasn't sure about love and all that stuff yet, but he knew one thing: Sara would always be his best friend. "Thanks, Sara," he said softly. Sara printed out a copy of Itchy's tickets, handed him the papers, and kissed him on the lips.

"We need to finish *Tamsen's Lost Journal,*" she said. "Can we do some before you go?"

"Yeah. We can always redo it when I get back."

He settled in next to Sara, and together they gazed at the screen as Tamsen's story continued.

Tamsen's Lost Journal

Chapter 12

(Itchy Donner note: this part will probably be different after I go down to Alder Creek and see all the stuff for myself. I can't wait. It's gonna be so cool!):

It's Christmas and I don't have anything to give to the children. The food is almost gone. We're eating hides, and I've been boiling the hides to make soup. It's horrible. It's like eating paste. But the children don't complain. They're such very good children. They even play, even though I'm afraid we'll die here. Little Eliza tried to show me a sunbeam the other day, and she cried when she couldn't hold it in her hand. I cried when she wasn't looking because it was so sad. If I could die instead of the children, I would. George is getting sicker and sicker, and his hand doesn't look like it's going to get better. I'm so afraid. I wish we were back in Illinois right now. We'd be sitting in front of our warm fireplace, we'd have lots of food and we'd be safe. That's what I really want now. I want to be safe.

Sara and Itchy stared at the screen. "I don't think I like this part very much," she said.

"It only gets worse after this."

"I'm afraid about what happens."

"But you know how it ends," Itchy said. He felt bad, too, but it puzzled him why Sara would be scared. "If you already know how the story ends, what's to be scared of?"

"But *we're* telling the story," Sara said. "It's different. It's like it's really happening right now, and we can change the ending if we want. Maybe it's because you're going there. That's scary. I mean, you'll be where everything happened! You'll be at the same places where they died." Sara's eyes filled with tears. "It's scary, Itchy."

Itchy wasn't sure what to do. In movies and on T.V. this is where the guy would hug the girl and tell her everything was going to be all right, don't be afraid, we'll be okay, all that stuff. Itchy felt kind of stupid doing that, though, because he was just a geeky kid. But he clumsily put his arm around Sara's tiny shoulders anyway, and she pressed tightly against him.

"I'm afraid about what happens," she repeated.

"We'll...finish it together and it'll be okay."

"Be safe, Itchy. I mean when you go down there. Be safe."

Itchy nodded and held Sara tight. He was scared, but he didn't want her to know it. But he was excited, too, because his dream, the thing he'd wanted for so long, was about to come true.

In seventy-two hours he'd be at Alder Creek.

Irene hadn't slept much Thanksgiving night, and she called Jacqueline Friday morning and told her she wouldn't be coming in to the salon. It didn't matter much, anyway, because they only had a couple of appointments.

"You take it easy, honey," Jacqueline told her. "Gotta get over what that dirtbag did. Is Itchy okay?"

Irene stared into the ripples on the surface of her coffee. "He's still in bed. He came home pretty late from Sara's, but he seemed all right."

"Good. He's a good boy. You just relax, honey. I'll hold down the fort."

Irene sat in the singlewide's dingy kitchen. It still smelled of last night's turkey, of gravy and mincemeat pie. It smelled happy. Irene lifted the coffee to her lips. Her hands shook. She sipped, but the coffee tasted sour and bitter.

Red. She couldn't flush the Red thoughts no matter how hard she tried. She felt stupid. Used. Like somebody had pulled a nasty practical joke and now the whole world was laughing at her. Donner Party. Shit. All those years, and she believed him. Read the books to Itchy, studied the history like it mattered. And it was just a big lie, one designed to humiliate her and Itchy. While Red was gone for eleven years he didn't know that his lie would root so deeply—or maybe he knew but didn't care. And now she got to clean up the wreckage. One thing was for sure, Irene thought: No matter what Red said or did—even if he came crawling back for forgiveness—as far as Irene was concerned, Red Donner was history. She hoped he'd be too ashamed to come back, but knowing Red—and his knack for shamelessness—he'd soon show up at the door, grinning, swearing, begging forgiveness, trying to worm his way back into the family. Wasn't going to happen. Not this time. Irene Donner—make that Weatherly from now on, she decided—won't be fooled again. She and Itchy would go somewhere far away, someplace where Red couldn't find them. They'd try to forget about it all—the lies, the deceit, the embarrassment. That was the worst part. Feeling like a fool.

She sat and sipped her sour coffee until it cooled. It was late. Time to wake Itchy up. But Irene couldn't force herself to get up from the table. Let him sleep a little longer. Kids need lots of sleep.

She sipped her cold coffee and stared out the window.

Itchy had been awake since five o'clock, but he didn't want his mom to know. He quietly—very quietly—gathered what he'd need for the trip to Alder Creek. His backpack would be filled to bursting—extra clothes, a digital camera that Sara was letting him use, his notebook and copy of the unfinished *Tamsen's Lost Journal.* He figured he'd read it, and re-read it, on the bus ride down. Get him in the mood. Not that he really needed to, but might as well do something useful for all those hours.

As Itchy packed a strange sensation gnawed at him. Something out of whack, a weird feeling that things weren't right. It took him awhile to realize that Uncle Jimmy's accusation that they weren't really Donners still bothered him. Itchy had been able to crush his doubts after the initial shock passed. He knew that Uncle Jimmy—and his dad—were dead wrong. But the very idea that somebody related to him could deny their Donnerhood—that wasn't right. It was like telling a black person that they were really white. It was so obviously wrong and stupid that you could laugh in their face, but it still disoriented you because it was just so weird. Itchy shook his head. Sad, really. When he and Sara finished *Tamsen's Lost Journal* maybe he'd sit down with his dad and call Uncle Jimmy and let them in on the truth. Poor guys. Denying reality. Itchy felt sorry for them. Sometimes the really religious kids at school, the ones who went to Pastor Earle's church, would try to convert other kids and get laughed at or beat up. Itchy thought their religious stuff was stupid—after all, the only religion that made any sense was Catholic—but he understood how they felt. If you were sure something was right you wanted to convince everybody else who didn't believe. In those kids' case what they believed was dopey. In Itchy's case, his—and his dad's—connection to the Donner Party was the one and *only* truth. He'd convince Dad and Uncle Jimmy eventually. Just give him time.

He finished stuffing his pack. He'd decided to wear his big parka, and he'd jam a few granola bars in the outside of the pack for the long walk down to Elk Creek. It was six miles, and to get there in time to catch the bus at three-thirty tomorrow afternoon, he figured he'd have to leave by ten. He'd never walked six miles before, but he was sure he could do it. He'd been tempted to see if Stan the Man or somebody else might give him a ride, but he didn't want any grown-ups to know where he was going, so walking was the only real option. He toyed with the idea of hitchhiking, but that seemed spooky—and besides, whoever picked him up might tell his mom. He'd walk. Tamsen walked all the way from Illinois to California, so there wasn't any reason why her great-great-great grandson couldn't walk six lousy miles downhill.

Now all he had to do was wait. Spend all day hanging around today, try to sleep tonight, and tomorrow morning he'd be on his way.

He'd go over to Sara's later. That'd help kill some time.

And then tomorrow....

The Donners must've felt the same way right before they left Illinois. Excited and a little frightened. Itchy felt more a part of them than he ever had before.

Thank God he was a real Donner. He wouldn't have had the courage otherwise.

"Did he call the cops?" Red asked as he rubbed his throbbing temples. He remembered now one of the reasons why he finally quit drinking. He hated the fucking hangovers. That's why it was best to stay drunk 24/7.

Pencil wheezed as he peered in through the storeroom door. He flipped on the light and Red flinched at its brightness. He'd let Red stay there last night after the fight and Red had slept—or passed out—on a stack of flattened cardboard boxes.

"I talked him out of it," Pencil said. "He's a weird little fuck, but you shouldn't have done what you did."

"He hit on Irene."

"Still...."

"Yeah, yeah, I know. I'll send him some flowers or somethin'." Red slowly stood. "I gotta throw a mean piss. Thanks for lettin' me stay here, Pencil. You're a good guy."

"I'm a fuckin' prince. Irene toss you out?"

"Yep."

"Gonna get back with her?"

"Dunno. She's pretty pissed."

"This was a one-shot deal, Red. You're gonna need to find someplace else to stay. And don't be fuckin' with my customers. It's bad for business."

"Gotcha, buddy." Red strode past Pencil, headed for the men's room. He gave Pencil a friendly clap on the shoulder.

"Hey, Red?" Pencil said as he passed. Red stopped and turned. "None of my business. But if you got a brain in that fuckin' thick head of yours, you don't let Irene and Itchy get away from you this time. Be the dumbest thing you ever did."

Red nodded. "And I done my share of dumb-ass things. I'll fix it."

Pencil couldn't help but wonder: Do guys like Red Donner ever go through life without fucking up?

Father Ray splashed his face with cold water. He toweled off gingerly, because everything hurt. Red had given him a nasty shiner—his eye was swollen to a purplish slit. His upper lip flopped twice its normal size, and all his muscles—and his balls—ached. He imagined this is what it felt like to survive a horrible car crash. Still, he savored the pain. Sweet, divine punishment. Father Ray wondered if he was a masochist. Maybe he was really saintly, like those medieval freaks who used to flay themselves for Jesus. Yeah, right. Good old Padre Ray, getting his ass kicked in a sleazy bar by the jealous ex-husband of a cute little parishioner he'd lusted after. Some future pope was sure to beatify him for that, you betcha.

He couldn't wait to get the fuck out of here. He'd hide out in the rectory for the rest of the day, then hit the road tomorrow morning. Wonder what the bishop's gonna say when he sees the state I'm in? Father Ray wondered. Probably wouldn't even mention it. It'd be the elephant under the carpet. Father Ray smiled. Good for a laugh. Maybe he'd tell them he had to fight off unruly Baptist fundamentalists from torching the church. Sure, pin it all on Pastor Earle and his biblical literalist fruitcakes. The diocesan big boys might buy that.

It didn't matter. He'd be on the road tomorrow, away from this place, off to new adventures. Good. New is good. Humans crave change, even candy-ass ones like Father Ray. *Tsk-tsk-tsk*, he thought. Bad self image. Got to work on that. Love yourself, Father Ray. Sure. And maybe love cute little Irene Donners when you get to wherever you're headed....

Shouldn't be a priest. Need a woman. Quit, dump it, tell the bishop you want out. Do it, Ray, do it!

Father Ray sighed. He knew he wouldn't. He'd go down there, get called on the carpet and have his wrists slapped, lie his way out of trouble, and he'd be sent someplace else, probably a larger parish with a grumpy old chain-smoking priest to keep an eye on him. So be it.

Life sucked.

But the pain felt good. And when Irene Donner's face muscled its way back into his mind, he let her stay. Because, in spite of everything, she sure was cute.

And he liked thinking of her. Picturing her.

Shit.

Itchy couldn't sleep. He tried, but sleep wouldn't come. The past day had dragged, even though he'd spent most of it at Sara's house. They surfed the web for new Donner stuff but didn't find anything. They talked a little, played video games, and then, when it came time for Itchy to leave, Sara cried. She gave him a sweet, slow kiss, said, "Be careful, Itchy," and her tears wet his cheek. Then he went home.

He looked at his clock. One-thirty in the morning. He'd be exhausted when he left, but so what? He could sleep on the bus. It's just that, lying awake in the inky darkness, second thoughts crept in. Was this a stupid idea? He'd be in big trouble when he got back, that much was for sure. His mom would kill him. But she'd have to understand how important it was, how he *had* to see Alder Creek for real. Since the blow-up with his dad chances were they'd never get to go down there, so Itchy had to take matters in his own hands. She'd understand. Sure.

Sure....

Itchy thought about new *Tamsen's Lost Journal* chapters, how he and Sara would finish the book. When he saw Alder Creek, when he got a feel for the place, then he'd know how to end the saga. Whether Tamsen was murdered by Keseberg or froze to death in the creek. He'd know. Alder Creek would tell him its secrets.

His thoughts began to scatter in that way thoughts do as you drift off, and he finally settled into a light, restless sleep.

He dreamt of Tamsen.

*   *   *

Dear Mom,

You're going to be really mad. I'm sorry. But I have to go for awhile. I'll be okay, so you don't need to worry. I'll be back Wednesday probably. I'll explain everything then. You'll understand and I think you won't be mad when you understand.

Love,

Itchy

Itchy read the letter for the third time. It wasn't as eloquent as he wanted, but it was the best he could do. He felt bad that his mom would be worried, but he hoped that the letter would calm her down a little bit. He carefully folded the paper and put it in an envelope.

He slipped it into her dresser drawer, on top of her underwear. He figured that since she changed her underwear every day (she did, didn't she?) that she'd find the letter. She was working at the salon today, so she wouldn't be home until late afternoon. And by then Itchy would be on his way.

Ten o'clock. Time to go. He pulled on his fluffy parka, put on his Tamarack Loggers ball cap, and slung the backpack over his shoulders. Okay, he thought, here we go. This would be the farthest he'd ever been from home. He took a deep breath, looked around the singlewide, hesitated—

And then he left for Alder Creek.

Two hours later, Itchy had already gone four miles. He walked alongside the road, only ducking into the woods when he heard a car or truck coming. Luckily, Saturdays were light traffic days, with no logging trucks and few cars, so he could stroll on the pavement most of the time. He was too hot in the parka, so he tied it around his waist. It was unusually warm for a late November day, with bright sunshine and a clear blue sky. Perfect. This wouldn't have been any fun if it had been snowing, Itchy thought. It would've been more Donner-esque, but it was okay with him to have non-Donner conditions.

He was deep in thought about great-great-great Gramma Tamsen when a car careened around a curve on the road behind him. He didn't have time to hide. It had come up too fast, and Itchy barely made it into the muddy roadside ditch as it sped by. He peered over the leafless blackberry brambles hoping that the driver wouldn't stop. He held his breath.

And then he heard the car slow and stop; the transmission ground into reverse. The car was headed backwards toward him.

Father Ray had been shocked to see someone leap off the side of the road as he approached. Good thing whoever it was did, because Father Ray's vision through his one un-puffy eye had left his driving a little dodgy. He debated whether or not to stop, but the way the person acted was weird, and Father Ray still had enough of the do-gooder parish priest left in him to want to stop and offer assistance if needed.

He backed up to where the person had hidden and got out of his car. He saw a crouched figure down in the blackberry bushes. "You okay?" he asked. The figure didn't move or respond. "Hey," he called out. "Are you all right?!"

When he saw the telltale rashy red patch and bony profile of Itchy Donner peer up at him, Father Ray relaxed.

"Hi, Father Ray," Itchy squawked, trying to sound normal, as if they had just passed each other on the sidewalk. He'd gotten scratched by the blackberry thorns and a couple of bloody rivulets trickled down his arms.

"Why are you hiding in a muddy ditch?"

"Um, I don't know."

Classic stupid kid's answer, Father Ray thought. The exact kind of thing he would've said at the same age. "Do you need a ride?"

Itchy frowned as he considered. Father Ray immediately regretted making the offer, because the very idea of any member of the arch-nemesis Donner clan riding in his car was repellent. But he'd asked, so he couldn't really change his mind now.

"Okay," Itchy said. "I just need to go to Elk Creek." He scrambled up out of the ditch. His pants were caked with mucky goo and his hugely over-sized fake Nikes had so much gunk on them they looked like chocolate sneakers.

"Mind scraping some of that off before you get in the car?"

Itchy nodded and chunked off the biggest pieces, but he was still a mess. Father Ray sighed. Now he'd have to clean the MG when he got down to Boise.

Itchy climbed in, his fat backpack and puffy parka taking up a surprising amount of space in the front seat of the tiny car. Father Ray got in, fired up the noisy engine, and they sped off.

They drove for a minute, neither saying anything. Father Ray wasn't in the mood to talk, but curiosity finally got the best of him and he asked, "So why are you going to Elk Creek?"

Itchy said vaguely, "Um, just because."

Father Ray downshifted as they took a tight curve; he hugged the inside edge of the lane. He was really going too fast for the road, but that was part of the joy of owning a sports car. He liked to hit the corners fast, keep his RPMs up, squeal some rubber and feel the car labor to hold the road.

Itchy smiled. "This is a cool car."

"I like it."

Itchy looked over at him. "Did you get in a fight or something?"

"Actually, your dad did this to me."

Itchy's eyes widened. "He did?! Why?"

"Ask him."

"I don't know if I'll see him much," Itchy said, sounding sad.

"How come?"

"He had a fight with my mom. She thinks he lied about some stuff. She said she isn't going to let him stay with us anymore."

Father Ray nodded. That would explain the ass-whupping. The white-trash shithead was taking out his frustrations on me, Father Ray thought. Would've been a whole lot easier if the asshole had just gone to confession.

Father Ray glanced over at Itchy. Down at his backpack. Back up to his face. "Are you running away from home, Itchy?"

Itchy blushed. "No," he said, his voice cracking. "Not really."

"Where are you going?"

"I have to go see something."

"Where?"

Itchy squirmed and looked out the side window. "I just need to go some-where."

"Your mother will be worried."

"I left her a note."

"I shouldn't be helping you."

Itchy turned back toward Father Ray. Tears glistened in his eyes. "Please don't tell on me."

"If something happens to you it'll be my fault."

"Nothing's gonna happen. I promise."

Father Ray double-clutched as they hit another curve. He was almost to Elk Creek, and he had to make a decision. This kid was going to do something stupid, and Father Ray needed to step up and stop him.

Or did he?

"How old are you?" Father Ray asked.

"I just turned twelve."

"Not really old enough to be on the road by yourself."

"Please Father Ray," Itchy pleaded. "I *have* to go somewhere. I'll be okay. Please don't tell my mom."

They pulled into Elk Creek. Father Ray parked in front of the tiny post office. He shifted into neutral and kept the MG running. "If I don't say anything to your mother I'd be seriously derelict in my duties as a priest and as an adult."

Itchy said nothing. He stared at Father Ray. For a moment Father Ray thought that the weird kid didn't understand what he'd just told him, but then Itchy said in a quiet, almost threatening voice, "I heard that you kissed my mom."

"My superiors already know about that," Father Ray snapped, his heart beating faster as anger rose in him. "Get out of the car."

Itchy gathered up his pack and parka and quickly got out. Before he closed the door he peered back in at Father Ray. "Don't tell on me," he said. But he wasn't begging this time. His voice was sure, and Father Ray saw some of that Red Donner arrogance. This scrawny little shit had a nasty dose of his old man in him.

Father Ray grabbed the door handle, slammed it, and sped off. He looked in his rearview mirror at the shrinking image of Itchy Donner standing on the sidewalk. Watching.

Father Ray stomped on the brakes and screeched to a stop in front of the Elk Creek General Store. A pay phone in front. *Get out and call her.* You don't leave a twelve-year-old kid on his own. Got to be some kind of liability, some kind of law against it. But then, what did he really do wrong? Gave a kid a ride. Actually protected him from the danger of walking on a road by himself. Wasn't his business what the kid was up to. Shit, kids younger than Itchy rode four-wheelers all over hell up here, these mountain kids grew up early. Had to. He'd seen kids not much older than Itchy driving their parents' pickups. This was primitive country, kids had to grow up early. And if some little mountain cracker needed a ride from Tamarack to Elk Creek, so what? Maybe he was going down there to buy his mom a birthday present or something. Was that Father Ray's problem? Why should he give a shit?

Father Ray stared at the pay phone. Then looked in his mirror. Itchy was still back there, standing in front of the Post Office, staring at him. Waiting. Taunting. Daring him. Call her...don't call. Do the right thing...don't care. Irene Donner. A moment's softness, a moment of regret. Red Donner. Motherfucker.

Father Ray. This is your moment of truth. Whatcha gonna do?

Father Ray gunned the engine. Reached for the gearshift. Jiggled it. *Call her.* Tell her where her son is.

Red Donner kicked your ass. Irene Donner's mother ratted you out to the bishop.

Consider...consider....

When Father Ray jammed the tranny into first and sped off, he surprised himself by smiling.

By the time he hit the edge of town, the smile had turned to laughter....

Itchy watched with relief as Father Ray roared off into the distance. That was the first time he'd ever beaten an adult at something important. It felt good.

Like the times he knocked his dad off the log when they were practicing for Logger Days. His secret was safe. Close call, though. Now he had a couple of hours to kill before the bus came. Good. This was turning out better than he expected.

He walked down to the general store, bought a Mountain Dew and a bag of Doritos, and settled on a sun-drenched bench to wait for the bus. As he crunched happily on the chips he read through *Tamsen's Lost Journal* yet again.

"Here," Itchy said as he handed the ticket to the driver. The elderly black man nodded disinterestedly and Itchy climbed on board. He half expected somebody to yell at him, somebody to stop him, somebody to scream, "Hey, kid, you can't go to Alder Creek by yourself!" But nobody noticed or cared. The driver hadn't bothered to glance at his face for more than a second.

Only a few people were on the bus. A couple of old ladies sat together—one snoring softly, her head tilted sideways as a cord of drool dangled from her slack mouth. Itchy quickly turned away from that gross-out scene. A few grubby looking guys, young and old, all bored, stared blankly out the windows. A girl—who didn't look all that much older than Itchy—sat with her ugly little sleeping baby sprawled on the seat next to her. She glanced at Itchy and then went back to reading a dog-eared copy of *People*. That was it for his busmates.

Itchy moved to the rear of the bus, back by the bathroom, and settled into a seat. He wanted to stay in back so he could keep an eye on the other riders. It wasn't that he was scared, but this was his first time out in the world alone and he wanted to be extra careful.

The driver climbed tiredly back on board, the door squealed shut, and they were on their way. Itchy leaned back in the seat. He had to concentrate to control his breathing. He was so excited he couldn't stand it. He was on his way, he'd done it! A little over twenty hours and he'd be there. A tear leaked out of his eye, a happy excited tear. He was relieved nobody saw it, because they would've thought he was a goof. This was *so* cool! Itchy Donner, man of the world, on his way to finally meet his past.

Cussing was stupid, but he couldn't resist murmuring to himself one of his dad's favorite expressions: *"Fuckin' A, Bubba."*

Irene was weary. It'd been a long day of hairdressing at the salon. They'd been busy for a change, and in some ways she preferred the dead days. She needed the money, but she was so, so tired.

"Itchy?" she called out as she got home. It was after five o'clock and already dark outside. The warm day vanished with the sun, and a biting cold had settled over Tamarack. "Are you home?" she said.

No response. It annoyed her that he hadn't come home yet. He knew the rules: be home by dark and help her with dinner. She picked up the phone and punched in the numbers for Sara's house. A. Jackson answered, "'Lo?"

"This is Irene Donner."

"How you doing, Irene?" A. Jackson asked pleasantly. He seemed nicer to Irene since the business had failed. Failure had taught him some humility.

"I'm fine, Mr. Flynn. Is Itchy over there?"

"Just a second." She heard him call out to Sara and ask if Itchy was around. "Sara says he hasn't been over today, Irene."

"Oh. Okay. Thank you."

"You bet. You have a nice Thanksgiving?"

"Yeah. Well, interesting, at least." She didn't know him well enough to go into the gory details, and she needed to track down Itchy. After a few more pleasantries she hung up and called Stan the Man and Mart's place.

"Me and Stan haven't seen him all day. Maybe he's with Red," suggested Mart.

"Probably," Irene sighed. "Just what I don't need to deal with right now. Do you know where Red is?"

"I heard he's been hanging out at Pencil's."

"I'll call over there."

"Lemme know if you need help rounding him up." Mart paused. "Are you doing okay?"

"Just tired. We were busy today."

"How about...the Red business?"

"I'm fine," Irene said. She was too tired and annoyed to talk about it. "If you see Itchy tell him to get back here."

"Will do," Mart said.

Irene hung up and stared at the phone. Where could he be?

Red sat hunched at the bar, sucking up Jack Daniel's like water. Pencil had reluctantly let Red sleep in the storeroom again last night, but he told him in no uncertain terms that tonight Red had to find someplace else. Red nodded sullenly and kept drinking. It was like the old days, Pencil thought, except Red wasn't fun anymore.

When Irene stormed into the bar and demanded, "Where's Itchy?" to Red's hunched back, he'd flinched as if struck. "I swear to God if you're pulling something stupid like trying to take him away from me—" she threatened.

"I dunno where he is," Red said in a thick, slurred voice. "Ain't seen him since the other night."

"I can't find him!"

Red set his glass down and slowly turned to face her. He looked terrible. Puffy bags hung under his eyes, and his hair was matted and greasy; a dull, sad expression pulled at his mouth. "You check with Sara?" he asked.

"Of course I did. I checked everywhere he might be. I can't find him." She tried to keep the screechiness out of her voice, but heads turned anyway toward the embarrassing little domestic spat.

"Huh," Red said. "He'll turn up. Probably out starin' into the sky and dreaming 'bout Donners."

"Enough of the goddamn Donners! Will you please get off your ass and help me find him?"

Red finished his glass and slowly swayed to his feet. "All right. Let's go track him down."

"How much have you been drinking?" Irene asked.

"Enough," Red mumbled.

"I'll send Stanley and Mart out drivin' 'round to look for him," Jacqueline said. Irene had called her after she and Red had knocked on doors all around Tamarack, asking if anybody had seen Itchy. Nobody had a clue. Irene's panic was rising.

"He's so dreamy, honey, you know how he is," Jacqueline continued. "Probably got his nose buried in a book someplace."

"We checked the library," Irene said. She tried to stifle hysteria's nasty little probing fingers. "Nobody's seen him today."

Red stood by Irene, nervously shifting from foot to foot. They'd come back to the singlewide after their unsuccessful search of Tamarack. It was seven-thirty.

"We'll find him, don't worry," Jacqueline assured her. "Red there with you?"

"Yes."

"Drunk off his ass?"

"He was. He's getting better now."

"Lemme talk to him."

Irene handed Red the phone. "Hey, J.W.," he said.

"Listen to me, and listen good, you asshole. I didn't want to stir up Irene, but you and me both know something bad's goin' on here. Call the sheriff's office as soon as we hang up and get 'em looking for him."

"Okay."

"And whatever you do, don't upset Irene any more than she already is. Step up and be a goddamn adult for a change."

"Lighten up, J.W., okay?" Red was going to say more, but Jacqueline slammed the phone down. He turned to Irene. "I'm gonna call the cops," he said. "Not that I want to make a federal case outa it or anything. Just so we have more eyeballs lookin' for him."

Irene nodded, her movements jerky. "What if something's happened?..."

"He's okay. We'll find him." Red looked up the number of the sheriff's office and called them. As he explained the situation, Irene stood off to the side, her arms wrapped tightly around herself.

Breathing was hard.

A few more passengers got on the bus along the way, but no one sat near Itchy. Fine with him. It was after midnight, and as the endless miles clicked off along twisty Highway 95, Itchy closed his eyes. He wanted to sleep, but he was still too keyed up to relax. Every bump popped his eyes open. There wasn't much to see, even though a full moon glowed over the deserted landscape. But Itchy knew by the time morning came they'd be close to the California Trail. Once they hit Winnemucca and Interstate 80, they'd be following the trail, seeing the same mountains, the same valleys, the same rivers that his ancestors had seen. Itchy couldn't believe he'd be following in their wagon ruts. How could he possibly sleep?

But after a time he finally drifted off, and he slept hard. When he awakened, sunlight warmed his face. He rubbed the sleep from his eyes. He'd slept so late! They were still on a two-lane road, so that meant they hadn't gotten to Winnemucca yet. The desert country was so isolated and treeless...Itchy had never seen anything like it before. He imagined what it must have been like to come through such places walking alongside a wagon train. Those people were so tough.

He got up, peed, rinsed his face, then went back to his seat and ate a couple of granola bars and his leftover Doritos. He watched the desolate mountains pass by, the scrubby brush, the occasional ranch in the distance clinging to the slopes of dusty, faraway hills. The air was dry here, and it smelled of sage. His lips had already begun to chap.

He was getting closer and closer. And the amazing, incredible thing—he could feel it! He could sense the approaching past. Somehow, it felt like his body was changing, becoming more...Donner. It was like he was in a time machine, each mile peeling back months, years, getting closer to 1846. Such a weird—and wonderful—sensation.

The bus stopped at a weather-beaten little ranch town near the Oregon border. A young, muscular guy climbed on board and plopped down a couple of seats in front of Itchy. Itchy watched him closely. He had thick black hair, deep brown skin...was he an Indian? Itchy wondered. Wow. Getting closer to Alder Creek, almost to the California Trail, and now he saw his first Indian! Itchy wanted to ask the guy if he was a Paiute or Shoshone, if he knew anything about *his* ancestors. For all Itchy knew, this guy's great-great-greats had stolen cattle from the Reeds, or followed along behind the Donner wagons and scared Tamsen! Amazing. This was better than Itchy could've imagined.

But he didn't say anything to the Indian. He might be pissed that his land had been taken, and, who knows, he might get mad if Itchy told him he was a descendent of the Donners. He knew that the Indians were still pretty sore about everything that happened to them. He couldn't blame them, really. So he left the Indian alone. Better to imagine than confront.

He settled back in the seat and waited for the bus to get to Winnemucca. He'd have to change to another bus there, and then he'd be on the trail of the Donners. Getting closer and closer and closer....

It had been the longest night of Irene's life.

A couple of deputy sheriffs came by after Red phoned, and, seeing that an Itchy absence was so unusual, had called in a volunteer search and rescue team.

A. Jackson, with the help of the deputies, had organized more search teams, and soon groups of loggers and millworkers combed the nearby woods looking for Itchy. By midnight the entire town of Tamarack was hunting for Itchy Donner. Red was out with them, flitting anxiously from group to group. A. Jackson finally told him he was getting in the way and to go home and be with Irene.

Mart and Jacqueline waited at the singlewide with Irene. Mart hated to be stuck inside with the women; he wanted to be out helping. Red came back at three-thirty in the morning with no news, and they glumly waited together in the living room. Mart ignored Red; he couldn't look at him without wanting to smash him in the face. Jacqueline chain-smoked, Irene waited, hollow-eyed, leaping up to look out the window at the slightest sound, Red paced, and Mart...Mart sat uselessly in his goddamned wheelchair and seethed.

"Anybody want something to eat?" Jacqueline asked at one point to no one in particular. Nobody responded.

The night passed, the sun rose, and still no word. A. Jackson came by to tell them that the teams were still out searching. "Maybe with the light...." he trailed off. "Itchy's tough, he's lived here all his life. I'm sure if he's out there he can take care of himself. Don't worry. We'll find him."

Irene nodded. A. Jackson's take-charge attitude reassured her. A little.

"'Preciate all your help, A.J.," Red said.

"We gotta stick together while we can, Red. That's the best part of Tamarack."

After A. Jackson left, Irene went into the bathroom and splashed cold water on her face. The gnawing worry, fear...she'd never felt so alone. *Please let him be okay*, she prayed. As much as she didn't want to, maybe she'd call Father Ray later. She needed holy help, even if it was from somebody like Father Ray. She realized it was Sunday; she probably wouldn't go to mass. But she'd call him later. Or maybe sooner. He could have everybody at mass pray for Itchy. If anybody went, that is. Most of them were already out looking for him.

She decided to shower, to try and wash the weariness away. It didn't work, but as she toweled off she felt hunger pangs. Wherever Itchy was he must be starving, she thought. She began to cry. *Let him be okay, please let him be okay!* Big, gaspy, anguished cries, *oh God this can't be happening!*

Irene forced her breathing to slow. Forced herself to calm down, to level out.

She went into her bedroom and pulled open the dresser drawer. Grabbed a pair of panties. Her hand brushed against something. She looked into the drawer. She gasped and let out a muffled little scream when she saw it.

An envelope with one word in Itchy's scrawled handwriting:

MOM.

The bus change at Winnemucca was uneventful, and as Itchy surveyed his new travelling companions he didn't see anybody interesting. The Indian wasn't continuing on, and Itchy watched him walk off down the street. That was too bad, Itchy thought, because he'd been working up his courage to talk to the guy. Now he'd never know if he was a Paiute or a Shoshone. Or even an Indian at all.

But Itchy soon forgot about the Indian—and everything else—because they were headed west on Interstate 80, and he was now following the California Trail.

He gazed out the window, fascinated, trying not to blink because he was afraid he'd miss something, a vista that George and Tamsen might have seen. The Humboldt River came into view. Itchy's heart pounded. The very same river they followed! His mouth went dry, he couldn't breathe, the excitement was too much. He knew every twist and turn of the trail now, and as scrubby mountains to the east and west swept into view, he knew all their names. *Ohmygosh, 4G Tamsen looked at this very same view!* Pesky tears bugged him again, the emotion of finally seeing this was too much. He blinked them away, they blurred his view and he couldn't let that happen, he had to absorb every detail, every twist of the river, every chocolate-colored hill, every green patch that unexpectedly burst forth from the desert floor around unnamed springs.

Closer, closer, the bus sped past the Humboldt Sink, the forbidding, puddly lakebed where the Humboldt spilled and died and evaporated into alkali dust, Itchy gasped, they camped *here* in October, 1846! *Then they had to cross the Fortymile Desert, they had to get to the Truckee River, they knew they were getting close, but it was late in the year, and ohmygosh, maybe right over there by that hill is where the Paiutes killed all those cattle that belonged to Mr. Eddy!*

Itchy couldn't help it, he cried now, all the years, all the books and web-sites and pictures and dreams and he was here, *here,* where they'd been, and soon the bus would pull into Reno, then climb up the Truckee River canyon, and then, at the top, Truckee itself. He'd be so close. He wiped away tears, imagined the landscape of over a hundred-and-fifty years ago, it wouldn't have looked much different, and Itchy was overwhelmed by the connection to his ancestors—so strong, so impossible *not* to feel. How could his dad and Uncle Jimmy say that it was a lie? They were crazy! His dad's lie wasn't a lie, it was true, if only they came to see and feel for themselves!

The interstate followed the Truckee River into Reno, and Itchy's over-heated imagination saw wagons and Indians and pioneers around every bend. The bus stopped downtown, but Itchy didn't get off. *C'mon, c'mon, let's go!* he thought. When the bus finally pulled out of the station with a full load of pas-sengers and drove past the casinos and high-rises, Itchy didn't care. The city meant nothing to him—even though he'd never been in one before. All he wanted was to get back on the trail.

The bus climbed the onramp, back on the interstate, and Itchy stared up at the gray wall of the Sierras looming ahead. It was the scariest thing he'd ever seen. How could they have even considered getting over those? Wispy mares' tail clouds swept above the summits, and early season snow capped the very highest peaks. Itchy was in awe. Here it was, the formidable wall that stopped his ancestors—and killed some of them. Absolutely, positively incredible.

The bus began climbing. Itchy knew that the old trail was north of here, so he was less impressed with the views since Tamsen and the rest hadn't been along this route. He looked with idle curiosity at the railroad tracks clinging to the canyon's wall—that was where the transcontinental railroad first came in 1869—and old log flumes, but that history didn't interest him. Donners, 1846, the only history that mattered.

The bus reached the summit. Itchy peered out the window. They'd soon be at Truckee. He stretched to look over the seats in front of him, he craned his neck to see through the windshield. Far in the distance, a higher ridge of mountains. Snow-capped. Itchy gulped. He *knew* those mountains, that slight notch in the middle—

He was looking at Donner Pass.

Even though Irene had found Itchy's note, the search teams continued to hunt for him on the off chance that he'd run away to go camp out somewhere in the woods.

"The good news is that we know he meant to leave," A. Jackson told her. "So we can stop worrying about accidents and kidnappings and things like that."

"This is all his fault," Jacqueline griped, pointing at Red. "If you hadn't—"

"Drop it, J.W.!" Red snapped.

"What matters is finding out where he went," A. Jackson said, trying to calm the situation. He looked over at Irene. Since she'd found Itchy's note she was more angry than anything else. She wanted to smack Itchy from here to Boise. "Any ideas, Irene? Does he have any favorite places to go?"

"I dunno, we've looked everywhere I can think of around here."

"Would he go someplace else?" A. Jackson asked.

Irene thought for a moment. She looked down. Then her head snapped up. "Oh God!"

"What?" A. Jackson asked.

"We need to talk to Sara...."

Sara sat at her computer, idly surfing. She didn't really see the colorful websites flashing before her. All she could think of was Itchy. And how much trouble he was going to be in when he came home.

Sara had been amazed at the way the grown-ups overreacted about this. She and Itchy hadn't really thought things through; it never occurred to them that police and search teams and bloodhounds would be out looking for him. At least Mrs. Donner finally found Itchy's note, but that didn't calm things down much. Sara was scared. Not for Itchy—she figured he was okay, and he should almost be to Truckee by now anyway. No, Sara was scared for the adults. They were all acting crazy, even her daddy. Why didn't they just take Itchy at his word? He said he'd be back Wednesday, why didn't they just relax? Adults were so weird.

She heard the door downstairs open, and footsteps thumping up the stairs toward her bedroom. It sounded like a bunch of people. Her door swung open, and there stood her father, glaring. Irene and Red and Jacqueline stood behind him.

"Sara!" A. Jackson barked. Sara knew she was in big, big trouble.

"Yes, Daddy?"

"Itchy's mom would like to speak to you."

"Okay," Sara said in a weak little voice.

Irene slowly moved past A. Jackson. She pulled up the small desk chair that Itchy always sat in when he and Sara surfed the web together. "Can I sit down next to you, Sara?" she asked gently.

"Okay." Sara's head felt spinny. She missed her mom. She wasn't exactly sure why.

Irene sat close to her, then reached over and clicked off the computer. The room was utterly silent. "I'm really worried about Itchy," Irene said. She tried to keep her voice calm and friendly.

"He's probably okay," Sara said.

"I need to know where he is. Do you know where he is, Sara?"

Sara hesitated and looked at the floor. "No," she whispered.

"I think you do."

Sara looked at her father for help. He glared at her with the sternest look she'd ever seen. He wasn't going to rescue her. Red and Jacqueline glared. She had no allies.

"I don't know," she said, but her voice quavered and her eyes leaked tears.

"Sara," growled A. Jackson. "We don't have time for this!"

Irene held her hand up but never took her eyes off of Sara. "I know you and Itchy are best friends, and I know you want to be loyal to him."

Sara nodded slowly.

"And I know he probably made you promise not to tell. But this is important, Sara. Itchy's only a little kid, and he might get hurt. You don't want anything to happen to him, do you?"

"No."

"Neither do we. That's why we have to know where he went. I think I have an idea, anyway. But you need to tell us."

Sara looked desperately around the room. The adults stared at her and waited. She couldn't betray Itchy, he'd kill her, and she'd promised. Why didn't they just relax, why didn't they just take it easy, he'd be back, he was fine, why didn't they—

"Sara," Irene said in a whisper. "Tell me where he is."

The tears turned on; Sara couldn't stop them. "I promised...." she moaned.

Irene gently reached around Sara's tiny shoulders and pulled her close. She caressed Sara's thin hair. "It's okay, sweetie...it's okay. Just tell us, everything'll be okay. We won't be mad at you."

Sara couldn't stop crying. She had a hard time getting the words out. "I'm sorry," she cried. "I promised Itchy."

"Tell us," Irene said.

"Itchy's...." Sara's voice caught in wet, convulsive sobs, and she couldn't speak.

"It's okay, honey," soothed Irene.

And when Sara finally forced out the dreaded words they slammed Irene so hard she thought she might hit the floor.

Sara had looked at her with haunted, betraying eyes and said simply: "Itchy's at Alder Creek."

Mother took me to a hole where I saw smoke coming up through the snow, and she told me that its steps led down to Uncle Jacob's tent, and that we could go down there to see Aunt Betsy and my little cousins. I stooped low and peered into the dark depths. I was afraid to go there since I had not seen them since the day we encamped. Then, they were chubby and playful. Now, they were so changed that I scarcely knew them and they stared at me as if a stranger. I was glad when mother took me back to our own tent, which seemed less dreary because I knew the things that were in it, and the faces about me.

Eliza Donner

January 15, 1847

Chapter Thirteen

Itchy stood on the sidewalk in downtown Truckee as the bus pulled away and shrouded him in a smelly brown diesel cloud. He couldn't move. He was finally here! He couldn't believe it. Only a few miles separated him from his past.

He was more frightened now than when he'd left Tamarack. He'd made the long trip all by himself, that should've been the scariest part, but now that he was here, alone, zipping his parka against the late November chill, he trembled with fear. Why?

It must be anticipation, he decided. Like that fluttery feeling you get before you do something really cool, like opening Christmas presents—or reading a new Donner book.

Itchy started walking. He had a couple of hours of daylight left, and he needed to get to the Donner Memorial. He wanted to check that out, then find someplace to sleep, and first thing in the morning head up to Alder Creek.

Semis roared by on the nearby interstate, and as Itchy walked past gas stations and stores no matter how hard he tried he couldn't get in the moment.

Too much twenty-first century intruded. He'd lost the sense of 1846 he had on the bus ride. He tried to block it all out, the cars speeding by on Donner Pass Road, the *thumpthumpthump* of some bozo's boomy subwoofer blaring rap in his lowered Honda Civic, the airplanes buzzing overhead—

Get back to 1846!

He spotted the agricultural inspection station on the interstate. He stopped and stared at it. That's where the Graves family cabin had been. Now the site was under a freeway. Itchy shook his head sadly. How could they have just paved over a holy place? He couldn't make himself see it as it was, couldn't conjure up a dream image of a hundred-and-fifty years ago. Disappointed, he moved on.

Itchy forced his imagination to see the area pristine again, and if he looked up, saw only the hills, the sky, concentrated on the cold, stinging air, then, just then, he could catch a tiny whiff of the past. 1846...desolation, alone, 1846, *1846*....

He walked quickly. The Donner Memorial was close. He crossed a bridge over the interstate, following the signs—although he didn't need to—and then, through the trees, he saw it—

The top of the statue. Itchy froze in mid-stride. His breath caught in his chest with a sharp, painful stitch. *Ohmygoshfuckin'ABubba there it is!*

The pioneers seemed to float in the trees, the man's brawny back, his arm raised, hand shielding his face from the sun so he could see the future, the woman huddled close to him, child at his leg. Itchy walked slowly alongside the road. Almost there. He approached the statue from behind, and as he got closer he could see the stone pedestal—twenty-two feet high, the same depth of the snow that winter of 1846-47—on which the sculpture stood.

He crossed the road. Gasping, but not tired. Stunned at the hugeness of the memorial. He'd seen pictures a million times, of course, but the reality of it, the immensity, so much bigger than he realized.

The present dropped away. The sounds of the highway vanished. Itchy stepped gingerly on the pine needles blanketing the ground. A few sad patches of early snow lay hidden in the shadows of rocks and brush, but Itchy didn't notice. His eyes stayed locked on the memorial.

He moved to the front of the huge statue. The familiar plaque, its words long burned into his memory, only a few feet away. He gazed up at the words he knew better than any prayer: *Virile to risk and find; kindly withal and a ready help. Facing the brunt of fate. Indomitable—unafraid.* He'd never really understood all the words, but two of them, they were the important words, and they meant everything to him and his Donnerness—*Indomitable* and *Unafraid.*

Unafraid.

Itchy set his backpack down and reached out to touch the pedestal's stones. Tears returned. Underneath the monument was the site of the Breen cabin. Terrible things had happened here, mere inches from his feet. Some thought that most of the bones had been buried underneath. Itchy closed his eyes. He felt the strong presence now, tugging at him, he was in the past. Even though this place wasn't where the Donners had spent much time, he knew the other families well enough—almost as well as he knew the Donners—that he felt part of their history, too. The Breens, the Graves', the Reeds, the Murphys, even Keseberg—all were part of Itchy Donner, and by being here now, he *knew* they were with him.

He gazed straight up at the huge statues far above. The man, stalwart, strong, indomitable, just like the plaque said. Itchy studied the fierce bravery in the man's bronze face. The woman, leaning hard toward the west, straining to get there, carrying an infant, she had an unstoppable expression of "Let's get where we're going, I've got things to do!" and Itchy could imagine that it was Tamsen, impatient to open her school and publish her botany book and journal. The girl, hiding behind her father's muscular leg, only she looked a little unsure.

327

But then, Itchy figured, she was a kid, so she wasn't quite as brave yet as her parents. But, one way or another, they'd get her safely to their new home. The silent statues spoke to Itchy. They were his ancestors. His present existed because of their past.

He sat on the pedestal's rock ledge. He sniffed back tears. He had to control his emotions, he knew that. This was just the beginning. He'd completely lose it at Alder Creek if he didn't buck up. *Be a Donner!* he told himself. He sat for a few minutes at the memorial, then he scooped up his pack and slowly backed away, not taking his eyes from the statues until he'd reached the parking lot.

He forced himself to turn away. The small Emigrant Trail Museum was in his view now. No cars in the lot—that amazed him. One of the most incredible places in the world, where you could touch and feel and *be* the past, and nobody visited on a Sunday afternoon? He couldn't believe it. What was wrong with people?

He decided he'd go into the museum after a trip to the site of the Murphy cabin. He walked along the short path that led to the site. Slowly, savoring the smells, the view, everything. He'd been here before, so many times he'd made this walk in his mind. Now it was real.

The wide gravelly path wound through the forest, and Itchy knew that around the next bend he'd see it. He slowed down, he wanted it to come into view gradually, like a movie fading in at the beginning.

The hulking gray boulder lay just ahead. Itchy slowly moved toward it. The forest was utterly silent. The sun had already settled behind the mountains' crest and the chill intensified; it seemed to muffle Itchy's footsteps on the path. Itchy shivered. He stopped walking. The huge stone scared him. It seemed so intimidating, and to know that families had lived against it during that long, cruel winter, that children died there, that bodies—including Tamsen's—were cut apart and eaten...seeing the rock, a tangible, remaining piece of that winter—it made everything real.

Itchy pulled the digital camera Sara had given him from his pack and took a couple of pictures as he got closer to the boulder. He stood directly in front of it. Where he was standing was right in the middle of the cabin they'd built against the stone's face. He squatted down and touched the soil. He closed his eyes. Just a flash, a chilly shiver, but for an instant, the cabin was there again, he was inside, it was so cold, so dreary, so...filled with the odor of death, he—

His eyes popped back open and he jumped to his feet. "Jeez!" he gasped. For that instant it was real. Too real.

He backed away. A bronze plaque affixed to the side of the boulder listed the names of the Donner Party. Itchy hesitated, then made himself move back to the stone. It towered above him. He read the plaque even though he already knew the words: *The face of this rock formed the north end and the fireplace of the Murphy cabin....*

He read on until he got to the names of the survivors and the dead. He knew them all. Knew their stories, the good and bad. Itchy took a tentative step toward the boulder. Speckly lichens spattered its surface, the gray roughness mottled as though it was old flesh. He reached out to it, because he *had* to touch it. He needed to feel the stone as they had felt it. He needed to touch it because this is where Tamsen's life ended. She'd come down to the lake camp after George died, and Keseberg was the only one left living here, everybody else was either dead or rescued, and here, right here, Keseberg...ate bodies. Including Tamsen's.

His hand shook. Slowly, his fingers outstretched, he touched the surface. Cold, rough, he placed the palm of one hand on the rock, then the other hand. He leaned against it. So cold. So rough. He knelt in front of the rock, his hands sliding down its face, and he felt like he should pray but he didn't know what prayer to say, a *Hail Mary* or *Our Father* or *Glory Be* seemed so ordinary, so instead he just drifted through the past. He gazed at the stone, knowing that they had gazed at the same place so long ago as they huddled in the squat, hide-covered cabin, how many of them had touched this very spot? Had Tamsen? Had Simon Murphy, only eight-years-old, leaned against the rock here, had he huddled with his brothers Landrum and William, had his mother Lavinah comforted him, had she caressed his head as it rested against the stone?

Again, the tears came. Itchy was overwhelmed by it all. Not scared anymore, just unbearably sad. To know what those people went through, to think that twenty-foot snow banks buried this spot, that they ate charred mice and boiled rotten buffalo robes and leather straps to survive, that Keseberg ate pieces of Tamsen...to finally see and feel the place. He couldn't stop crying.

He sat, leaning against the rock, for a long time. He cried for them all. They had probably leaned against the very same spot and wept, too, he thought. He owed them his tears. Tomorrow, when he was at Alder Creek, he'd be ready. It would hit him even closer than here, he knew, because that's where the Donners had been, but he could take it. He was tough. The tears made him tough.

He was *a Donner.*

"Hello," the ranger said. The plump, pleasant looking lady sat behind the counter reading the paper. She peered over it and smiled as Itchy walked in. He recognized the smile as one of those eager, teacher-like grins that older people give kids when they're overanxious to help or want desperately to make you learn something you don't really want to know.

"Hi," Itchy said. He'd stopped in the bathroom after his emotional stay at the Murphy cabin site, and after a face-wash he was feeling better.

"Did you need some help or information?" she asked.

"Um, I'd like to go into the museum."

"It costs one dollar."

Itchy dug through his pockets and pulled out a grimy, crumpled bill. "Here," he said.

"Are you all by yourself?" she asked.

"Um, my parents will be here in a little while. They dropped me off while they went to get gas."

"Not as interested in history as you are, huh?"

"No. Not really."

"Do you know much about the Donner Party? We have some pamphlets and books."

"It's okay." The lady was nice, but she was beginning to bug him. He wanted to go into the museum and look at stuff.

"All right, then. There's a slide show, too, if you'd like me to start it for you."

"It's okay. Thanks." Itchy decided it was time to be decisive, so he just smiled at the helpful ranger and walked on into the museum.

It was a dimly lit room, and not all that big. The first exhibits were about Indians, then displays about Chinese workers on the transcontinental railroad—but Itchy passed them by without a second glance.

He hurried to the Donner Party section. Encased behind glass, so many fragments of the past—even shards of china—could they have belonged to Tamsen? Buttons, salt and pepper shakers, reading glasses...if this stuff hadn't been connected to the Donner Party, it would've just been ordinary junk. But as Itchy stared wide-eyed at the debris on display, his breath caught just like at the Murphy cabin site. He wanted to touch, to feel the glossy smooth surface of the china pieces, to flip a button in his hand—had that button held 4G George's coat closed? But everything was protected from his touch, and he could only peer through the glass. Another display case, there's the rifle William

Eddy used to shoot the grizzly bear on November fifteenth, it helped feed the Reed and Graves' families. Itchy pressed his face against the glass and studied the rifle's barrel, its stock. He imagined its blast as Eddy shot the bear, he smelled the gunpowder...he wanted so much to touch it.

He ached to get closer to the artifacts, looking wasn't good enough, he *had* to touch them, to feel them, maybe that nice ranger lady would open up the cases and let him reach inside, maybe if he told her he was a Donner that would make a difference—after all, shouldn't descendents get some extra privileges?

Itchy read the museum captions explaining the displays, but they told him nothing he didn't already know. He stared at the replica of Patty Reed's creepy-looking doll that she kept throughout the ordeal—the real one was over in Sacramento at Sutter's Fort—and he studied minute pieces of charred bone fragments and other archaeological debris that had been sifted from the various sites over the years. He was so immersed in it all that when footsteps sounded behind him he didn't hear them. The only sounds in his head were from the past.

"Are you Itchy Donner?" a male voice asked.

Itchy was roughly snatched from 1846 and pulled into the deep, dark nightmare of the present. He closed his eyes. *Don't make me come back to now. Whoever you are, please go away!*

"Itchy?" the voice asked again.

Itchy sighed. This wasn't good. He slowly turned away from the display case, away from the broken pieces of his past. He faced the voice. And the present.

The first thing Itchy noticed was the gun. Even holstered, it looked huge. He studied the big belt—cops always had lots of jangly things hanging off their belts—and the perfectly creased pants. He slowly looked up into the face of the Truckee city policeman. The big cop smiled.

"Your folks are pretty worried about you," he said.

Itchy frowned. "Who's Itchy?" Might as well give lying a shot, he figured.

The cop shook his head and grinned. "Nice try. You need to come with me, son."

"Can I just look at some of this stuff a little longer?" he pleaded. The nice lady park ranger slipped into the museum and stood behind the cop. Her pitying look told Itchy everything he needed to know: they didn't understand. They thought he was a loser spaz.

The cop glanced back at the ranger. "Anything he can see that isn't out front here?" he asked.

"We have a few items he might find interesting," she said. She came to Itchy and put a motherly arm around his shoulders. "I hear you're quite the Donner Party scholar," she said as she led him through a door into a workroom behind the museum.

"Not too long, now," the cop called out.

The park ranger nodded. "There's some more pottery fragments back here. Things you can touch."

Itchy brightened. He'd been busted, but at least they were being cool about it. The only problem left now, though, was getting to Alder Creek.

He'd find a way.

The windshield wipers of Red's beater pickup slapped uselessly against the stabby, icy rain.

"Shoulda put in some new goddamn blades before we left," he griped.

Irene said nothing. She stared out the passenger window at the dark silhouette of distant mountains.

"'Course, bein' in such a hurry when we left and all, I couldn't really get the rig ready for a big-ass road trip. Sounds like they're takin' good care of Itch for us, though, don't it?" Silence. Irene didn't move. "We're makin' good time considering the shitty weather," Red continued, glancing over at her. His conversation had that forced quality of someone straining to fill the void. Still no response from her.

They drove a few more miles in silence. It was late at night, somewhere in the wilds of southeastern Oregon. The rain alternated between chubby semi-snow blobs and a straight-on downpour. They'd been driving forever it seemed to Irene, and they still had so far to go. She couldn't sleep. The truck was cold and uncomfortable, and she was too wired to sleep anyway.

"I'd go faster," Red said. "But there ain't much rubber on the tires, so I want to be careful."

Irene kept staring out the window. She wouldn't turn toward him. "You don't need to talk," she said wearily. Red's voice made her head hurt.

"Just tryin' to break up the trip."

"Don't bother."

"Jesus, Irene, you gonna punish me for-fuckin'-ever?"

She said nothing.

"I mean," Red continued, "Itchy's okay, he just got a silly notion to run away, shit, lots of kids do dumb-ass things like that, it ain't the end of the world."

The rain began to let up, and Irene could see the moon's bluish light shining through cloud breaks in the distance. "Why do you suppose he got that 'silly notion'?" she asked.

"Well, okay, I'll admit it's kinda my fault."

"It's *all* your fault." Irene didn't have the strength to argue. Her words came out flat and unemotional.

"That ain't fair."

"Red—"

"I mean," he said, "I ain't perfect. We all know that. The Donner fib just got away from me, that's all."

"I'm tired, I don't want to talk about it."

"A little forgiveness wouldn't kill you, Irene."

It surprised Irene that the absurdity of his weaselly self-pity didn't have her yelling at him. Maybe she was too tired, or maybe she didn't care about Red anymore. She didn't know. All she said was, "Just drive, okay? Once we bring Itchy back, I don't want to see you again. If you want to visit Itchy—and if he wants to see you—fine. But I don't want anything to do with you. I don't want to talk to you, I don't want to listen to you, I don't want to look at you, I don't want to know you exist. When we leave Tamarack you're welcome to stay in touch with him. But not me. Ever. Understand?"

Red flinched. "That's harsh."

"It's the way it is." She turned away from him and went back to staring out the window.

"Once you cool down we'll talk about it. I know you're not—"

"Please be quiet."

"Adults gotta discuss problems. Shit, Irene, I still love you."

"I don't love you. I'm not sure I ever really did."

Red sighed. He drove for awhile without saying anything. The occasional semi blew past, spraying them with sheets of muddy water.

"Remember that little fossil I gave you last Christmas? The fern?"

She didn't answer.

"Pops into my head all the time," he continued. "It's like when I see somethin' pretty, somethin' delicate, I think of the outline of the little fern on the rock. And then I think of you. I can be out workin', and I get a view for just a second, somethin' beautiful, and you and that pretty little fern are in my head. Why do you 'spose that is?"

"I don't know." Why wouldn't he shut up?

"I think it's 'cause there's a place in your brain where important stuff lives. Not that a little rock is important, but it's a connection to you, you know? I got a Irene place in my head, and it's where I put everything that's beautiful, everything that matters. Sometimes the little stuff is just as important as the big stuff. Lovin' you, that's a big deal. But that pretty little rock, it's like it's part of you, too. And a pretty sunset, or a mountain peak, or a big bull elk bugling in the morning when I'm out in the woods—all that stuff goes into the Irene zone in my head. It's about beauty...it's the place where I keep the things I love. Itchy's there, too."

"Where do you keep your lies?"

"I'm tryin' to get rid of that place," he sighed.

Irene whispered, "Just drive, Red. Just drive."

It surprised Itchy that Officer Roy turned out to be a really nice guy. If he was going to be caught by a scary cop with a big gun, he could've done a whole lot worse than Officer Roy.

Mrs. Officer Roy—Itchy couldn't remember her name—had clucked and cooed and offered Itchy cookies when Officer Roy brought him home to stay with them.

Officer Roy had taken Itchy to the police station after he'd finished looking at—and touching—the artifacts in the museum's back room. Broken china, some gun parts, unidentified iron scraps...Itchy had studied and held them all. The park ranger patiently explained where the pieces had been found, what the scientists planned to do with them, how they analyzed everything...it had been great. Itchy was almost happy that Officer Roy had captured him, because otherwise he'd never been able to see all this. Itchy thanked the park ranger profusely as they left, and she said he was welcome to come back any time—although preferably with his parents.

At the police station Itchy had talked to Irene on the phone. He'd never heard her sound so furious. He was in bigger trouble than he realized.

"Are you all right?" was the first thing she asked.

"Yeah," he said. "Are you mad?"

"What do you think?" she snapped. "We're driving down there to get you."

"Is Dad coming?"

"Yes," she said. "We're both really disappointed in you. How could you do something so stupid?" She didn't give him a chance to answer. "When we get down there we're having a long talk, Itchy. This Donner business has to end."

"But you wouldn't believe the cool stuff I've seen!" he said. "I actually touched the rock at the Murphy cabin site, and they let me see some of Great-great-great Gramma Tamsen's china!"

"You're not related to those people!" Irene yelled into the phone. Itchy jerked the phone from his ear, and Officer Roy, standing nearby, heard it and winced. He felt bad for the scabby little kid. He liked being a cop, but anything that involved family troubles always bothered him. And it seemed that most of the trouble people got into had family roots.

"Your father lied, you know that. You're *not* part of the whole Donner thing, and I'm sorry I ever told you that you were. But it's over, Itchy. This has to stop. Something terrible could've happened to you. You have to forget about it. You're not a Donner."

Itchy didn't say anything. She'd never understand—but that was because she wasn't really a Donner like he was. He was tempted to try and set her straight, but maybe now wasn't the best time. She was pretty steamed. When they got here he'd show her the Donner sites, and his dad, too, and they'd understand the truth. *Not a Donner*. Sheesh. Sometimes people were so dense. He loved his mom, but she was being really dumb about this.

Irene went on scolding him, but he tuned her out. She told him to be nice to the people looking out for him, and then she told him she loved him and that they'd be there tomorrow night to get him. Weird. First she yells at him, then she tells him how much she loves him. It sounded to Itchy like she was crying when she said goodbye. He'd never understand parents.

Officer Roy wasn't sure what to do with Itchy. They didn't want him to spend the night in juvie with the hard cases, but he needed to be supervised until his parents picked him up. They considered stashing him with a foster family for the night, but when he called around Officer Roy found that none of the Truckee area families had a bed to spare. So, since Itchy seemed like a nice kid, Officer Roy offered to take him in. Officer Roy's wife Marie liked kids— although they'd never had any of their own—and he figured she wouldn't mind. Something about Itchy Donner touched Officer Roy. The usual runaways he dealt with were druggies or troublemakers, not dreamy twelve-year-olds with fantasies of being Donner Party descendents. When he told Marie about Itchy's predicament she immediately agreed to let him stay the night.

Marie had cooked a big dinner—pot roast and potatoes—and Itchy had gratefully devoured everything set in front of him.

"You've certainly got a big appetite, Itchy," Marie told him. She was a tiny woman, pretty and fragile. The exact opposite of her burly cop husband. They reminded Itchy of his own parents, except they seemed to like each other a whole lot more.

"I'm kinda hungry all the time," Itchy said.

"So you took a bus down from Idaho, huh?" Officer Roy said. He offered Itchy more potatoes. Itchy accepted.

"Yeah. My friend Sara got the ticket for me on the web with her dad's credit card."

Officer Roy shook his head. "Computers...amazing the trouble you can get into on the things."

"But there's lots of really good Donner Party sites on the web. I've learned all kinds of stuff there."

Officer Roy exchanged a glance with his wife. Irene had explained the situation to Officer Roy—that Itchy had been deceived by his father's lies about being a Donner Party descendent, and that's why Itchy was so obsessed and ran away to Truckee. Heartbreaking stuff, and when Officer Roy had told Marie it had made her cry. He wanted to smack Itchy's old man for lying to the kid. Growing up in this day and age was hard enough without parents filling their kids' heads with bullshit stories. Officer Roy wondered if Itchy's old man was some kind of backwoods, meth-head cracker or something...he'd heard stories about those people up in Idaho.

They'd enjoyed Itchy's Donner Party enthusiasm even if it saddened them. The kid was goofy but endearing. He'd fallen asleep on the couch shortly after dinner, and Marie had gently awakened him and led him off to the guest bedroom. He was asleep the second he slid between the sheets.

When Itchy awakened he didn't know where he was. Home? No, wait, Truckee, that's right. Sleeping in the spare room of Officer Roy's house.

Itchy sat up in bed and rubbed the sleep out of his eyes. The dinner last night sure was good, and now the sweet scent of bacon wafted through the house. He liked staying with these people.

He pulled open the curtain and peered outside. Yesterday's blue skies had been replaced by a leaden, featureless gray sky. It looked like Tamarack winter weather, Itchy thought. Too bad. It was much nicer sunny.

He got dressed and went out to the dining room. The house was cozy and small. Marie was busy cooking French toast and humming to herself.

"Hi," Itchy said.

"Good morning, Itchy! Did you sleep well?"

Itchy nodded. Mrs. Officer Roy sure was cheerful. "Where's Mr., uh, Officer Roy?"

"At work."

"Oh."

"Hungry?"

"Sure."

She dished him up bacon and scrambled eggs, three thick slabs of French toast drizzled with butter and syrup, and a huge glass of orange juice. Itchy was in heaven. Maybe he should run away more often.

"Your parents should be here early this evening," she said. "Do you miss them?"

"Yeah. I guess. But I've only been gone since Saturday."

"They must've been very worried when they didn't know where you were."

Itchy chowed down. He looked outside, through the scrubby pines that surrounded the house. "How far is Alder Creek from here?" he asked.

"Just a couple of miles up Highway 89. Why?"

"Just wondered."

"You know, that's called the Donner Camp. Where the Donners stayed."

Itchy resisted the urge to be a smart-ass and say "Duh!"—she was a nice lady and he liked her food—so he just nodded.

"But I suppose you already knew that, being the Donner Party expert that you are."

Itchy gulped down a huge mouthful of French toast. "Could I go there today? Could you take me?" he asked. "Before my parents get here, I mean."

Marie hesitated. "I'm not sure that's a good idea, Itchy."

"How come?"

"Well, I'm just not sure, that's all. We'll see."

The dreaded "We'll see." Itchy knew what that meant.

"I'll call my husband and see what he thinks, okay?" she offered.

Itchy nodded. Officer Roy was a good guy, he'd let him go. Cool. He'd see Alder Creek before Mom and Dad got here, then everything would be all right. He'd get back to Tamarack and he and Sara could finish *Tamsen's Lost Journal.* He'd be in trouble, grounded for life (not that it mattered), but his parents would get over it, and he'd have done what he set out to do. Mission accomplished.

"Could you call him now?" Itchy asked. He hated to be pushy, but he needed to get to Alder Creek.

Marie nodded weakly and called her husband.

He told her he didn't think it was a good idea, seeing that Itchy's parents didn't want the Donner fantasy to continue. "Just keep him in the house, let him goof around on the computer or something," Officer Roy told her.

When she told Itchy that they couldn't go to Alder Creek, Itchy pretended it was okay, no big deal.

But he'd go to Alder Creek before his parents got there.

He had to.

"Wanna stop?" Red asked.

Irene stretched and yawned. She'd watched as dawn blushed over the barren desert mountains. It should've been pretty and pleasant, but for some reason it bothered her. The sage covered desert, so open, so empty, was beautiful in its desolation, but Irene found the wide expanses off-putting. Tamarack, with its tiny, closed-in valley, tree-filled and shadowy, felt reassuring and safe. The miles and miles of nothing and the huge open sky out here seemed alien and scary.

"How far do we have to go?" she asked, yawning again.

"'Nother eight hours or so."

"If you see someplace that's not too gross, we can stop."

"Hungry?"

"I suppose."

A thick wall of dark clouds loomed to the south. "Hope we ain't drivin' into more bad weather," Red said. "We'll be losin' the sun pretty soon, looks like."

Too bad, Irene thought. She needed sun today. She had enough gloom in her life.

Red coughed and stretched in the seat. "Gonna have to surgically remove my ass from the upholstery once we stop," he said.

His tone and casual chatter annoyed Irene. "Does anything ever really bother you?"

"Sure."

"How come you never show it? Your son just ran away because of you

342

and rode a bus thirteen-hundred miles, doesn't that concern you?"

"Sure it does, but—"

"But if it's not about you, it doesn't really matter. That's it, isn't it?"

"C'mon, Irene, I don't wanna fight."

"I'm not fighting. I'm just observing."

"You're ball-bustin' me. Nothin' I say or do is gonna make a difference to you right now."

"Probably not," she said. "I just don't understand you."

"Never will, neither. Can't ever understand another person. That's just the way it is."

The sun slid behind the clouds, and what little early morning warmth its rays had generated vanished. Irene shivered. "Turn up the heat, please."

"Already got it up all the way," Red said, fiddling with the control. "Colder 'n' shit outside." He leaned forward and looked up at the gray sky. "Yep, got some nasty weather in our future."

"Wonderful," Irene said. She leaned her head against the window. Her breath fogged a triangular patch of glass, shrinking and growing with each inhale and exhale. "Now that I think of it," she said, "I *do* understand you, Red."

"Oh yeah?"

"Sure. It's easy to figure you out. You're nothing but a pathetic liar."

Red didn't say anything. They drove in silence until they came to a dusty little ranch town. They stopped for breakfast at a Basque café.

They ate in silence.

Itchy brought out every protective instinct Marie possessed.

She wanted to help the odd little boy, she wanted to give him something for that nasty rash, she wanted to feed him and bulk him up, she wanted to get his mind off the Donner Party fantasies...she wanted to mother him.

He reminded her of a mangy stray dog, abandoned and lonely, looking for a bowl of food, a bath, and an ear scratch.

She watched as Itchy's fingers danced over the computer keyboard. He was emailing his little friend at home, the girl who bought him the bus tickets.

"Would you like something to eat, Itchy?" she asked. He'd eaten lunch two hours ago, but knowing his appetite Marie assumed he was ready for more.

"Sure!" Itchy said. His fingers never stopped typing.

"I'll make you another sandwich. And how about some more chips?"

"Sure, thanks Mrs. Officer Roy."

Marie grinned. "You can call me Marie, Itchy."

"Okay," he said, not really hearing. He was too busy telling Sara about his adventures so far.

After she left the room, Itchy stopped typing. It was almost two o'clock. He needed to get going if he was going to see Alder Creek before his parents showed up. He figured it'd take forty-five minutes to walk there, another hour or so to soak it all in and...feel the place, and if he really hurried he might get back to the house in a half-hour. Three hours total. He'd have to leave soon, because it got dark around six. He considered. He hated lying to Marie since she was so nice, but sometimes you did what you had to do without worrying about hurting somebody's feelings. Nobody ever said being a Donner was easy.

He devoured the sandwich and chips she brought him, and he was about to try and come up with some lie to get him to Alder Creek when Marie inadvertently came to his rescue.

"I need to run some errands, Itchy," she told him. "Would you like to come along? I'm going over to Tahoe City. You could see Lake Tahoe."

"Thanks, Mrs....Marie. I think I'll stay here and use the computer. If that's okay."

Marie agreed and left him some apples and another bag of chips. "I should be back in a couple of hours or so," she said as she left.

Itchy watched her drive down the gravel driveway and turn onto the main road. The minute she was out of sight, he pulled on his parka and stuffed his backpack with his notebook and digital camera and copy of *Tamsen's Lost Journal*. He wrote a note and left it on the dining room table:

Marie, I'm really tired so I'm taking a nap before my parents get here. Can you wake me up at seven o'clock if they're not here yet? Thanks, Itchy.

That should give him plenty of time. Of course, when he got back everybody would be mad at him again, but tough luck, they'd get over it. And he'd finally have his visit to Alder Creek. It's all that matters, he kept telling himself. *It's all that matters.*

He stuffed the bed with spare pillows and a blanket so that if she peeked in the door it'd look like he was there. He'd seen it lots of times on T.V. and in the movies, and the fake body-in-bed always seemed to fool prison guards and bad guys, so Itchy figured it would work with a nice lady like Marie.

It was almost three-o'clock when he started toward Alder Creek. He hurried through the woods, staying out of sight of Highway 89, its noisy traffic always within earshot.

Itchy was sweating, even though the biting cold numbed his ears and nose. Tamarack never got this cold this early in the year, and Itchy wished he'd brought mittens. He stuck his hands in the parka's pockets, but having his arms immobilized made moving quickly clumsy. Forget it, he decided, it didn't matter if his fingers hurt. Cold hands were a small price to pay to visit Alder Creek, so he pulled his hands free as he ran, letting the frigid air chill his fingers to the bone. *Be a Donner! Indomitable, unafraid!*

And as he ran through the trees, as he got closer to Alder Creek, each footstep led him back, just like before at the memorial, the years, the decades, peeled away. Closer, closer, it didn't matter that his hands were freezing, *be a Donner!*, he was almost there, he knew it, he could feel it, and as he reached the Alder Creek parking area, he didn't see the asphalt and bathrooms and signs and traces of the twenty-first century, it was all invisible to him, he was completely unaware because:

Itchy Donner had just arrived in 1846.

"Cock-sucking, motherfucking bastard!" Red shouted as steam blasted his face from underneath the truck's open hood. "Fucking radiator hose blew. Piece of shit!"

Traffic roared by on the interstate. They were stranded in a dry canyon ten miles outside of Reno.

"Can you fix it?" Irene asked. She stood off to the side of the road, watching Red and shivering in the cold.

"No, I can't fucking fix it, Irene, I don't have a fucking replacement hose!"

"Lose the attitude," she said coolly.

Red muttered and cussed, fiddling uselessly under the hood. Irene glanced upward. The sky looked ominous; the clouds had that gray, ugly thickness about them that usually meant snow.

Red stared into the engine compartment for awhile, and eventually both he and the engine cooled down. Irene got back into the cab and waited.

"We're gonna need to catch a ride into Reno," he told her.

"Fine."

For half-an-hour Red stood by the disabled truck, his thumb dangling with the well-practiced nonchalance of a seasoned hitchhiker. A semi finally stopped, and the chatty driver—a Mississippi native named Bobby Lee—gave them a lift into Reno for the price of listening to his life story of finding Jesus. They bought a new radiator hose and a couple of gallons of Prestone, paid a cab for a ride back to the truck, and two hours later were on their way once again.

Irene was so exhausted she could barely keep her eyes open. It was only late afternoon, but it felt to her that night had already closed in.

"We should've called that policeman who's taking care of Itchy," she said.

"He'll be fine. We'll just be a little late. It's not that big a deal."

Irene didn't answer. She didn't have the energy. She fought desperately to keep her eyes open, but weariness overtook her. Her chin touched her chest and her eyes fluttered closed.

She didn't see the first tiny snowflakes strike the windshield.

Tamsen and Elizabeth Donner

They gave unselfishly, their fortunes and their lives that their children should survive. Near this site, in the winter of 1846, two pioneer women gave up their lives for their families....

Itchy tried to catch his breath as he quickly read the bronze historical marker. The parking lot was deserted. He skimmed the other signs, nothing he didn't already know, although it disgusted him that one sign said that the Emigrant Trail was now a mountain bike path—didn't people have any respect?—and then he quickly moved on to the narrow gravel pathway that led to—

—Where it all happened.

Itchy inhaled deeply. The air was so cold it hurt, but that didn't matter. The clouds had lowered, and it seemed later than it was. So dark already. But

Itchy didn't notice or care. He forced himself to walk slowly, each step crunching in the soft gravel, he needed to savor the feeling, and to understand, to go back, to...be with the Donner ghosts who still lived here.

The path led through huge pines—these trees were old, they had to have been here in 1846! He stopped and gently touched their trunks. They'd probably been saplings back then, maybe Tamsen had brushed against them, maybe Eliza had absently plucked needles from their branches, maybe....

Itchy moved forward. A meadow to his left. That area had been searched and excavated by archeologists a few years ago, he knew, and they'd found artifacts there. Some of the things he'd touched back at the museum. He gulped. His heart thumped against his chest. He pulled out the digital camera and took pictures. The autoflash popped because it was so dark out already. The clouds were the color of raw liver, low and frigid and ugly. Itchy shivered. His fingers were numb.

He moved on. The trail followed the meadows' edges. There were scattered trees around, some big ones (those *had* to have been here in 1846!), and low hills, but the area was more open than he expected. Off to his right he saw the Alder Creek valley floor, covered in a blanket of dusky-colored, frost-killed grasses. Some patches of snow hid beneath the trees and in shadowed draws.

Itchy stopped walking. Complete silence, except for his gaspy breaths. He couldn't believe he was actually at Alder Creek. *Concentrate, go back, be with them.* He closed his eyes. The cold penetrated even his oversized parka. How must they have felt back then, trying to stay warm with their thin, meager clothes? Rotten old buffalo robes they eventually tried to eat, dirty and tired and sick and freezing—how had they survived as long as they did? Itchy kept his eyes tightly closed. He was getting closer, he was feeling how they felt, sensing—

Then, a gust. Chilly, frigid, it brushed his cheek like a gentle slap. The silence was broken as a sudden wind whistled through the trees. A cold, bitter wind.

Itchy opened his eyes. Shivering, he hurried down the path. Past gray, bone-like snags of long-dead trees, toward the place, and now, oh yeah, *fuckin' Abubba,* this was it, now he had it, the feeling, Alder Creek, Tamsen and George, Itchy was home—

Ahead, the big snag. The Donner Tree. Itchy moved slowly, reverently toward it. Broken off, its bark stripped away, a charred cavern at its base, this was the tree that had been claimed for over a hundred years as the site of one of the Donner camps. Itchy knew that it probably wasn't really the place—the archeologists hadn't found much evidence there—but it still had the symbolism, and that mattered. Itchy ignored the plaques and signs and went to the huge stump. It towered over him, long dead but still majestic. He touched it, wishing his fingers weren't numb so he could better feel its roughness. This tree had been here when *they* were, and even if they didn't camp against its trunk they certainly saw it every day, passed by it, considered it a neighbor.

Itchy circled the tree, studying it from every angle, taking pictures. How many people had come to this tree, touched it, said prayers for his family?

The wind blew harder. He pulled up his parka's collar and tugged his ball cap tighter against his head. It didn't help. The searing cold cut through everything.

He knew he'd have to leave soon, but not just yet. He had the feeling, but, somehow, it wasn't enough. He needed more. Something was missing.

Itchy backed away from the Donner Tree, and as he did, something caught his eye. About a hundred yards to the northeast, in a stand of trees, he saw an incongruous patch of color. Something unnatural. What was it?

He left the path and hiked across the brushy area, pushing through soft dirt and ankle high scrub. As he got closer he saw flowers, red and yellow flowers. That didn't make any sense—not in November, not in the mountains. Then he saw the small white cross. He froze. What was this?

He stepped closer. Fading silk flowers, carefully arranged, surrounded the crudely made wooden cross. Itchy slowly knelt down on the dirt. This must be the place! He'd read that the real spot, the real area where they'd camped was near the Donner Tree, but left unmarked. Somebody—maybe other Donners?—had left this tiny, makeshift memorial at *the* spot.

Itchy touched the earth, then scraped up a handful of the pebbly dirt and let it slowly sift through his fingers. The howling wind scattered the dust into a long trail, its grit carried far away....

Itchy couldn't stop shivering. This was the spot. Right here, *right here*, Tamsen and George and the family had stayed, he knew it, he'd never been more positive of anything in his whole life. Itchy didn't notice the first snow spatters hit his back, he didn't feel the wind gain strength, he didn't sense that the daylight had dimmed, he shivered with emotion, with being a Donner on *the* spot where Donners lived and died, where Tamsen gave up her life to tend to George, where the children huddled for those long miserable months before they escaped, where....

Where Itchy was convinced his life began a century and a half ago.

He pulled out his notebook and pen, huddled against a tree trunk, and began to scribble notes, notes that Tamsen would've made. He'd rewrite it with Sara when he got home, but right now he had to get it on paper. The wind whipped the notebook sheets, his hand, like a claw, could barely grasp the pen, he had to squint to see what he was writing, and the words came out squiggly and almost unreadable because of the wind and his shivering and then—

The snow.

Snow like Itchy had never seen, blowing sideways, and suddenly so heavy, he had been in lots of Tamarack storms, but nothing like this, an instant whiteout, snow blowing so hard it found its way inside his parka, he pressed against the towering tree trunk, but it didn't help much, and frozen trickles worked down his neck and back, it's okay, he thought, this is it, this is the way it was for them! Now he knew for sure what it meant to be a Donner, this was incredible, how could he have been so lucky? He tried to write it all down, but the pen blobbed and streaked in the cold, and the pounding snow spattered the paper and smeared, and his hand just didn't seem to want to work right, and the noise of the storm got in the way of thinking, and he pressed against the tree, time to get out of here, he realized, but when he stood he couldn't see anything and he knew if he started running he'd get lost because it was impossible to see, better stay right here until it passes, so he huddled against the tree, hugged it, he'd write things down later, shivering, so cold, so, so cold, Tamsen and George were right here, they felt this, the same thing, the same wind, the same snow, they heard this, it's 1846 again, Itchy was part of it now—

Indomitable, unafraid.

He curled tightly against the storm, brought his knees to his chest, pulled his arms in tight, tucked his nose down into his parka, his ears so cold, *jeez, it's cold*, he thought, and what to do now? It'd pass, he'd be fine....

Think of them. That's important, think about the Donners, how this felt to them. Think of Tamsen. That's it, think of Tamsen. What would she be doing right now? *Okay, I'll think about Tamsen, and when the storm ends I'll write down what I thought about. I can think in her voice. That's what I'll do.*

Itchy shivered. The storm raged.

And he closed his eyes and imagined what Tamsen would've thought....

"Shit," Red said. The traffic on I-80 crept slowly up the Truckee River Canyon into the jaws of the blizzard. "Stupid flatlanders. They could be goin' a little faster."

"And end up sliding off the road," Irene said. She was sick of listening to Red. She'd awakened from her nap feeling even worse than before, all headachy and queasy and grouchy.

"Yeah," Red agreed reluctantly. "Maybe so."

"How much farther?"

"Ten miles. Gonna take forever, though. Sure the snow don't get any better higher up." Red paused. "Bet Itchy's lovin' it. Probably starin' out the window thinkin' that's the kind of storm that the old Donners went through." He chuckled at the thought.

"If that's supposed to be funny, it isn't."

Red's grin slowly faded. "No, 'spose not."

The defroster fought a losing battle to keep the windshield clear, and Red had to rub a circle in the glass every few minutes to see out. The snow was coming down so hard and fast they could barely see the taillights in front of them, and the road was quickly disappearing beneath swirling dustdevils of blowing snow.

The traffic stopped, and red lights flashed ahead. "Gonna make us chain up, I bet," Red said. "Just what I fuckin' need."

Irene leaned back and closed her eyes. She just wanted this to be over. She wanted Itchy back, Red gone, her life in order. Soon.

Soon, everything would be fine.

The shivering stopped.

Itchy forced his eyes open to slits, but the storm still raged. Why'd the shivering stop? he wondered. How come he wasn't cold anymore?

He squinted and tried to blink, but his eyelids felt strangely heavy, like they were fat and lazy. He couldn't get his brain to work right...he tried to think of someone, a familiar name...Tamsen...who?—had he been sleeping?—but his thoughts jumbled into bizarre colors and sounds and....

He suddenly felt warm. Almost hot. *Great parka.* This storm was nothing. As soon as it stopped he'd walk back to...where? He couldn't catch the memory. Where was he? Tamarack? That didn't seem right. Something happened. Wasn't home. Where? Tamsen? George? Eliza? Why did those names seem familiar? *Who...wait, I'm...Alder Creek? Donner. I'm a Donner. What's a Donner? Warm. Hot. Windy. Take off the coat, get cool, too hot, burning up, why can't my eyes see anything? Is it snowing? Am I outside? Mom? Tamsen? Who...I don't know where I am. Donner? Wind. What was that?! Am I a Donner? I am a Donner, aren't I? What's a Donner?*

Is somebody there?—

"Child?"

Itchy lifts his face from inside his parka and peers into the blizzard. The sudden warmth is gone, he's so cold now he's numb, he's very drowsy and just wants to sleep and he knows he shouldn't. But then, all of a sudden, he starts to get warm again. Weird. Doesn't make any sense. That's very strange.

"Child? Are you well?" the woman's voice asks urgently.

Itchy squints to see. It's dark, snow pelting him so hard he can barely keep his eyes open, the wind howls, and yet somebody's out here talking to him.

"What?" he says.

"You must come inside from the chill," the woman tells him.

Itchy still can't see who it is, but a tiny hand reaches toward him, and he reaches out and takes it. He doesn't see what happens next, but he's aware that he's moving through the snow, being led by someone. So dark, so scary, wind like he's never heard, snow coming down like a solid mass, he almost falls, but the strong, small hand grasping his pulls him forward and he couldn't stop if he wanted to.

Inside. The wind doesn't blast him anymore. His eyes are closed. His hand is warm now, and the hand holding it gives him a gentle squeeze.

"There," she says. "You are safe now."

Itchy tries to open his eyes, but the lids don't work. Melting snow trickles down his face, it feels like he's standing under a shower. The wind howls outside, near yet far, and it's now that the stench assaults his senses, a sickeningly sweet, decaying, rotten smell. He's smelled it before, from bloated, road-killed elk he's seen around Tamarack.

"Open your eyes," the woman says. "You may if you'd like. You needn't be afraid."

Itchy strains, and finally the lids pull apart. He rubs his eyes; it's like they're filled with dirt. "My eyes hurt," he says.

The woman's hand gently touches Itchy's forehead, caressing, moving his hair, and his eyes don't hurt anymore. He looks up.

She's a tiny woman, not much taller than Sara. But she's old—over forty, even older than his mom. She's dressed weird, a long, old-fashioned, threadbare dress, grimy shawl pulled tightly across her shoulders. Her face is round, and if she were better fed she'd have rosy cheeks. But she looks so tired, haggard, sallow. Purplish rings under her eyes, eyes that have suffered. She smiles at Itchy, and through her pain he sees friendliness, love even.

The light is so dim. A single candle flickers weakly. And that smell...what is it? Itchy wants to look around, see where he is, but he can't take his eyes from the smiling, kind-faced little woman.

"Who are you?" he asks, but he already knows because he's the one dreaming this and he can make it happen any way he wants.

"The storm is terrible," she says. Again, that knowing, friendly smile. "You shouldn't be outside in such weather."

"I didn't know it would be bad. I wanted to see—"

A horrible wet, crackling cough, *a wheezing, painful moan. Itchy turns to the noise.*

The old man is bundled in hides. The yellow candlelight isn't strong enough to really see

354

him other than in silhouette. His breathing is labored. Another moan. Bearded, gaunt, waxen.

"Is he okay?" Itchy asks.

The little woman now stands over the dying man. Itchy didn't see her walk there. Strange.

"He will soon be with the Lord," she says. "As will I."

"Where are your children?" Itchy asks.

"They left yesterday. They will live long lives if God wills it."

"They'll be okay. I know they will." Itchy is tempted to tell her what will happen to them all, but he can't get the words out. This probably isn't the time or place anyway.

The man groans, then throws off the hides. Itchy recoils at the sight of his arm, swollen grotesquely, purple and black and huge and horrible. As the man thrashes the odor—that's the smell, it's him dying—gets worse, and Itchy covers his nose.

Tamsen gently soothes George, quietly talking him back into calm, and she pulls the hides back up over him. He mumbles and hisses in delirium, but Tamsen is able to quiet him. Itchy looks around the tent. Much smaller than he thought it would be, it's pitched against a tree, and snow leaks in through tiny openings in the rotting oxhide. He's not going to ask 4G Tamsen about the whole cannibal thing, but he glances around the tent and doesn't see anything gross. Good. He knew it wasn't true, but now he has proof.

Later. Time has passed, but Itchy isn't sure how much.

Tamsen sits near George, whispering soothing words in German. Itchy sits next to her.

"Can I read your journal?" he asks.

Tamsen gestures to a pile of clothing and debris in the corner of the tent. Itchy digs through it and finds a stack of yellowing, stained papers tied with rough string. He unties it, looks at the words. The Lost Journal! Except now, it's not lost anymore. But as he thumbs through the pages the words don't make any sense, he's not even sure it's English, something isn't right.

"You and the small girl are doing a fine thing," Tamsen says, now standing over him.

"Are we getting it right?" Itchy asks, looking up at her.

She smiles and says nothing. Itchy wants to hug her. He loves her. Like his mom.

Mom.

Tears wet his cheeks.

"Child?" Tamsen asks. "Why do you cry?"

Itchy shrugs. "I dunno. I guess—"

"She'll forgive you."

"For what?"

Tamsen just smiles. 4G George groans loudly, the smell worsens, and then wind invades the tent, the pages of Tamsen's Lost Journal are ripped from Itchy's hands, the tent is filled with swirling sheets of fluttering paper, Itchy, panic-stricken, tries to catch them, pull them from the air, but the wind is too strong, and the papers vanish into the blizzardy night.

Outside. Back at the tree. Itchy's in the same position as when Tamsen found him. He looks up. She's standing in the snow in front of him. Smiling at him.

"Goodbye, Child," she says. She reaches to him and caresses his forehead. Her touch is so soothing. He doesn't want her to ever stop. But she does. "Goodbye," she says.

And then she's gone.

The wind howls.

Snow.

Cold.

Tears trickle from his eyes as the lids flutter closed....

The blasting, wind-driven snow quickly built large drifts around the tree, and before long Itchy was completely covered.

He'd stopped moving.

From a distance, Itchy Donner was just an oddly shaped, snowy lump at the base of a huge tree....

Marie barely made it back to the house. She hadn't seen a storm like this in years, and even with four-wheel drive she slipped and slid all the way home. There'd probably be five feet of snow on the ground in the morning. Sometimes she dreamed of wintering somewhere besides Truckee, someplace with turquoise waters and warm, gentle tradewinds where nobody knew what a snow shovel looked like.

Two messages blinked on the answering machine, one a hang-up and one from Roy.

"Storm's gonna be huge and nasty, so I'm staying on after my shift for awhile," he said. "I'll bring Itchy's folks over when they show up at the station. Love you."

Marie smiled. Roy was the best, the ultimate manly guy who made everybody feel safe. Rough and gruff, but a big old softie on the inside. How many cops would've brought poor Itchy home? That's the kind of guy Roy was.

Marie found Itchy's note and smiled as she read it. The kid was so cute. Probably afraid of the chewing out his parents were going to give him, so he wanted to rest up before they got here. Good for him. Sure, he'd done something stupid, but that's the way kids are. Marie hoped his parents would understand. She wanted to talk to them, especially Itchy's mother. She felt that, even though she'd known Itchy for only a few hours, she'd formed a bond with the kid, and that maybe she could help somehow. He was so sweet natured, he just needed a little nurturing, some understanding. There were worse things than being obsessed by famous relatives—and his father had lied to him about that, so Itchy wasn't really at fault. He was just an innocent victim.

Marie got busy cooking up some burrito fixings. She knew Itchy would wake up starving, and his parents would probably be hungry, too, so they could all have a nice little Mexican feast. Burritos were the ultimate comfort food as far as Marie was concerned, and on a foul night like this they'd be just what the doctor ordered.

Roy came stomping in forty-five minutes later, shaking snow off and leading Itchy's parents into the house. Marie had finished two glasses of wine while she cooked, hoping it would calm her down. She was nervous, and she didn't know why. Roy introduced her to Red and Irene.

"It's very nice to meet you," Marie said. Red was what she expected; Irene wasn't. Although obviously exhausted, Irene struck Marie as a sweet girl, a well-meaning and loving mom. And exceptionally beautiful, too. Marie wondered how such a delicate beauty ended up with a woodsy guy like Red.

Irene managed a weary smile. "Thank you so much for taking care of Itchy," she said.

"Yeah," Red added, "'Preciate it. Boy's a little goofy, like his old man."

Officer Roy brushed snow off his shoulders. "Good thing they got here when they did," he told Marie. "CHP just closed the interstate."

"We get snow up in I-dee-ho, but ain't seen nothin' like this," Red said.

Irene glanced around the cozy little house. Marie studied her. Her movements were jerky. The poor girl was a nervous wreck, Marie decided. She wanted to hug her.

"Um, where's Itchy?" Irene asked.

"Oh, he wanted to take a nap before you got here. He was a little tired. And scared, I think. You know, of being in trouble and all."

Red nodded. "He's got good reason to be."

The sudden alarm in Irene's face frightened Marie. It was as if she'd seen something horrible.

"A nap?" Irene whispered. "Itchy's not a nap-taker. He never has been. Even when he was a baby." Panic flashed across her face. "Where is he?"

Marie gently took Irene's arm. "He's in the guest bedroom. We'll go wake him up." Poor sweet thing, Marie thought. She's so fragile.

Marie led Irene to the guestroom. She knocked lightly, said, "Itchy? Your parents are here," and then pushed open the door. She clicked on the light, and as soon as she did she realized what Itchy had done. "Oh dear...." she said.

The lumpy form in the bed obviously wasn't a person. Irene rushed forward and yanked the blankets off. Pillows and a wadded-up blanket where Itchy should've been.

"That goddamned little shit," Red mumbled, shaking his head.

Officer Roy glared at Marie. Irene spun back toward them and whispered in a hoarse, panicky voice:

"Where's Alder Creek?!"

The snow had drifted heavily, so Officer Roy told the highway department about the emergency situation and got them to plow the road into Alder Creek.

Red and Irene rode in Officer Roy's Chevy Blazer. They followed the slow-moving snowplow. They clung tightly to the plow's rear; if Officer Roy backed off more than ten feet the plow's blinking lights disappeared into the blizzard's white-out.

"If he's here he's probably in the bathrooms by the parking lot," Officer Roy said. "They're unlocked. I'm sure he's fine. It's a pretty small area, actually."

Irene only half listened. Her throat had squeezed shut and exhaustion and fear made her light-headed.

"I'll tell you, Roy, this kid's gonna be the death of me yet," Red said. He was in his good-old-boy mode, happily bullshitting like he didn't have a care in the world. Irene wanted to strangle him.

"Yeah. Well. I apologize for not keeping a closer eye on him," Officer Roy said. "My wife got fooled."

"He can be a sneaky little shit, that's for sure," Red said. "Ain't your wife's fault, though."

They followed the plow into the Alder Creek parking area. The pinkish sodium vapor lights on the restrooms glowed eerily through the swirling snow. Officer Roy pulled up in front of the small building, and before the Blazer stopped moving Irene jumped out and ran to the bathroom doors.

"Itchy!" she yelled, flinging open first the men's, then the women's. She turned wildly and shouted over the roaring wind, "He's not here!"

Officer Roy and Red joined her. Red watched Officer Roy closely. "Where else could he be?" Red asked.

Officer Roy looked across the snow covered parking lot, into the night, into the howling blizzard. "He might," Officer Roy shouted over the storm, "be out there!" He pointed in the direction of the Donner Tree, but with the blinding storm he wasn't sure he could find it even though it was only a couple of hundred yards away. "Lemme call in help," he said, and he hurried back to the Blazer and got on the radio.

Irene collapsed against the bathroom's wall. Red moved toward her, but she swung wildly at him. "Stay the fuck away from me!" she shouted.

"Irene—"

She ignored him, pushed past him, ran into the storm, the darkness, the wind shrieked, the snow pelted her so hard it stung, suddenly disoriented, blinded by wind and cold, she spun, fell into the snow, flailed, scrambled to her feet, tried to run but the mucky snow grabbed her ankles like quicksand, it was too deep, pulling at her, wouldn't let her move, lost, she didn't know what direction to turn, to run, no idea where to go, helpless, and then she screamed so loud something tore in her throat, a painful rupture that flooded her throat with blood, but she screamed through the pain—

"ITCHY!"

Her voice cut through the howling blizzard and for a moment, a *brief* second, she thought she heard something. Was it a cry for help, a faint plea of, "Mom...?" She listened.

And listened.

But it was only the wind.

My mother and Mrs. Murphy were talking in subdued tones, pouring the oil of sympathy into each others' gaping wounds. Neither heard the sound of feet on the snow above; neither knew that the Third Relief Party was at hand, until Mr. Eddy and Mr. Foster came down the steps, and each asked anxiously of Mrs. Murphy, "Where is my boy?" Each received the same answer: "Dead."

Eliza Donner
March 14, 1847

Chapter Fourteen

As far as Father Ray was concerned, the whole diocesan "you've been a very bad boy" wrist-slapping was nothing more than an exercise in complete and utter bullshit. They'd jerked him around for almost three days now, shuttling him back and forth between Catholic shrinks and smarmy church lawyers and grumpy monsignors, feeding him lots of "Christ teaches forgiveness," along with ominous threats of giant lawsuits lurking just over the horizon. He'd stopped listening. Or caring.

It was Wednesday afternoon, and his last meeting was scheduled with an archdiocese auxiliary bishop, a guy who reminded him of a fish and whose name he could never remember. He sat in the bigshot's cramped office, staring out the window, waiting for his majesty to come back from a vital hallway chat with another priestly mucky-muck. What a bunch of garbage.

This was the meeting where they'd give Father Ray his next assignment. He didn't care, he'd just smile agreeably and go where they told him to go. Maybe down the road he'd make important decisions about his future, but not just yet. He wasn't ready to think for himself. Eventually. Sure. Someday.

The auxiliary bishop wandered back, gingerly rubbing a nasty sunburn on his bald head. Probably got it golfing at some bishops' conference in Maui, Father Ray thought bitterly. These guys were just like any corporate higher-ups—they got all the perks and goodies while the grunts in the trenches did the shit work.

"Well," Most Reverend Sunburn said. "This shouldn't take long." He sat down behind his desk and shuffled through a chubby manila folder. "By the way," he added, "Father Feeney called and wanted you to know one of your parishioners passed away."

"Oh?" Father Ray said. Probably one of the ancient Bents; half a dozen of them had been ready to ride off into eternity for years.

"Yeah. Um...Jacob Donner was the name, I believe."

At first Father Ray didn't know who it was. Jacob? Was that some elder relative of Red's?

"Apparently he ran away, then something happened. He got caught in a storm and froze to death. Awful stuff. Father Feeney thought you'd want to know." The auxiliary bishop nonchalantly shuffled through the papers in Father Ray's folder. "Oh," he said. "I notice that the complaining parishioner's name was Donner. Any relation?" He looked up just in time to see Father Ray slump in the chair and all the color drain from his face

"Itchy?" Father Ray whispered.

"Excuse me?"

"It was...." Father Ray's voice broke. *"Itchy* Donner."

"I see."

Father Ray tried to breathe but his lungs weren't working. Where did all the oxygen go? *Itchy...Donner....dead.* And he could've stopped him, he could've made a call and saved Itchy's life.

Do something, pray, beg for forgiveness, do something, you useless piece of shit!

"Are you all right?" the auxiliary bishop asked. "You look ill."

Father Ray slowly stood on wobbly legs and walked out of the office.

"Ray?!" the auxiliary bishop called out after him. But Father Ray didn't answer.

He moved blindly through the building, somehow made it outside, got into his MG, fumbled for his keys, gasping deep, painful breaths, seeing stars like he'd faint, *ohsweetJesus, Itchy's dead!*, fired up the engine, floored it—

And he sped away in a smoky cloud of burning rubber.

The archdiocese never heard from him again.

The morning of Itchy's funeral was surprisingly warm.

It felt like an Indian summer September day. Pleasant and sunny. Happy. Mild. The kind of day you played hooky from school or called in sick to work. The kind of day you spent lazing in your yard, or fishing in the creek.

Not the kind of day you buried your son.

Irene sat slumped on her bed. She hadn't slept since...that night, not really. Some unconscious stretches filled with grotesque nightmares, but no real sleep. She wasn't sure she had enough energy to even get dressed. But she had to, she had to force herself to move.

Because Itchy's funeral was in two hours.

Jacqueline would be over shortly. She'd help. Jacqueline would cut through Irene's fog of grief, pull her to her feet, dress her, clean her up, support her, protect her, she'd do everything a strong, loving mother could do—and everything Irene *didn't* do for Itchy—Jacqueline would step up and take care of it all. Everything except—

She couldn't bring Itchy back.

Irene wept. She didn't think she had any tears left, but they kept returning. Along with the ghastly memories of Alder Creek.

She'd run straight into the blizzard that night, Red chasing after her, and he finally caught her. She fought him hard, but he picked her up and dragged her back to the parking lot.

"We don't need to lose you, too!" he'd yelled.

The rest of the night was a blur to Irene. Police arrived, she remembered lights and sirens and shouting, men in huge parkas and boots and snowshoes stomping off into the woods with high-powered lights, and then dogs, and the night wore on, the blizzard wouldn't stop, the snow piled so high, and then—

Two guys running back to the parking lot. Carrying something.

Itchy.

They rushed past her into the waiting ambulance. She climbed in.

And she saw that Itchy was dead.

He was blue and waxy. The EMTs worked on him, but Irene knew it was futile.

Her beautiful boy. Delicate snow crystals encrusted his long eyelashes. A peaceful expression, like he'd fallen asleep. That reassured her. Frozen tear-drops on his cheeks.

She touched his forehead. Cold. Icy.

She'd never forget the touch. Never forget....

She sat on her bed and wept. She couldn't stop. Burying her Itchy baby today. No....

The rest of the aftermath was even more of a blur. Red consoling, pushing him away, why couldn't *he* be dead and not Itchy? Jacqueline and Stan the Man appeared, comforting her, making arrangements. Keep Red away. That mattered. *Keep Red away*, she told them. She didn't know where he was or what he was doing. He wasn't her problem anymore. He'd have to grieve on his own.

She recalled now, the flight home from Reno with her mother and Stan the Man. She remembered the long drive to Tamarack from the airport. She remembered picking out a casket....

And finally, in a few hours, Itchy would be buried and that was that. Gone. Forever. People would pick up and move on. But not Irene. She'd never be able to say goodbye to her Itchy baby.

No matter how hard she tried she couldn't make the weeping stop.

"C'mon, honey," Jacqueline said softly. "Gotta get dressed."

Jacqueline gently pulled Irene to her feet. Irene hugged her desperately. "I can't do this," she whispered in a hoarse croak. She'd ruptured her vocal cords screaming for Itchy, and the doctor had told her it'd be months before her voice came back.

"We'll get through it together, darlin'," Jacqueline said. She helped Irene put on a simple black dress and then she combed out her hair. "Should get you a perm, maybe do some highlights," she remarked. "Always been so pretty. Looks a little drab all of a sudden."

Irene stared at her reflection as Jacqueline worked on her hair. She'd never seen herself look so rotten. Dull, red-rimmed, pouchy eyes, pasty skin, new wrinkles. She'd aged years in days.

"God, I look terrible," she said. She tried to force a smile but one wasn't there.

"'Terrible' is what *I* see in the mirror every mornin'," Jacqueline told her. "You're still out-of-this-world gorgeous. Always will be, too." Jacqueline kissed her on the top of her head. "I love you, honey."

"I love you too, Mom," Irene said. New tears.

"C'mon now. Save those. Don't waste 'em on me."

Irene wiped her eyes. "Anybody seen Red?"

"He's back," Jacqueline said. Her voice dripped bitterness. "His rig broke down in Oregon and he hitched back up here. Stayed with Pencil last night, I heard."

"Will he be...?" Irene couldn't make herself say "funeral."

"Dunno. I'll make sure Stanley keeps him away from you if he is."

Irene nodded. She looked down at the tabletop. The little etched fossil fern that Red had given her sat propped against the mirror. She picked it up and turned it over in her hands. It was lovely and smooth. And cold. Very cold. Jacqueline stopped combing her hair.

"Honey?" Jacqueline asked.

Irene handed her the rock. "Give this back to him."

Jacqueline took it and slipped it into her purse.

Irene closed her eyes. The soothing, rhythmic strokes of the brush through her hair calmed her. She'd get through this. She'd find a way.

She didn't have any choice.

A. Jackson tapped on Sara's closed door. "Sara? Are you getting ready? We need to leave in a little bit." No response. "Sara?" he repeated.

"Okay," came the weak reply. He stood by her door but didn't go in. He didn't know what else to do.

Sara sat at her computer and stared at the screen. She had gone to one of Itchy's favorite Donner Party sites, one with lots of links and pictures and historical info. They'd spent hours together surfing through it.

She began to cry again.

It wasn't supposed to happen this way. It was supposed to be easy, Itchy should've gotten his Alder Creek research and come home, they should've finished *Tamsen's Lost Journal* and everything would've been okay. Now, nothing was okay. And Sara knew it was mostly her fault. Her dad and everybody else told her not to feel guilty, but she did anyway. If she hadn't helped Itchy get those bus tickets, if she hadn't encouraged him to go, if, if, if....

Now her best friend in the whole world was dead and gone and it was her fault. The adults could say whatever they wanted, they could sugarcoat it and patronize her, but it would never change one, undeniable fact: Itchy was dead and she helped kill him.

"Sara?" her father said from outside the door. "You need to get ready, sweetheart."

"Okay."

Sara reluctantly switched off the computer. Going to Itchy's funeral was going to be the hardest thing she'd ever done. Itchy's family would be mad at her. She was afraid to see Itchy's mom. Would they say anything?

As she got dressed she cried.

Maybe she could ask Mrs. Donner if she could finish *Tamsen's Lost Journal* for Itchy. That might be a nice thing to do. Kind of like a farewell present.

But, as she thought about it, maybe that wasn't such a great idea after all. Maybe she'd just shut up, maybe she'd just cry for Itchy and try not to feel too guilty.

She missed him so much. This was going to be terrible.

And it was all her fault.

*　　　　*　　　　*

Mart carefully tied his tie. The knot was okay, but the tail was too long and he had to start over again. He hated getting dressed up, but on the rare occasion when he did, he wanted to look perfect. Getting the stupid tie length right was always the dealbreaker.

Mart had been waiting at Irene's when Stan the Man and Jacqueline brought her back from Alder Creek. He wanted to hold her and comfort her, but being trapped in the chair meant all he could do was mumble condolences and wait for Irene to lean over so he could give her a weak, commiserating hug. He wasn't even sure she realized he was there; her eyes were so glazed and faraway that everything she did had the quality of a dream, of somebody acting on instinct.

"Thank you, Mart," she whispered, and then she went inside without a second glance.

"She's pretty far gone at the moment," Jacqueline told him, patting his shoulder. "But she'll need you to get through this."

Mart understood, but still it stung. Mart needed her, too. He hadn't realized until Itchy died that he'd loved the kid. He'd miss his Sunday Scrabble buddy and junk food partner-in-crime, he'd miss the long Donner Party history lessons, he'd miss everything about the goofball. Itchy had become like his little brother.

He got the tie right on the third try. He rolled out onto the porch to wait for Stan the Man. The sunny warmth surprised him, but it felt good. At least they didn't have to bury Itchy on a miserable, overcast day. Thank God for small favors.

Stan the Man drove up right on time, and Mart rolled down the ramp to the street.

Mart felt a sudden surge of fury toward Red. This was all his fault. Asshole. Mart took a deep breath. Wouldn't do any good to get crazy right before the funeral.

Let it go. Irene is all that matters.

"Red?" Pencil flipped on the storeroom light and peered in.

Red sprawled on the floor, snoring wetly. He'd gotten plowed last night after he arrived back in town. Pencil didn't want to turn him loose on the world, so he took pity and let him pass out in the storeroom.

"Hey, Red!" Pencil repeated. He wore an ancient, fat-lapelled '70s-style suit, the only one he owned. "Let's go. Need to get up."

Red blinked and squinted at Pencil with a drunk's night-after confusion. "Whatcha all dressed up for?" he asked.

"Your boy's funeral."

Red slowly sat up and ran his hands through his hair. "Oh."

"Clean up as best you can, I'll give you a lift to the church."

"Probably best I don't go."

Pencil stepped into the storeroom and stood over Red. His huge belly strained against the buttons of his frayed jacket, and he glared down at Red with the frighteningly intense glare of a drill instructor ready to stomp a green recruit into shape. "If I have to," Pencil wheezed, "I'll drag your no-good ass there. You're nothin' but a pathetic fuck-up. But you owe it to your boy to be there to bury him. So get up, clean up, and we're goin'."

Red didn't argue. He rinsed off in the bathroom, found a shirt that wasn't too rumpled, and he and Pencil headed to the church in silence.

Father Feeney said all the right words, but they provided no comfort.

Irene listened to the elderly priest's platitudes, but she didn't really hear.

She stared at the casket. She couldn't look away. Jacqueline sat next to her and gripped her hand. Jacqueline dabbed at tears, but Irene was cried out for the moment.

The small church was packed to standing-room-only, and halfway through the mass Irene heard noise in back. She turned. Red had just come in with Pencil. Red looked terrible, and when his eyes met Irene's he gave her a grim nod. She turned away.

She closed her eyes.

Just let this be over.

The Tamarack Cemetery perched on a tree-shaded hillside overlooking town, and it was packed with tombstones—some fancy old ones with carved, hovering angels, but mostly just crooked little markers overgrown by weeds. Sara wondered why they bothered covering the dirt pile from Itchy's grave with fake grass. Most of the grass in town had already turned brown, and the cemetery didn't have all that much to begin with anyway. The fluorescent green stuff that looked like ugly shag carpet just seemed wrong to Sara. So fake.

Itchy would've hated it.

A. Jackson kept a protective arm around Sara's shoulder as Father Feeney said the graveside prayers and sprinkled holy water. Sara's eyes moved between Itchy's casket and Irene. Sara had never seen anybody that despondent before. She looked so sad. Sara pressed tightly against her father.

Red stood at the rear of the mourners with Pencil. He squinted at Itchy's casket from time to time, but mostly he just stared at the ground. Pencil wasn't religious, but the priest's prayers and Irene Donner's sad, beautiful face made him mumble his own clumsy requests to God—just in case. *Please help that pretty little woman be okay,* he prayed.

Father Feeney finished the service. He went to Irene, took her hand, muttered condolences and some priestly advice, and then the official part of Itchy Donner's funeral—and life—was over.

Irene slowly moved to the grave. She took a rose from the floral arrangement that A. Jackson had bought and placed it on the casket. She didn't cry. A weary exhale, her hand brushed the casket's dark surface, and then she stepped back.

"Goodbye, Itchy," she whispered.

Jacqueline hugged her, and together they slowly walked away. Stan the Man pushed Mart's chair over the bumpy ground as they and the other mourners followed.

Irene stopped and turned. Sara and A. Jackson stood awkwardly nearby. Irene said, "Just a second," to Jacqueline and went to Sara.

Sara saw her coming and panicked. This was what she feared most: Mrs. Donner was going to yell at her and blame her for what happened. She pressed harder against her father's side.

"Sara?" Irene whispered hoarsely. "Are you all right?"

"Yes," she said in a thin little voice.

Irene squatted down to Sara's level. She gently touched Sara's face. "Please don't feel guilty," she said. "What happened wasn't your fault."

"Yes it was," Sara moaned, and she began to cry.

"No, it wasn't. You were Itchy's best friend. You made his life better."

"I did?" She wiped her eyes with her sleeve.

"Yes. He needed you, and I know you meant everything to him. Without you he wouldn't have been very happy. Just remember that, okay? I don't want you to feel guilty. Just remember that you were best friends. Promise me that."

Sara looked into Irene's eyes. Even sad she was such a pretty lady. Itchy was lucky to have her for a mom. Sara wished her own mom was more like Irene.

"You're not mad at me?" Sara asked.

Irene shook her head and hugged her, then she stood and smiled tightly at A. Jackson. "Thank you," she whispered.

A. Jackson nodded. "Anything you need, Irene, you let me know."

Irene went back to Jacqueline, and together they left the cemetery.

Red stayed behind. Nobody acknowledged him except for Pencil.

"Need a ride back, Red?" Pencil asked.

"I'll walk."

"Okay then."

Pencil gave him a tentative pat on the shoulder, then left. The cemetery was soon empty, except for the two workers who waited for Red to leave so they could lower the casket into the grave and cover it up. They sat a short distance away. One of them smoked; the other leaned against the backhoe reading the paper.

Red stared at the casket.

A beautiful fall day. Warm. Pleasant.

Red took a step toward the grave. Hesitated. Then, he slowly reached out to Itchy's coffin. He touched the surface; it had been warmed by the mild sun. The touch was like an electric shock, and he jerked his hand away.

He wanted to say goodbye, to say a prayer, to reach out to his boy.

But he didn't know how, he didn't have the right words. Anything he said would've probably been a lie. Just like his life.

Liar.

He backed away. Tears burned his eyes.

Liar.

The wake was odd in the way wakes always are, the sense of an incongruous disconnect with reality—lots of food and the feeling of a strange, somber Christmas party. Irene made the best of doing the social grief thing, playing both hostess and bereaved.

A steady stream of visitors came and went, and the little singlewide bulged with unaccustomed guests. Irene accepted condolences, hugs, offers of "If there's anything I can do...." with grace. She looked like she was holding it together.

But Mart knew better. He watched her as he sat in the living room and nibbled at the covered dish masterpieces left by friends and neighbors. Itchy would've loved all the junk food, he thought. Strange, somebody dies and we pig out. Mart didn't understand that. It must've had to do with comfort. A full gut took away the pain.

Mart marveled at how well Irene hid her sorrow. Jacqueline, through her Marlboro fog and forced hospitality, couldn't cover the grief. But Irene, she was both sad and in control.

A few times Irene asked him, "Are you all right? Do you need anything?" with a gentle touch on his shoulder. As if Mart was the one who needed help right now.

Mart was wondering how long the wake would drag on when Stan the Man came up behind him and softly said, "Red's outside. I think maybe he wants to talk to you."

"I don't want to talk to him."

Stan the Man reached into his pocket and pulled something out. "Jacqueline would really appreciate it if you took care of this," Stan the Man said nervously. "I ain't real good at these kind of things." He handed Mart the fossil fern rock. "She said to give this to him. He knows what it is."

"I don't—"

"I think Irene wants you to do it, too," Stan the Man said.

"Fine," Mart said through gritted teeth.

He rolled outside. Red sat on the log he'd set up for Itchy's Wimp o' the Woods training. He stared off into the distance.

"What do you want?" Mart said.

Red seemed far away. It took him the longest time to look down at Mart. His face had an odd blankness. "How you doin', buddy?"

"What the fuck do you want?"

Red sighed and shook his head. "Seems like everybody hates ol' Red now, huh? Don't seem like anybody remembers that Itchy was my boy, too. That maybe I'm feelin' pretty shitty 'bout losin' him."

"He wouldn't be dead if you hadn't come back," Mart snapped, but he regretted saying it the second the words left his mouth. Red was right; he deserved some sympathy, even if he was a fuck-up.

"Yeah, 'spose that's true. But at least we got to know each other. That's worth somethin', don't you think?"

Mart held up the little stone. "I'm supposed to give this to you."

Red reached down and took it. He looked at it for a moment, then shook his head and smiled wistfully. "Pretty, ain't it? Amazing the pretty things you can find out in the woods." Red slipped it into his shirt pocket. He hopped off the log. "Tell Irene goodbye for me, will you, Mar-teen?"

"Sure." Mart's anger had rapidly dwindled, which annoyed him. He didn't want to feel pity for Red.

"Tell her I'm sorry. It's about all I can say."

Mart nodded. Red held out his hand. Mart reluctantly shook it.

"Where you going?" Mart asked.

"Someplace where I ain't fucked things up yet."

Red ambled off. At the street he looked back up the hill, gave Mart a friendly wave, and then he was gone.

Mart sat outside for a long time.

The sun felt good.

By late afternoon the last of the mourners had passed through the singlewide, and Irene was left with her family and an enormous amount of leftover food. It had that Sunday get-together feel—only Itchy wasn't complaining about his lousy Scrabble tiles and going on and on about the Donner Party.

Stan the Man sampled the casseroles while he and Jacqueline covered them with foil and Saran wrap. Mart sat in the living room with Irene and watched her gaze silently out the window. Her arms were folded tightly against her body.

The sun dipped below the hills, and the day's unusual warmth vanished. Mart studied Irene's profile in the fading twilight. What was she seeing right now? Her expression was fixed and hard, as if she was glaring at something—or someone.

"Irene?" he asked.

"Yes?" she answered in her husky, damaged voice. She didn't look away from the window.

"Can I get you something?"

"No, thank you."

Mart wasn't sure if now was the time, but he needed to fill the silence. "Red's gone. He said to tell you he was sorry."

Irene nodded, and her chin quivered. "Did he say anything else?" she whispered.

"Just goodbye."

Irene nodded. Then, in a voice that Mart could barely hear, she said, "Father Feeney told me that God never gives you more than you can handle."

"Yeah."

"Other people said it, too. Half the people at the cemetery whispered it in my ear."

"It's one of those dumb things people say when they don't know what else to say."

"Don't you believe it, Mart?"

"I didn't think I could handle being crippled. But I'm still here. Don't know if God had anything to do with it, though. You do what you have to do to survive, that's all. You don't have any choice."

"I think it's a lie," Irene said. *"I can't handle this."* She turned and looked at Mart with haunted eyes. "There's no way I can handle it...."

She rushed past him and went into Itchy's room.

She closed the door behind her.

Jacqueline and Stan the Man finished cleaning up, and with Mart they waited in the living room for Irene to come out. A half-hour passed, then an hour. Jacqueline chain-smoked, Stan the Man sat with his arms folded and sighed a lot, and Mart stared at Itchy's door.

"Go check on her, Mart," Jacqueline finally said.

"Maybe we should leave her alone."

"She's had enough alone. Go in there. She needs you."

Mart slowly wheeled to Itchy's door. He tapped lightly. "Irene?"

"Yes?" Her voice was raspy and hollow.

"Can I come in?"

Silence.

"Irene?"

"Okay," she finally said.

Mart opened the door and maneuvered his chair into Itchy's tiny, cluttered room.

Irene sat on Itchy's bed, surrounded by his Donner books and assorted Donner Party memorabilia. It had gotten dark out, and she hadn't turned on any lights. Mart switched on the desk lamp and its feeble yellow glow lit the room like an old candle.

"What are you doing?" he asked.

Irene slowly looked over at him. She seemed calm. She hadn't been crying, which surprised him.

"What if he really was a Donner?" she asked. "What if he was right? What if Red's lie was true?"

Mart didn't know what to say.

"I guess it doesn't matter," she sighed, answering her own question. "When he was little I used to tell him all the stories I read about them, about what brave pioneers they were, about how strong Tamsen was. It made his life better, don't you think Mart?"

"It made him proud."

"That's not bad, is it?"

Mart wheeled closer to the bed. "You were...*are* a great mom, Irene."

"I never would've lied to him," she said, her voice hissing painfully. "If I'd known...."

"Itchy couldn't have had a better mom. You did everything right."

Tears trickled down her cheeks. "I never would've lied to him...." Her voice trailed off. She looked down at a stack of papers on the bed. She picked them up. "He had this with him at Alder Creek," she said. "It's called *Tamsen's Lost Journal.* He and Sara were writing it."

"I know. He told me about it."

"Would you read it to me please?" she whispered.

She handed Mart the papers. He looked at the first page. It was crinkled and the ink smeary—he assumed from the Alder Creek blizzard. He swallowed hard. This was a tangible part of Itchy, something he'd created and left behind, a legacy they could always remember him by.

Mart began to read: "*The Unknown Story of the Donner Party as told to Itchy Donner by his Great-great-great Gramma Tamsen in her Lost Journal, by Itchy Donner, her Great-great-great Grandson. (Itchy Donner note: Me and Sara decided to shorten it to just 'Tamsen's Lost Journal' because it's easier to say.)*" Mart and Irene both smiled at Itchy's painfully baroque title. Mart continued, "*The way I started this before it went 'Great-great-great Gramma Tamsen said that the Donners never ate anybody. She said that Keseburg, and the Breens, and the Reeds and lots of other people ate people. But not the Donners. I believe her.' But once Sara started helping me with it we decided to write it like 4G Tamsen was talking, so this is the way it goes now: 'I'm so excited to be heading west. George and the girls want to go, and even though I'm sad about leaving Illinois, I think things will be even better for us in California. Nothing bad can happen there....*" Mart continued to read the first few pages. He stopped, though, as the sound of Irene's weeping gradually filled the room.

"You want me to go on?" he asked.

She nodded. Mart reached over and gently brushed the tears from her cheeks. For the first time since Itchy died she looked him in the eye and held his gaze. He caressed the hair from her tear-moistened face, then took her hand.

Their fingers intertwined.

"I'll never leave you, Irene," he whispered.

She squeezed his hand—

And together, amidst the clutter of Itchy's shrine to the indomitable, unafraid Donner pioneers, Mart slowly read Irene the remaining words of *Tamsen's Lost Journal...*.

Epilogue

Red walked alongside the road, stumbling every so often over rocks and roadside debris. His big boots sunk into the soft gravel shoulder. It felt like he was walking through quicksand, but he couldn't make himself lift his feet any higher. Each step was impossibly heavy. So, so heavy.

His pack was slung carelessly over his shoulder, hanging lightly with his few belongings. When a car or truck approached he casually dangled his thumb without bothering to turn around.

Nobody stopped to pick him up.

No snow yet, he realized. That surprised him. The storm that pounded the Sierras—and Alder Creek—had stayed well south. A snowless Tamarack this time of year. Weird.

He looked up at the towering trees lining the road. Cedars. White pine. Nice second growth, plenty big enough to cut but left alone so enviros or wandering flatlanders would look at the pretty trees and not notice the clearcuts behind. A game A. Jackson played. A lie.

Lie.

Red stumbled and dropped to his knees. He couldn't get up. He didn't want to get up.

Lie.

The lie held him down. It wouldn't let him stand.

He didn't have any tears left, or even emotion. Dead and cold and bitter inside. But he couldn't kneel by the side of the road forever. He'd have to get up eventually. Have to move on. Go somewhere. Somewhere new. Somewhere he wasn't known, where people wouldn't point and whisper, "There's that fucking liar Red Donner. His lie killed his son." Was there a place where people wouldn't know? Where they wouldn't sense his unforgivable lie?

He tried to stand. He made it halfway up, then his knees buckled.

The weight. Too much weight.

He tossed away his pack. That must be the problem.

But still, he couldn't stand.

His head felt so heavy. Like lead. Filled with....

The lie.

Red knew the lie would never leave him. He'd never purge it, never wash it away, never forget it. "I'm Red Donner, descendent of the famous Donner Party, those not-really-cannibals from the past, ain't it cool? What's your name? Care to dance?" And it fucking worked every time. A little white lie, a lie that didn't matter to anybody, a lie that got him laid, a lie that didn't hurt anybody.

Except Itchy.

The lie killed Itchy.

"Liar, liar, pants on fire," Red said, sing-songy. "Liar, *LIAR PANTSON-FIRE!*"

Wind through the cedars. A whispery rebuke.

Cheaters never prosper. What happens to liars?

Their kids die.

"Stand up, pussy," Red told himself. He struggled to his feet. Stayed standing. Swayed. Like he was drunk. Was he? Might be. Couldn't remember.

He only remembered the lie.

"Yeah, my Gramma told me stories she heard from her gramma about the Donners. How they ate the leather straps from their rescuer's snowshoes, yep, old Granny told me...."

LIAR!

Could somebody forgive him? Not that fuck-ass priest. Shit. Not Irene. She shouldn't forgive him. He didn't deserve forgiveness from her. What about Mart? Would Mart forgive him someday? Nah, never. Too much had happened. Too much.

Lie.

Red's chin touched his chest. Time to move on, time to hitchhike someplace to forget. Get away from Tamarack.

"I'm sorry Itchy...I'm so fucking sorry...." Red whispered. And his eyes began to water. Tears. Finally, more tears. He could feel again. "Forgive me, Itchy. Please...." Red pleaded.

The wind whistling.

No forgiveness, though. Just rebuke. Condemnation.

Red Donner, descendent of the famous pioneers, those brave, tragic people, so tough, so—

Oh, Red Donner *isn't* related to the real Donner family. He's just a white-trash loser, a gyppo logger who's fucked up everything he ever touched, a loudmouth good-old-boy who had a little charm and enough smarts and a famous last name he used to get himself into big trouble.

You can't make the lie go away, Red. Lies are forever.

Shouldn't have let it loose. Now look what it got you.

Red lifted his head, opened his eyes. Looked into the clear, hard sky.

And he had an idea.

A truck approaches. Big diesel, Red thinks. Double-clutch, shift, the brrrrrp/growl *of the engine.*

He turns.

A log truck. Full load. Might even be some logs that he'd cut, who knows?

Wonder who's driving? Doesn't matter, really.

Just hope whoever it is don't hold a grudge.

The truck approaches. Moving pretty fast.

Full load.

No stopping on a dime.

The truck is almost to him.

Almost, almost.... Red hesitates, watches, considers.

This would make the lie go away.

The truck is almost to him.

Should he step in front of it?

He takes a step into the road. Airhorn blares at him.

Do it! End it!

But he doesn't. Can't.

Coward.

The truck blows by, horn still blaring, the driver flips him the bird, Red recognizes him, it's one of the Bents.

Standing alongside the silent road now. Alone. Chickenshit. Didn't even have the courage to end it, to join Itchy. To be a man. A Donner.

Chickenshit.

"Where'd you say you were headed?"

Red leaned back in the passenger seat of the eighteen-wheeler. The cheerful, chubby-faced driver—was his name Wayne? Red couldn't remember—had picked Red up on Highway 95 south of New Meadows. Now they were headed east on I-80, into a blinding, bloody sun rising over the barren Nevada wastes.

"That's still kinda up in the air," Red sighed. Red hadn't felt much like talking. Usually he enjoyed shit-shooting with anybody who had ears, but not now. Not anymore.

They drove for another hour, Wayne chattering happily, Red grunting occasional answers. Red stared ahead at the miles of pavement, the barren mountains, alkali sinks, offramps leading to sad, dusty little towns.... A sign reading, "Emigrant Springs Historical Area, 2 Miles" flashed by as Wayne passed a slow-moving RV.

"Did you know," Red said slowly, "that this highway follows the old pioneer trail?"

"Uh, yeah, I guess so," Wayne said.

"Wagon trains used it on their way over to California," Red said.

"Huh."

"My boy told me all 'bout it." Red hesitated. "He was a real expert on that stuff."

Wayne caught the melancholic undertone in Red's voice and said nothing.

"The Donner Party come right through here," Red added. He stared into the desert. The next words came out automatically. "You know, I'm related—" he began, then the words curdled in his throat.

"What's that?" Wayne asked.

Red coughed, roughly shook his head, and said nothing more. He rolled down the window and prayed that the desert's chill morning air would chase the lie from him.

Red closed his eyes.

The windy roar drowned out everything.

But the lie was still there.

It always would be.